CONFEDERATES IN CANADA

A Civil War Romance

Nikki Stoddard Schofield

authorHOUSE®

AuthorHouse™
1663 Liberty Drive
Bloomington, IN 47403
www.authorhouse.com
Phone: 1 (800) 839-8640

Published by AuthorHouse 02/23/2016

ISBN: 978-1-5049-8022-7 (sc)
ISBN: 978-1-5049-8023-4 (hc)
ISBN: 978-1-5049-8024-1 (e)

Library of Congress Control Number: 2016902861

Print information available on the last page.

This book is printed on acid-free paper.

PRAISE FOR NIKKI'S BOOKS

I loved it [Savannah Bound] from start to finish. I hated to put it down. I liked the intrigue in it, and I have to say there were parts in which I actually cried. When you can write where the reader's emotions are touched like that, you know it's good. I also enjoyed the history part of it.

--Ms. Jean Burns, Flint, Michigan

Nikki is an excellent researcher and one who is driven to exhaust as much knowledge as possible about her work. She has enhanced her skills over the years and produces an excellent product as a result. Nikki's focus on the Civil War period of our history gives her considerable credibility as a teller of tales with that time as a backdrop.

--John P. Price, Esq., Indianapolis, Indiana

I highly recommend all the books that Nikki has written. She researches the historical facts of that time period to make the storyline come alive to the reader. I have always been captivated by each novel's characters and couldn't wait to see how the story ends.

--Ms. Paula Settle, Stanton, Kentucky

Nikki's passion for history and romance, her focused research skills, and her Christian commitment combine to make interesting and pleasurable reading. The unexpected twists and turns of her plots keep the reader's attention and curiosity for the next page. Reading her descriptive novels is like taking a walk through the past that gives an appreciation for the present.

-- Ms. Jan Watts, Louisville, Kentucky

PREVIOUS NOVELS BY NIKKI STODDARD SCHOFIELD

Bondage & Freedom

Guerrilla warfare in East Tennessee is the setting for Nikki's first novel in which Captain Brinton Good compassionately cares for Lydia, a nurse suffering elective mutism and post traumatic stress due to the horrors she has seen in Civil War hospitals.

Alas Richmond

During the final days of the Confederacy, Giles Tredwell, an Englishman serving as a spy for the Union, and Verity Scott, a Southern belle who opened her mansion as a boarding house, become friends as they deal with boarders, slaves, children, and people affected by the fall of Richmond to the Union army.

Treason Afoot

The Indianapolis Treason Trials resulted in an 1867 United States Supreme Court decision which is still studied in law schools today. Wounded veteran Jay Hadley befriends Emeline Tanner and hires her to work in his bookstore. They become involved in the dramatic events surrounding the Knights of the Golden Circle and the Sons of Liberty which occurred in Indiana's capital during 1864.

Savannah Bound

Lanson Barrington escapes from Andersonville Prison and meets Adelaide Draycott when her train is attacked outside of Savannah, Georgia. They care for a four-year-old boy, Theo, whose mother was killed by train robbers. Sharing the same house, Lanson and Adelaide confront the problems arising from his false identity and her search for her long-lost mother, while General Sherman marches his vast army toward Savannah.

In memory of my parents,
Lois Elizabeth Burns Stoddard
and
Maynard Good Stoddard

CONTENTS

PREFACE

While researching a first-person portrayal, I became fascinated by the story of the Confederates in Canada. Susan Pendleton Lee (1832-1911), whom I portrayed before Civil War Round Tables, was the daughter of General William Nelson Pendleton (1809-1883), an Episcopal minister and chief of artillery for the Army of Northern Virginia, and Anzolette Elizabeth Page Pendleton (1810-1884), from Lexington, Virginia. Susan's brother was Lieutenant Colonel Alexander Swift "Sandi" Pendleton (1840-1864), who served as Stonewall Jackson's chief of staff. In studying the lives of Susan and her husband, Brigadier General Edwin "Ned" Gray Lee (1836-1870), second cousin once removed to General Robert Edward Lee, I learned that Ned was assigned to replace Jacob Thompson as head of the Confederate secret service based in Canada. The escapades of those daring young men in that long-ago era were intriguing. As I told Susan's story before Civil War audiences, I had no thought of one day writing a novel about the dare-devil experiences of the Confederates in Canada.

Gary W. Gallagher, in his book The Confederate War, 1997, quoted a scholar who estimated "85,000 to 90,000 Americans in all fled to Canada during the war, either to dodge enrollers, to avoid the draft or to desert the army." (Page 31) Imagine what that large number of men might have accomplished if they had been in the armies, both Northern and Southern. Our history might have been written differently.

In April 2014, I took a research trip to Canada, visiting Guelph, St. Catherines, and Ft. Erie, returning via Clarence, New York, and Port Gibson, Ohio. The journey was enlightening not only for the books and maps which I collected along the way but, more importantly, for the conversations with the local people, who were helpful and friendly. I mention some of them in my Acknowledgements which follow.

ACKNOWLEDGEMENTS

I would like to thank Renee Bennett, Martha McDonald, Phyllis Walters, and John Gilmore for their close reading of the original manuscript. Renee also provided her wisdom concerning child psychology. Martha has proofread my four previous novels. Phyllis is a retired librarian. John, a Civil War scholar, attends my church.

Historian Barry Sheehy of Gabarus, Nova Scotia, read the manuscript electronically. He has researched the Confederate secret service in Canada for his next book, <u>City of Secrets</u>, based in Montreal in 1864 and 1865. He recognized many of the characters in this book as figures he knows intimately. The only mistake which Barry found was that Mrs. Thompson was probably not in Canada with her husband, but joined him in Europe when he escaped there. However, I chose to leave her character in the story for the sake of Jacob having someone in whom he could confide.

Mary Donahue was my final proofreader. After all the other corrections were made, she had the manuscript for a last look. Without the help of these friends, this novel would undoubtedly have typos and errors, many of which were caught by their careful reading. I am so appreciative of their diligent work and good suggestions.

During my April 2014 trip to Canada, I gained valuable information from Melanie McLennan, who operates the London House Bed and Breakfast with her husband Andy at 80 London Road West, in Guelph, Ontario. Because of its convenient location, I was able to walk to the First Baptist Church of Guelph, which was built during the Civil War, as well as the hilly downtown. In St. Catherines, I stayed at the 1840 Inn on the Henley "Stokedale," owned by Ross Gale, who gave me much interesting information about the history of the area. In Ft. Erie, Ontario, Annie Hall (she said she had the name before the movie), who runs an antiquarian bookstore, shared facts about the Niagara River and the town. Bart Erwin, owner of Our Sunset Place Bed and Breakfast in Port Clinton, Ohio, told me about Lake Erie (which the B&B borders), the islands, and books on the area's history.

I want to thank my family and friends for their support of my writing. Their encouragement helps during the gray days when the words just don't seem to flow.

ABOUT THE AUTHOR

Nikki Stoddard began her serious writing career when, at the age of sixteen, she became Thursday's editor of the Shortridge Daily Echo, one of five high school daily newspapers in the world at that time, 1959-1960. At the awards ceremony in May 1960, at Shortridge High School in Indianapolis, she was presented with the Al J. Kettler Award for Journalism. From that time, Nikki has been writing.

Ms. Schofield is the mother of two sons, Rob who lives with his wife Vicki in Ohio, and Gaven who lives with his wife Christine and three daughters in Virginia. She has five granddaughters, Bridget, Stephanie, Abigail, Gabrielle, and Lily; one grandson, Nicholas; one great-granddaughter, Bella, and three great-grandsons, Gonzalo, Elias, and Sebastian.

From 1974 to 2012, Nikki was the law librarian at the Indianapolis office of Bingham Greenebaum Doll LLP, formerly Bingham Summers Welsh & Spilman. Upon entering phased retirement, she took a second job as the Staff Genealogist at Crown Hill Cemetery, where she works on Fridays. Also at Crown Hill, the third largest private cemetery in the country, Nikki serves as a tour guide specializing in the Civil War personalities.

In October 2011, Nikki began volunteering one day a week at the Indiana State Library, Manuscript and Rare Book Division, where she processes collections and creates finding aids which are available on the Internet. Many of the items Nikki summarizes in these finding aids are from Civil War collections. This work enables her to read what people of that era wrote and thought, thus providing authenticity to her novels.

Her latest endeavor is serving as a docent at the Indiana Medical History Museum located in the old Pathology Building on the grounds of the former Central State Hospital. She began training in June and gave her first tour in August, 2015. Nikki hopes to use her knowledge from this volunteer service to write with more accuracy about Civil War medicine.

A member of Speedway Baptist Church, Ms. Schofield is chairman of the deacons for 2016, moderator of the business meetings, adult Sunday school teacher, and assistant treasurer. For five years, she served as one of two representatives from the North Central region on the Coordinating Council of the Cooperative Baptist Fellowship with which her church is affiliated. In April 2014, she was elected Moderator of the North Central Cooperative Baptist Fellowship.

As president of the Indianapolis Civil War Round Table for three terms, Nikki has also served the club as director for the annual trips, secretary, and newsletter editor.

For many years, Ms. Schofield gave first-person presentations of Civil War women including Belle Boyd, Confederate spy; Mary Surratt, Lincoln conspirator; Mary Ann Morrison Jackson, wife of Stonewall Jackson; Helen Pitts Douglass, the second wife of orator and abolitionist Frederick Douglass; Anzolette Page Pendleton, wife of General Robert E. Lee's chief of artillery, General William Nelson Pendleton; Susan Pendleton Lee, wife of Edwin Gray Lee, Confederate commissioner to Canada; Lucinda Morton, the wife of Indiana's Civil War Governor; Susan Slater, Confederate spy; and several others.

Ms. Schofield is a member of the Baptist History & Heritage Society, the Fellowship of Baptist Historians, and the Society of Civil War Historians.

ABOUT THE COVER ARTIST

Gabrielle Elizabeth Schofield was born in 2002 to Christine and Gaven Schofield of Richmond, Virginia. In 2015, she entered 7th grade. Gabrielle enjoys playing the piano, riding horses, reading, and interacting with her two sisters, Abigail and Lily. She is active with her family at church. Gabrielle won the competition for the back cover picture of her elementary school 2012-2013 yearbook. Her tree design showed all four seasons with the theme: "Great and Getting Greater!" Gabrielle also won the city-wide competition for the James River Poster Contest sponsored by the James River Association. Her picture was used as a Christmas card in 2015. The purpose is to promote environmental awareness of a clean river. Her reward was $100 which she plans to spend on art supplies.

CHARACTERS BY CHAPTER

In order of appearance

Chapter 1 – Hotels Ablaze

Lieutenant John William Headley, historical, born 1840 in Hopkins, Kentucky, agent of the Confederate Secret Service

William B. Brown, alias of John Headley

Anathea Sarah Brannaman, fictional, born 1844 in Louisville, Kentucky, heroine

Beatrice Cutter, fictional, born 1858, daughter of Mayfield and Adelle Cutter, orphan

John F. Carlton, historical, owner of the United States Hotel, New York City

Mayfield J. Cutter, fictional, born 1834 in Guelph, Ontario, Canada, father of Beatrice and Freddie; son of Joan and Varney; husband of Adelle

Frederick "Freddie" Cutter, fictional, born December 1861, son of Mayfield and Adelle Cutter, orphan

Raiford Miles Young, fictional, born 1840 in Goshen, Indiana, hero

Colonel Norman Eddy, historical, commander of the 48th Indiana Volunteer Regiment

General Ulysses Simpson Grant, historical, born 1822, General in Chief of the Armies of the United States

Gov. Oliver Perry Morton, historical, born 1823, governor of Indiana, 1861-1867

General William Tecumseh Sherman, historical, born 1820, commanded the Military Division of the Mississippi

Colonel Joseph Newcombe, fictional, born 1815, Department of the East, U.S. Army, stationed in New York City

Captain Hector Smith, fictional, aide to Colonel Newcombe, born 1839

Major General John Adams Dix, historical, born 1798, commander of the Department of the East from July 18, 1863 to 1865

Junius Brutus Booth, historical, born 1796, died 1852

Junius Brutus Booth, Jr., historical, born 1821, son of Junius Brutus Booth and Mary Ann Holmes

Edwin Thomas Booth, historical, born 1833, son of Junius Brutus Booth and Mary Ann Holmes

John Wilkes Booth, historical, born 1838, son of Junius Brutus Booth and Mary Ann Holmes

Mr. Leonard, historical, Superintendent of Firemen, New York City

Joan Cutter, fictional, born 1810, mother of Mayfield Cutter, in Guelph, Ontario, Canada West

Varney Cutter, fictional, born 1804, father of Mayfield Cutter, in Guelph, Ontario, Canada West

E. L. Pearson, fictional, born 1819, manager of Cutter Industries, Guelph, Ontario, Canada West

Chapter 2 – Fire Refugees

Chapter 3 – Rebels! I Knew It!

James Buchanan, historical, born 1791, president of the United States, 1857-1861

Bennett G. Burley, historical, Confederate agent from Glasgow, Scotland

John Yates Beall, historical, born 1835, spy for the Confederacy, hanged at Fort Columbus, New York, February 24, 1865

Lenore Young, fictional, born 1841, wife of Raiford Young, died 1859

Brigadier General Edwin "Ned" Gray Lee, historical, born 1836, head of the Confederate Secret Service in Canada from January to April 1865

Susan Pendleton Lee, historical, born 1832, wife of Edwin Gray Lee

Dr. John Wakefield Francis, historical, doctor in New York City

Colonel Robert Maxwell Martin, historical, born 1840, from Louisville, Kentucky, in the Confederate Secret Service

Milo Clark, fictional, constable in Guelph, Canada West

Chapter 4 – Train Jumper

Harmon Utley, fictional, leading citizen of Guelph, Canada West

Dolly Utley, fictional, daughter of Harmon Utley

Lieutenant James Chenault, historical, from Kentucky, in the Confederate Secret Service

Lieutenant James T. Harrington, historical, from Kentucky, in the Confederate Secret Service

Lieutenant John M. Price, historical, from Maryland, in the Confederate Secret Service

Lieutenant John T. Ashbrook, historical, from Kentucky, in the Confederate Secret Service

Lieutenant Mechum Esling, fictional, born 1840, from Tennessee, in the Confederate Secret Service

Delphina Esling, fictional, born 1841, wife of Mechum, mother of Maggie and baby Mechum

Mechum Esling, Junior, fictional, born 1864, son of Mechum and Delphina

Maggie Esling, fictional, born 1862, daughter of Mechum and Delphina

Chapter 5 – Suspension Bridge

Oscar Bolton, fictional, neighbor of Varney and Joan Cutter in Guelph, Canada West

Saida Bolton, fictional, wife of Oscar, neighbor of Varney and Joan Cutter

Thomas Briggs, historical, chief clerk of Roberts & Co. bank in London, murdered in a first-class carriage on the North London Railway

Franz Muller, historical, a German tailor in London, hanged for the murder of Thomas Briggs in 1864

Jesse Shilliday, fictional, born 1820, doctor in Guelph, Canada West

Harriet Shilliday, fictional, born 1824, wife of Dr. Shilliday

Adelle May Cutter, fictional, wife of Mayfield J. Cutter, mother of Beatrice and Freddie

Rev. Kensey Johns Stewart, historical, born 1817, Episcopal minister, Confederate secret agent in Ontario, Canada West

Emma Louisa Stewart, historical, born 1821, wife of Rev. Kensey J. Stewart

Jefferson Finis Davis, historical, born 1808, President of the Confederate States of America

Dale L. Stewart, historical, born 1852, son of Kensey and Emma

Emma P. Stewart, historical, born 1854, daughter of Kensey and Emma

James B. Stewart, historical, born 1855, son of Kensey and Emma

Kensey J. Stewart, Jr., historical, born 1860, son of Kensey and Emma

Mary P. Stewart, historical, born 1863, daughter of Kensey and Emma

Zurelle Wyatt, fictional, birth year unknown, wife of Ochran, runaway slave

Ochran Wyatt, fictional, birth year unknown, husband of Zurelle, runaway slave

Nelson Bartmess, fictional, worker at Cutter Foundry

Josiah Igoe, fictional, worker at Cutter Foundry

Eustus Wright, fictional, worker at Cutter Foundry and husband of Jennet Burleigh

Frank Burleigh, fictional, worker at Cutter Foundry and cousin of Bennett Burley

Elmore Pearson, fictional, born 1848, son of E. L. Pearson

Jennet Burleigh, fictional, twin sister of Lynnet, wife of Eustus Wright, resident of Guelph, Ontario

Lynnet Burleigh, fictional, twin sister of Jennet, resident of Guelph, Ontario

Dalby Wyatt, fictional, born 1858, son of Ochran and Zurelle

Willene Wyatt, fictional, born 1860, daughter of Ochran and Zurelle

Fernancy Wyatt, fictional, born 1862, daughter of Ochran and Zurelle

Chapter 6 – Falling Scaffolding

Fides, historical, Federal agent

FitzHenry, fictional, Federal agent

Garrett, fictional, Federal agent

Olive Branch, fictional, code name for Raiford Young

Bennett Henderson Young, historical, Confederate leader of the St. Albans Raid

General John Hunt Morgan, historical, Confederate cavalry commander

Jackson Wade, fictional, Federal agent

Chapter 7 -- Providential Delay

Nesbit Payne, fictional, corrupt Toronto policeman

William Mittleberger, fictional, lawyer in Guelph, Canada West

Chapter 8 – Guelph

John Huggins, fictional, cab driver in Guelph, Canada West

John Galt, historical, founder of Guelph, Canada West

Deering Lister, fictional, neighbor of Varney and Joan Cutter, in Guelph, Canada West

Chapter 9 – The Buffalo Raid

Anzolette Page Pendleton, historical, wife of William, mother of Susan

Rev. George Grafftey, historical, pastor of First Baptist Church, Guelph, Canada West

Seth Simons, fictional alias for Raiford Young

Reddick Wagley, fictional, second alias for Fides

J. B. Bowles, historical, prisoner on Johnson's Island

Lt. Wheeler, historical, prisoner on Johnson's Island

Cassius F. Lee, historical, uncle of Edwin Gray Lee, Hamilton, Canada West

Daniel Bedinger Lucas, historical, friend of Edwin Gray Lee, Lexington, Virginia

Judge John W. Brockenbrough, historical, Lexington, Virginia

Hannah Lee, historical, sister of Edmund Lee, first wife of Kensey Stewart

Edmund Jennings Lee II, historical, born 1797, father of Edwin Gray Lee

Chapter 14 – The Orphans Come

Hilda Peacock, fictional, citizen of Guelph

Mrs. Grafftey, historical, wife of Rev. George Grafftey

Chapter 15 – Blizzard

Abijah Jennings, fictional, workman at Cutter Foundry

Mrs. Jennings, fictional, wife of Abijah

CHRONOLOGY OF HISTORIC EVENTS

1864

November 24 – Nineteen New York City hotels set afire by eight Confederates from Canada

November 25 – Six of the eight Confederates, who set fire to the hotels, met for the last time at their Central Park cottage

November 26 – General John A. Dix issued General Order 92

November 27 – St. Alban's Raiders moved from St. Johns to Montreal

November 30 – Battle of Franklin fought in Tennessee

December 5 – Jacob Thompson sent his report to C.S.A Secretary of State Judah P. Benjamin in Richmond, Virginia

December 10 – Ned and Susan Lee left Smithville on the S.S. Virginia

December 13 – St. Alban's Raiders released at end of first trial

December 13 – Lieutenant Wheeler and J. B. Bowles escaped from Johnson's Island

December 15 – Buffalo Raid to rescue seven C.S.A. generals in route from Johnson's Island prison to Fort Lafayette in New York Harbor

December 15-16 – Confederates lost the Battle of Nashville, Tennessee

December 16 – John Yates Beall and George S. Anderson arrested near the Suspension Bridge over the Niagara River, New York

December 21 – Confederate General William J. Hardee evacuated Savannah, and General William T. Sherman entered the city

December 27 – St. Alban's Raiders began second trial

December 29 – Robert Cobb Kennedy arrested in Detroit, Michigan
December 30 – Ned and Susan Lee docked at Halifax, Nova Scotia

1865

January 10-24 – Susan and Ned Lee traveled from Halifax to Toronto

January 23 – Robert Edward Lee appointed general-in-chief of all Confederate Armies

January 31 – U.S. House of Representatives passed the Thirteenth Amendment to the Constitution abolishing slavery

February 1-8 – John Yates Beall's trial at Fort Lafayette, New York

February 3 – River Queen at Hampton Roads hosted a failed peace conference

February 14 – Commissioner Jacob Thompson departed from Toronto

February 24 – John Yates Beall hanged at Fort Columbus, New York

March 4 – President Abraham Lincoln delivered his Second Inaugural Address

March 10 – Confederate President Jefferson Davis declared a day of fasting, humiliation and prayer

March 13 – Confederate President Davis signed the Negro Soldier Law authorizing the enlistment of slaves as soldiers

March 25 – Robert Cobb Kennedy hanged at Fort Lafayette, New York

March 31 – General Edwin Gray Lee visited St. Alban's raiders in Montreal Jail

April 3 – Richmond, Virginia fell to federal troops

April 5 – St. Alban's raiders released at end of second trial

April 9 – General Robert E. Lee surrendered his Confederate Army of Northern Virginia to General Ulysses S. Grant's federal army at Appomattox Court House, Virginia

April 14 – Jacob Thompson departed from Montreal for Europe

April 14 – John Wilkes Booth assassinated President Lincoln at Ford's Theater, Washington City

April 15 – President Lincoln died

April 26 – John Wilkes Booth died at Locust Hill Farm owned by Richard H. Garrett southwest of Port Royal, Virginia

April 26 – Confederate General Joseph Eggleston Johnston surrendered the Army of Tennessee, the Department of the Carolinas, Georgia, and Florida, and scattered commands to Union Major General William Tecumseh Sherman at Bentonville, North Carolina

May 4 – Confederate Lieutenant General Richard Taylor surrendered the Department of Alabama, Mississippi, and East Louisiana army to Union General Edward Richard Sprigg Canby at Citronelle, Alabama

May 26 – Confederate Lieutenant General Simon Bolivar Buckner surrendered the District of Louisiana to Union Major General Peter Osterhaus in New Orleans

June 2 – Confederate General Edmund Kirby Smith surrendered the last Confederate force, the Trans-Mississippi Department, at Galveston, Texas, to Union General Edward Richard Sprigg Canby, and the Civil War ended.

CHAPTER ONE

HOTELS ABLAZE

*Wherein Confederate spies set fire to nineteen
New York City hotels; Raiford and Anathea rescue
Beatrice and Freddie; a young father dies; and
New Yorkers condemn Southern terrorists.*

On Friday, November 25, 1864, Lieutenant John William Headley, a Confederate spy working out of Canada, signed the register of the United States Hotel as William B. Brown, and mounted the stairs to the top floor. Located at Fulton and Water streets, two blocks west of the East River, the six-story hotel was one of the oldest in the city and considered a tinderbox. Built in 1833, it had a marble façade which disguised its totally wood construction. Although the hotel was old and creaky, it was comfortable. Patronized by ship captains and merchants, the hotel's most prominent feature was the cupola on the roof, which gave guests a panoramic view of New York City and the East River.

John Headley left the key on the outside of the door to room 550 in case he had to make a quick getaway. In the room, the young man lit the gas light. Seeing the window was open, he closed it and thought: *I don't want smoke to be seen too soon. The fire must have time to do its damage.*

Mr. Headley draped the bedclothes over the headboard and piled two chairs, drawers from the bureau, and the washstand on top of the bare mattress. This done, he carefully opened a bottle of Greek fire and poured the volatile chemical compound onto the pile. The phosphorus in bisulfate of carbon blazed up instantly. The entire bed was in flames by the time John exited the room ten minutes after entering. Locking

1

the door, Mr. Headley pocketed the key, walked along the hallway, and down the stairs.

* * *

Next door, in room 552, Anathea Brannaman set her watch brooch on the bureau. *Eight twenty-five. Good. I can read in bed awhile and make an early night,* she thought as she took the pins out of her hair, fluffed her chignon loose, and picked up the brush. Sitting in the chair by the window while brushing her long brown hair, she thought: *I wonder what they are saying about me now? Probably, a puff of trash as blown away in the wind, or the devil got her at last. But I won't think about those people any more. I don't care what they think of me.*

Anathea turned her thoughts to the family she met in the lobby earlier that evening. When she came from the hotel dining room, Anathea had seen a man bend over in a chair and cough into a handkerchief, while two crying children clung to his knees. Anathea had noticed red spots on the man's handkerchief and immediately thought of her mother. *Blood on the handkerchief. Consumption. He's dying, just like Mother did,* Anathea had thought as she approached the little family and asked to help.

The little girl had looked up with an expression of anguish and said, "We need a room, but there isn't one."

Anathea had gone to the front desk and asked John F. Carlton, the hotel's owner, if she could give the family her room.

"No need," Mr. Carlton had said. "A chambermaid is making a room ready for them now."

In a short time, Mayfield J. Cutter and his children Beatrice, age six, and Frederick, age two almost three, were given the key to room 559 on the 5th floor. Anathea, who had waited with them, mounted the stairs with the family. Because Mr. Cutter had to stop often to catch his breath and cough, their progress had been slow. Anathea had thought: *What beautiful children. Will I ever have beautiful children like these?*

At their door, the ailing man had thanked Anathea and introduced himself and his children before going into the room adjacent to John Headley's.

Now, as she put her brush back on the bureau, Anathea wondered: *Where is the mother? Maybe they are going to see her. She should be taking care of her husband. He needs to see a doctor. How much longer can he live?*

Because sad thoughts of the consumptive man reminded her of her mother's illness and death, Anathea focused on the current problem of finding a job. Twisting a single braid, she recalled her misfortune of arriving the day before, which was Thanksgiving when businesses were closed. Thus, she was not able to seek employment on the holiday. Today, she had sought jobs but found none.

Suddenly, Anathea stopped braiding. She smelled something. Looking around, she saw smoke seeping through the crack between the baseboard and the floor. Anathea rushed to the door, pulled it open, and looked to the right. Smoke crept under the door of the next room.

"Fire!" she screamed. Lifting the hem of her brown dress, she ran to room 550. Anathea banged on the door. "Fire! There's a fire in your room! Get up! Get out! Fire!" She rattled the knob. The door was locked.

Two gentlemen appeared at her side and, after several tries, bashed the door open. The room was empty. The bed was aflame. Flames raced across the ceiling. The three staggered back from the heat and smoke. Another man in a robe pushed past them into the smoke-filled room. All of them were coughing. The third man grabbed the pitcher from the wash stand and poured water on the flaming bed.

"Get the drapes!"

"Use the rug!"

"Beat out the flames!"

One man tore down the drapes while the other man yanked up the rug. The man in the robe said, "I'll get more water," and ran out. Anathea yanked open the bottom bureau drawer, tugged out the extra blanket, and beat the burning bedstead. She felt her braid coming loose. They coughed as they worked.

"Wake the others!" one of the men said to Anathea as he shoved her toward the door.

"Open the window!" said one of the gentlemen.

"No!" said his companion. "It will increase the fire!"

Stumbling into the hall, Anathea bumped into the man in the robe returning with a pitcher of water in each hand. She hurried past him and began banging on doors while yelling: "Fire! Fire!"

Hotel guests exited their rooms and raced for the stairs. Several men stayed to help fight the flames.

"Get the firemen!"

"Notify the desk!"

"Tell Mr. Carlton!"

"Get out!"

Anathea pushed past the people, pounded on doors, and shouted. Her eyes stung from the smoke. People banged into her in their hurry to escape.

The Cutter family! I don't see them! Anathea thought.

"Where's the fire?"

"Appears to be confined to one room!"

"Bring all your water pitchers!"

"Need more water!"

The voices in the hall did not awaken Raiford Young, in room 560. Because he had slept little in the past two days, he was now in a deep sleep. He imagined the noises were part of his dream of battle. The thudding on his door sounded like a distant cannon.

* * *

As the son of a Baptist mother and Mennonite father in Goshen, Indiana, Raiford Young joined the 48th Indiana Volunteer Regiment upon the promise of Colonel Norman Eddy, commander, that he would not be required to kill another human. Raiford served first as a supply wagon driver, a stretcher bearer, a hospital steward, and once on a burial squad. In the month of May, 1863, after the 48th joined General Grant's army, Raiford lost his conscientious objections and took a rifle for the purpose of killing the enemy. He could not remember which battle it was. All he remembered was people were killing his friends and he needed to stop them.

In January 1864, while stationed in Huntsville, Alabama, the regiment reenlisted as a veteran organization. They were given a veteran furlough and welcomed in grand style in Indianapolis on February 8. Governor Morton and other dignitaries made speeches about their service and bravery. Remaining in the capital city during his furlough, Raiford volunteered at City Hospital. This was preferable, he thought, to facing the pacifists in Goshen, especially his father. He resolved to delay that eventuality until war's end.

Back in Huntsville, Raiford's duties changed. He was raised in rank to Captain and placed on the staff of General Ulysses S. Grant. Sound reasoning under fire, as well as good penmanship, were qualities admired by the military. When General Grant needed a courier to take a message to General William Tecumseh Sherman, who was waging battles around Atlanta, he sent Raiford. In early November, General Sherman called the daring young courier to take a message to New York City. Raiford well remembered the interview.

"Tell Colonel Newcombe that he need not send any more supplies," General Sherman said, as he bent over a map on his folding table.

"No more supplies," Raiford repeated to be certain that he heard correctly.

"That's right. I intend for the men to live off the land."

Raiford knew General Sherman was planning to move his vast 62,000-man army soon but did not know where. Nevertheless, he was pleased with the assignment. Having witnessed carnage and bloodshed during the battle for Atlanta, he was grateful to be away. Images of war had begun seeping into his dreams. He jumped at unexpected noises. He had no desire to return to General Grant who faced the Army of Northern Virginia at the siege of Petersburg. He longed for peace.

New York City – the war has not reached that far north. Oh, yes, they did have those draft riots in the streets last year after Gettysburg. That's all died down now. It should be calm in the streets there. Thank you, Lord, for this means of escape while still being obedient to duty.

Raiford, feeling guilty about leaving friends, walked away from headquarters with a lighter step. A few days later, he arrived in New York, took a cab from the station, and entered the U.S. Army headquarters at 49 Bleeker Street where Captain Hector Smith greeted him.

"I would like to see Colonel Joseph Newcombe," Raiford said.

"I'm his aide," the thin young man said, extending his hand and saying his name.

"Captain Raiford Young, courier."

"Colonel Newcombe is with someone right now, but he won't be long. Would you like coffee? How was your trip?"

Raiford accepted the mug of coffee and, feeling ebullient, began telling a tale about being attacked by Indians while coming through Cumberland Gap but fighting them off with his trusty two-edged sword. Five soldiers in the office, along with Hector, stood spellbound as they listened to the fanciful narration. When Raiford concluded, the men laughed and three of them clapped.

5

"What's the applause for?" asked the colonel, coming out of his office with his visitor.

Hector introduced Raiford and added, "He's just told us a lively story. We might have found the kind of man you've been looking for, Colonel."

The slender captain held the door open for Raiford, who entered Colonel Newcombe's office, took a chair, and listened to Hector briefly repeat his story. The older man smiled as he heard his aide's rendition.

"You said we need a good storyteller," Hector concluded.

"Indeed we do," said the superior officer, forming a tent with his hands on top of his paper-strewn desk. "So tell me, young man, are you good at lying?"

"I don't call my travel story lying exactly," said Raiford. "I was just spinning a yarn."

"Can you spin a yarn in a tight spot, such as …" he paused, "if you are caught by the enemy?"

"Yes, sir, I can." Raiford told the two men about his capture by Confederates while driving a supply wagon, the false story he told his captors, and his release the next morning because they believed him.

Colonel Newcombe picked up a paper from the top on a pile, handed it to Raiford, and said, "This is a telegram from Major General John Adams Dix, commander of the Department of the East. Dix wants more courageous, clever men to serve as spies in Canada."

Canada! Raiford said, "I didn't know we had spies in Canada."

Hector said, "We have spies, police, and detectives of well-established character, but not as many as the Confederates have."

"And the Rebels up there are not of well-established character," said Joseph.

"Draft dodgers, prison escapees, and ne'er-do-wells," added Hector.

"In truth, we don't know how many Confederates are in Canada," said the colonel. "We need more information. We need men stationed in more places. Our lines are spread too thin."

"Isn't Canada neutral?" asked Raiford.

Colonel Newcombe nodded and lowered his eyes. "It's a sad day when we have to violate the neutrality of a friendly nation. England won't join either side. We should honor her stance but how can we? If Confederates are in our northern neighbor, getting weapons, planning evil acts against us, we need to know!" He pounded his desk.

Hector asked, "Do you have a family?"

"No, I'm a single man."

"I'd go myself but my wife became frantic when I suggested it."

The colonel said, "I need you here, Hector." Turning toward Raiford, the officer asked, "Are you interested in being reassigned?"

Immediately, Raiford responded, "Yes." *Away from the killing.*

The older man said, "This work requires caution, tact, and bravery. You would be detached from your regiment for an unknown length of time, perhaps until the end of the war."

Raiford sat forward on his seat and said, "Wherever I can serve, I am willing."

Shuffling through his papers, Joe Newcombe began handing them to Raiford one by one as he talked. "We know Rebs are buying gunboats manufactured in England. We think they're getting rifles and cannons and who knows what else from Canada. We don't know how Englishmen are working with Canadians or if they are. Maybe it's only Rebel skulkers in Canada who are undermining our efforts."

Hector said, "We're caught in a pincer with Rebels to the south and also north of our borders."

"I read about the handful of Rebels who raided St. Albans, Vermont, and escaped to Canada," said Raiford.

"We think that was only the tip of the iceberg," said Hector.

"There could be thousands," said Joseph.

"That many?" Raiford looked from one man to the other.

"We don't know. We just don't know," said the colonel, leaning back in his chair. "That's why we need more of our detectives there to follow up on leads, to confirm or dispel rumors."

Captain Smith said, "If we can nab these men, we think the officials in Canada will prosecute the culprits for violating their neutrality."

Raiford listened to the two officers explain details as he perused the papers handed him. Hector sent a telegram to Atlanta that day, requesting the reassignment and asking for confirmation of Raiford's good record. Two hours after the captain's wire, General Sherman wired back that Raiford was highly regarded and his reassignment was approved. Raiford began immersing himself in the intelligence about espionage north of the border. He prepared for a week.

Today, he had studied reports from seven a.m. to seven p.m. and was exhausted when he lay down on his bed at the United States Hotel.

* * *

Anathea could hear nothing from the interior of room 559 as she listened between knocks. "Mr. Cutter! Children! Get up! You must get out!" Anathea pressed her ear against the door and held her hand over her other ear to muffle the hall noises. "Beatrice! Freddie! Mr. Cutter!"

Maybe he's already dead, thought Anathea. *I must get the children.*

Suddenly, she felt light headed.

Oh, not now! Please, Lord! Don't let it happen now!

Anathea's panic attacks had subsided recently. She had not experienced one since fleeing from Kentucky. Hoping to stave off the symptoms, which she knew too well, she resolved to focus on the problem at hand and not succumb to the dizziness.

The door was locked. She turned to room 560 across the hall and struck the wooden barrier with her fist. No answer. She turned the knob. The door opened. Rushing in, Anathea saw the silhouette of a man atop the covers. The dark room was lighted only by the gas lights in the hall.

Why hasn't he awakened? Is he drunk?

"Get up! I need your help, sir!" Anathea shouted as she leaned over the bed and shook his shoulders. The motion made her head swim. *Not now. Don't faint now.* She felt his muscles tense beneath the fabric of his cotton shirt. Without forewarning, Raiford reached up, clutched her upper arms, and rolled them both off the bed. Thud! They landed on their sides.

Who is attacking me? Raiford felt the mass of tangled hair against his face. *It's a woman!*

Anathea gasped and thought: *I can't breathe.*

Raiford yanked her by one arm as he stood up. Attempting to gain her balance, Anathea leaned her forehead against his chest. He took her other arm and held her firmly. Their bodies were inches apart.

"Fire. Help," she mumbled. Turning toward the door, she fumbled for his hand, found it, took hold, and guided him into the hall.

"A man … consumption … children… room locked," she said.

They both coughed as smoke reached their lungs. The hallway was bedlam. Anathea ignored her light-headedness. She had a mission. At the door of 559, Raiford released her hand and tried the knob.

He's not drunk. His actions are steady, Anathea thought as she watched him.

Raiford shoved his shoulder against the door to no avail. He kicked the panel near the keyhole. The wood splintered.

"Mr. Cutter! Beatrice! Open the door!" Anathea shouted through the broken opening. Raiford reached into the jagged hole, scraped his wrist on the splinters, felt the key, and unlocked the door. Blood trickled from his cut wrist onto his white cuff.

Anathea and Raiford, coughing and stumbling, pushed against each other as they entered the darkened room. A single candle burned on the little table by the window.

"There's a fire! You must get out!" Anathea declared.

"Papa can't get up," said Beatrice. Wearing only a nightgown, the little girl stood beside the bed and gripped the blanket which was pulled up to Mayfield's chin.

"I'll help him," said Raiford.

"Where's your brother?" asked Anathea.

"Hiding," said Beatrice.

"Here I am," Freddie said, crawling from under the bed. His nightshirt snagged on the bed frame.

Raiford scooped up the little boy, tearing the hem of his nightshirt. Holding Freddie with one arm, Raiford flung the blanket off Mayfield and reached down to help the man rise. Anathea took the quilt from the foot of the bed, tossed it over Beatrice's thin shoulders, and pulled her by the hand toward the door.

"I can manage," said Mayfield in a weak voice. "Take the children." He pushed Raiford's hand aside and motioned toward the door.

Raiford snatched up the father's blanket, flung it around Freddie, and said, "Hurry!"

When Raiford exited the room, he could see Anathea and Beatrice at the head of the stairs before they disappeared amid the people starting down. Mayfield staggered to the doorway and froze. Breathing the smoky air into his diseased lungs, he coughed and coughed.

"Come on, Papa," Freddie said over Raiford's shoulder as he was carried down the stairs. This was the boy's last sight of his father.

"Loosen your hold, little man," Raiford said, turning the corner on the landing. "You're choking me."

The boy obeyed. Raiford moved the boy's chubby legs to encircle his waist, pulled him securely against his chest, and continued the descent in the crowded stairwell. Ahead of them, Beatrice used both hands to hold her quilt, so Anathea kept her hand on the child's shoulder and guided her amid the rushing people. Fearing she might fall, Anathea held the railing and thought: *I hope I can find them when we get outdoors. There are so many people. Don't let me faint, Lord.*

Reaching the lobby where Mr. Carlton directed the frightened guests into the street, Anathea stopped and waited, but only for a few moments. The hotel guests were eager to escape the burning building. Anathea and Beatrice were swept out with the crowd.

* * *

In the distance, fire bells rang loudly. At the Winter Garden Theatre at 624 Broadway, near the Astor Hotel which was also burning, three sons of the famous English thespian, Junius Booth, were performing together for the first and last time in the play *Julius Caesar.* The eldest, Junius Brutus Booth, Junior, was playing Cassius. Edwin Booth had the part of Brutus. And the youngest of the three, John Wilkes Booth, was portraying Marc Antony. The performance was a benefit to raise money for a statue of William Shakespeare in Central Park.

When a coil of smoke seeped into the theater from the LaFarge Hotel next door, the audience of two thousand wondered if this was part of the drama. The smoke rose from under the stage.

"Fire!" shouted a man's voice from the darkened theater.

In the dress circle, Superintendent of Firemen, Mr. Leonard, stood up and yelled, "That's only a drunken man! Go on with the play!"

While the actors continued mouthing the words of Shakespeare, Mr. Leonard ran to the basement where he and stage hands extinguished the flames.

* * *

As Anathea and Beatrice left the 220-room hotel, they moved to the edge of the crowd. Anathea could not stop coughing. Her legs felt like rubber. She feared collapsing.

I cannot faint in this crowd. I would be trampled. I must remain calm for the little girl's sake. Don't faint. Don't faint.

Many of the people were coughing. They breathed in the cold night air. Anathea looked behind and around her, searching for, but not seeing, the stranger with Freddie and Mr. Cutter.

"We will wait here and watch," Anathea said, keeping a firm grasp of the girl's shoulder.

"I can't see from down here!" protested the child. "Everyone's in the way."

"I can. I'll tell you when I see Freddie."

"And Papa, too," Beatrice said. "He's very sick."

"Yes, I know. But the man who has Freddie will help him."

"He's going to die."

"Oh, I hope not." Anathea noticed that the center part in Beatrice's blonde hair was uneven and supposed that the girl had fixed her hair by herself. To distract her, Anathea asked, "Where's your mama?"

Taking in the cool air helped alleviate Anathea's dizziness. *I am not going to faint. Thank you, Lord.*

"She's with Jesus," the little girl answered.

"I'm sorry, Beatrice," she said with sincerity. "My mother is with Jesus, too."

The little girl said, "Maybe they know each other."

"Perhaps," said Anathea, smiling for the first time since the fire started.

In order to get the child's mind off the drama around them, Anathea asked, "Where are you and Freddie and your papa going?"

"To see Grandma and Grandpa."

* * *

Joan and Varney Cutter lived in Guelph, Ontario, Canada West. They had received a letter from their son Mayfield, telling them of his medical furlough due to consumption and that he was bringing his children to them. Joan read the letter aloud to her husband, who simply smiled and nodded as if she was reading a poetic Bible passage.

A tall, lanky man, Varney Cutter enjoyed robust health and a busy schedule until last year when his mind began to decline. As owner of Cutter Industries, Varney became forgetful, even to the extent of forgetting to go to work. He could talk about people and events from years ago but not remember the hour just past. His employees saw less and less of his stately gray head moving among them. They put his absence down to old age and prosperity. He simply did not need to come to work every day. The company was doing well with manager E.

L. Pearson and bookkeeper Kirk McCarrell in the office on Farquhar Street.

Plump and pleasant, Joan Cutter, Varney's wife, was happy to have him home more often, but distressed by his mental state. Joan endeavored to keep Varney's condition secret from neighbors and church friends. She wanted to shield him from embarrassment.

"He's not feeling up to his usual self," Joan said several times a week when someone inquired about Varney.

Although the large mansion required several servants, Joan did not replace the live-in help when they took other jobs. Instead, she hired day workers and was careful to keep Varney in another part of the house when they came.

When Joan learned of her son's fatal disease, she felt weighed down by despair. No one shared her anguish -- certainly not her husband. When his wife mentioned their only child, Varney spoke of Mayfield as a little boy.

While Joan and Varney's granddaughter Beatrice waited outside a burning hotel in New York City, they went to bed early. Joan was coming down with a cold.

"It's too early to go to bed," Varney protested in his soft voice.

"I know, dear, but I don't feel well." She crawled under the covers of the big bed they had shared for 35 years. Before closing her eyes, she added the statement she had made every night during those years: "I love you, dear."

Varney repeated the endearment without emotion.

* * *

In front of the United States Hotel, the press of the crowd made Beatrice and Anathea move farther away from the entrance. Anathea insisted Beatrice hold her quilt with only one hand so she could hold her other hand.

"I'm afraid we might get separated," said Anathea, taking the little hand.

"Do you see Papa and Freddie yet?" asked Beatrice, who left her hand limp in Anathea's grasp.

"Not yet. Tell me about your grandparents. Where do they live? In New York?"

"No. In Canada. Papa left the army to take us there."

"Where have you been while Papa was a soldier?"

"At the house of mean old Mrs. Ritterspaugh." Beatrice's tone indicated her dislike of the woman. "We called her Bitters-spew." The little girl spit out the last syllable as she made a face.

Anathea smiled briefly before asking, "Why was she mean?"

"She had too many children and she didn't like any of us," answered Beatrice.

"Where was that?"

"Newark." Beatrice strained to see above the crowd and asked, "Do you see them yet?"

"Not yet," Anathea said as her mind went to the headmistress at the Louisville Home for Friendless Girls. *She had too many children and didn't like any of us either.*

* * *

Anathea Sarah Brannaman went to the Louisville Home for Friendless Girls, an orphanage with a rich patroness and staffed by strict older women, when she was twelve years old. Her mother, Anna, a widow suffering from tuberculosis, entered the poor house where she died a week later. Anathea's only sibling, her brother Adam, was apprenticed to a hat maker and hated it. On his days off, Adam visited his sister until one day in 1859, when she was fifteen. On his last visit, he told her he was going to the gold fields in California to make his fortune. She cried when they parted. As for her father, she knew that he was a poor, itinerant preacher who died when she was two.

Living in the red brick orphanage on State Street, Anathea was eager for the day when she turned sixteen and, by law, could leave the unhappy place. She had a friend among the staff, Miss Barbara Dell, who taught reading, spelling, and penmanship. Anathea intended to write to Barbara when she was settled. The watch brooch which Anathea treasured was a wedding and farewell gift from Miss Dell.

After Adam departed, Anathea had to change her plans because they could no longer include her brother. She harbored no dreams of riches from California gold fields. The idea of such a long journey frightened her.

* * *

Adam Brannaman also changed his plans because, when he arrived in California, he quickly saw the men making the money were merchants not miners. He began by clerking in a store in Sacramento, then buying into part ownership, and eventually owning the business. He and Anathea wrote to each other but months separated each letter. Adam had intended to stay in the far west until the lady he was courting accepted another man's marriage proposal. That startling event spurred him to make plans for selling his store and returning home. By August, he arrived at the Great Salt Lake. Becoming acquainted with the Mormons there, Adam pondered his sister's life at the Shaker settlement in Kentucky.

He wondered: *Are Shakers like Mormons? Will they allow me to enter their village? It's not a city like this place. Maybe they forbid outsiders admittance. Will I like her husband? She wrote nothing about him in her last letter. Why would that be? 'We are well and working hard' was all she wrote at the conclusion. Perhaps she was tired. Won't she be surprised to see me?*

* * *

Anathea met Monro Emmert when he came every Monday and Friday to deliver fresh vegetables to the Friendless Girls' kitchen. Anathea, shy in the presence of men whom she seldom saw, chatted with Monro and soon looked forward to Mondays and Fridays.

The headmistress thought well of Monro Emmert, who was polite and soft-spoken. The other girls teased the couple. Monro took the jesting in his stride. When Anathea asked him about jobs she could do when she moved out of the orphanage, he became apprehensive, telling her that Louisville was not a place for a young single lady. When Monro proposed, Anathea thought it was her best option. They were married in July 1860. He referred to her as "my good deed" because he had rescued her from the evils of the city by bestowing the status of a married woman upon her.

Anathea's first letter to Adam after leaving the orphanage told about her marriage and new life at the Emmert farm. The next letter was about the couple's move to the Shaker community near Harrodsburg. And the last letter Adam received from his sister did not mention Monro.

* * *

On crowded Fulton Street in front of the United States Hotel, a metropolitan policeman said, "Move back please! All of you move back!"

At five feet three inches tall, Anathea could not see the hotel entrance over the heads of the people.

"I can't see them coming out," said Anathea.

"I'm going to the door!" Beatrice pulled away from Anathea.

"No! Come here!" Anathea grabbed for the girl. When someone pushed Beatrice, Anathea kept her from falling.

"We must wait. Hold my hand. We will move closer to the door together." Anathea wiggled her way among the milling bodies as she led the little girl.

Firemen, pulling their truck on foot, arrived on Fulton Street. Another truck, from a different station, came to the Water Street entrance. Bystanders made way for the firemen who raced into the wooden hotel. Anathea and Beatrice were blocked from going further.

Will they find us? Where are they? Will they get out?

The quilt was slipping. Anathea leaned down to pull it closely around the little girl.

"You're not looking," Beatrice said.

"He will find us. You need to keep warm." Anathea spoke while pushing the hair out of her eyes. Her braid was completely undone.

The night wind was cold. Although it had rained that morning, the afternoon had been clear. The city's first snow on November 15 was all melted by the 30-hour rain storm on November 20.

Anathea had a sudden thought: *What would the headmistress say if she knew I was in public with my hair down, blowing in the wind like this? What a silly thing to worry about. At least, Miss Dell would understand. And, besides, I didn't faint.*

Bending over the child, Anathea said, "Let's pray." Without any word of agreement from the girl, Anathea said, "Please, Lord, bring them safely out of the hotel – Freddie and his father and the stranger."

A young couple near them added their prayers. A teenager prayed. A circle of peace descended on the small group amid the confusion of the crowd.

Although the fire was confined to the top floor, the entire hotel was aroused and almost all of the guests evacuated. Besides hotel guests in the street, neighbors descended into the mob. The buzz of voices filled the night.

Nearly 4,000 men served as volunteers in the New York City Fire Department. They were divided into fifty engine companies, fifty-six hose companies, and seventeen hook-and-ladder companies. Strong competition existed among the fire companies. Each company wanted to prove it was the fastest and the best at putting out fires. If a man served in the right company with good political connections, he might get a patronage job that paid well. Besides, these men loved the excitement.

Anathea saw a hose company do nothing as it awaited the arrival of its favorite engine company. A fireman stood on a hose to reduce water pressure of a disliked fire company, and another fireman slugged him in the chest to knock him off the hose.

Turning her attention from the firemen to the people, Anathea searched faces and silently prayed.

"I see him!" Anathea said to Beatrice as she waved one hand and held tight to the little girl with her other hand. "Here we are! Over here! Freddie! Frederick!" *What's his name? The stranger? I'd call his name if I knew it.*

Freddie released his hold on Raiford's neck and fluttered his hands near his shoulders, as was his habit when he was exited. "I see! I see!"

"So do I. Hold onto me," Raiford said to the little boy, who grabbed him around the neck once more. The man pushed his way through the crowd.

"Here! Take him!" Raiford said as he thrust the boy toward Anathea.

"No! Don't go!" cried Freddie, reaching out, which made it difficult for Anathea to hold him. "Raiford! Come back!"

Anathea struggled to keep from dropping the frantic child.

"I'm going to get their father!" Raiford called over his shoulder and disappeared.

* * *

Historic Note: Only eight Confederates created the mass panic in New York City on November 25, 1864. The Southern patriots were angered by Union General David Hunter burning the Shenandoah Valley and General William Sherman starting his destructive trek across Georgia. Although the hotel fires did not do the extensive damage the Confederate officers had planned, they did accomplish one goal—fear of the enemy across their northern border. Many northern Americans had become immune to the war in the south until now. But with Manhattan's commercial district ablaze, that immunity changed. Confederates were now on their doorsteps creating terror. At last, citizens recognized the desperate need for a peace conference that might result in two separate countries.

CHAPTER TWO

FIRE REFUGEES

*Wherein Raiford and Anathea care for
grieving children; a church offers aid;
Raiford and Anathea pray.*

"I want Raiford! I want Papa! I wanna go home!" Freddie wailed amid coughing. He wiggled and twisted out of Anathea's hold.

"Your sister is here," Anathea said, setting him on the ground.

As soon as Freddie saw Beatrice, he flung his arms around her. Beatrice hugged him and declared, "We're orphans, Freddie! We're orphans now!"

"You don't know that," Anathea said in an attempt to sooth the distraught children. "That man – what did you call him – Raiford? He went to get your papa." *Please, Lord, let it be so.* "Everything will be all right."

Or will they both burn to death?

Freddie had dropped his blanket when he hugged his sister. Anathea wrapped the blanket around both children and took the quilt for herself. She looked around to see if anyone needed the quilt, but those near her had on coats or covers of some kind. Being mindful of the needs of others had been a part of orphanage life which stayed with Anathea even after leaving the place.

Two white-coated waiters carried glasses on silver trays and called, "Water! Water anyone!"

Anathea took a glass and held it for Freddie to drink first. His coughing eased. With half the glass full, Anathea offered it to Beatrice.

"Share with her," Freddie admonished his sister as he pulled the glass away.

Anathea gratefully finished the few swallows remaining.

"Where's Papa? Why doesn't he come?" wailed Beatrice.

"Maybe he's too tired," said Freddie.

"I am sure Mr. Raiford will bring him down," Anathea said. "We must watch for them."

A waiter took the empty glass from her.

"Lift me up! I can't see," said Freddie.

Keeping the quilt edges in her fists, Anathea wrapped the boy in her arms and held him up. Freddie did not wiggle but clung to Anathea like a little monkey.

Moving away, Beatrice complained, "I can't see."

"No! Stay close to us! We don't want to get separated!" Anathea called.

"Come back, Beatrice!" Freddie yelled, and his sister returned to hold the boy's ankle.

"Are we orphans?" Freddie looked down at Beatrice.

Before she could answer, Anathea said, "No, you're not orphans. I'm certain Mr. Raiford will bring your papa out."

Please, Lord, not orphans. Not like me.

Beatrice rested her head against her brother's leg. Anathea lifted him slightly to have a better hold.

"You're a heavy little boy," she said, smiling at him.

"I'm a big boy."

"How old are you?"

"Two almost three."

Anathea asked Beatrice the same question in hopes of getting her mind off the drama before them.

"Six," said Beatrice in a crisp voice. "Can you see them yet?"

"Not yet," said Anathea.

"Freddie, can you see them?" the sister asked, as though Anathea's answer was not adequate.

"Nope," said Freddie.

Anathea prayed: *Lord, watch over Mr. Raiford and Mr. Cutter. Protect them. Thank you that I haven't fainted.*

A Bible story came into Anathea's mind. Because Freddie was getting heavy, she knelt down and set him on his feet as she asked, "Do you know about Daniel's friends in the fiery furnace?"

"Daniel was in the lions' den," Beatrice said.

"Not that story. This story is about Daniel's friends."

Anathea summarized the Bible story and hardly finished when Beatrice said, "Stand up and look for them."

As soon as she stood up, Anathea saw Raiford.

"Here we are! Over here! I have the children!" Waving, she repeated her words until Raiford moved toward her.

Raiford, his face and beard smudged with soot, squinted in the gas light. His dark eyes were watery from the smoke. He was coughing hard. And he was alone.

"Where's Papa?" Beatrice grabbed his shirt sleeve.

Raiford took the girl's hand, leaned over, and found Freddie's hand. Anathea put her hands on the backs of the children.

Raiford said, "I carried your father to an ambulance."

An ambulance! Then he's all right, thought Anathea. But his next words ended her moment of elation.

"Your father is resting now in the arms of Jesus," Raiford said softly.

Beatrice burst into tears. When Freddie saw his sister crying, he too began to wail. Raiford put his arms around Beatrice and Freddie at the same time as he knelt on one knee on the cold bricks. Anathea felt tears trickle down her cheeks.

I want to comfort them, too. What can I do? Lord, guide us now.

Anathea touched Freddie's soft hair and would have done the same for Beatrice, but the girl pulled away when she felt the woman's hand on her head. Raiford, who continued to cough, looked at her and shook his head.

Does that mean there was no hope? Was Mr. Cutter dead when he got to him?

Another fire crew arrived. The crowd shifted to make way. Anathea was pushed aside. Immediately, Raiford snatched up Freddie and said to Beatrice, "Give me your hand, honey."

Beatrice obeyed. Raiford moved toward Anathea, who was unable to return to him and the children because of the flow of people.

Suddenly, a young man carrying a notepad and pencil appeared at Anathea's side. He said, "It appears you were in the fire. Can you tell me what happened?"

When she stared at him, he added, "I'm a reporter with the *New York Tribune*."

Anathea felt a surge of panic. *A reporter! My story published! No!*

"What room were you in when the fire started?" asked the young man, holding his pencil over the small pad.

"I would rather not say." Anathea froze. *If I give my room, he can check the register for my name. Monro might read it. He might find me.*

"Were you harmed?" the reporter asked.

"Please talk to someone else," Anathea said. Her mouth felt dry. Her head began to spin.

Raiford, having heard the reporter's questions and her replies, recognized fear in her voice, and said, "This has been an ordeal for her, sir. If you don't mind, talk to others, please."

At Raiford's words, which were spoken politely, the *Tribune* reporter nodded and retreated.

Why wouldn't she answer his questions? Is she shy or hiding something? Raiford asked himself.

Metropolitan police were directing people to allow space for the new firemen and their equipment. Both Beatrice and Freddie were crying softly.

A man with a gentle voice said, "Would your family come with me?" Raiford turned and faced a middle-aged man wearing a black hat and overcoat. "We have shelter in my church. It's just around the corner. I'm Pastor Ralph Higdon."

The minister and his neighbor, Crane Williams, were going among the crowd and inviting them to Calvary Baptist Church on Pearl Street. Raiford caught Anathea's eye and tipped his head slightly in a gesture which asked permission. Without hesitation, she nodded.

"Thank you. We will," Raiford said to the pastor, who shouldered his way through the crowd to lead his newly-acquired flock to shelter.

"Can you carry him?" Raiford asked, as he held the chubby boy toward Anathea.

When she took the boy in her arms again, Raiford picked up Beatrice who rested her head on his broad shoulder and wept. Anathea's hair blew wildly in the breeze. Raiford walked in his stocking feet and patted the little girl on her back. A blood stain on Raiford's cuff gave evidence of his cut wrist. Men's angry voices surrounded them as they walked.

"It's the work of Rebels!"

"Bet they came down from Canada!"

"Richmond said they would!"

"I heard there's a hoard of 'em living up there."

"We ought to cross the border and smoke out the devils!"

"Hang them from the lamp posts!"

"No good arsonists!"

"We should burn them at the stake!"

"Cowards! All of them!"

"Setting fire to innocent civilians!" said a woman.

"They can't fight on the battlefield like our brave boys are doing!"

"Dirty cowards resort to making war on common folks!"

"They've substituted the torch for the sword!"

"Nothing like this in the annals of barbarism!"

* * *

John Headley, having lit similar fires at the City Hotel, the Everett House, and the Astor House, was walking down Broadway when he saw a crowd at Barnum's American Museum. Pandemonium reigned. Visitors to the museum, which was owned and operated by Phineas Taylor Barnum, climbed down ladders from the second and third floors to escape the blaze.

"Get my animals out!" shouted the museum's manager.

A stampede from the burning building knocked down bystanders. Three portly girls, two dwarfs, three giants, and Indian warriors fled. Twenty-five hundred from the lecture hall audience also ran from the museum.

Mr. Headley was surprised about the Barnum fire because none had been intended there. Only hotels were scheduled to be burned. Nevertheless, Captain Robert Cobb Kennedy, having set fires at the New England House, Lovejoy's, and Tammany Hotel, took it upon himself to set the famous showman's place afire, too.

As planned, young Headley went down Broadway to the North River wharf, where he hid in the shadows and tossed bottles of Greek fire in six different places. One of the ensuing fires was on a barge filled with hay which made a huge conflagration. Going to the City Hall, John caught a street car and rode to Bowery Street, opposite the Metropolitan Hotel.

After walking half a square, he saw his cohort, Captain Kennedy. There was no mistaking the Louisianan's limp. He had been wounded in the thigh on the first day of the Battle of Shiloh.

Intending to play a trick, John came behind his friend and slapped him on the shoulder. Rob squatted as he drew his pistol.

"Whoa there," said John, laughing.

Recognizing his fellow Confederate, the captain said, "I ought to shoot you for giving me such a fright."

The two men shared their experiences. Robert told John that he had broken a bottle of Greek fire on the edge of a step at the Barnum's Museum, because he said, "There would be fun to start a scare."

As the two conspirators talked, the occupants of the museum ran helter skelter into the street.

* * *

The fire at the United States Hotel was quickly extinguished, but other hotel rooms smoldered for hours before the fires were detected. Nevertheless, all nineteen hotel fires were put out sometime in the night. Churches, boarding houses, and other hotels offered alternative accommodations for the displaced people.

At Calvary Baptist Church, Catherine Williams, Crane's wife, offered glasses of water to the new arrivals as her husband pumped water in the basement kitchen. Prudence, the pastor's wife, offered soap and clean towels to wash off soot and grime. Pastor Higdon told the newcomers where things were in the large stone building.

"Come and have some bread and grape juice," invited the pastor, motioning the bedraggled people toward the kitchen as soon as they were all indoors. "Prudence, dear, let's give them those leftovers from yesterday."

The Baptists had held a Thanksgiving Day communion and prepared more than needed. The pastor's wife retrieved the broken pieces of bread from the tightly-closed tin, while Catherine got out the ceramic jug of grape juice. Ralph helped Crane set out basins of water for washing.

Anathea, Raiford, and the children washed before sitting down at a long table. Although the grieving children had lessened their sobbing, when the pastor praised the Lord for everyone's safety, they started crying again.

"Papa burned up!" cried the little boy on Anathea's lap.

"You lied to us!" Beatrice glared at Anathea, who sat beside her.

In explanation, Anathea told Raiford, "I said you would rescue their father. I just wanted to..." She could not continue her sentence because of the lump in her throat.

I did lie to them. Lord, forgive me. Anathea's thoughts made her heart ache. She wanted to cry with the children, but she also knew that she must be strong. Suddenly, she was back at the orphanage, watching children cry and trying to hold herself above the agony. *Be strong. Don't let it affect me. It's not my father who just died.*

Nevertheless, Anathea felt tears sting and reached up one hand to cover her eyes. Prudence put a dish towel in Anathea's hand, sat down beside her, and asked gently, "What is it?"

Because Anathea was unable to answer, Raiford told the pastor's wife about the death of the children's father.

"Will you sit on my lap?" Prudence asked Freddie as she took the boy so Anathea could dry her tears.

Rev. Higdon sat across the table from the grieving children and spoke about heaven into which their father just entered. The children listened to the pastor's gentle words as the fire refugees washed, ate pieces of bread, drank water and grape juice, and endeavored to recover from the trauma they had just experienced.

Crane showed some men the donations room where blankets and pillows, given for soldiers, were piled. From these, beds were made for the refugees. They set up folding screens to create alcoves in the large basement. Gas lamps on the walls and candles on the tables provided light. A large pot-belly stove in the center of the big room offered heat for those near it, but the warmth barely reached the edges of the fellowship hall.

With the Cutter children quiet now, their crying having subsided for the moment, Rev. Higdon went to the head of the table and announced to the twenty-three people: "You can take your bedding upstairs and sleep on the pews or down here if you prefer. We will light the stove at the back of the sanctuary. Make yourselves at home. Take what you need from the donations room. Let my wife and me, or our neighbors, Mr. and Mrs. Williams, know how we can help you."

The pastor's wife, sitting near Raiford, asked, "Is that blood on your shirt?"

"It's nothing," Raiford said.

"I'll get you some salve and a bandage," Prudence said, setting Freddie on the seat as she rose.

Anathea, who turned down the proffered bread, drank a small glass of grape juice and observed the children. Freddie was rosy cheeked with bright blue eyes and tousled blond hair. He appeared healthy as could be. Beatrice, on the other hand, was slender, with sad blue eyes and prominent cheek bones. One of her braids had lost its tie and was coming undone.

"Won't you eat some bread?" Anathea encouraged the girl.

"Freddie can," said Beatrice.

Freddie picked at the small pieces of bread placed in front of him. Raiford encouraged both children to eat and drink.

Prudence brought a tin of salve and strip of bandage to the table, Anathea opened the container and reached for Raiford's hand. Something needed to be done and she had been taught to do whatever was needful. Without a second thought, Anathea pushed up his shirt sleeve and asked, "How did you do this?"

"The broken door."

"Oh, yes, I remember now."

She proceeded to apply salve with her right hand while cradling his large hand in her left one.

What a soft hand for a man. Monro's hands were not soft. They were calloused like his heart.

Catherine Williams said, "I've found some jam to put on your bread," and proceeded to add the delicacy to bread pieces. The children chewed slowly. They were intent on the voices of the people at the table and did not hear Anathea's whispered question to Raiford.

"What's to be done about their father?"

Raiford said softly, "I will ask Brother Higdon about burying him."

Her touch is gentle. What pretty hands she has -- such lovely long fingers. And her hair is beautiful.

"He had consumption." She replaced the lid on the tin and took the strip of white cloth.

"That explains it." Raiford held his hand up so she could reach underneath as she wrapped the bandage around and around. When she came to the end of the fabric, Anathea leaned down and tore the end with her teeth. Her unbound hair draped over his arm. Once again, the thought came to Raiford.

What beautiful hair. And a new thought: *I wish I could touch it.*

Raising her head, Anathea ripped the cloth so she could wrap it in both directions and tie a knot.

"Thank you," said Raiford. "I think we should introduce ourselves. My name is Raiford Young."

"Freddie said your name was Raiford. I didn't know if that was a first or last name."

"It was my mother's maiden name."

"I'm Anathea Brannaman. The children are Beatrice and Freddie Cutter."

"Are you related to them?"

"No. I just met them in the lobby earlier this evening."

Anathea looked into his dark, expressive eyes. His brown wavy hair touched his collar. His neatly-trimmed beard and moustache, the same brown as his full head of hair, did not obscure his lips. With a patrician nose, high forehead, and tanned cheeks, Raiford Young was a handsome man.

Raiford took in the appearance of the young woman sitting beside him. Soot streaks on her cheeks did not mar her pretty features. Her light brown eyes shimmered in the candle light flickering on the table. Her long, thick hair cascaded around her shoulders and appeared to have copper highlights amid the brown. She wore a simple cotton dress with no hoop. Her breasts were small. Her hands were slender. Her mouth had a pleasing shape.

Raiford thought. *I wonder what it would be like to kiss her.*

He mentally shook himself to dispel the thought, and attributed it to the fact he had been in the army so long and away from females.

Some people began taking their bedding upstairs.

Raiford asked Anathea, "Would you like to sleep on pews or down here?" He tilted his head slightly as he awaited her decision.

"Here, I think," she said. "Pews are narrow. The children might fall."

Nodding in agreement, he asked, "Do you need anything from the donations room?"

"No. I'll sleep in my dress."

When Raiford told the children they would sleep on the floor of the church basement, both children began crying again.

"I want to sleep with Papa!" wailed Freddie.

"I want to go back to the hotel," sobbed Beatrice. "Papa is waiting for us there. He's worried about where we are."

Raiford picked up Freddie, holding him against his chest with one arm, and reached for Beatrice's hand, as he led them to an alcove bordered by two screens which had children's paintings of Bible scenes. Sitting on the blanket Crane placed on the floor for them, Raiford waited for Anathea to sit down too.

"You know your papa is not at the hotel. An ambulance took him. He was very sick," Raiford spoke softly. "His lungs were not healthy. That made it especially hard for him to breathe amid that smoke."

"Where is Papa?" asked Freddie in such a pitiful voice that Anathea wanted to cuddle him.

He's trying hard to be brave. They both are, she thought.

Raiford said, "Papa is where he will never, ever be sick again. Only his body is here on earth in a place called a mortuary."

"Is he in heaven?" asked Beatrice, who had heard the pastor's explanation but still needed confirmation.

"With Mama?" asked Freddie.

Before either of the adults could answer, Beatrice said, "We should not go to Canada after all. We should go to heaven and be with Papa."

Raiford caught Anathea's eye and saw the alarm in her expression. Quickly, Raiford took Beatrice's small hands in his large ones, looked at her, and said, "The Lord decides when we go to heaven. We do not make that decision ourselves. Your mama and papa are together in heaven, but God wants you and your brother to be together here on earth."

Freddie snuggled close to Raiford and asked, "Are you sure Papa found Mama? Heaven is a big place."

Raiford smiled, released one of Beatrice's hands so he could embrace the boy, and answered, "Heaven is a big place. That's why angels are there to help people find each other."

"Do you think an angel helped Papa find Mama?" asked the girl.

"I think Mama was already waiting for him," the man said.

Anathea felt as though she was observing a living tableau in which the characters spoke lines assigned in a script. Although she sat close and heard the dialogue, she had no lines to speak in her role.

"Would you like to pray for your parents before going to sleep?" Raiford asked. When the children said they would, Raiford moved from a sitting position to one on his knees. Anathea and the children did the same. Next, he took the children's hands and waited for them to reach out to Anathea, making a circle.

Raiford prayed, "Blessed Lord, I pray now for Mr. Cutter, the loving father of Beatrice and Freddie. He was a good earthly father to them, the same as you are a good heavenly father to us. Grant that he and Mama will be together without any delay. Make their new home, whether it's a cottage or a castle, a joyous place with friends and feasting. Give Papa the abundant rewards for serving you here below as he took care of Freddie and Beatrice." Raiford paused. "Miss Brannaman, do you want to pray?"

Monro never asked me to pray. He always dominated. I always submitted.

Anathea cast aside her unhappy thoughts and prayed, "Lord, help Beatrice and Freddie to remember their papa and not let his memory fade. Help them to know he is in a better place. Comfort them."

After a brief silence, Raiford said, "Amen."

The prayer calmed the children. Nevertheless, they cried themselves to sleep. This crying was soft-sounding sniffles as tears dampened their pillows.

Raiford pulled the covers over Freddie's little shoulders and slid down to lie next to him. Beatrice held her brother's hand under the covers. Anathea lay on the far side next to the girl, who wiggled away from the woman and snuggled with Freddie.

Raiford wondered: *Is this providential, Lord? Why have you brought these people into my life at this time? Have you forgotten that I have an assignment for the Union Army in Canada?*

He smiled to himself at the thought of God forgetting the job assigned to him.

* * *

Historic Note: British North America shared a border of nearly 4,000 unguarded miles with the United States of America. Peace existed between the two countries at a time when Civil War raged in the States. Several British colonies were lumped together in popular jargon as Canada. Canada West was Ontario where the Toronto Globe, the leading newspaper, gave support to the northern states. The French-speaking province of Quebec was Canada East, where the Montreal Gazette sided with the Confederacy. Canadians were fearful that a civil war could occur in their territory unless a strong national government took control.

CHAPTER THREE

REBELS! I KNEW IT!

Wherein fire refugees experience hospitality at
Calvary Baptist Church;
Raiford consults with his commander; and
Bennett Burley is arrested.

After midnight, the fellowship hall of Calvary Baptist Church became quiet as exhausted fire refugees fell asleep. The thick stone walls of the basement kept street sounds from intruding. Anathea and Raiford, however, were wide awake.

Anathea suddenly realized that she was sleeping with a man. *What would Monro think if he knew? I don't care what he thinks. Oh, when will I get him out of my thoughts?*

Although Raiford's body was weary, his mind was alert. *What a strange situation this is. I never expected such a turn of events. But then, I never imagined the tide of circumstances would bring me to New York.*

"Are you asleep?" he whispered into the darkness.

"No," Anathea opened her eyes.

"I want to thank you for awakening me in my room. I could have burned to death." He kept his tone low so as not to disturb the sleeping children.

"You must have been very tired to sleep with all the noise in the hallway."

"I have not had much rest in the last few days." After a moment, he added, "I've been preparing for my business trip."

I wonder what his business is. Instead of asking, Anathea said, "I should be thanking you for helping us."

"I could do no other."

"You could have simply saved yourself."

"No. I could not have done simply that." He smiled in the darkness.

She thought: *Why not? Monro probably would have.*

He thought: *If not for this woman, I could be in the city morgue with Mr. Cutter.*

Rev. Higdon extinguished the last wall lamp. Only a kitchen lantern provided light in the cavernous basement.

"Was it intentional – the fire?" Anathea whispered.

"I think so. The Rebels threatened to retaliate for what we've been doing in the South." Turning on his side toward her, he saw her shadowy form and knew that if he reached over the children, he could touch her. He changed his gaze to the black ceiling and said, "I've never been in a burning building before."

"Nor have I." She closed her eyes.

He pulled Freddie's little body against his chest and asked, "Why are you in New York?"

"To start a new life," said Anathea.

"A new life?" he pondered, and asked himself: *Is she a war widow?*

"Yes," she said without elaboration. *A new life without Monro. A new life without any man dominating me. A new life in which I make my own decisions.*

"What about you?"

"I have business taking me to Canada."

"Canada?" Opening her eyes, she turned her head toward him.

"Yes. I have some urgent matters awaiting me there."

"That's where the Cutter family was going."

"They were?"

"Yes. The children's grandparents live there."

Raiford said nothing.

Anathea thought: *Would he consent to escorting us? If not, could I make such a trip with these children alone? I was afraid to travel to California with Adam, but I've come alone to New York with no harm done me. But how can I provide? My paper money might be burned or stolen. But whatever my finances or lack thereof, these children must not go to an orphanage. Not there!*

Raiford thought: *This is not part of the plan I've been discussing these past few days. A woman and two children are stranded. Can I desert them? Certainly not! I must speak to the officers first thing tomorrow.*

Anathea's final thought before falling asleep was: *My plan was to disappear in the bowels of a big city, where Monro would never find me. But, whether this man helps me or not, Canada would be a better hiding place than New York.*

* * *

At the door of an elegant suite in the Queen's Hotel, Toronto, Canada West, a bellboy delivered a telegram to Jacob Thompson, currently Commissioner of the Confederate secret service based in Canada and formerly a U.S. Senator and Secretary of the Interior under President Buchanan. The distinguished-looking, middle-aged man with dark beard read the message, frowned, tipped the boy, and returned to the large living area where five men milled around, drinking, smoking, and talking.

"What is it, Colonel Thompson? Bad news?" asked one of the men.

Although Jacob had no official military title, the Confederate draft dodgers and escaped prisoners of war who gathered around him used the title of Colonel.

"It's not good. Our man in Guelph is being followed." Mr. Thompson handed the message to the nearest man, who read it and passed it on.

"What's he doing in Guelph?" asked another young man.

"Bennett Burley is getting torpedoes manufactured for us," Jacob answered.

"Bennett Burley," said a man by the wide window. "Haven't I heard that name before?"

"Undoubtedly," replied Jacob. "Mr. Burley was second in command of Captain Beall's abortive expedition to rescue our men on Johnson's Island."

"Does he need help up there in Guelph?"

"I can go."

"I would be glad to give him assistance."

"I know a little something about torpedoes."

"I can get those federals off his tail."

Each of the young men spoke before Jacob raised his hand to silence them and said, "I need some time to consider this."

"What are we going to do with those torpedoes?" asked a man puffing on a cigar.

"We could blow up the walls on Johnson's Island and free two thousand officers."

"Or blast that federal gunboat, the *Michigan,* out of Lake Erie."

"Why not explode one of their arsenals?"

"More than one – explode five or six."

"Gentlemen, I'll tell you the purpose," the older man said, as he sat down in a large upholstered chair. "My plan is to open up the Mississippi. Those torpedoes will be attached to rafts sent into the federal gunboats now patrolling our great river. That Union blockade must be broken up so our ships can sail again."

"The Mississippi River is a lifeline to our country," said a young man near the cart of liquor and glasses.

"What about winter? Canada has harsh winters. How will you transport the torpedoes? It's already November."

"Originally, I thought we could go through the Great Lakes but you're right. Things are starting to freeze," said Mr. Thompson. "Trains will have to be the route now."

"The South must break the stranglehold those Yankees have on our commerce."

"The Mississippi is the life line to our troop movements."

"Supplying our soldiers, too."

"Shipping cotton."

"We have to break that naval chain the Union has wrapped around us."

"We must have access to the outer world."

"Let me go to Guelph and see what I can learn from Mr. Burley."

"No, let me go. I know the weapons business."

"Where are the torpedoes being made?"

"A place called Cutter Foundry," said Commissioner Thompson.

* * *

In the morning, Raiford awoke to the smell of coffee. He moved from under the covers slowly so as not to awaken the woman and children.

"You need some boots," Rev. Higdon greeted Raiford when he padded into the kitchen.

"I didn't have time to put them on last night."

Raiford and the Baptist minister chatted as they stood near the stove. The two men agreed on a plan. After a quick breakfast and cleaning up, which included tugging on a pair of donated shoes, Raiford was ready.

Rev. Higdon told his wife where they were going, and Raiford said to her: "Please tell Miss Brannaman and the children that I will be back soon."

At the parsonage stable next door, Raiford hitched the horse to the two-seat Tilbury Buggie while Pastor Ralph fed two stray cats. The pastor, in the driver's seat, stopped at a corner for Raiford to purchase a copy of the *New York Times* from a newsboy.

"What's it say about the fires?" asked Rev. Higdon.

Raiford read aloud from the front page: "The city was startled last evening by the loud and simultaneous clanging of fire-bells in every direction, and the alarming report soon spread from street to street that a pre-concerted attempt was being made by rebel emissaries…"

"Rebels! I knew it!" declared Ralph as he flipped the reins. "Go on. What else?"

"Rebel emissaries, in accordance with the fiendish programme recently set forth by the Richmond papers, to burn New York and other Northern cities, in retaliation for the devastation of rebel territory by Union armies."

Once more, the minister interrupted Raiford's reading. "They mean Hunter's burning the Shenandoah Valley and Sherman's burning Atlanta."

"No doubt."

"Read on."

Raiford read: "The facts gathered by our reporters appear to confirm the truth of these reports."

"No one better than *Times* reporters," mumbled the pastor.

Raiford started the next paragraph. "The plan adopted by the incendiaries was to set fire at once, or nearly at once, to the principal hotels and other public buildings in the city." He skimmed down the list to find the United States Hotel. "Our hotel is not mentioned."

"Does it say how they did it?"

Raiford read, "In several instances, beds in vacant rooms were found saturated with phosphorus and filled with matches."

The Baptist minister said, "I talked to a fireman last night who said the windows of the rooms where the fires started were closed. The arsonists were not smart enough to know that fires need oxygen to spread."

"We were fortunate then," said Raiford. "If they were smarter, it could have been much worse."

Raiford had read the entire article by the time Rev. Higdon dropped him off before going on to the morgue.

* * *

When Anathea awoke and saw Raiford was gone, she felt a surge of panic. Clutching her arms across her chest to keep herself from trembling, she sat up and looked around the hall. *Maybe he's in the kitchen or another room. Would he have left? Why should he stay?*

Slipping from under the covers, she pulled the blanket securely over the sleeping children. In the kitchen, three church ladies were preparing breakfast. They spoke in low tones so as not to awaken others. Anathea looked around but did not see the pastor's wife.

* * *

At 77 Bleeker Street, Raiford went directly to the office of Colonel Joseph Newcombe, knocked, and entered upon command.

"Are you ready for your departure today?" the genial commander asked.

"Perhaps not today," said Raiford. "Something has come up."

"Oh," said Joseph, motioning for the younger man to sit. "What?"

Hector Smith entered without knocking in time to hear Raiford say, "I was in one of those blazing hotels last night."

"Were you hurt?" asked Hector, taking the chair beside Raiford.

"No. I'm unharmed," Raiford answered, and briefly told about his experience at the United States Hotel and Calvary Baptist Church.

"You're just in time to catch those foul incendiaries!" exclaimed the colonel. "Some believe they are still in the city, but I think they're heading back to their lair in Canada."

Hector asked, "Why must you delay?"

"The woman and two children need my assistance." Putting his hand on Hector's forearm, Raiford asked, "Can you prepare travel papers for them?"

"I could," he said, glancing toward the colonel, "if I had orders."

Raiford faced Joseph and said, "This would be a perfect cover for me. You told me that good spies need believable covers. They usually travel alone and thus are easily spotted. I think this is providential."

"Hum-m-m." Joseph leaned over his intertwined fingers on his desk and repeated. "Providential. Could be. Yes, it could be providential."

Hector said, "The Lord often works in our lives in just such unusual circumstances."

Joseph said, "But as a fictional family man, won't you be hindered? You will have to tend to them and not your work."

"I disagree," said Raiford. "The woman seems to be very capable. She will be an asset not a liability."

"Women have made good spies," said Hector.

"Nevertheless, you must keep your true mission a secret from her," said Joseph, scowling.

"They don't even know I am in the army," Raiford replied. "I turned in my uniform because I won't need it where I'm going."

The senior officer failed to notice that Raiford did not agree to keep his spy mission a secret from Anathea. Raiford thought: *He doesn't know her. I think she might be helpful to me.*

"Are you certain they will not be a burden?" asked the colonel.

"When I need freedom for any reason, Anathea can take care of the children. As soon as Freddie and Beatrice are safely with their grandparents, I can part company with them. They will not be a burden."

"I have a family," said Hector. "They're not at all a burden."

Joseph chuckled at his aide's remark and asked Raiford, "Where are the grandparents?"

"I don't know yet. I'm hoping to find information at the hotel."

The colonel nodded and admonished Raiford, "Now, when you get to Canada, don't venture off into some tundra area where we cannot reach you. Remember to telegraph but..."

Raiford finished the older man's sentence: "But send detailed reports by way of trustworthy messengers. Yes, Hector explained all that, sir."

The three men rose from their chairs and started toward the closed door.

"What excuse could you use for traveling with a family?" Joseph asked Raiford.

"The same one I had already planned. I'm going to a cool, dry climate for my health. Only now, I will say it's for my daughter's health. The little girl appears sickly, compared to her healthy brother. Her real father had consumption."

"He died in the fire, you said?"

"That's right, sir. The pastor who gave us shelter last night is seeing to the burial."

"All right," said the colonel as Hector got up and opened the door. "Prepare the additional travel papers for her and the children, Captain Smith. Can you leave on tonight's train?"

"Yes. We just have to attend the graveside funeral this afternoon," said Raiford.

Going toward his desk, Hector said, "Give me their names. I can bring the documents to the depot."

"Also, issue a draft for more money," said Joseph. "Families can be expensive."

* * *

In Guelph, Canada West, Joan Cutter got up late. She usually arose as soon as the sun was up. Because she had coughed frequently in the night, Mrs. Cutter did not sleep well. Hearing Varney banging pans in the kitchen awakened her. She put on a robe, went downstairs in their large brick house, and made tea and toast.

"Can we go for a walk?" Varney asked as she shuffled out of the kitchen.

"Not today, dear." She called over her shoulder. "I'm too sick. You must stay in the house today. All right, dear? Stay indoors."

"All right, dear," repeated Varney, who had no idea what he had just agreed to do.

* * *

When Raiford returned to the Calvary Baptist Church basement, he saw Freddie and Beatrice were still sleeping. Searching the large room, his eyes fell on Anathea. Her hair was neatly brushed and held back with a tie at her neck. She was setting a bowl of oatmeal in front of an elderly woman at the table where several people were eating.

I liked it better when your hair cascaded around your lovely face, he thought as he approached her. *I remember Lenore when her hair was down. She was never lovelier.*

Looking up, Anathea saw him approaching. Raiford noticed the redness of her eyes.

"You've been crying," he said softly as he came to her side.

How does he know?

No one had seen her cry. She had sobbed briefly in the ladies' room with the door closed. Her current situation had overwhelmed her. She felt deserted. Realizing she might faint, she had splashed cold water on her face and did not collapse. She thought that evidence of her tears had washed away.

"What's the matter?" Raiford took her upper arm and led her behind a folding screen where recent sleepers had been.

"I thought you were gone." Anathea looked at the tile floor.

Where did he get those shoes? They look shabby.

Raiford rubbed his hand from her shoulder to her elbow, and said, "I told Mrs. Higdon to let you know."

She backed away until his hand dropped from her arm.

"You did?" she asked, and lifted her gaze to meet his.

"Yes. Did you see her?"

"No. Mrs. Williams said she's busy upstairs."

Raiford told her, "Pastor Higdon dropped me off to see about some business before he went to the morgue."

At the word *morgue*, Anathea's eyes widened.

Raiford continued, "The pastor will perform a graveside service for Mr. Cutter this afternoon. Before that, if the children are up to it, we need to go back to the hotel and see about our belongings."

Nodding her consent to his plan, she started toward the table. Raiford walked beside her and said, "Miss Brannaman, this is not a problem that has been given to you alone. When you sought my aid in rescuing the Cutter family, you involved me. I believe the Lord wants me to help you. Therefore, I will not desert you and the children as long as you are in need of my help."

"Thank you," she murmured as she sat down in front of a spoon and empty bowl.

"I will see to their safe delivery to their grandparents. I promise you." He sat beside her. They waited for Prudence to serve oatmeal into their bowls.

"Well, here's another country heard from," said the pastor's wife, acknowledging the appearance of Beatrice and Freddie, hand-in-hand, coming toward the long table. She went to get more bowls.

The children, sleepy-eyed, stood in front of their rescuers as Beatrice made the declaration: "We're leaving!"

"Where are you going?" Raiford asked in a calm voice.

"We're going to the street," Freddie said in a determined tone.

His sister added, "We will make our own way to Grandma and Grandpa's."

Freddie said, "We're not going back to Mrs. Bitters-spew." Again, he made a face.

"Who?" Raiford asked.

Anathea said to him, "Mrs. Ritterspaugh was a neighbor who cared for them while their father was in the army."

Raiford nodded and said, "Let's talk about this over breakfast." He rose to pull the bench out for them to be seated. As he did so, he put his hand on Anathea's shoulder to steady her since she sat on the bench. "Are you hungry? The ladies have made oatmeal."

Freddie climbed onto the bench and sat close to Anathea. Mrs. Higdon placed two bowls of porridge on the white tablecloth and returned to the kitchen. As Beatrice sat down beside her brother, Raiford said, "Street life is not very comfortable at this time of year. The weather is starting to turn cold, you know." He sat beside Beatrice.

"We have coats," said the girl. "They're in our hotel room."

Reaching for the girl's hand, Raiford said, "Take your brother's hand so we can pray."

When Beatrice took Freddie's hand, Anathea took the little boy's other hand as Raiford blessed the food. As they ate, Raiford told them of the plan to return to the United States Hotel.

"We will get your coats and whatever else we can. Some things might be smoke damaged."

"What's smoke damaged?" asked Freddie.

"Things will smell like smoke," said Anathea.

"I don't care if our coats smell like smoke," said Beatrice. "We're leaving."

"Becoming vagabonds is not a good plan," Raiford told the children.

"Will we be bag-a-bons?" Freddie asked his sister.

"No," she said. "We will be ourselves."

Raiford patiently compared the life of a vagabond to that of a soldier. "Both soldiers and vagabonds sometimes must sleep on the ground. They don't always have enough to eat. Sometimes, when it rains or snows, their blankets are wet and don't keep them warm." After a slight pause, he said, "I have a better idea!"

The children ate as they listened to Raiford's soothing voice.

"How would you like to be our niece and nephew?" He glanced at Anathea to see if he could detect her reaction. She simply stared at him.

"Niece and nephew?" Freddie lowered his blond eyebrows in puzzlement.

"I would be your Uncle Raiford and this kind lady would be your Aunt Anathea. We would take you to your grandparents. How does that sound?"

Raiford had intended to discuss the idea with Anathea before mentioning it to the children. Although he had told Joseph and Hector that he would pretend they were his family, Raiford had second thoughts about that scheme. It would require that he and Anathea behave as husband and wife. He concluded that uncle and aunt would be easier and more proper.

"You're not really our uncle and aunt," said Beatrice, scowling.

"That's true," said Raiford. "It will be a game. Can you keep a secret?"

"I can," said Freddie.

Although Beatrice nodded consent to keeping a secret, she was remembering her mother's lover who called himself their uncle and also requested that she keep a secret.

* * *

In Lexington, Virginia, Brigadier General Edwin Gray Lee, who was called Ned, awaited word from his application for a long sick furlough. When he sent the request to Richmond last week, Ned was serving as commander of the Shenandoah Valley District's reserve forces. However, his poor health made it impossible to continue with the strain of those duties.

Having married Susan Pendleton on November 17, 1859, Ned worked as a lawyer in his home town of Shepherdstown, Virginia, which became West Virginia during the Civil War. In October 1860, on his doctor's advice, Ned Lee had gone to New York City to consult with Dr. John Wakefield Francis, who diagnosed tuberculosis. Among the physician's recommendations, one seemed a remote possibility – live in a cold, dry climate such as Canada or New England.

Now, however, the prospect of moving to Canada was clearly in his future. He resolved to take his wife with him, although sailors objected to a woman on board, claiming they brought bad luck, and luck was required for running the blockade. Ned did not relish the idea of putting his wife in such danger, nor could he imagine leaving her behind. He knew that his poor health prevented him from working in the field again. He could, however, serve the Confederacy in Canada, and that was what he intended to do. As soon as the furlough arrived, he would make definite plans.

* * *

At Fort Laramie, Wyoming, Adam Brannaman had become the driver for a young woman, whose driver departed the wagon train. It was mid September when they left the fort, with Adam's horse tied behind her wagon. The woman, escaping a polygamist marriage, was eager to reach her family in St. Louis. She talked and talked while Adam listened patiently. Adam had thought about courting the woman but she was too bitter about men. When he left her in St. Louis, he was grateful for the silence.

* * *

Before leaving Calvary Baptist Church, the little family went to the room of donated clothing to find coats.

Prudence Higdon came up to Anathea and said, "I forgot to give you Mr. Young's message about his errand this morning. I was busy upstairs with some people who needed me."

Anathea nodded. *So he did leave a message that he would come back. Why did I doubt him? Have I become distrustful of all men because of Monro?"*

Once again, she shook off the unwanted thought of her former husband.

Anathea and Raiford observed the way Beatrice tended to Freddie like a little mother. They learned that Freddie was smart, had a good vocabulary, and occasionally resented his doting sister's attention.

While helping Freddie find a matching mitten, Raiford asked, "Where do your grandparents live in Canada?"

"Ontario," said Beatrice.

"Ontario is a large area. Do you know the town?"

"No."

"Maybe papers in their room will give the town," Anathea said.

Rev. and Mrs. Higdon helped the children try on coats while Raiford tried on several coats that were too tight in the chest. During the coat searching, Raiford explained his plans to Rev. and Mrs. Higdon.

"We will see what can be salvaged among our belongings at the hotel. After shopping and lunch, we will meet you at the cemetery. Do you know the time when the grave can be ready?"

"Two o'clock," said Ralph.

Prudence said, "Don't hire a cab. Use our carriage."

Crane Williams, the pastor's neighbor, who was showing an older couple the donations room, said, "Your Tilbury is too small for all of them, Sister Higdon. Our six-seat rockaway would suit better. I will be happy to serve as your driver."

"Can I sit in front with you?" Freddie asked the pleasant middle-aged man.

"If your folks approve," said Crane, smiling behind his bushy beard.

Raiford tipped his head as he eyed Anathea, who gave her consent with a single nod. Within the hour, they were riding in the Williams' carriage, first to the train station to see about tickets.

"The train to Albany does not leave until nine tonight. It has fold-down beds so we can sleep while we travel," Raiford reported when he returned from the depot's ticket office to the carriage at the curb.

"I always wondered what it was like to sleep in one of those trains," said Mr. Williams as he flicked the reins on the horse's back.

"What's a fold-down bed?" asked Freddie, turning around in his seat.

As Raiford explained, Anathea remembered seeing the beds folded up during her recent trip from Kentucky. Because she could not afford to pay for a bed, she envied those who could during her walk through the sleeping car on her way to the dining car.

"Do other people see you sleeping?" asked Beatrice.

"There are curtains," answered Raiford.

"Like we had those things last night?" said Freddie.

"They're called screens," said his sister.

The carriage moved through the heavy traffic from the depot to the United States Hotel. With back wheels larger than the front ones, the rockaway carriage was the first of its kind that Anathea had ever ridden. Wagons had been her usual mode of transportation. In fact, her journey from Louisville to New York City was the first time to ride a train. Having enjoyed the adventure, she looked forward to another train ride.

* * *

In Guelph, Varney Cutter put on his coat and hat and went for a walk, as was his habit every morning when weather permitted. Joan was asleep. Although the bedroom door was left open so her husband could come and go, Joan heard nothing of the front door shutting softly. The heavy oak door with a stained-glass panel in the upper half was too far away from the upstairs bedroom, and Joan was too soundly asleep to hear.

* * *

The little family arrived at the United States Hotel shortly after ten o'clock when Robert Martin and John Headley were eating a late breakfast at a restaurant on Broadway near Twelfth Street. The two young Confederates read the morning papers while blocks away hotel guests sorted through the smoky-smelling items in their rooms.

In the hotel safe, Raiford had left his money in a tan leather wallet. Retrieving the wallet before going upstairs, he briefly flipped through the greenbacks. Anathea, unaccustomed to hotel amenities, said, "I didn't know they would keep your money for you."

"You left yours in the room?" he asked.

"Yes. I hope it wasn't stolen."

In truth, Anathea's three ten dollar bills and two one dollar bills were still in her reticule when she scooped it off the bureau and searched the contents. She had taken money which she determined, by careful calculation, was owed in payment for her work among the Shakers, and had left a receipt before escaping from Pleasant Hill. Besides the money, she had a single piece of paper, folded into a four-inch square, at the bottom of her drawstring purse. Monro had handed her the paper, a bill of divorcement, when they entered the gates of the Kentucky commune. No one who lived at Pleasant Hill was allowed to be married. From that day, she had not been a wife.

Raiford, coming to her side in room 552 and seeing her silently count her few bills, said, "You need not be concerned regarding expenses. I have enough to provide for us."

"I will pay my own way," she said, turning to face him as she stuffed her money back and felt the much-folded paper in the bottom.

"Very well, but I will pay for the children," he answered in a firm tone.

I guess he can pay for the children if he wants to, Anathea thought as she went about the room and gathered up her meager belongings.

In his room, Raiford exchanged his shabby shoes for his sturdy black boots which had his secret journal tucked in the lining. His brown leather satchel, as well as the clothes within, smelled of smoke, as did the children's clothing which he helped Anathea collect.

"Phew!" declared Freddie as he watched his sister and the two adults.

"I agree," said Raiford. "That's why I think we should give our smoky clothes to the church and buy all new things."

Anathea said, "The church ladies can wash out the smell and needy people can still use them."

"We're needy people," said Beatrice.

"No," Raiford said as he stroked the girl's soft hair. "You are not needy. You will have the food and clothes that you require." Smiling at her, he added, "I think we should also get you and your brother a few books and toys to occupy you during the trip."

Happy to hear this, Freddie began talking to his sister about what he wanted.

Anathea said to Raiford, "I will buy a blank book to keep track of costs."

"If you wish," he said, knowing that his tiny secret journal could not be used as a family account book.

Before leaving room 559, Raiford took the packet of letters and papers belonging to Mayfield Cutter and put them in his satchel. *I'll read them later,* he thought.

* * *

At the Cutter Industries office, a small stone building to the left of the main gate, Kirk McCarrell put down the *Guelph Gazette* when manager E. L. Pearson entered the office and asked, "Did you know Bennett Burley was arrested?"

Snatching up the newspaper dated Saturday, November 26, Mr. Pearson, a heavy-set man with a bushy beard and bull neck, said, "When? Why?" He quickly scanned the short article Kirk pointed out to him.

Kirk, a nice-looking young man with dark blond hair, a thin moustache, and hazel eyes behind wire-rimmed glasses, recalled meeting Bennett Burley, cousin of Frank Burleigh, a foreman at the foundry. He had entered the office last week and cut short the conversation among the three men.

"We're desperate for weapons," Bennett had said before seeing Kirk and firmly closing his mouth.

The men had stopped talking. Frank had introduced his cousin Bennett who said he needed to purchase a sled.

"Did you know he was a Confederate spy?" asked Kirk.

"How would I know that?" E. L. snarled as he tossed the *Gazette* onto the work table.

In truth, E. L. Pearson did know that Bennett Burley worked for the Confederacy, because the man had ordered torpedoes to be manufactured at the foundry after hours. "Utmost secrecy," Frank's cousin kept repeating. E. L. assured the cousins that the sale would not appear on Mr. McCarrell's carefully-maintained account books.

Ignoring his boss's angry tone, Kirk picked up the *Gazette* and said, "I wonder if the reporter got the spelling wrong. Frank spells his last name B-u-r-l-e-i-g-h but he has this Bennett's last name spelled B-u-r-l-e-y."

"Frank's cousin was just buying a sled here. You remember that," mumbled Mr. Pearson.

Kirk did remember that was the excuse given, but he also knew that no sled was sold to Bennett Burley. The phrase "desperate for weapons" stuck in his mind. He thought: *I need to report my suspicions to someone. Who? Mr. Cutter? What help could he be? Constable Clark? But I have no proof of anything untoward. I know who.*

As soon as the work day ended, Kirk hurried to the home of his fiancée.

* * *

Historic Note: Queen Victoria declared Canada's neutrality by a proclamation dated May 13, 1861. This piece of paper, with its fancy penmanship and official seal, only gave England's notice of what was already apparent in the British provinces. The mother country had set a policy of strict neutrality weeks before by forbidding the sale of guns to either the North or the South. Canadians feared the Yankees might capture their steamships on the Great Lakes, or Southerners might board their Atlantic vessels and raise the Rebel flag. In 1833, Great Britain had abolished slavery in all of its colonies, but that action did not put them, officially, on the Northerners' side in the American Civil War. The British were uncommitted and intended to stay that way.

CHAPTER FOUR

TRAIN JUMPER

Wherein Mayfield Cutter is buried;
the little family departs from New York City;
Mechum Esling jumps from the train;
Mr. and Mrs. Bolton find Varney Cutter.

In A. T. Stewart's Marble Palace, the largest department store in New York City, Raiford helped Beatrice select a pink flowered carpet bag while Crane and Freddie decided on a small tan leather one which the little boy could carry by himself. Anathea asked for the cheapest carpetbag, but Raiford chose a maroon and black brocade one with an elaborate design and leather handle.

I have never owned anything so stylish, she thought. The one she brought from Kentucky was fabric with a wooden handle.

"I can't afford that," Anathea whispered to him.

"I'll pay for it," he whispered back.

"I will reimburse you."

"If you wish," he said as he smiled.

"Aren't you getting a new bag?" Freddie asked Raiford.

"No. Mine is adequate. The smell of smoke is not as bad in leather as it is in fabric."

When it came to buying new clothes, the children had an argument about a sailor outfit which Freddie wanted.

"It's not practical," said Beatrice. "You know Mama said to buy practical clothes."

"But I want it," said Freddie, stamping his little foot.

Raiford settled the disagreement by telling Beatrice that one impractical outfit was all right and that she should select one for herself. Delighted, Beatrice chose a peach-colored dress with three rows of ruffles on the skirt.

"I never saw such a pretty dress," Beatrice whispered to the saleslady as she folded the garment in tissue paper.

Anathea could not keep from smiling when she saw Raiford resolve the dispute to the satisfaction of both children. Crane, too, was impressed, and patted Raiford on the back.

"Mr. Williams, would you take the children to the section with toys?" Raiford asked. "I'll join you shortly."

Raiford took Anathea's arm and escorted her to the women's department, saying, "I won't be long selecting my clothes. The men's department is just over there. You get whatever you want."

* * *

Kirk McCarrell met his future father-in-law, Harmon Utley, proprietor of the largest general store in Guelph, owner of three packet boats on the Speed and Eramosa rivers, plus other real estate, as he was leaving for home. The two men walked slowly as Kirk told the older man about this morning's conversation with his boss about the arrest of Bennett Burley.

"So you think Cutter's manufactured those weapons Constable Clark seized when he arrested Bennett Burley?" Harmon lowered his bushy eyebrows over his deep-set eyes.

"Why not? They had to be made somewhere," said Kirk.

"There are other foundries in Guelph."

"But Cutter's is the biggest and best. Besides, I don't trust Mr. Pearson."

"Why is that?"

"He keeps a locked drawer in his desk. He doesn't tell me about some orders. I get enquiries that I know nothing about. I can tolerate his ill treatment of me, but I hate the secrecy."

"Dolly has told me about your problems with Pearson."

"I want to do well there, to be successful, so I can support her in a proper manner."

"You're a smart young man. You will succeed wherever you decide to work," said Harmon. The men had reached the pathway to the Utley house. "Come to dinner tonight? We'll talk more."

Kirk readily accepted the invitation. Dolly greeted her fiancé at the door with a quick kiss on the cheek. When her father lowered his eyebrows at her, she giggled.

* * *

Raiford was correct when he said he would not be long shopping in the men's department. Within ten minutes, he had returned and found Anathea fingering a corset held by a sales clerk, a prim older woman dressed in black.

"You don't need that," he said, coming to her side.

Startled, Anathea blushed. *What is he doing here? He should not see such things.*

Miss Prim said, "A well-dressed lady needs foundational garments."

Raiford replied, "No corset and no hoop. We will be on a train and a hoop skirt would be inconvenient."

"Yes, but a corset..." The Marble Palace clerk did not finish her sentence because Raiford shook his head and led Anathea to a rack of dresses.

"What do you like?" he asked.

Anathea was overwhelmed. She had never had a dress from a department store rack. Her clothes had always been homemade, and often hand-me-downs which were hemmed or patched. Even when she was married, she made her own clothes.

"This one is pretty," Raiford said, looking at a lavender skirt and blouse with purple braid at the cuffs and waist. Holding the padded hanger with both garments, he considered the size and said, "It should fit you."

In no time, Raiford helped her select two outfits. She wore the dark green skirt with gold fringe four inches from the hem, and the matching jacket with fringe from the shoulders to the waist in a vee pattern. The saleslady folded her old brown dress along with two new blouses, one white and one ecru, and two skirts in a separate package from her second new outfit, the lavender and purple.

In the toy area, which was a corner of the children's clothing department, Anathea and Raiford joined Mr. Williams and the children, who were talking with delight about the shelves of German-made toys.

"Freddie wants a spinning top," said Crane. "But I told him that he could not play with it on the train."

"We'll get the top and something else you can play with during our trip," Raiford said. "Here's a tin jar of modeling clay. It has miniature tools with it."

"May I have this tea-pot with cups and saucers?" Beatrice asked shyly as she pointed to a porcelain set with dainty painted flowers.

Raiford said, "All right, but you will need a doll to have tea with you."

Beatrice's big smile changed her entire face. Anathea was pleased to see the little girl's delight as Raiford took her hand and led her to the shelf of dolls. Selecting a twelve-inch doll with bisque face, hands, and feet, and a stuffed body, Beatrice cradled the doll in her arms like a baby and said, "I'll name her Victoria Stewart after the queen and this store."

"Next, we need books, drawing paper, and colored pencils," said Raiford. Before leaving the toy area, he also bought a checker set.

At the glove counter, the children got mittens, Raiford selected leather gloves, and Anathea chose a fur-lined muff. They planned to return their borrowed outerwear to the church donation room.

Every time Raiford made a payment, Anathea tucked the receipt into her reticule, after telling him the first time: "I will tally up the costs when we're on the train."

Their last stop was the stationery department where they purchased a blank book. When they stowed the packages into Mr. Williams' carriage, Anathea said, "Thank you, Mr. Young."

"Please call me Raiford," he said as he smiled at her.

From Stewart's, they went to the Mulberry Lane Restaurant which Crane recommended, ate a filling meal, and listened to their kind chauffeur talk about how his church was helping the soldiers and their families. His talk reminded Anathea of how charitable ladies helped the orphans with whom she lived after her mother died. She resolved to write to Miss Dell, the kind teacher at the orphanage, and to her brother Adam, as soon as she was settled.

* * *

Adam Brannaman became ill in St. Louis with food poisoning. Because the restaurant was in the hotel where he had a room, and which he concluded was not very clean, he moved to a boarding house. There, the doctor visited daily and the landlady tended him as though he were her own son. Therefore, Adam remained longer in the Mississippi River city than he had intended.

* * *

At the graveside that afternoon, Raiford, Anathea, the children, Mr. Williams, Rev. and Mrs. Higdon, two gravediggers, and two men from the morgue gathered around the rectangular wooden box beside the recently-dug hole. As the pastor read from First Corinthians chapter fifteen, the children cried. Raiford knelt and embraced both of them as they wept on his shoulders. Anathea used her handkerchief to wipe away tears and thought: *He's a good man. Thank you, Lord, for bringing this good man to us.* Prudence put her arm around Anathea. Pastor Ralph closed his well-worn Bible and patted Raiford's back.

As they wound their way among the gravestones, one of the men from the morgue came to Raiford and said, "We found these things in his coat pockets." He handed Raiford a silver watch and chain, a well-worn wallet, and a daguerreotype of a young woman in a wedding dress standing behind the chair of a man in a dark suit. The sight of their parents' wedding picture made the children cry again. As Raiford put the items in his pocket, he remembered the packet of letters he found in the Cutter's hotel room and thought: *I need to read those letters. They should give me some clues about this family.*

* * *

Lieutenant Headley and Colonel Martin met with their comrades at the Bowery Street headquarters cottage, which Robert Martin had rented. As the young Confederates arrived, one by one, they greeted each other with delight.

"So they didn't catch you, huh?" said Captain Kennedy, who walked with a limp from an old wound in his foot.

"How did you escape the noose?" asked Lieutenant James Chenault, a Kentuckian.

"It wasn't from training," laughed Lieutenant James T. Harrington, also from Kentucky. He was referring to the fact that there had been no advanced preparation before the men came down from Canada.

"Glad to see you made it!" said their leader, Colonel Martin, who walked stooped over from a chest wound.

When all eight men were present, the colonel said, "Apparently the newspaper reports of arrests all over the city are untrue."

John Headley, second in command, said, "Those Yankee journalists can't be trusted."

"Just trying to scare us," said Lieutenant John M. Price.

"Did you achieve your goal?" Robert asked.

John Headley told about firing the hotels assigned to him and then meeting Captain Kennedy who spoke next. Lieutenants Harrington and John T. Ashbrook gave brief descriptions of their success with the Greek fire and the hotels they set ablaze. John Price and James Chenault briefly summarized their exploits.

The final speaker was a quiet man with wide-set eyes and light brown hair. No one knew what state he was from. A Tennessean, Lieutenant Mechum Esling was well aware of the divided loyalty back home. He had relatives fighting on both sides.

Mechum said, "I fired the hotels assigned to me. I am certain no one was hurt. I went back to check and listen to the bystanders talk. Everyone got out safely."

"That's why we set the time for eight o'clock," said Colonel Martin. "Remember? We wanted everyone to be awake and get out."

John Headley added, "We were not intending to kill civilians."

"Yes, I remember that being said." Mechum nodded and stared at the floor. "But I'm not certain this has accomplished anything to shorten the war."

"You wait and see," the leader said. "The newspapers will put fear into its readers. The Yankees will imagine a large army over the border ready to pounce."

"Can we count the scoundrels in that army?" asked James Chenault, chuckling.

The others chuckled, too, even Robert, who said, "There are no scoundrels among us."

James Harrington said, "Those Yanks will sit down for a peace conference any day now."

"In case Mr. Lincoln is still not persuaded to talk peace, I wonder what scheme Mr. Thompson has for our future," John Price pondered aloud.

"That brings us to the next order of business," said Colonel Martin. "We need to depart from the city as soon as possible. We can leave in pairs but not as a group. Be watchful. Stay on your guard."

Captain Kennedy warned, "The train stations will be crawling with detectives."

* * *

Varney Cutter tripped over a twisted branch in the patch of woods behind his large brick house on Quebec Street where he often walked with his wife. When he fell, he hit his forehead on a log and cut a gash over his left eye. Varney crawled a short way as blood dripped on the ground. When he got to his feet, the old man held his hand over the wound and both eyes.

"Where are you?" he called, but did not know who 'you' was.

He put his hand down and tried to find his way home. The house was not in sight. Only trees surrounded him. He was lost. Varney wandered.

* * *

At the Baptist parsonage, Anathea and Raiford packed the new clothes while the maid heated water in the kitchen. Prudence insisted the guests take baths to rid themselves of the smoke smell in their hair. Beatrice bathed first in the little room off the kitchen, followed by her brother, then Anathea, and lastly Raiford.

Anathea was combing her wet hair by the kitchen fireplace when Raiford emerged from the bathroom. He stood in the doorway, rubbing his hair dry with a small towel, and watching her. Anathea's back was to him so she did not see his appreciative gaze.

Her hair is not at all like Lenore's, he thought. *Lenore's was blonde and straight as a string. Anathea's hair is dark, thick, and curly. How I would enjoy running my fingers through those tresses. Get a hold of yourself, man.*

Coming toward the fireplace, Raiford asked, "Should we donate all our old clothes to the church?"

Anathea turned to face him as he stood beside her and said, "Yes, I think so. Our new clothes are more than we need."

"I disagree. We need to buy more clothes in Toronto," Raiford said.

"But an extra outfit was all the children had in their bag at the hotel," Anathea said.

"I know, but I want them to be well-dressed and cared for when they arrive at their grandparents," he told her.

Anathea nodded her agreement and thought about her own new clothes. She had never owned two new outfits at the same time and never anything so elegant. Twisting her hair into a bun at the back of her head, she said, "I have not owned such pretty clothing."

"You should have many pretty things," he said softly.

Anathea glanced at him and away, as she saw the intense look in his eyes. Raiford sat on the low stool by the fire and watched her fix her hair. After a few moments of silence, he asked, "How can you do that without seeing your reflection?"

Anathea inserted a hair pin, glanced at him, and said, "Mirrors were a luxury we didn't have in the orphanage."

Raiford wanted to know more about her life in an orphanage, but Prudence and the maid entered, followed by Beatrice carrying an armload of brown paper with A. T. Stewart's logo printed boldly on each.

"Do you save wrapping paper?" the girl asked.

"Always," Prudence replied as she took the pieces, placed them on the table, and began folding each paper.

"What for?" asked Beatrice, following Prudence's lead while the maid went to empty the bath water.

"There are all kinds of things to do with wrapping paper. We must not be wasteful," said Prudence.

Anathea thought: *Just like the Shakers who made use of everything possible. Good economy, they said. I did learn some worthwhile habits from those people. Too bad they were so misguided in their understanding of marriage.*

Beatrice said, "Papa taught us not to waste things, too."

"What did your papa do for a living?" asked Anathea.

"He was a shoemaker until he joined the army," said Beatrice.

Prudence said, "I heard that a great many Canadian men joined the Union Army."

"As many as 50,000, I believe," said Raiford. "I met a few when I helped in a hospital."

"I wish Papa was in a hospital," said Beatrice, "instead of a hole in the ground."

The girl's lower lip began to tremble, but her brother's sudden entrance broke the spell of her oncoming grief.

Freddie, waving his little hands at shoulder level, declared, "I'm all ready! When do we ride the train?"

* * *

At eight o'clock, just as darkness was settling over the New York Central Railroad Station, on Saturday, November 26, John Headley and Robert Kennedy got someone else to buy their tickets because they feared being apprehended. With tickets in hand, the two Confederates moved through the bustling crowd toward the sleeping car. Uniformed policemen were prominent. Federal detectives, dressed both as gentlemen and as laborers, were also present but not known by any tell-tale uniform.

"It's this track. Down here," said John.

Pulling his hat lower on his forehead, Robert replied, "Coming."

They had to wait an hour before the sleeper opened. As they slipped unnoticed to their seats, neither spy was halted nor questioned.

Raiford searched faces for Hector Smith, but could not spot him among the travelers.

"Can we get on the train?" asked Freddie.

"Why are we waiting?" Beatrice tugged at Raiford's hand.

"A man is bringing papers you need to travel into Canada," said Raiford.

"Papa didn't have any papers to travel," the girl said.

"He was a citizen of Canada," Raiford explained. "He didn't need them to go home, but President Lincoln is strict about who travels in and out of the country. We have to carry travel permits."

"What happens if we don't?" asked Beatrice.

"Soldiers shoot you," said her brother.

"No one will shoot you," said Raiford. "The border guards will just stop you."

Anathea said, "Describe the man you are looking for."

As soon as Raiford finished a quick description of Hector, she pointed and asked, "Is that him?"

It was. Raiford waved his arm and started to call but realized that he should not bring attention to himself. "Stay right here," he said as he hurried toward Captain Smith. After receiving an envelope which contained the permits and a letter of credit for the Bank of Ontario, Raiford shook hands with the young man and assured him, "I'll telegraph as soon as we're settled."

Returning to the woman and children, Raiford thought: *She was good to find him in the crowd when I could not see him. Anathea might prove to be an asset in this spy work.*

A black porter helped Raiford stow the four carpetbags underneath benches opposite each other. The porter lowered the two bunk beds above the windows and pulled the curtains out from the wall. The dark blue curtains could be pulled across in front of the beds, giving privacy to the sleepers.

As Raiford tipped the porter, Beatrice went to see the crying baby in the next sleeping area. The baby was in a basket on the aisle floor and her mother busy with a toddler. Cajoling the infant until the harried mother could pick up her daughter, Beatrice remembered the stillborn infant that caused her mother's death. With a sad face, the girl returned to her seat.

"Can I get in my bed now?" Freddie asked, as he started up the narrow ladder.

"Don't climb up there! You might fall and die!" Beatrice reached toward her brother to pull him down.

Raiford picked up Freddie and plopped him onto the bunk while saying, "The beds are safe, Beatrice. No one will fall from them."

"Get in your bed," the little boy said and pointed to the other high bunk.

"No! No! I'll sleep on the floor!" the child stated.

Raiford demonstrated the sturdy beds but finally agreed to let her sleep in the bunk under Freddie's, saying, "I will sleep above your bed, Aunt Anathea, if you don't mind." Seeing that Beatrice was truly frightened of the high bed, Anathea consented.

The train departed on schedule and without incident, which would not be true when it came time for them to leave from Toronto.

Before Beatrice was tucked into her bed, Raiford said, "Time for bedtime prayers."

"Time to bless everyone," said Freddie.

Raiford said, "Come down, Freddie, so we can hold hands." When the little boy did, Raiford took his small hand and then Anathea's. Standing by the children's bunks, with Anathea holding Beatrice's hand, the adults listened to the children ask God to bless mama and papa, Uncle Raiford, Aunt Anathea, Rev. and Mrs. Higdon, Grandma and Grandpa, and finally the trainmen.

"Give us a safe journey, Lord," Raiford prayed.

"Provide peaceful sleep," prayed Anathea.

"Don't let anybody fall out of bed and die," added Beatrice.

"Amen," said Raiford, smiling.

The rocking of the train car lulled the children to sleep easily. Anathea watched the lights of the city fade and wondered: *What lies ahead? A few days with these people, and then I will be free again. Can I find work in Canada? Are jobs available? Maybe I can work in a hotel or restaurant, but I think I would prefer a private home to a public place. It would be more peaceful and I would see fewer people. Yes, I would prefer that – fewer people.*

Raiford was thinking: *How will this turn out? Can I accomplish anything worthwhile for my country? Should I return to Georgia? I'm sure General Sherman can use me now that he's on the move? Would I even be able to find him in order to join them again? Perhaps I can do more here. Lord, guide me. Make my efforts count for good.*

* * *

The next morning, in the dining car, as they ate breakfast, Raiford asked, "When the children are home, will you stay in Canada or return to New York?"

Swallowing, Anathea said, "I think I would like to find a job in Canada and stay there, but I don't know much about the country. Do you?"

Raiford tucked Freddie's napkin into his collar and answered, "A little, although this is my first trip there." Handing her napkin to Beatrice, he asked, "What do you know about Canada, Little Lady?"

Beatrice smiled and said, "I know it has provinces instead of states."

"Very good," Raiford commended. "They are British provinces because the head of their government is the Queen of England."

"Victoria," said Beatrice, patting her doll beside her on the seat.

"What are the names of the provinces?" Anathea asked Raiford.

"The five stretching from the Atlantic Ocean to Lake Superior are..." Raiford counted them off on the fingers of his left hand. "Canada West and Canada East, which make one province, called the United Province of Canada, although they are divided geographically and culturally."

"What's that mean?" asked Freddie.

"In Canada East, the people speak French, but in Canada West, they speak English."

"I speak English," said the little boy.

"That's right, and so do your grandparents because they live in Ontario, which is Canada West."

"What are the other provinces?" asked Beatrice.

Pointing to his next fingers, Raiford named: "New Brunswick, Nova Scotia, Prince Edward Island, and Newfoundland." When he said Newfoundland, he held up his thumb.

Anathea recalled a previous thought: *What nice hands he has.*

"There's also the vast territory belonging to the Hudson Bay Company," he said, picking up his coffee cup and drinking. "It's called Rupert's Land."

"Rupert's Land! That's funny," said Freddie, giggling.

Glad to see the boy amused, Raiford was grateful for the information Hector Smith provided him in preparation for the journey. *At least, it is funny to Freddie.*

When they were finishing their meal, Anathea excused herself to use the lavatory at the end of the car. Upon returning to her seat, she was suddenly jolted as the train took a sharp curve. She fell toward Mechum Esling who was dining alone. The Confederate captain grabbed Anathea around the waist, stood up quickly, and held her steady while the train straightened out.

"Excuse me, ma'am," Mechum said as he removed his hands. "No offense intended."

Hurrying back to the table, she was aware that Raiford had observed the incident. His eyes were fixed on her. Anathea's cheeks were red from embarrassment.

Standing up politely as Anathea resumed her seat, Raiford said, "He kept you from falling."

"I know," she said, avoiding his eyes and gripping her hands in her lap.

Rather than sit down again, Raiford moved slowly along the aisle, stopped beside Mechum, and spoke softly to him.

What is he saying to that man? Anathea wondered. *Is he chastising him for touching me? Monro would have. In fact, Monro might have thrown a fist. He had an evil temper and was always so jealous.*

Already, Raiford was coming back. No blows had been struck. Neither man appeared angry.

"I thanked him," Raiford said as he sat down.

Anathea could only stare at the man sitting close to her. *Monro would never have done that.*

Mechum turned his gaze from the grateful man and pretty lady to the scenes outside the window and thought about his wife Delphina and two little children at home in Tennessee. He missed his family and wondered: *Could she make the trip to Canada to be with me? That mother is traveling with her two children. Maybe Delphina could, too.*

* * *

In Memphis, Delphina Esling sat at the writing desk in the parlor of her parents' home and wrote to her husband. The envelope, addressed to a post office box in New York City, was propped against the lamp base. She wrote: *Please consent to our joining you wherever you might be. Our separation is becoming unbearable for me. Your infant son longs to meet his father for the first time. Little Maggie asks about her papa every day. My bags can be packed in no time. I only await your word.*

Mrs. Esling put down her pen and daydreamed about her husband's loving ways and words. She decided to finish her letter in the morning. That would be soon enough to deliver it to the courier tasked with placing letters in the northern post. Since Mr. Lincoln had halted mail between the seceding and loyal states, this message would take an indirect route. And since the postmaster in New York did not know Mechum's new address in Canada, the envelope would be many days in transit before Mechum received it.

* * *

Joan Cutter woke with a sore throat. Her nose was so stuffed that she breathed through her mouth. Nevertheless, she had to get up. She did not know where her husband was. Silence reigned in the house. She put on her robe and exited the bedroom.

"Varney!" she called, but her hoarse voice did not carry far in the mansion. Holding tightly to the walnut railing, she went down the front curving staircase and passed beneath the dead eagle with wings spread as though flying through the stairwell.

"Varney, Varney, where are you?"

Going by the buffalo head in the hall, Joan entered the large front parlor where the mounted head of a black bear faced her. In the small parlor, a stuffed white owl and other birds sat on high shelves. From here, she wandered into the dining room and kitchen.

"Varney, don't hide from me."

Coming into the back hall, she stumbled over the bear-skin rug before catching herself. Across the hall, she searched the storage room, the guest bedroom, the office and library overlooking the wide front porch. Joan climbed the back stairs and searched the six bedrooms, the linen closets, the two servants' rooms off the back hall, and even went up to the attic.

After an hour of futile searching, she sat down on the edge of her rumpled bed and wept.

* * *

Coming through the dining car, the conductor called: "One hour 'til Albany."

"I need to redo your braids," Anathea said to Beatrice.

"We'll go back to the sleeping car," said Raiford.

Suddenly, there was a commotion. Two men confronted Mechum Esling. One man grabbed for his collar. The other man declared loudly: "Federal detectives! You're under arrest!"

Everyone in the car focused on the three men. A lady spilled her tea. A baby cried at the loud voices.

"Put your hands out!" The second detective held up a pair of handcuffs.

Having no intention of wearing those restraints, Mechum pushed violently against the two men, knocking them backwards. He raced between the tables and onto the outdoor platform. The detective with handcuffs raced behind him. The train was going thirty miles an hour. Scenery sped by. Raiford and the other detective arrived on the platform in time to see Mechum jump.

"Look at that man!" exclaimed Freddie, gazing out the window and fluttering his hands near his shoulders.

Mechum tumbled down the embankment, scrambled to his feet, and ran through the snow.

"Pull the alarm cord!" the first detective yelled to the passengers inside.

"Go after him!" shouted the second detective.

"I'm not jumping at this speed! You go!"

"Will someone pull the cord?"

An older man reached up and yanked on the overhead emergency cord. An earsplitting blast shot out of the steam whistle. The train screeched to a halt. Five men, including Raiford, jumped into ankle-deep snow and headed along the tracks.

Two conductors entered the car and quizzed the passengers, who were abuzz with conjectures about the escaping man.

* * *

Historic Note: General John Adams Dix, commander of the Department of the East, issued General Orders 92 on November 26, 1864, which read in part: "A nefarious attempt was made last night to set fire to the principal hotels and other places of public resort in this city. If this attempt had been successful, it would have resulted in a frightful sacrifice in property and life. The evidence of extensive combination, and other facts disclosed today, shows it to have been the work of Rebel emissaries and agents. All such persons engaged in secret acts of hostility here can only be regarded as spies, subject to martial law, and to the penalty of death. If they are detected, they will be immediately brought before a court-martial or military commission, and, if convicted, they will be executed without the delay of a single day."

CHAPTER FIVE

SUSPENSION BRIDGE

Wherein Varney and Joan Cutter are helped;
Anathea and Raiford discover Adelle's secret; and
Jacob Thompson sends a telegram.

As the train pulled into the Albany depot, the people were still talking excitedly about the train jumper. Having arrived on Sunday, which had an abbreviated schedule, there were no trains into Canada until evening. They left their luggage in the baggage room and walked to the nearby church.

* * *

Mechum Esling ran until he was so exhausted that he collapsed in a snow drift. When he caught his breath, he sat up and looked around. In the distance, he saw a barn and said aloud, "Where there's a barn, there must be a house."

In a short time, he was resting beside the roaring fireplace of an elderly couple who offered him coffee and toast in exchange for news from the outside world. Mechum claimed that he had lost his way after his horse died in the night. They accepted his explanation and offered him their hospitality. Mechum was grateful.

* * *

In Guelph, Canada West, Mr. and Mrs. Oscar Bolton were on their way to St. Bartholomew Catholic Church on Church Hill in the center of town.

"Give me your scarf. I forgot mine," Saida said to her husband.

The small man, five feet four inches tall and weighing 130 pounds, handed over his wool neck scarf without a word.

Saida Bolton snatched the fabric and wrapped it around her double chin and fleshy neck. She was a head taller and fifty pounds heavier than Oscar.

Townspeople considered them the most mismatched couple in appearance. This was Saida's second marriage. Her first husband fell down stairs and broke his neck. Oscar, a bachelor for forty years, married the overweight woman because she was a good cook and fussed over him. That was, at least, until they wed. Now, she did nothing but abuse him.

"Look there! Who's that?" asked Saida, pointing toward the trees where Varney Cutter was wandering.

"Where?" asked Oscar.

"See him, stupid?" Saida cupped her hands and shouted: "You there! Are you lost?"

Varney turned, saw the couple, and ambled toward them.

"Why, it's Mr. Cutter!" exclaimed the little man. "What's that on his face?"

"It's blood," said the big woman.

* * *

In Albany, New York, Raiford held open the door of the gray stone Lutheran church and said, "I've never worshipped with Lutherans. Have you?"

"No," said Anathea, brushing past him, and thinking: *With Methodists, with Shakers, what difference does it make?*

They had seen the steeple of the church from the depot, and, at Raiford's suggestion, came to worship.

Anathea was surprised and pleased by the service, which was nothing like what she had known among the Shakers at Pleasant Hill, Kentucky. The orderly worship service and sweet-sounding organ music dispelled her recent memories of anguish amid the religious group where her former husband now lived. Several of the well-dressed people spoke cordially to them after the hour-long service.

* * *

In Guelph, Saida and Oscar Bolton did not attend St. Bartholomew's that Sunday, as they had intended. Instead, they took Varney Cutter, who was completely disoriented, to the doctor's house on Cork Street East where they stopped the medical man before he and his wife left for their church. While Dr. Jesse Shilliday tended to Varney, his wife Harriet and Mrs. Bolton went to see Joan Cutter in the brick mansion on Quebec Street.

* * *

At the Hudson House in Albany, Raiford, Anathea, and the children ate dinner in the restaurant on the ground floor. Over a dessert of vanilla pudding topped with whipped cream, Raiford suggested they get a hotel room for the afternoon.

"The children didn't get to bed until late," he said. "No sense in sitting on those hard benches in the depot when we can rest in a comfortable room."

"Isn't that an extravagance for only a few hours?" Anathea asked him. *Monro was never extravagant. He was tight with his money -- his money, never mine.*

"Not at all," Raiford said, and wiped a dab of cream from Freddie's face.

The clerk reported that a room would be ready in half an hour, so they went around Quackenbush Square to the station to get their bags. When they entered the hotel room, the children lay down on the rug. Freddie played with the checkers as though they were soldiers, calling the black ones Rebels and the red ones Yankees. He spun his new top amid the checkers and called it cannon fire. Beatrice set up a tea party for her and Victoria.

Sitting in chairs by the window, Anathea and Raiford shared the *Albany Express*, trading the newspaper pages back and forth as they finished each one. It was Saturday's news because no paper was published on Sunday.

When Anathea had read all that she wanted, she sat with the paper on her lap, stared at it, and thought: *Monro never shared his newspaper with me. He believed a woman had no mind to understand current affairs. The female brain is weak, he had said. A woman should not meddle in a man's world. How different Raiford is from Monro.*

Raiford noticed her distracted look, set his paper on the nearby table, and asked, in a lowered voice, "Have you heard of the Thomas Briggs murder case in England?"

"You mean the London banker who was attacked in his first-class train carriage?"

"Yes." Raiford scowled and said, "They hanged the man who was on trial." He kept his voice low so as not to upset the children with this tragic story.

"The German tailor?"

"That's right. Franz Muller. I think he was innocent."

"Why?" she asked.

They proceeded to discuss the investigation and trial which had been much publicized since the crime on July 9th. Pleased that Raiford listened to her comments, Anathea spoke easily about her thoughts on the case. At Pleasant Hill, when she cleaned the rooms, she secreted the tossed-out newspapers and read them alone. Only the Bible was permissible reading for the women.

Raiford made several remarks in affirmation of her deductions on the Thomas Briggs investigation and thought: *She has a good head on her shoulders. Her powers of reasoning are better than average, I would say. Her thinking is not wishy-washy. She would make a good spy herself.*

"They never discovered blood on Mr. Muller's clothes," she concluded her overview of the murder case.

"Indeed so," said Raiford. "That is just one of the oddities about this whole thing. Witnesses saw him before and after the murder in the same clothes with no evidence of blood stains. Just my cut wrist produced a blood stain on my cuff."

"I should look at your cut. Maybe you can go without the bandage," she said, reaching toward his hand resting on his thigh.

Raiford held his bandaged wrist toward her. She unwound the fabric and said, "It's all healed. You don't need this anymore."

As she wadded up the cloth, she carried it to the wash stand. Anathea put the bandage in the basin and poured water on it.

"I don't think that bandage will be dry before we have to leave," Raiford said.

"Then it can be discarded, I suppose," she said, and thought: *Brown wrapping paper, used bandages, I cannot save everything. Sorry, Shakers.* She smiled at her thought.

Beatrice shrieked when Freddie's top spun into her tea party. The adults quickly inspected the overturned dishes, determined nothing was broken, and attempted to assuage the angry sister.

"I'm sleepy," said Freddie, in hopes of avoiding punishment by changing the subject.

"Take off your shoes!" his sister snapped.

In a soothing voice, Raiford asked, "Would you like to hear a story?"

While the children removed their shoes and climbed atop the brass bed, Raiford pulled his chair close and proceeded to relate <u>The Pilgrim's Progress</u>. "A man named Christian lived in the City of Destruction. He was dressed in rags, had a book in his hand, and a great burden on his back."

"What was the book?" asked Beatrice, remembering her new book.

"It was the Bible," said Raiford.

"What was the burden?" Freddie wanted to know.

"The burden was his sins," answered the storyteller. "Do you know what sin is?"

"All the bad things you do," said the girl.

Anathea was intrigued as she listened. She was unfamiliar with John Bunyan's classic tale. Soon after relating Christian's encounter with a man named Evangelist, the children were asleep. Anathea wished Raiford would continue the story, but instead he went to his leather bag and retrieved a packet.

"These are Mr. Cutter's letters. We should read them while they are sleeping so it won't make them cry again."

He placed the small bundle on the round table by the window, moved his chair from the bedside to near Anathea, sat down, and unfolded the first paper. He held the letter out so they could read at the same time. The document was a furlough for ill health granted to Private Mayfield J. Cutter, Guelph, Canada West.

"That gives us his home town," said Raiford. "Most likely his parents live there."

"If not, someone in Guelph should know where they are," said Anathea.

The second paper was Mayfield's enlistment, which gave a physical description and his age in 1861 as twenty-seven. Raiford re-folded this paper and set it atop the medical furlough. The third item, in a woman's feathery penmanship, began: *My Dear Husband.* The single sheet concluded with the words: *Your loving wife now and forever Adelle May.*

After reading the short letter, Raiford dropped it on the table, turned to Anathea, and said, "The poor man."

* * *

In Guelph, Saida Bolton and the doctor's wife took turns knocking on the Cutter's heavy oak door. The stained-glass panel depicted a sunny country scene. When no one answered, Saida turned the brass handle and pushed. "It's open. We can go in."

"Mrs. Cutter!" called Harriet, looking around the empty hallway and shivering at the sight of the huge buffalo head protruding from one wall.

"Joan Cutter!" shouted Saida, stomping forward until she was under the spread-winged eagle above the stairwell. "Joan Cutter, are you up there?"

"I'll go up," said Harriet.

"I'll look down here," said the big woman, picking up her voluminous skirt.

In the next minute, Harriet yelled over the banister: "She's up here! She's in bed!"

Within the hour, Harriet had fetched her husband who diagnosed influenza. While Saida sat in the sick room, the doctor and his wife went to the kitchen to make the special gruel which Jesse had devised for flu victims.

"Where are their servants?" asked Jesse, as he opened cupboards and drawers.

"They just have day workers," his wife said, setting a tin of corn meal on the big oak table.

"They need people here night and day." Jesse pumped water at the sink while his wife brought a mixing bowl from the shelf.

The Shillidays, who had a young, live-in couple working as maid and handyman, relied on their servants for more than housekeeping. Varney Cutter was in their care right now.

"I agree." Harriet spooned corn meal into the bowl.

"Can you organize ladies to take turns in nursing her?" Jesse poured water into the bowl. "I don't want Saida Bolton here. She's no good as a nurse."

"She will want to be involved." Harriet looked for sugar in the large room.

"Busybodies usually do," the doctor said, stirring the gruel.

Harriet smiled, nodded her agreement, and named several women who would be good nurses, to which her husband agreed.

When they brought the tray to the sick room, Dr. Shilliday said, "I will see you home, Mrs. Bolton. Harriet is staying. Other ladies will relieve her."

Despite the large woman's protests, the doctor escorted her home. But she did not stay home. She had too much gossip to spread.

"Before Joan Cutter took to her bed, she beat her husband until he bled. The poor old man fled for his life," Saida told first one neighbor and then the other.

Although people disbelieved this story, Mrs. Bolton was adamant. The rumor quickly spread through town. Each bearer of the tale usually would add: "Saida Bolton says."

Saida enjoyed pointing fingers at others. It kept them from pointing at her.

* * *

At the Hudson House hotel in Albany, Raiford and Anathea stared at one sentence of the letter from Adelle Cutter to her husband Mayfield. That sentence was: *I carry a child not yours.*

"You say poor man but I say poor woman," said Anathea. "How devastating that must have been for her. What a tragedy."

Raiford turned his gaze from the letter and focused on her face.

"Why do you say that?"

"If I were in her place…" She blushed and could not continue.

Looking back at the letter's date and the dates of Mayfield's enlistment and discharge, he said, "This letter is over a year old. Mayfield wasn't there when the child was born."

Anathea whispered, "She must have died giving birth."

Raiford said, "I wonder if the baby's father was with Adelle."

Who was he? A soldier? Where is he? Still in Newark? Did he know he was going to be a father? Raiford wondered.

Glancing at the bed where the children were sleeping, Anathea spoke her thoughts aloud, "Do you suppose Beatrice understood?"

"Not at her age, I shouldn't think," said Raiford, folding the letter. "But perhaps something about her mother reminds her. Perhaps that is why she shows such disinclination toward you."

At Raiford's statement, Anathea stared at him and said, "You have noticed that?"

"Haven't you?"

"Yes. I have." She paused before adding: "But how would that … I'm not certain…."

"May we speak plainly?" Raiford tilted his head in the way he had when asking permission. Anathea nodded and he continued. "If Beatrice knew her mother had a child by a man other than her father, she might have disliked, perhaps even hated her mother. Do you see that as a possibility?"

"Perhaps." Anathea met his eyes. "But there's another possibility."

"What?"

"I spent my teenage years in an orphanage where children came from homes in which they had been beaten by one parent or another. They arrived with bruises and cuts. Almost always, if they spoke of their parents at all, it was to defend them."

"Really?" Raiford had no experience with parents abusing their children, so this statement surprised him.

"Yes. It seems strange, I know."

Raiford pondered his next thought for only a moment before voicing it. He said, "Beatrice's mother was with a man to whom she was not married; but, if her daughter defends her, even though she's dead, Beatrice is defending her memory. Now you appear in her life, living with me, a man to whom you are not married. Perhaps Beatrice is transferring her dislike and disapproval from her mother to you."

"I wonder." Maintaining eye contact, Anathea realized what sympathetic, kind eyes Raiford had.

"Can you think of another explanation?" he asked.

"I don't know. In the past, when someone didn't like me, I could ignore them and befriend someone else. There were several dozen of us at the Home for Friendless Girls. But I don't want to ignore Beatrice. I want to be her friend."

"That's good," said Raiford, nodding once.

"But how?"

"Be her aunt not her mother."

"I never had an aunt," said Anathea.

"I have seven." Raiford scooted his chair an inch closer and said, "May we go back a moment. You started to say if you were in Adelle's place, but did not finish your sentence. Tell me what you would have done."

"I would not have told my husband," she said in a whisper.

"How could he not know? After the war, when he came home, he would realize that the baby was not fathered by him."

"Maybe I would have left him, before he came home," she said. "Maybe she found life with her husband so intolerable that she preferred to escape."

"Escape?" Raiford found her choice of that word to be odd. "You mean divorce him?"

"No. Just escape," she whispered. Changing the subject, Anathea said, "Tell me about your seven aunts. Do you have many nieces and nephews?"

Raiford recognized her quick shift in topic and obligingly told her about his large family in Goshen, Indiana. She made comments on how orphanage life was somewhat similar as well as dissimilar.

"How old were you when you started living at the Home for Friendless Girls?" he asked.

"I was twelve. My mother was impoverished and dying of tuberculosis. This was her only option for me. My brother Adam had left for California, and we had no word from him."

"Did you have a favorite among the caretakers at the orphanage?" Raiford asked.

"Yes. Miss Barbara Dell. She gave me this brooch watch when I left." She touched the dainty watch which she wore near her shoulder.

Raiford said, "It's very pretty" and reached for the next paper. "We will take things slowly. Knowing what we know now will help us to understand." He unfolded the paper, held it out, and read: "Dear Son." The letter from Mayfield's mother told them that his parents were sorry to hear about his wife's death and his poor health. They consented to his coming home with his children, whom they were eager to meet. *Our home awaits your soon arrival,* were Joan Cutter's last words on the much-folded paper.

"Where is Guelph?" Anathea asked as she read the back of the letter which served as an envelope.

"I will get a map of Canada when we cross the border." Raiford opened the last letter telling about the death of a friend at the Battle of Gettysburg. The final paper was a passport verifying Mayfield's citizenship as a Canadian.

I might be able to use this for myself, Raiford thought as he studied the details on the official document.

"Three letters and three official papers," said Raiford as he returned them to his bag. "Not much to show for a man's life."

"He had these two beautiful children to show for his life," Anathea said.

* * *

That evening, at the New York Central depot, where the tracks had been extended from Albany to Buffalo, Raiford met Rev. Kensey Johns Stewart, who was boarding with his flustered wife, Emma Louisa, and five children, the youngest of whom was a one-year-old baby in a large basket.

Dr. Stewart had enlisted as a chaplain in the Confederate army when the war began, but now thought he had a higher calling. After meeting with President Jefferson Davis and discussing a scheme which the clergyman said would be kept "a profound secret," Davis approved a draft of $20,000 in gold to finance Stewart's operations. Parson Stewart thought he was taking Jacob Thompson's place as commissioner of the Confederate secret service. However, he would soon learn that was not the case.

Mrs. Stewart held her baby's basket close to her breasts as she watched her older children crowd the train steps.

"Going to Toronto?" Rev. Stewart asked Raiford in a friendly manner.

"Yes, we are," said Raiford.

Kensey put his hand on his oldest child's shoulder and said, "You first, Dale."

"As are we," said the bewhiskered man, smiling at the younger man who held a little girl's hand and the pretty woman beside him. She held a boy's hand.

Emma Stewart said to her son, "Help the younger ones, Dale."

The twelve-year old reached down from the platform to help his siblings up the metal steps as Raiford and Kensey exchanged introductions.

When Beatrice heard the name Stewart, she said, "My doll's name is Victoria Stewart."

"Named for the department store in New York," Anathea said.

"And the queen," added the little girl.

"Are you related to A. T. Stewart?" Raiford asked.

After replying in the negative, the pastor asked, "Have you been to Toronto?"

"No. Have you?"

The adults watched the Stewart children climb the steps toward Dale.

"First trip for us as well. Come now, Emma, dear, hand me the baby."

"Could you recommend a hotel?" Raiford already knew about Toronto hotels from his indoctrination by Hector Smith. The purpose of his question was to engage the man in conversation.

"We plan to rent a house, but will be staying at the Queen's Hotel until we find a place large enough for us," replied the Episcopal minister, taking the baby basket from his wife.

Queen's Hotel, thought Raiford. *Where Jacob Thompson resides.*

"I heard the Queen's is expensive," said Raiford.

"The best place in the city," said the friendly minister.

How is a minister with a big family able to afford the best hotel in Toronto, thought Raiford before he said: "I heard the Metropole Hotel is a nice place. We might stay there."

"I know nothing about the Metropole," said the minister.

As Mrs. Stewart lifted her skirt a few inches in order to step up, Raiford took her arm and said, "Allow me." He gave her a boost for which she thanked him. The couple and their children moved toward empty seats.

Turning to Anathea, Raiford said, "I hope the Metropole will be to your liking." He lifted Beatrice to the first step.

Anathea said, "Any place will be fine," and thought: *Monro never cared if a living space was to my liking.*

She watched Raiford lift Freddie to the steps and expected him to take her arm as he had done with Mrs. Stewart. To her surprise, Raiford put his hands on her waist and picked her up as he had done with the children. Anathea held her breath until his hands released her body. Letting out a sigh, she climbed the other two steps and hurried after the children.

* * *

In Guelph, Ontario, Canada West, Dr. Jesse Shilliday repacked his medical bag in preparation for departure. To his patient, who was sitting up against two feather pillows, he said, "Stay in bed now, Mrs. Cutter. Keep warm. Take this gruel I've made for you. It will stick on your stomach and not come back up."

"I'm so sorry about all of this, Doctor," Joan said in a wispy voice. "You have been so kind. I didn't mean to burden you."

"Now, now." The middle-aged doctor with sympathetic brown eyes came to the bedside and patted her frail hand atop the covers. "You have been no burden."

"But Varney…"

"We have enjoyed having him with us. He's no problem whatsoever."

"I didn't want people to know," said the old woman as her chin trembled. "I'm so ashamed."

Jesse sat on the edge of the bed and put both strong hands around her frail one as he said, "There is no shame in this. Varney is in his dotage. That's not shameful. You have good friends at church and among your neighbors who have been worried about you. They are willing to help. You don't have to bear this burden alone."

As though she had not heard his kind words, she asked, "Will he ever come out of his dotage?"

"No. Most likely not." Jesse's voice was low and consoling. He thought: *I hope she does not hear Saida Bolton's latest slander.*

"Has Varney asked for me?" Her voice quivered.

"Mrs. Cutter, you know his condition," the doctor said gently.

"Yes. Yes. I know." She gripped his hand. "I miss him. When can he come home?"

"When you are better," said the doctor. "You don't want him to get this influenza, do you?"

The old woman shook her head.

"Now I want you to meet someone," said Jesse, going to the hall door. "Although the ladies have been helping, you need servants here full time." He opened the door and motioned to the couple waiting in the hall. When Zurelle and Ochran Wyatt entered the room, the doctor introduced them.

"They have just arrived from Alabama," said Jesse.

"On your Underground Railroad?" asked Joan in a barely audible voice.

"That's right," said the medical man. "That mysterious route to freedom has brought them to your doorstep. They can help you and Varney. This big house needs them."

Ochran, a muscular black man with pants held up by one suspender came to the bedside and said, "We work mighty hard for you and the massah."

"Not master," Jesse quickly corrected. "There are no masters and slaves in Canada."

Dr. Shilliday was a leader in the British and Foreign Anti-Slavery Society, which aided runaway slaves to newfound freedom in Canada. Zurelle, Ochran, and their three small children arrived in Guelph only last week after an exhausting and fearful trip through the United States. When Jesse thought they were recovered sufficiently, he suggested they work at the Cutter house. Ochran had readily accepted.

"I'd be pleased to do for you," said Zurelle, moving shyly to stand beside her husband.

Joan lifted her hand toward first Zurelle and then Ochran as she said, "I am happy to meet you."

The couple offered weak handshakes. This greeting was too new for them. Not until reaching Canada had they ever shaken hands with a white person.

Dr. Shilliday said, "You rest now, Mrs. Cutter. We'll get this family settled."

"You know where the servants' rooms are?" Joan's voice was so enfeebled that only the words *servants' rooms* were heard.

The medical man gave the family a tour of the mansion and explained, "Mr. Pearson manages the Cutter Foundry. I'll speak to him about your salary."

"Salary?" asked Ochran.

"Your wages. The money you both will earn while working here."

"Me, too?" asked Zurelle.

When Jesse assured the young woman that she would earn money, she began to cry. Her husband comforted her against his chest and said, "This is all a wonder to her, Doctor. We never dreamed of such a place. Feels like we done gone to heaven."

Jesse laughed and Ochran smiled.

* * *

On Monday morning, as four men trudged through the snow to Cutter Industries, they discussed the recent news of Bennett Burley's arrest.

"How will we get paid now with your cousin in jail?" asked Nelson Bartmess.

"Yah, I heard he might be transported to a federal prison," added Josiah Igoe.

"He can't do business behind bars," said Eustus Wright, a nice looking man who was youngest of the group.

"Let me answer! Will you?" snapped Frank Burleigh, first cousin of the arrested man. The other three were silent as their leader continued. "The Confederacy needs those torpedoes we're making. Someone else will come and pay for them."

"Who?" asked Eustus.

"I don't know who. Someone!" Frank glared at the young man.

"What if he talks," Josiah said. "They could arrest us next."

"Bennett won't talk," said Frank.

"What about Pearson?" asked Nelson. "He can't be trusted."

The men slowed their pace as they neared the entrance to the factory.

"He's a loose cannon," said Josiah. "He'll do anything for a half dime. He would sell these weapons to the North if they offered him more."

"He's not stupid. He knows how to keep down low," said Frank.

"Does he?" Eustus looked around and lowered his voice as fellow workers went by. "I wish we could get rid of these iron monsters and quit the business."

"Still don't like handling explosives, huh, kid?" said Nelson.

Eustus simply shook his head, and Josiah answered, "None of us do. We don't have the experience with explosives. Bennett did."

"We know," said Frank. "Not so loud."

The men, now surrounded by workers going through the Cutter Foundry gate, were silent. Before separating, Frank Burleigh said, "I'll talk to Pearson."

* * *

At the same time that the clandestine torpedo workmen met with the foundry manager, Kirk McCarrell searched for a key to Pearson's locked desk drawer. He had not found it when the office door opened and his boss bellowed, "What are you doing at my desk?"

"Looking for ink," said Kirk in as calm a voice as he could manage.

E. L. reached into a cubby hole, pulled out an ink bottle, and handed the accountant the bottle of writing fluid.

Dr. Shilliday knocked, entered the office, and saw the exchange of the ink bottle as well as the scowl on the older man's face.

"Dr. Shilliday, how are you?" Kirk greeted. "Would you like some coffee?"

The medical man accepted the hot cup and sat down.

Mr. Pearson asked, "How is Mr. Cutter? We heard he was injured."

Jesse was always amazed at how fast news traveled in the town, even before publication in the *Guelph Gazette*. He told the two men about Varney's fall, Joan's flu, the new servants, and the fact that Mr. Cutter was staying at his own house to avoid contracting his wife's illness.

"Will Mr. Cutter be going home soon?" asked Kirk, filling a second cup of coffee for himself.

"In a few days, I should think, when his wife is well," said Jesse, sipping his coffee. "The Wyatts are doing a good job but it's a big place, as you know. Mrs. Cutter, at her age, was not up to managing with only daytime help. Her husband needs almost constant attention."

"She didn't really hit him until he bled, did she?" Kirk's question was more a statement.

"No, she did not. That Mrs. Bolton!" He scowled and added, "Varney said he fell in the woods."

The young man asked, "Have the new servants been paid?"

"I paid them. In fact, I came to talk about their wages."

As the doctor spoke, the door opened and Elmore, E. L.'s teen-aged son, entered and asked, "Who's getting wages, Doc -- more of your runaway slaves?"

Jesse politely answered the slovenly boy with acne who leaned against the wall.

Elmore grumbled, "Why don't you use the money the old man has stashed in the house?"

The doctor told the teen, "Because Mr. Cutter is in charge of that money and he is not home. He's staying with me so he won't come down with Mrs. Cutter's influenza."

Kirk added, "Besides, that's only a rumor about Mr. Cutter having money at his house."

Elmore humphed, turned toward his father, and said, "You forgot to leave me any money this morning."

"Everyone wants money," snarled E. L., reaching into his jacket pocket and withdrawing a wallet. As soon as he had cash in hand, Elmore left.

Jesse placed an invoice on the desk beside Kirk and said, "This itemizes my medical costs as well as the wages for Mr. and Mrs. Wyatt."

"I'll write a check," said Kirk, proceeding to do so. "Mr. Pearson will have to co-sign it."

As E. L. added his signature below Kirk's he said, "I don't know why they need live-in help. Those Burleigh girls do for them."

Just then, a messenger boy arrived and gave a telegram to Kirk, who was nearest to the door. After handing him a tip, Kirk read aloud: "Replacement arriving soon. Jacob Thompson." Staring at his boss, he asked, "Who is Jacob Thompson?"

Snatching the telegram, E. L. growled, "Never you mind!"

* * *

The Burleigh sisters, who were twins, met Zurelle Wyatt when they came into the kitchen for their weekly pickup of dirty laundry and delivery of the clean clothing. Because the door was unlocked, they walked in as usual.

"Who are you?" Jennet Burleigh asked the black woman.

"Z-z-zurelle. I'se work here."

"Well, we do the laundry," said Lynnet Burleigh. "Mrs. Cutter didn't tell you to do the laundry, did she?"

"Miz Cutter didn't tell me 'bout my work a 'tall," said Zurelle, bobbing her head back and forth between the twins, who were not identical but very similar in facial features. Jennet had naturally curly hair while Lynnet's light brown hair was straight. They wore it the same, tied at the nape of their necks with a ribbon. They were both pretty with wide-set eyes and full mouths.

Putting her basket down, Jennet said, "In that case, we will continue our service until dismissed."

Lynnet took a tin of freshly-baked molasses cookies from the top of her laundry basket, placed it on the table, and removed her outerwear.

Jennet went to the stove to set the kettle on and said, "Join us for tea. We're cold and need to warm up. Mrs. Cutter always has us stay for tea. Tell us about yourself. We heard Mrs. Cutter is sick and Mr. Cutter is at the doctor's house."

"Hush, Jennet, and let her get a word in," admonished Lynnet.

Dalby, Willene, and Fernancy, who had been playing in the upstairs back hall, came down to the kitchen, and shyly huddled together. The Burleigh sisters quickly made friends with the children, who had never seen twins before. The friendly young women also engaged their mother in conversation.

"Our cousin was arrested here and put in jail, but don't think we're a bad family," said Jennet.

Lynnet stirred three half cups of tea as Jennet filled them with milk. After dropping a cube of sugar into each cup, the young twins served the children. Only Dalby accepted the tea without coaxing.

Zurelle took the cups from first Lynnet and then Jennet and gave them to her daughters as she said, "They ain't never had nothin' give 'em by white women afore."

"You will find things are different up here in Canada than where you came from," said Jennet.

"We know that," said Dalby, keeping his eyes focused on these strangers.

When they were all seated around the big table, drinking their tea, and eating the molasses cookies, Zurelle hesitantly asked, "Why was your cousin arrested?"

"He's accused of being a Confederate spy," said Lynnet.

"But we don't know what he really did wrong," said Jennet. "I suppose there will be a trial to determine that."

"We don't know if his trial will be in Canada or the United States," said her twin, just as Ochran came in from shoveling snow.

Zurelle introduced the local sisters to her husband, who warmed himself by the big fireplace.

Jennet said, "We better put the clothes away so we can get on with our errands."

"I do that," said Zurelle. "Doctor Jesse says folks ought not to visit Miz Cutter while she be so poorly. You might catch the flu, too, he said."

The twin sisters thanked Zurelle, shook hands all around, and left the mansion.

* * *

As Anathea came back from the ladies room at the end of the train car, she grasped the handles on one of the seat corners when the train took a curve. Holding tight to the metal bar until the train was on a straight course, she overheard two men in the seat near her.

"Cut the loaves down the center," said the first man.

"Not baked inside?" questioned the second man.

"Certainly not," replied the man nearest the window. "Scoop out the crumbs, insert the explosives, and glue the sides closed."

"It has to be done neatly so the seams don't show."

The train straightened out. The man nearest the aisle looked up at Anathea and she moved on. As soon as she sat down beside Raiford, she wanted to say something to him, but waited until Rev. Stewart, who had been rambling about Southern rights, excused himself to referee a disagreement between Dale and James.

"I just heard the most unusual conversation," Anathea whispered to Raiford.

"What?" Raiford asked as he turned to face her.

Anathea repeated the two men's words. Neither the children nor the adults nearby overheard because Anathea spoke softly.

"Why would men put explosives in bread?" Anathea wanted to know.

"There are evil schemes afoot," Raiford answered.

Rev. Stewart resumed his seat across the aisle and asked, "What evil schemes are those?"

Raiford exchanged glances with Anathea before he answered. "She overheard something unwholesome."

"What might that be? Do tell? Whose conversation?" The minister became animated as he looked from one to the other.

Reluctantly, Raiford said, "Those two men in the forward seats."

Once Kensey had confirmed which two men, he left his seat, hurried down the aisle, leaned over, and spoke in lowered tones to the men.

Anathea asked Raiford: "Do you think he is counseling them against sinful acts?"

Raiford was silent for a long moment before he said, "I don't like that man."

Just then, Freddie, who had been looking out the window, waved his hands at shoulder level and exclaimed with delight: "I see the big bridge!"

* * *

Historic Note: William Hamilton Merritt long dreamed of a suspension bridge over the Niagara River. Stone masons from Scotland built the two massive towers from which the cables were hung across the Niagara Gorge. Finally, in 1855, the engineering marvel was completed. The bridge was a double-decker with the upper level for trains of the Great Western Railway and the lower level for horse traffic – stagecoaches, carriages, and horseback riders. By bridging the Niagara River, legitimate commerce not only benefited but also illegitimate activities, such as those carried out by Confederate operatives who needed easy access to the safety of British North America.

CHAPTER SIX

FALLING SCAFFOLDING

Wherein Raiford tells the legend of the Maiden of the Mist;
Anathea has a panic attack;
Headley and Martin report to Thompson;
Raiford meets fellow federal spies and learns about
Jackson Wade's incarceration; and
Kirk voices his suspicions about E. L. Pearson.

At the Suspension Bridge, all passengers had to detrain because the New York Central Railroad ended and the Great Western Railroad of Canada began. The two men who spoke about putting explosives in loaves of bread disappeared in the crowd. While waiting for the passengers to change trains, Raiford told the children the legend of the Maiden of the Mist.

"What's mist?" Freddie asked, before Raiford said more than a few sentences.

"It's the water that sprays up from the falls when it hits the river below," the man explained.

On the platform, the conductor motioned people, a few at a time, onto the train, while others listened to Raiford's pleasant voice tell the ancient folk tale.

"A Seneca Indian girl lived with her family in a village beside the Niagara River," Raiford continued. "Indians did not know the one true God until missionaries came to tell them. Therefore, the Seneca girl, called the Maiden of the Mist, believed a powerful creature named Hinu lived in the cave behind the waterfall and controlled events. The Senecas thought Hinu could make thunder and rain."

"Could he?" asked Beatrice.

"No. Only God controls nature," Raiford assured her. "This is just an old story."

"Let him tell it," Freddie scolded his sister.

"One summer, many of the Indians became sick," said Raiford, who noticed the people around him were listening. Anathea smiled when she caught his eye and realized that he was aware of his unintended audience. "So the Indians sent canoes bearing gifts of flowers and food down the river and over the falls to please Hinu so he would stop the sickness. However, the sickness did not go away. Then, the Maiden of the Mist decided she would canoe down the river and try to convince Hinu to free her people from the curse."

"Did she drown?" asked Freddie.

"No, because she was rescued," Raiford answered.

"Who rescued her?" Beatrice was wide-eyed.

"Hinu's son. He saw the brave Maiden swept over the great falls. The roar of the falls deafened her. The spray of the water blinded her. But she was not afraid. She felt peaceful as she floated down, down, down to the Niagara River, where Hinu's son caught her in his arms."

Raiford's expressive narration added to the drama. Anathea thought: *What a romantic story. If only such things were true.*

"Did she marry him?" asked a stranger, a young woman, at Raiford's side.

"Yes, but not before they helped her people," said Raiford.

"How?" asked another stranger.

"The Maiden asked Hinu's son why his father did not stop the sickness of her people," answered Raiford. "The young warrior told the Maiden that there was a monstrous horned snake that poisoned the river and caused the sickness. Hinu was not strong enough to kill the evil snake."

When the conductor motioned for some people to enter the train, they shook their heads and said, "Just a minute," as they awaited the end of Raiford's story.

"The Seneca chief and his warriors, joined by Hinu and his sons, battled the wicked snake, defeated him, and flung him toward the waterfall, but the snake's body became wedged among the rocks." Raiford looked around the group surrounding him and concluded the tale by saying: "That is why the falls have the shape of a bent bow.

The snake's writhing body collapsed the boulders and created the shape that you see today when you look at Niagara Falls."

The people who had heard Raiford's dramatic rendition applauded politely. Raiford smiled and nodded to them as they moved toward the train car where the conductor waited impatiently.

"They were listening to our story," Freddie whispered into Raiford's ear, when he picked up the boy to carry him onto the train.

"That's all right. It's good to share stories with people," Raiford said.

Anathea, finding her seat across from Raiford, marveled at his boldness. *I could never tell a story like that amid strangers who were listening to me. Where did he learn how to do that? Was he taught that in school? At the orphanage, we never learned how to speak in public.*

When the train departed and the children were engaged in looking out the windows, Anathea asked Raiford, "Where did you hear that story?"

"I ran across it while researching in preparation for this trip."

Once again, Anathea wondered about his business that took him to Canada.

* * *

Following a scenic route skirting Lake Ontario, the Great Western entered the port city of Toronto, which had twice been the capital of the Province of Canada. That distinction ended six years ago when Quebec became the capital.

With good water and rail transportation, Toronto housed the world's largest whiskey factory, Gooderham and Worts Distillery. Immigrants swelled the population to more than 50,000, about 1,000 of whom were black. The city permitted black and white children to attend the same schools. Three churches were exclusively for black people, two Methodist and one Baptist, although they could attend the white churches if they wanted. Finding freedom in Canada, runaway slaves who arrived in Toronto made their homes in the northwestern section of the city.

* * *

On the day Raiford, Anathea, and the children arrived in Toronto, Monday, November 28, 1864, Edwin Lee received his six-month furlough. Relieved of command of the reserve forces in the Shenandoah Valley, Ned showed the single paper to his wife, Susan.

"This should avert suspicion of my real business in Canada," he said as he kissed her lightly on the cheek.

They were staying at Sue's family home, the parsonage of Rev. William Nelson Pendleton, Episcopal pastor at Lexington, Virginia. William was Chief of Artillery of the Army of Northern Virginia and not at home when the telegram arrived for his son-in-law. However, his wife, Anzolette Page Pendleton, was at the parsonage on the hill. Susan hurried to consult with her mother about what to pack for her trip to Canada, while Ned sat down and wrote a letter to Secretary of War James Alexander Seddon, in Richmond, Virginia. Edwin asked what ships were available to sail to Canada.

* * *

The trek from Kansas City to St. Louis was cold and miserable for Adam Brannaman's wagon train. Upon arriving in the city, he rented a room at the Lewis & Clark Hotel where he slept in a comfortable bed for fifteen hours straight. When he awoke, he wrote a letter to Anathea, telling her to expect him soon. At a tailor shop, he ordered two new suits which would be ready in a few days. The day of his departure, while carrying the bundle with his new outfits, a street riot caused him to divert his route and get lost. By the time he arrived safely back to the Lewis & Clark, he had missed the last steamer of the day. The following day, when he inquired about passage, he learned that another boat could not accommodate him for three days. On that day, snow began falling at dawn but the *S.S. Bluebird* was only two hours late in leaving the dock.

* * *

As they rode in a cab from the Great Western depot to the Metropole Hotel on Front Street, the children exclaimed about the snow.

"There's more snow here than in Albany," said Beatrice. The little girl showed an interest in the map Raiford had obtained at the border and sat near him to see their locations as they traveled.

"Does it always have snow on the ground?" asked Freddie, who sat by Anathea.

"No. Canada has warm summer days the same as we do in the States," said Raiford.

"But Canada's summer is shorter," added Anathea.

"Shorter like me, you mean?" said the little boy, which made them laugh.

At the Metropole, as Raiford paid the cab driver, he overheard quarreling by workmen constructing a building next to the hotel. He was glad Anathea and the children were already inside the lobby because several foul words were spoken. Looking up at the brick-layers on the scaffolding fifteen or so feet above the street, Raiford saw the older of the three men take a flask from his coat pocket, guzzle a long drink, and return the liquor to its hiding place.

Raiford entered the Metropole, signed the registration book, sent their luggage up, and escorted the children and Anathea to the restaurant connected to the lobby by a wide archway. They ate a hardy noon meal for which they were grateful after the train's less-than-gourmet food. Leaving by the restaurant door to Front Street, they avoided the workers on the scaffolding in the opposite direction.

At Ye Olde Bookshop on Duke of York Street, Anathea purchased a blank book with a flower design etched on the cover as well as a biography of Anne Hutchinson, who was tried for heresy in Massachusetts in the colonial era. Raiford purchased three books: a small pocket diary, William Wilberforce's A Practical View of the Prevailing Religious System of Professed Christians, and a King James Bible. He also bought a carrying case with two pens and a bottle of ink. They placed their purchases on the counter and went to help the children decide on their books. Freddie got a book of nursery rhymes and an alphabet book, while Beatrice chose A Little Pretty Pocket Book and Tales by Hans Christian Andersen.

"Is this too much?" Anathea whispered to Raiford as he withdrew his wallet to pay the bookstore clerk.

He smiled, shook his head no, and repeated the adage: "If you pour your money into your mind, you can never be robbed."

The clerk said, "Ben Franklin's words. Wise advice. Would you like me to wrap those or do you prefer a canvas bag?"

Raiford asked Anathea, "Which?"

"A bag, please," she said, and was once again reminded that he asked her opinion which Monro never did.

* * *

In Guelph, Varney Cutter wondered who these people were. They were kind. They gave him good food. His bed was warm and comfortable. But he did not know them.

"Where is this?" Varney asked when he came into the living room.

"You are in our home, Mr. Cutter," said Harriet Shilliday, picking up her knitting.

"I brought you here," said Dr. Shilliday, pointing to a rocking chair where Varney was to sit.

Obediently, Varney sat down and began to rock, saying, "I don't remember that. Why did you bring me here?"

"You were out wandering," said Harriet. "We think you might have been lost."

"We will take you home as soon as Joan is well," said the doctor.

"Joan?" Varney scowled as he tried to remember why that name sounded familiar. He asked, "Is Joan sick?"

"Your wife is recovering from the flu," said Jesse.

"You don't look sick," Varney said to Harriet.

"I'm not Joan. I am Harriet Shilliday, the doctor's wife. Your wife is home in bed with the influenza. Ladies from the church are taking turns sitting with her, and your new servants are there as well."

"She should not be out of bed yet, but she's getting stronger every day," said Jesse.

"Who is she?" asked Varney, looking from one person to the other.

"Your wife, Joan Cutter," the doctor said slowly.

Joan's husband nodded and lowered his eyes. Jesse and Harriet exchanged knowing glances. They both remembered how active and hard-working Varney Cutter had been only a few months ago and were sorry to see his decline.

* * *

Having crossed Front Street, Raiford, Anathea, and the children returned to the Metropole from the direction of the building under construction, which meant they had to pass beneath the scaffolding. The brick-layer with the flask of whiskey was drunk. His two fellow workers were arguing with him.

"Your work is terrible!"

"Go on home!"

"I'm not gonna," shouted the belligerent man.

Some walkers avoided the scaffolding not only because of the mess around it but also because of the shouting overhead. Just as Anathea, Raiford and the children came near, the drunken mason stepped too far back, grabbed the nearest pole, and brought the entire structure of boards, bricks, mortar tubs, tools, and scaffolding down in a clatter.

Sudden fear surged through Anathea. Black outlined her vision. She saw falling bricks. A man's body flew before her eyes. Crashing noises filled her ears. She could not breathe. Her vision narrowed smaller and smaller. A tiny pinhole of light was the last thing she saw. All went black. She fainted.

Meanwhile, Raiford had pushed the children into the hotel doorway, away from the falling debris. When he saw Anathea slide to the sidewalk, he grabbed her before she landed. Turmoil surrounded the scene. Passersby hurried to give aid. Raiford lowered Anathea to the sidewalk and scanned her body for blood. He saw none. Her eyes were closed. She was as still as a corpse.

Nothing hit her. She's not bleeding. Why is she unconscious? Raiford thought as he pushed her bonnet off to see if her head was bleeding. Freddie and Beatrice came to each side of Raiford. "Here. Take her bonnet," Raiford said, handing it to Beatrice as he ran his hand through Anathea's hair, bringing her chignon into disarray.

"Too tight lacing," said a woman watching the couple.

Immediately, Raiford felt of Anathea's back, running both hands from her shoulder blades to her waist. "No corset," he said to the concerned woman.

"Anathea, wake up." Raiford stroked her cheek with his palm. "Breathe, Anathea. You're all right. Breathe." Pulling her closer to his chest as he knelt on the brick-littered sidewalk, he rocked her gently.

"Is she dead?" asked Freddie.

"No, she's not dead," his sister said. Touching Raiford's shoulder, she asked, "Is she?"

Anathea awoke to a strange sensation. She could feel Raiford's heart beating against her cheek. She heard kind, gentle words. Cradled in Raiford's arms, she felt a swaying motion and opened her eyes.

"Breathe like this," said Raiford. "Take deep breaths this way." He showed her what he meant by breathing deeply. She felt his chest expand and contract against her face. Slowly, she took shallow breaths. She felt lethargic.

I don't want to move. Feels so good. Raiford is holding me. Monro never held me when I fainted. So different, so pleasant, to be held.

Freddie asked, "Did a brick hit you, Aunt Anathea?"

"We don't see any blood on you," said Beatrice.

"I… I'm all right," said Anathea in a shaky voice.

"Do you think you can stand?" asked Raiford.

"Yes," she murmured. "It … it startled me." With her feet ensnared in the hem of her skirt, she stumbled but Raiford kept his arm securely around her waist as she untangled her feet and stepped toward the lobby.

The construction boss came and shouted, "Get out of here, you drunken sot!"

The mason who caused the calamity was unhurt and departed quickly.

"Get bandaged up," the boss said to the other two masons who had a minor cuts.

None of the walkers on the sidewalk was injured. Raiford kept a firm hold of Anathea's waist as he led her up the wide staircase to their second floor rooms.

* * *

In an elegant suite at the Queen's Hotel, on that same Monday, November 28, John Headley and Robert Martin gave a full report of their activities to their commander, Colonel Jacob Thompson.

John said, "Our attempt to burn hotels in New York was not as successful as Sherman's burning of Atlanta."

"The Greek fire was defective somehow," added Robert.

Jacob, studying the young men, asked, "Was it intentional, do you think? Were you given bad concoctions on purpose?

"I don't know," said John, slowly sipping his whiskey. "I picked up the Greek fire from a basement on the west side of Washington Place, at the address Captain Longmire gave me. The old man handed me the valise without a word. It was so heavy that I had to change hands every ten feet in order to carry it. I boarded a crowded street car and set the valise on the floor at my feet."

Robert said, "The car went up Bowery Street toward Central Park."

"Before long, I noticed a foul smell," John continued. "The people around me were also aware of the odor."

"Were the bottles corked?" asked Jacob.

"Yes," John told him. "When I got off, I heard a passenger say: 'There must be something dead in that valise.' It smelled like rotten eggs."

"Did one of the bottles break?" asked their leader.

"No," said John. "But you would have thought so by the smell."

"He had twelve dozen four-ounce bottles," said Robert. "None of us knew a thing about Greek fire except that, when exposed to air, it would blaze up and burn whatever it touched."

"It did do that," said Jacob. "At least, the newspapers report nineteen hotels afire."

"But only minor damage," said Robert. "We had hoped to accomplish more. General Sherman burned Atlanta to the ground. Our blazes were a bonfire in comparison."

* * *

In Guelph, the Wyatt family was settling into the Cutter mansion.

"Laws-a-mercy, I never did see such a fine house," Zurelle said to Ochran as they moved a small mattress from the attic to the children's room, one of the two servants' rooms at the back on the second floor. Their children bounced a rubber ball in the hallway between the rooms. It was the first ball they had ever played with.

"The massah's ol' clapboard house could fit inside this here brick one and have room to spare," said Ochran.

"That's for sure," said his wife. "The doctor's mighty good to bring us here."

"I'll say Canada is big as the sun better than being sold south."

Ochran was referring to the deciding event which put him and his family on the road heading north. When their master died in August, his son-in-law intended to sell Zurelle and her children but keep Ochran, who was a strong, obedient workman. Ochran heard this news from one of the house slaves and his resolve was set. He would not allow his family to be sold away from him. Instead, he would follow the North Star and seek freedom in Canada.

"Why can't we just go to some northern state?" Zurelle had asked when Ochran had told her of his plans. "I heard Canada is far, far away, more miles than a body can walk in a lifetime, and it snows every day."

"We can't go to a northern state because they ain't free neither," her husband had replied. "Since they passed that Fugitive Slave Law, only Canada is free."

Thus, the young couple made the arduous trip on the invisible Underground Railroad, receiving much help along the way, and arrived in Guelph tired but joyful.

The children's ball bounced through the door as the parents dropped the mattress on the floor.

"What do you think about your new home?" Ochran asked as he tossed the ball back to his son.

"I like it" said Dalby, who looked as much like his father as a boy could.

"Will we live here always?" asked Willene.

"We don't know about that," said her father.

"I don't like the roof," said little Fernancy.

"The roof?" questioned Zurelle as she picked up her daughter.

"It's in the way. I can't see the stars," replied the two-year-old.

* * *

In the Metropole Hotel, rooms 205 and 207 had a connecting door but were of unequal size. In the larger room, number 205, were the usual hotel furnishings plus the luggage. The smaller room had only a single bed, wash stand, candle stand, and pegs on the wall. Raiford led Anathea to the cushioned rocking chair by the window in room 205.

"I'll get you a glass of water," he said, going to the bureau. "How do you feel?"

Freddie hovered near the chair and wrinkled his brow. "Are you better now?" He patted her hand which was on the arm rest.

Ignoring Anathea, Beatrice explored the two rooms.

"Yes. I'm all right," Anathea said as she took the glass Raiford handed her and sipped slowly.

"Why did you fall down?" Freddie wanted to know.

"I was frightened."

"Nothing hit you," the little boy said.

"No, nothing hit me. I guess I was afraid something would."

Standing close, Raiford listened to Anathea's explanation and asked, "Has this happened before?"

"A few times." Looking up at him, she added, "I'm all right. Truly. There is no reason to make a fuss."

Beatrice came to Raiford and asked, "Who gets the big room?"

"You ladies, of course," said Raiford, bowing slightly. To Freddie, he said, "Gentlemen always defer to ladies. That means, ladies get the best room."

Fluttering his hands near his shoulders, Freddie asked, "You mean I get to sleep with you and not my sister?"

Smiling, Raiford said, "That's right. We men have to stick together."

"But I want to share a bed with my brother," protested Beatrice, stamping her foot.

Raiford sat in the chair by the writing desk, motioned the girl to his side, and said, "We cannot do that, young lady."

"Why not?" Beatrice scowled.

"Think about it?" he said softly as he took her hand. "If you and Freddie have one bed, who will have the other one?"

Beatrice looked from him to Anathea who got up and put her empty glass on the bureau. "Not her and not you."

"That's correct," said Raiford, nodding.

Anathea stood in front of the bureau's mirror and fixed her disheveled chignon.

Freddie went to get his new books.

Raiford said, "You know such a thing would be improper because Aunt Anathea and I are not married."

Hunching her shoulders, Beatrice nodded her head while avoiding Raiford's steady gaze. Raiford added, "I know you love your brother and want to be with him, but he will not be far away."

"Can we keep the door open?" Beatrice asked, lifting her eyes to the man's face.

"Certainly." Raiford kissed the child on the cheek and said, "Now go look at your new books. I need to talk to your aunt."

Coming up behind Anathea, Raiford said, "I have to meet some men about business. If I can take care of everything this afternoon, we can leave for Guelph in the morning. Will you be all right?"

With her hair back in place, she faced him. "Yes. I'm fine."

"You're not dizzy? No harm done?" He studied her face.

Anathea repeated her statement. Raiford turned to say good-bye to the children. Kissing Freddie on the cheek and saying, "I'll be back soon" was a simple matter. The little boy was busy with his new books. However, parting from Beatrice was another matter. The girl clung to him.

"Don't leave! You won't come back!"

"Yes, I will," Raiford said firmly as he picked up Beatrice and carried her to the corner where the bag of books sat on the floor.

"Papa didn't come back!" she wailed.

Freddie, turning pages, showed little interest in his sister's distress.

"I promise I will come back in a few hours," Raiford said in a soothing voice.

Beatrice gripped his hand in both of hers and said, "Why do you have to go?"

"I have business that I must take care of. Aunt Anathea will be here with you."

At this, Anathea came toward them and said, "Let's read your books."

"I want Uncle Raiford to read to me!" the girl demanded.

Both adults tried to calm the child. Failing to do so, Raiford pulled Beatrice into his embrace as he knelt on the floor and said, "We are going to pray and then I will leave. Close your eyes now and be still."

As soon as he saw her close her eyes, he prayed, "Lord, I ask for your wisdom now. Give Beatrice peace. Help her to understand that I will come back just as I have promised to do. Thank you for brave Freddie who knows I will keep my promise. I am sorry that Beatrice does not believe me. Help her to ..."

But Raiford was not able to finish his prayer because the little girl wiggled out of his embrace, flung her arms around his neck, and cried. "I'm sorry! I'm sorry! I believe you! I do!"

Five minutes later, Raiford walked out the front door of the Metropole and entered a waiting taxicab. He gave the driver the address he had memorized.

* * *

I wonder what his real name is, thought Raiford as he walked up the stone steps to the row house and tried to get thoughts of the distressed little girl out of his mind. *Fides. Where did he come up with a name like that? My code name is easy to understand. Olive Branch —a peace offering extended to the enemy.*

The federal detective named Fides answered the door of his modest brick rental house. After identifying himself and giving the password, Raiford was admitted to the smoke-filled parlor where two men waited. One was smoking a cigar.

"This is FitzHenry and Garrett," Fides introduced Raiford as Olive Branch, whom they had been expecting.

As he shook hands with the men, Raiford said, "Your smoke reminds me of my hotel in New York."

Immediately, Garrett extinguished his tobacco. FitzHenry quizzed the new arrival about the November 25th hotel fires. The four men, young and intelligent, talked as though old friends. After discussing the New York City fires, Raiford told them about the train jumper, the overheard conversation of bombs in loaves of bread, and Rev. Stewart's strange plans.

"The reverend said the previous schemes of the Confederates failed because they were not blessed by God," Raiford informed his fellow spies.

"I'd say their attack on St. Albans succeeded fairly well," said Garrett. "They robbed the banks and got away with the money."

"But they didn't burn the town as they undoubtedly intended," said Fides.

The men were discussing the October 19th raid on St. Albans, Vermont, in which Bennett Henderson Young, formerly of General John Hunt Morgan's command, and his small gang of Confederate soldiers robbed the town's banks of $220,000 and escaped across the border into Canada. Fourteen of the robbers were captured and put on trial in Montreal Police Court on November 2, 1864. A recess was granted for one month to allow the raiders time for preparing their defense.

"But their plan to free prisoners at Camp Douglass during the Democratic Convention in August did fail," said FitzHenry.

"Enough about the past," said Fides. "We have an immediate problem. We were in the midst of discussing a possible jail break for a friend of ours." Fides went into the kitchen, calling over his shoulder: "I'll put the kettle on so we can have tea and tell you about it."

"I didn't know we got involved in jail breaks," said Raiford. "What did your friend do?"

The other three men followed Fides into the kitchen. Garrett got cups down from the shelf. FitzHenry opened the tea tin as he answered Raiford's question. "Jackson Wade was rounding up draft dodgers and deserters from the Union army. The Toronto constabulary charged him with crimping."

"Crimping?" Raiford wrinkled his brow.

"That's right," said Garrett. "Illegal recruitment."

"Shanghaiing," said Fides.

Raiford voiced his thoughts to be certain he understood. "You mean Mr. Wade was arresting federal soldiers who had deserted?"

"Or men who had been conscripted but refused to serve," said FitzHenry.

"And for this he was charged as a crimper?" Raiford took a piece of sweet bread from the tin Garrett handed him.

"That's right," said Fides. "We've been proposing methods of breaking him out of jail."

"And discounting each proposal as too risky," said Garrett.

"The most hopeful aspect of a successful escape attempt is the corruption of an official we know," said FitzHenry. "In other words, some lawmen will accept bribes."

"We want to exploit that weakness," said Fides.

The four men sat at the kitchen table, drank tea, ate sweet bread, and discussed various schemes for a jail break.

"Will Jackson Wade have a trial?" Raiford asked, setting down his empty cup.

"It's scheduled for next week, so we have some time," said Garrett.

Fides said, "I intend to meet with Nesbit Payne, our crooked constable, at a pub he frequents. I need to find out how much money a successful escape will cost."

"When?" asked Raiford.

"Tonight if he's there," said Fides.

"He's there every night," said Garrett.

"Are you available to help us, Olive Branch?" asked FitzHenry.

Raiford said, "I need to escort two orphans to Guelph."

"Guelph!" exclaimed Fides. "That's where Burley was arrested."

The men followed Fides into the front room, where the leader shuffled through papers on the side table and held up one of them.

"We got word from a man there named…" Fides looked at the bottom of the message and read: "Kirk McCarrell. He asks for our help in ferreting out the Confederate sympathizers in town."

"I could see Mr. McCarrell when I'm there," Raiford said.

"Burley was up to no good," said Fides, handing the letter and envelope from Kirk to Raiford. "Said he was visiting relatives, but you can see by that newspaper clipping enclosed that he was caught while attempting to ship a crate of torpedoes on the train to Detroit."

"Just because Burley's been stopped, doesn't mean more torpedoes are getting out of that town," said FitzHenry. "We don't know much about the place."

Garrett said, "We can use someone to find out where these weapons are being made."

Fides added, "And find out who is responsible. Was Burley a lone duck or are there more?"

Before parting, the men agreed to meet tomorrow afternoon at Garrett's boarding house. Raiford said he intended to leave tomorrow, so would not be at the meeting.

On his way back to the hotel, Raiford stopped at the telegraph office where he sent two messages. The first one went to Hector Smith and advised that the delivery of stoves was completed. This was the code previously decided to confirm that he had arrived in Toronto and met with his fellow federal detectives. His second wire was to Mr. and Mrs. Cutter in Guelph. *I hope there is only one couple named Mr. and Mrs. Cutter,* Raiford thought, as he paid the operator. *What will they think, getting a telegram from a stranger? Will they assume their son is dead? I cannot convey that dreadful news over a wire. They need to be told in person.*

* * *

In Guelph, Kirk McCarrell left his boarding house and went to the home of his fiancée, Dolly Utley, to escort her to a young people's taffy-pulling party. The Utley family greeted him warmly as usual. The Cutter Industries bookkeeper appeared distracted, and not until he and Dolly were walking in the cold evening air did he come out of his mental fog.

"What's bothering you?" Dolly asked, as she put her hand through the crook of his arm and moved closer.

"I must tell you about something I've done. It could affect our future. I might get fired." Kirk put his gloved hand over her furry mitten which rested on his arm.

Dolly's blue eyes became wide with alarm. "What did you do?"

"I sent a letter to Toronto, addressed to men our Constable Clark told me about."

"What men?"

"Men working for the United States government."

"What did the letter concern?" she asked.

"Workmen at the foundry who have been there late without turning in overtime slips. Pearson never authorizes overtime, but I think he's involved." Kirk spoke in a low tone, although no one was near on the icy street. "The shed where they work is locked and the windows covered over. I heard them one night when I worked late."

"What were they doing?"

"I think they were making torpedoes."

"That's what Mr. Burley was arrested for – shipping torpedoes."

"That's right, and I think he got them from us."

"Oh, dear."

"If Mr. Pearson finds out what I did, if those federal men come here to investigate, well, darling, I could be in trouble."

"But you did the right thing," Dolly squeezed his arm. "You could not have done otherwise."

"But there might be retaliation," said Kirk. "We got a telegram from a man named Jacob Thompson saying a replacement is on his way. If federal investigations catch this replacement… You know I've told you how Pearson loves money. If he finds out that I have spoiled his money-making plans…"

Dolly interrupted him by saying, "No harm will come to you. We'll tell Father!"

A couple arriving in a horse-drawn sled called to them to hurry inside.

Kirk called back, "We're coming!" In a whisper, he agreed with his fiancée to tell his suspicions to Harmon Utley when they returned from the taffy-pulling party.

* * *

The four torpedo-makers met with E. L. Pearson but none of the men were satisfied. The foundry manager, his arms crossed and his back against a shed door, did not tell the men about the telegram concerning a replacement arriving. Instead, he shouted: "Just keep working and keep your mouths shut!"

Still angry when his son Elmore came to ask for money, E. L. bluntly refused. Kirk had never seen the father refuse to give his son money.

* * *

At the Metropole dining room that evening, as they were eating bread pudding, Raiford set the Great Western's timetable beside his knife and said, "The train leaves at three o'clock tomorrow. We will go to the station right after lunch."

He thought: *I would like to delay and help get Jackson Wade out of jail, but getting these children to their new home must take priority.*

Anathea thought: *Once these children are home with their grandparents, I will be on my own again. Finally! I can make my plans for the future.* She picked up the timetable and looked for possible destinations for herself alone.

Beatrice asked Raiford, "Will you leave us there?"

"In Guelph with your grandparents, yes," said Raiford.

"What if they don't like us?" she whined. "What if we don't like them?"

Anathea said, "Certainly you will like each other. Don't you remember them?"

"We've never seen our grandparents," Beatrice informed the adults.

"There is always a kinship among relatives, even if you have never met," Raiford assured the girl. "You need not worry."

"Where will you go?" Beatrice asked the man.

"I'll stay a few days until you're settled," he said.

Freddie asked Anathea, "Will you stay, too?"

"For a few days, if you wish," she told the boy.

* * *

When the children were asleep, Anathea asked Raiford, "Did your telegram tell Mr. and Mrs. Cutter that their son was dead?"

"No. I thought it would be better to speak to them in person," Raiford said, as they faced each other across the small table on which the lamp lighted the books each of them had been reading.

Anathea returned to her story about Anne Hutchinson, but Raiford only glanced at his book by the English abolitionist. Lifting his gaze to her face, he said, "Tell me about your fainting spell."

Anathea met his eyes and replied, "I was frightened. That's all."

"Do you faint often?"

"I never did until…"

He waited a long moment before asking, "Until when?"

"When something happened that I felt powerless to change," she said slowly, being careful not to reveal anything about Monro.

The experience, her first fainting spell, flashed into her mind. It was the day they walked through the front gate of the Shaker village and he informed her that they were no longer married.

To dispel the memory, Anathea said, "It frightens me to feel I have no power over a situation, like when I see falling bricks and scaffolding."

"What's it like when you faint?"

Why is he asking me these questions? What is his purpose?

"First, everything appears to be outlined in black. The blackness closes in as though I'm in a tunnel or a cave. It happens quickly. Everything becoming black is also the time when I cannot get my breath. That's when I faint."

"I knew of a lady in Goshen who fainted when she was expecting a child."

"I am not expecting a child," Anathea responded firmly.

"I was not suggesting you were. I'm just trying to understand how I might help to prevent this."

"Why?"

Puzzled, Raiford asked, "Why do I want to keep you from harm?"

"I wasn't harmed."

"You could have been if I didn't catch you."

Anathea averted her eyes. Closing her book, she set it on the table and stood up. Raiford did the same and stopped her from moving away by taking her wrist and saying, "You do have power."

"How?"

"You can scream for help. You can run. You can escape the danger."

"But I was raised to accept…" *I do not want to reveal too much to him. I should not say more.*

"In the orphanage, you mean?" Raiford slid his fingers from encircling her wrist to hold her hand.

Anathea pulled her hand out of his gentle hold and said, "Yes, in the orphanage." *But more especially in my marriage to Monro.*

Raiford bid her good-night and carried Freddie from the spot beside his sister where he had fallen asleep into the adjoining room. There, lying in the narrow bed with Freddie snuggling close, Raiford thought about Anathea and her fainting spells, about Beatrice's dependence on him, about Bennett Burley's arrest, and about Jackson Wade's incarceration.

Anathea, falling asleep beside Beatrice, thought about the scene of the child's begging Raiford not to leave her. The recent experience melted into a vision of Monro leaving her, walking away from her body lying at the gate of the Shaker village where she had fainted. In her mind's eye, she saw Monro's feet stomping away from her as though she was an ant with its ground-level view. She saw dust rise from Monro's foot falls. She saw bugs crawl near her face, but she could not escape them.

If I were standing, I would faint. No, I did faint. That's why I'm lying in the dirt. I'm paralyzed. I cannot get up. Don't go, Monro! Help me up! My voice sounds like Beatrice begging Raiford not to go. He's still walking away. I don't want to see him leaving me. I won't look at him. What's that crumpled paper?

In her dream, Anathea reached for the paper in the dirt, opened it, and saw three words: **Bill of Divorcement**.

While Anathea dreamed, Raiford mulled over possible schemes to rescue Jackson Wade from jail, and wished he would be available to help. These were his last thoughts before falling asleep. When he awoke the next morning, a concrete scheme had planted itself in his mind.

* * *

Historic Note: Schemes had been devised since Confederate President Jefferson Finis Davis and his trusted Secretary of State, Judah Phillip Benjamin, appointed three commissioners to work in British North America. Jacob Thompson, former Congressman from Mississippi, was the senior member, with Clement Claiborne Clay, a former U.S. and Confederate Congressman from Alabama, as a junior member of the Commission.

James P. Holcombe, a law professor from the University of Virginia, served as the third member of the group. Although they were not official envoys to British North America, because Queen Victoria's neutrality declaration refused to recognize the Confederate States of America as a true nation, they nevertheless worked within the borders of neutral provinces of Great Britain. They sought agents who would aid Confederate soldiers to return to the army, but soon learned that not many escaped prisoners or draft dodgers wanted to return south. Instead, they gathered at the elegant St. Lawrence Hall in Montreal, the only hotel in Canada which served mint juleps, and discussed war news while the three commissioners attempted to crystallize the anti-Northern sentiment that already existed in Canada and to win sympathy for the embattled South.

CHAPTER SEVEN

PROVIDENTIAL DELAY

Wherein Raiford tells Anathea about his wife;
they delay their departure; federal agents rescue a prisoner;
and Raiford runs for the train.

On Tuesday morning, November 29, Anathea, coming down the hall from the lavatory, wondered: *How can I manage a train trip today of all days? This will be so inconvenient. What should I do?*

Entering the room, she was unaware of the pained expression on her face. Raiford, who had been thinking about how he could pass along his rescue plot to Fides and the others before leaving Toronto, noticed her scowl before she crawled onto the mussed covers, curled into a ball, and covered her stomach with her hands.

"I'm not feeling well," she murmured. "Go to breakfast without me."

"Could we bring you something?" he asked, coming toward her.

Sitting on the floor, the children, already dressed, were putting on their shoes. They chattered about what the hotel breakfast might be.

"No. Nothing," Anathea said, closing her eyes.

Raiford sat at the foot of the bed and asked, "Is it that time of the month?"

Immediately, Anathea's eyes flew open. She stared at him. Her cheeks reddened with embarrassment. Turning her face into the pillow, she squeezed her eyes shut and refused to answer.

How could he know? Men should not speak of such things!

His next words shocked her. "My wife suffered much during her monthly time."

Anathea remained frozen in the fetal position.

Raiford added: "Lenore died in '59, three months after our wedding. I also have sisters."

I don't want to know this, Anathea thought. *You should not speak to me so. Just go away.*

As though he could hear her thoughts, Raiford stood up and said, "We will bring you toast and coffee. You must eat something."

* * *

In the dining room, ten minutes later, Raiford ordered for himself and the children.

"Is Aunt Anathea sick very bad?" asked Freddie.

"No too sick, just a little, so we will not leave today."

"But I want to go home," whined Beatrice.

"You said you don't even know your grandparents," said Raiford. "But now you want to go home?"

"Well, we can't live in a hotel forever," she declared.

Raiford smiled at the girl and said, "I will send another telegram and tell them not to expect our immediate arrival."

"What will we do here?" asked Freddie.

I will try to help get a man out of jail, Raiford thought. To Freddie, he said, "I would like to buy some candy and maybe another toy or two. What about you?"

The children became excited at the idea. The toys they bought at the Marble Palace department store in New York were the first manufactured toys they had owned, and candy was a rare treat.

"Do you know the location of a confectionary?" Raiford asked the waiter when he served their breakfast.

Throughout the breakfast, Raiford and the children talked about candy and toys. They were still discussing the possibilities when Raiford placed a tray on Anathea's bedside and said, "I'm taking the children to the Dettelbach Confectionary. It's not far. We'll be back soon."

"I'll pack while you're gone," she said, sitting up against the pillow.

"No," he said and smiled at her. "We will not leave today."

"What?"

"We will not travel until you are ready," Raiford said.

Anathea could not believe she heard correctly. *Is he changing his plans to accommodate me? Monro never did such a thing.*

"Do you need anything while we're out?" Raiford asked her.

Anathea had to collect her thoughts before answering.

"Can we get you anything at the store?" Raiford asked again.

"Some yarn and knitting needles," said Anathea.

"What color yarn?"

"Any colors the children like. I want to make them scarves."

* * *

In the afternoon, Anathea knitted while the children ate their colorful Necco wafers and played with their new toys. Beatrice had a set of beads and was busy making a necklace for Victoria. Freddie had a stuffed polar bear named Whitey and a drawstring bag of marbles.

Raiford's departure on business matters did not result in the trauma that yesterday's departure had. "I'll be back soon," Raiford said, kissing the children and touching Anathea on the shoulder as she sat in the rocking chair.

After he was gone, Anathea missed him.

Why should I miss him? He has been with me only a short time. But I do miss him.

As she watched her knitting needles move amid the red yarn of Freddie's scarf, she thought about the morning.

He should not have spoken to me the way he did – asking if it was that time of the month. No gentleman speaks to a lady of such a thing. How different he is. He postponed our trip until I can travel conveniently. Monro never considered my comfort. I remember when it was my womanly time; Monro treated me as though I had leprosy. Raiford, however, treated me with … what? Tenderness? Consideration? His wife was very fortunate. How sad that she died young. What did he say? They had been married only three months. What would it have been like to be married to Raiford? Oh, I must not think about such a thing!

* * *

Garrett was alone when Raiford arrived at his boarding house.

"I will not be leaving today," Raiford greeted his fellow spy. "The lady with whom I am traveling needs a few days at the hotel."

"Good," said Garrett, who was cleaning a Colt revolver. "The others should be here shortly. We can use your help. Sit down."

As Raiford watched Garrett clean the gun, he explained his rescue scheme which the other man thought had a good chance of success. When Fides and FitzHenry came, they went over details of the plot to bribe Nesbit Payne, the deputy constable at the municipal jail where Mr. Wade was held.

"What might go wrong and how can we alter our plans in that case?" asked Fides.

"We just scatter," said FitzHenry. "Every man for himself."

"Nothing will go wrong," said Raiford, but he thought: *If I am caught, what will Anathea and the children do? I must make preparation for such an eventuality.*

* * *

Harmon Utley went to visit Bennett Burley's lawyer, William Mittleberger, in his office on Cork Street, a block from MacDonell, the main street through Guelph.

"Harmon! It's good to see you," William greeted his friend. "Come in and warm yourself."

A clerk, who was writing at a high desk in the corner, spoke to the visitor and returned to his work. Harmon sat by the blazing fireplace and told the lawyer about his future son-in-law's suspicions and the fact he had sent a message to someone in Toronto.

"Kirk has asked for help from federal agents because he's afraid those torpedoes your client is accused of shipping from Guelph were made at Cutter's. Has Mr. Burley told you where he got the weapons?" Harmon extended his hands toward the flame.

"Mr. Burley claims those torpedoes did not belong to him," said Mr. Mittleberger, rubbing his long beard. "He claims to be innocent of violating our neutrality."

"Even though the shipping receipt was in his name?"

"He claims that was a forgery."

"What about that robbery from the *Philo Parsons*?" Harmon asked.

He was referring to the Confederates having captured the *Philo Parsons* last September, intending to use the steamer in an attempt to rescue prisoners from Johnson's Island. However, when the raiders realized that the *U.S.S. Michigan* crew, which guarded the prison camp, knew of their plans, they abandoned their leader, John Yates Beall, and his second in command, Bennett Burley.

William said, "He claims he's innocent."

"There are ample witnesses."

"The *Philo Parsons* affair will be the only charge against him in court," said the lawyer. "The ownership of the confiscated torpedoes cannot be laid at my client's doorstep."

Harmon said in a low tone, "You know he's guilty of both accusations. How can you defend him?"

"In my training, I learned that even a guilty man is entitled to a defense."

"That attack on the *Philo Parsons* was naked piracy," said Harmon.

"A judge and jury will make that decision."

"Will he be tried in Guelph?"

"Probably not," said the attorney. "Toronto is most likely, if the Americans don't get him back for trial there."

"How could they? He's a Canadian citizen," said Harmon.

"We have that Webster-Ashburton Treaty."

"Remind me what it says."

"The treaty says we will extradite criminals but not political offenders or belligerents involved in acts of war."

"Is that how you plan to keep your client from being sent back to the Americans?"

William smiled at his friend, giving the only answer needed.

Harmon said," Your client, Mr. Burley, is already being tried in the court of public opinion."

Mr. Mittleberger did not disagree.

* * *

That evening, after the children were asleep, Raiford wrote in his travel diary while Anathea carefully recorded their purchases and costs in the new blank book Raiford had bought for her. They each had a pen but shared the single ink bottle.

Raiford thought: *This is much nicer than when I have to write in my tiny secret journal.* He did that writing while in the latrine where no one would see.

Having finished her entries, Anathea took up her knitting. Raiford closed the ink bottle when he was done writing and picked up his book. Before long, Anathea interrupted his reading by asking, "Would you please put your finger here?"

Raiford looked at the table top where she was pointing to the china doll's hand. Victoria had one red mitten, which Anathea had knitted after the children went to bed.

"Just hold it while I tie a bow," she instructed.

"This is cute," Raiford said as he put a bookmark between pages, closed the book, and placed his finger on the doll's wrist.

As Anathea tied the yarn into a bow, she slipped it carefully under his finger. Their hands touched. Neither one moved. Both stared at their hands on the table. Anathea felt heat come into her cheeks. Breaking the spell, she said, "Thank you," and removed her hands.

"Can you knit the other mitten this evening?" he asked, as he slid his hand across the table and into his lap.

"Yes. I'm not tired," she said. "But don't let me keep you up."

"I'm not tired either." He set his book on the small stand by the window and asked, "Did those ladies' pills I got you do any good?"

After visiting the Dettelbach Confectionary that morning, Raiford had gone to an apothecary where he bought Dr. Spohn's Ladies Pills which the pharmacist recommended.

"Yes, remarkably well," she said, as she kept her eyes on her knitting to avoid looking at him and becoming embarrassed again. "I did not know there were such pills."

"Good." He went to the double bed to scoop up Freddie. "There is something I must do tomorrow. Do you mind staying alone with the children again?"

"Not at all. We got along fine today. They play well together. Beatrice didn't look out the window for you nearly as often as she did on Monday."

"That's good." He lifted the sleeping boy.

"When will we leave?"

"When you decide." Raiford carried Freddie to their bed in the next room.

I decide? Me? I have the authority to make the decision for the four of us? Monro never gave me authority to decide anything. Not even our wedding. Now, our departure date is my decision. How different this is.

* * *

Wednesday, November 30, Beatrice awoke to find red knitted mittens on Victoria's delicate hands and thanked Anathea. For the first time, the little girl smiled at the woman. Anathea joined the others for breakfast in the hotel dining room. After breakfast, Raiford played marbles with Freddie. They used a length of red yarn to make the circle from which the marbles were pinged. Beatrice watched Anathea knit and asked if she would teach her.

"I don't know if you can," said Anathea. "You are very young."

"Could I try?"

"Perhaps if we get you some big wooden needles," said Anathea. "You need needles bigger than mine." She told her about a little girl at the orphanage who could knit and added, "But I think she was seven or eight."

Raiford was glad to see Beatrice becoming friendly with Anathea. Leaving them in the afternoon was easier when he knew the little girl was not fretting about his return.

Before going to lunch, they played Button-Button-Whose-Got-The-Button and Blind Man's Bluff. Raiford continued his narrative, from memory, of the story of *Pilgrim's Progress*. To work up an appetite, Raiford suggested a walk in the crisp air. Anathea, pleased that the ladies' pills kept her from feeling any cramps, was glad to be outdoors despite the cold. Before returning to the hotel, they stopped in a store and purchased two large knitting needles.

After lunch in the hotel dining room, Raiford escorted the children and Anathea to their rooms. As soon as Anathea set her drawstring purse on the bureau, Raiford put several large bills into it. Beatrice saw what he did. Next, Raiford took Anathea's arm, escorted her into the smaller bedroom and closed the door.

"I don't know when I will return," he said in a suppressed tone. "If something prevents me, you have enough money for the trip to Guelph. I put money in your reticule."

"What would prevent you from returning?" Her eyes widened with alarm.

Raiford stepped close. Their bodies were inches apart. He whispered, "I might be arrested."

"Arrested?"

"I hope not but there is a possibility." He brushed past her and reached for the door knob. "You can manage. I have confidence in you."

He opened the door to be met by Beatrice. The little girl was standing directly in front of the door. Her arms were crossed over her chest. A scowl distorted her usually pretty face. Immediately, both adults had the same thought: *Her mother's lover.*

Raiford scooped Beatrice into his arms and carried her to the rocker where he sat with her on his lap. "What is it, sweetheart?"

"I saw you give her money," declared the girl.

"Yes. I did. It's for your trip."

Should I tell her that I might be arrested? No. I don't want to add to her anguish. What should I say?

"Does what I did remind you of someone else?" Raiford asked.

Anathea stood at the connecting doorway and held her breath. *Give us wisdom, Lord.*

"You're like him," the girl said.

"Who?" the man asked.

"Him. Mama's friend. He gave her money. He stayed overnight. I didn't like him. Freddie did. He played with Freddie. I ran away and hid from him."

Raiford rocked the chair slowly as he talked in a soothing voice. Freddie, on the floor, was organizing his red and black checkers in rows on the rug and ignoring the conversation.

"I'm not like your mama's friend," Raiford said. "You know that. I gave Aunt Anathea money so she would not have to depend on me."

"Mama's friend gave her money, too."

"I know but this is different. I do not stay overnight with Anathea. You do. I would not stay with a lady who was not my wife," Raiford said, and wondered: *Have I said enough? Have I said too much?* He glanced over at Anathea, who swallowed hard, and moved to the table where she took up her knitting.

"Uncle Raiford has business to take care of," said Anathea. "Here, let me show you how to hold your new knitting needles."

"You weren't in there very long," mumbled Beatrice, gazing at the floor.

"That's right," said Raiford. "I just had to speak to her for a moment."

"Can't you speak to me, too?" asked the girl.

"I'm speaking to you right now," said the man. "Don't you hear me? Freddie hears me. I'm certain that Victoria hears me."

"Don't be silly," said Beatrice.

Raiford hugged the child, stood up, and set her down in the chair.

"Now knit a scarf for Victoria while I'm gone." He kissed her on the cheek, bent down to kiss Freddie, touched Anathea on the shoulder, and left the room.

* * *

Carrying one of two identical briefcases, Raiford entered the Toronto Municipal Jail. People were coming and going. Some wore constables' uniforms. Some wore three-piece suits. Some wore ragged clothing. As planned, he met Nesbit Payne, the deputy constable, in his private office, a dingy room down the hall from the cells on the ground floor.

"You're new, aren't you?" asked Nesbit.

"Just arrived," answered Raiford.

"Got the money?"

"Right here." Raiford snapped open the leather briefcase and revealed stacks of bills. "Do you want to count it?"

"It's a thousand?" Mr. Payne lifted one bundle and flipped through them in order to see that they were not blank pieces of paper.

"Exactly."

"Looks to be right." Nesbit dropped the bundle back in the briefcase and fingered the top of each as he counted ten stacks.

"You escort Mr. Wade," said Raiford. "I'll carry this to your cab."

"I can carry it," said the corrupt official.

"That won't look right," Raiford said, without showing any alarm at the suggestion. "You need to hold a gun at the man's back, so it appears like a prisoner transport. I need to carry this so I look like a lawyer."

"Yah. Guess you're right." The lawman drew his gun from the holster on his belt and checked it for bullets. "Is the cab waiting?"

"In the back alley," Raiford confirmed. "I'll give you the money there."

Keeping the gun in his right hand, Nesbit grabbed the cell keys from the hook on the wall with his other hand. Raiford opened the office door and held it for the constable, who whispered, "Walk ahead so I can keep an eye on you and the money."

"Of course," said Raiford, going in front of the burly man.

When Jackson Wade's jail cell was unlocked, Mr. Payne growled, "You need to answer more questions. This lawyer here will represent you." He nodded toward Raiford, who smiled at Mr. Wade, a young man with shaggy hair and mussed clothes.

Instead of going back to his office, as the prisoner expected, Nesbit waved his gun toward the back door of the building.

Jackson thought: *He's going to shoot me, or this other man will.*

Nesbit was thinking: *This is going to work. I'll get the money and ride away in the cab. These two scoundrels will disappear. I'll say I was kidnapped by thugs. No one will ever know how much I profited from this escapade.*

Raiford thought: *I hope he doesn't see Garrett. What will I do if he sees him?*

The escape plan worked perfectly. As soon as Raiford exited the door which opened into the alley, Garrett, behind the door, exchanged briefcases with him. Nesbit Payne never saw the swap because he was focused on the taxi in which he was to make his getaway, presumably being kidnapped by men who came to rescue Prisoner Wade.

When Raiford handed the new briefcase, just obtained from Garrett, into Nesbit's hands, the greedy man shoved Jackson toward him, hopped into the cab, let out a harsh laugh, and shouted, "Go! Go!" to the cab driver.

As the carriage sped away, Raiford and Garrett grabbed Jackson's arms and ran in the opposite direction. They were around the corner and out of sight when Mr. Payne opened the replacement briefcase to find no money. Instead, there were newspapers to provide weight and a note. The crooked Toronto constable read: "Proverbs 15:27 – He that is greedy of gain troubles his own house, but he that hates gifts shall live."

Raiford and Garrett took Jackson Wade directly to the Great Western station where Fides gave him his ticket to Boston, and FitzHenry gave him a suitcase. The Union officer thanked his rescuers profusely before boarding. Within a few minutes, the train departed, and Raiford headed back to the Metropole.

* * *

Although a thin layer of snow covered Toronto's landscape, a heavy snowfall added six inches during the night. Cold wind blew from the northeast. By midnight, the mercury fell to zero. In the morning, Thursday, December 1, needle-like snow drifted into icy piles atop buildings, trees, sidewalks, and streets. Hotel guests talked about being snowbound for days.

Beatrice and Freddie, each looking out one of the two windows in room 205, chatted about the sights of people and horses struggling to walk amid the deep snow drifts. Raiford joined them and motioned for Anathea to "Come and see."

Thus, Anathea, Raiford, and the children spent the day indoors, enjoying the camaraderie of fellow snowbound hotel guests in the large lobby and, in their two rooms, playing games, reading, talking, knitting and napping.

Anathea, lying beside Beatrice as they napped, could hear Raiford talking softly to Freddie beyond the door which was ajar. She thought: *I cannot remember when I have enjoyed such a day. Just think, snowed in with strangers, but they don't seem like strangers now. Yet, how long have we known each other? A few days only. If I could ever have a family, I would like to have a family like this.*

Raiford, too, had similar thoughts after Freddie closed his eyes for a nap. Raiford thought: *If Lenore had lived, would we have enjoyed such days when snowed in? Would we have been parents to children like Freddie and Beatrice? Will I ever have such a family?*

* * *

The snow which enabled Anathea to have happy memories gave no such pleasant thoughts to her brother. Adam Brannaman's steamer, the *S.S. Bluebird,* sighted chunks of ice floating down the Ohio River before docking at Louisville. Upon debarking, Adam found a city in turmoil, completely unprepared for snow. Drifts were so deep that horses and trains had difficulty getting to their destinations. Adam soon realized that it would be impossible to continue his journey to the Shaker village.

I'll stop by the orphanage and visit with Miss Dell, he thought. *Perhaps she can give me some recent news of Anathea and suggest a hotel until I can proceed.*

When Adam alighted from the carriage and trudged up the steps to the large townhouse, he noticed the sign *Home for Friendless Girls* was missing a nail and hung crooked over the door. Also, no one had cleared the snow from the steps.

The building had been the home of a rich widow who converted the building into an orphanage for girls when she moved to a larger house. Having been an orphan herself, she wanted a nice home for girls without families. The orphanage housed twenty-two girls when Anathea had left. Now, there were seventeen.

Answering the door, Barbara Dell pulled her shawl closer and stepped out of the wind. "Yes. May I help you?"

"My name is Adam Brannaman, Anathea's brother."

"Please come in." She smiled and stepped back as he entered.

Twenty minutes later, they were sitting in the small parlor which served as an office, sipping tea, as Barbara shared her tale of woe.

"Our benefactress died last month and her son, a wicked man, has gone to court to make her will invalid." Barbara, a pleasant-looking woman with gray at her temples, held both hands on her tea cup to warm them. "Her will provided for the orphanage in perpetuity, which means as long as the money lasts. Her son won't stand for it. He came here ranting after the will was read and told us that we would not receive another penny. Our headmistress quit. She never liked the job or the girls anyway. I've had to take over everything. The older girls help. We cannot afford to hire anyone."

"How are you managing?" asked Adam.

"Small donations," she said. "My greatest concern right now is coal. We've burned the desks and chairs to provide firewood. I'm reluctant to burn any more furniture. By evening, this house will be freezing. I don't know what to do."

Adam put down his tea cup, stood up, and said, "I'll see to this. Don't fret." Retrieving his hat and coat, he left, to return shortly with a wagon-load of coal followed by a cart filled with firewood. As the men were unloading, Adam asked them to start fires in all the rooms. To the cart driver, he said, "Would you be willing to do some repair work around the orphanage?"

"I'd be grateful for the work, sir."

Adam gave money to the three oldest girls to buy food and stayed for supper. When he left to find a hotel, the orphanage was warm and the residents were joyful.

* * *

At supper that evening, Anathea overheard a waiter tell the man at the next table that some trains were running on schedule tomorrow, and asked Raiford, "Will we leave tomorrow?"

Having heard the same waiter, Raiford smiled and said, "Let's wait until Saturday. Won't that be better for you?"

She nodded and lowered her eyes. Still unable to acknowledge the fact that he knew about ladies' monthly times, Anathea did her best to conceal her embarrassment.

Fortunately, Raiford changed the subject and asked, "What will you do when the children are home?"

"I thought I would look for a job in Guelph or somewhere."

"You won't disappear forever, will you?" Freddie wrinkled his little brow.

"Not forever," said Anathea. "I would like to visit with you and your grandparents. Maybe I can find a job close by."

"What kind of job?" asked Beatrice.

"Perhaps housekeeping. That's all the experience I have. Cooking, cleaning, doing laundry. Those are the things we were taught at the orphanage."

"You are capable of more than housekeeping," said Raiford. "Look what a good job you have done keeping track of our expenses."

Anathea had shown him her completed entries in the blank book to confirm that she had not missed adding any of the receipts and to check her addition, which Monro always did. Raiford had complimented her on her work, as he did again, saying, "There were no errors in your arithmetic and your penmanship is excellent."

"That was due to Miss Dell. She was a good school mistress. The other women at the orphanage just taught domestic trades."

"You could be a reporter," Raiford said, as he took a taste of the cherry cobbler set before him.

"Ladies aren't reporters," Anathea protested, nodding her thanks to the waiter as he gave her a dish of cobbler.

"Why not?" He smiled at the children who beamed with delight at the whipped cream piles atop their dessert. "In Goshen, the editor's wife wrote most of the news stories. He just did the editorials."

"You could be a nurse," said Freddie. "You got my splinter out."

Amid Freddie's howling that morning, Raiford held the boy tightly while Anathea removed a splinter from his finger with a needle.

"And you took good care of my cut wrist," added Raiford.

"I know nurses are working in the military hospitals," said Anathea. "But I don't think I would like to see all those wounded soldiers."

An instant memory flashed into Raiford's mind. He recalled the hospital tents and wards in make-shift hospitals where he had tended the dying and wounded. *But that was when I was a conscientious objector, before I gave that up and began shooting my fellow men.*

Raiford dispelled that thought from his mind. He did not want to think about how his philosophy of war had changed.

"You could be a school teacher," said Beatrice. "You taught me how to knit and read better."

Pleased by these suggestions and compliments, Anathea said, "I will pray and seek the Lord's guidance."

"That's the best plan," said Raiford, smiling at her.

They finished their cherry cobblers, went into the large lobby, and enjoyed the group singing around the piano.

That night in bed, Anathea thought: *Newspaper reporter, nurse, school teacher – could I do any of those things? How exciting to do something outside the house, something that a man usually does. Is it possible?*

Raiford, too, was pondering his future as he walked to the depot to buy train tickets the next day. *Can I return to Goshen after the war? Would I be accepted after denying my principles? But those who stayed home don't know what war is like? They don't know what it does to a man to see his friends, day after day, maimed and killed. Anger builds. Rage takes over. Revenge screams in your mind. How can anyone understand unless he has lived it? My pacifist neighbors cannot possibly understand?*

Can they, Lord?

* * *

On Saturday morning, December 3, when Dr. Shilliday escorted Varney home, he spent several hours at the Cutter house, leading the older man around and talking to him about the place where he had lived for years but could not remember at all. Joan followed along, adding comments about what had occurred in this room and that room. Suddenly, the three people heard a child scream and rushed toward the sound.

Willene Wyatt stood in the front hall with her small fists clenched and stared wide-eyed at the stuffed animals on the surrounding walls.

While caring for Joan Cutter, Zurelle had kept her children close to her in the kitchen, the back stairs, and servants' quarters. Dalby, following after his father, had seen more of the house with its mounted animal heads on the high walls. But the two girls had not. This was Willene's first sight of the dead wildlife.

Jesse Shilliday reached Willene before her parents came running from the kitchen. He scooped her into his arms and, knowing instinctively what caused the screams, said, "It's all right. The animals won't hurt you. They're not real."

Willene clutched the doctor tightly around the neck as he carried her into the kitchen. Zurelle had to pry Willene's hands away from the man's jacket in order for Ochran to lift his daughter into his arms.

"We need to get rid of those things," said Joan. Turning to Varney, she asked, "Can't we get rid of them, dear?"

"Get rid of what?"

"The stuffed animals," his wife said. "You shot them all. Remember?"

"Why did the little girl scream?" asked Varney. "Does she live here?"

Before Dr. Shilliday left, he discussed with Ochran the work required to remove the stuffed animal heads throughout the house. With all the other work Ochran had to do, the two men agreed that such a dismantling of the mounted wildlife would have to wait. Instead, for the time being, the children would stay in the back part of the house and away from the furry and feathered heads that scared Willene.

* * *

That same morning, Raiford helped Freddie pack as Anathea did the same with Beatrice.

"I'm going down to the front desk," said Raiford. "I'll be right back."

Anathea knew he was going to pay the bill and reminded herself to enter the amount in her log book when he returned with the receipt.

Raiford picked up a newspaper in the hotel lobby and glanced at it while waiting for the clerk to take care of a family checking out. He read the headline: *Rebels whipped at Franklin, Tenn.*" He was so engrossed in the story about Union General John McAllister Schofield mowing down the marching Confederates who lost six thousand men, compared to the Union losses of just over two thousand, that he did not hear the desk clerk say, "Next. May I help you?" When the clerk tapped the newspaper, Raiford looked up and said, "We're checking out this morning."

After paying the bill, Raiford returned to the room. Anathea, who had been undoing her nighttime braid in order to fix her chignon, had to stop and arbitrate a disagreement between the children about the best way to pack their toys in the new fabric bag. Raiford, in order to help, dropped the paid, folded, hotel receipt on the bureau and bent down on his knees amid the scattered toys.

"You look very pretty," Raiford whispered to Anathea, whose hair was loose around her shoulders.

Flustered, Anathea said, "Thank you. I must fix my hair." She hurried to the bureau, pulled hair pins out of her reticule, and went to the washstand mirror, not noticing that a much-folded paper came out at the same time as the hair pins.

Raiford felt a moment of déjà vu. He recalled watching her arrange her hair in the parsonage kitchen in New York City.

With the toys safely stored in the bag, Raiford went to the bureau. His back was to Anathea who stood across the room in front of the wash stand. Raiford picked up the first folded paper he saw, which he assumed was the paid hotel bill. However, it was not. Unfolding the paper, he read: *Bill of Divorcement*. The single paragraph declared that Monro Emmert and Anathea Brannaman Emmert were no longer husband and wife, but were, as of April 4, 1863, legally divorced.

Quickly, Raiford refolded the divorce paper and grabbed up the hotel receipt as a cold chill raced down his spine. *That was over a year ago. What has she been doing since then? Has she been in New York? No, she said she just arrived on Thanksgiving Day. Did she lie to me? Surely not. But she didn't tell me she was married. Why should she? It's none of my business. Divorced! I've never known anyone who was divorced.*

Tucking the hotel bill into his wallet, Raiford moved away from the bureau and retrieved the carpet bags, which he set in the hall for the porter. Anathea and the children were cheerful as they headed to the depot amid the sparkling snow. Maintaining his usual pleasant demeanor, Raiford, however, had to push two nagging questions to the back of his mind. *Why didn't she tell me she was divorced? Why should she tell me?*

Anathea, unaware that Raiford knew her shameful secret, was reluctant to depart from the Metropole Hotel, where she had spent a happy week, despite her female infirmity. She enjoyed the cozy, family feeling of the days the four of them spent in the two rooms. She recalled the games, storybooks, and pleasant talks they shared. Especially, she treasured the quiet evening talks with Raiford after the children were asleep.

* * *

At the Great Western station, Raiford was startled to see Nesbit Payne.

What's he doing here?

The crooked constable was searching male passengers before they could board. Raiford ducked behind a pillar, turned his back, and stood still. Anathea walked a few steps further before she noticed he was not at her side. Immediately retracing her steps, she faced him and asked, "What is it?"

The scowl on his face told her something was wrong.

Raiford took her elbow, handed her the tickets, and said, "Get on the train. I'll join you." When she appeared puzzled, he pushed her away and said softly, "Go."

Anathea reached for Freddie's hand, which Raiford had been holding, and hurriedly followed the porter who pushed their luggage on a hand cart.

Raiford moved furtively among the crowd, keeping his gaze on the lawman whom he had tricked. The train whistle sounded. The wheels began to turn. Anathea and the children found seats.

"Where's Uncle Raiford?" asked Freddie.

"Isn't he coming?" Beatrice appeared ready to cry.

"Yes, he's coming," said Anathea, trying to keep her voice steady. She recalled his words earlier in the week – *I might be arrested. That's what he said. Is it true now? What could he have done to result in his being arrested?*

The train was moving, picking up speed. Nesbit turned his back, thinking all the men had been searched. Raiford made a dash for the train. He reached the last car. Grabbing the hand rail, he hauled himself aboard. The wind nearly blew his hat off. He held it on his head with his free hand. Going from car to car, he sought the pretty woman and two children who had become a part of his life in the past week. The moment Raiford entered their car, Freddie shouted, "Here we are!" and waved his hands near his shoulders.

Raiford picked up the little boy and exclaimed: "Hello, Puddle Head." He had given the nickname to the child a few days ago during one of their games. Sitting down with Freddie on his lap, Raiford smiled at Anathea and Beatrice in the facing seat.

"Where did you go?" asked Beatrice.

"I had to avoid someone, Princess," Raiford said. Beatrice had earned that nickname by having fancy tea parties with her doll.

Who? Anathea wondered but did not ask.

"I'm glad you obeyed me and got on the train without arguing," Raiford said softly to Anathea.

"Obedience was part of orphanage life," she said, and added in her mind: *And hammered into me by Monro and by the Shakers.*

Anathea was more relieved than she allowed Raiford to know. Although their separation was brief, her mind was filled with racing thoughts about what she would do on her own. She had not been on her own until she fled from Kentucky to New York, and had little opportunity to adjust to the change. She thought: *I must adjust to being without him. Just because he's here now doesn't mean that he will be for long. This simply cannot last. We will part company soon, when the children are settled. I must not rely too much on him. I must strengthen my resolve. I'm on my own. We are together only for a short time.*

When the train passed the town of Milton, the passengers saw two brown bears scampering across the snow-covered rolling hills.

"Look! Look!" exclaimed Freddie. "It's my Whitey, only bigger." He clutched his stuffed toy against his chest and pressed his nose against the window, watching the bears until they disappeared in the distance.

The other passengers were intrigued by the lumbering bears.

"What strange animals," Beatrice said to her china doll.

Historic Note: Many Canadians thought the proposed new government was a strange animal. Confederation was something they had never seen before. Just last month, from October 10th to the 28th, thirty-three men had gathered in the legislative library in Quebec and adopted a Constitution to form a unified Canada. Only Prince Edward Island had disagreed with the Canadian scheme for federation. But the provinces wanted to avoid what was happening to their neighbor south of their border. The American Civil War, they believed, resulted because they lacked a strong central government. By giving power to the states, the American form of government failed, and eleven of those states seceded. Such a thing would not happen in the parliamentary system in British North America if this new confederation was approved.

CHAPTER EIGHT

GUELPH

*Wherein Anathea, Raiford and the children arrive at the
Cutter mansion; Kirk McCarrell and Harmon Utley confide in
Raiford; Mechum Esling joins the Buffalo Raiders.*

In the afternoon of Saturday, December 3, when Raiford escorted his
little family off the train in Guelph, he went to the cab stand and asked
the friendly driver who greeted him: "Do you know where Mr. and
Mrs. Cutter live?"

"Yes, suh, shor do," came the black man's reply. "Let me hep you
with those bags. Name's John Huggins."

In a few minutes, Mr. Huggins had the luggage stowed and
passengers seated in his large sleigh. He gave them thick furs to cover
their legs. Bells on the two horses jingled as they left the depot and
headed up the gradually sloping hill.

Anathea, looking out the window of the covered sleigh, said, "What
a pretty little town."

Guelph was founded on April 23, 1827, by John Galt to provide a
headquarters town for the Canada Company, a large, private, British-
chartered, land development company which had been incorporated
two years earlier to aid the colonization of Upper Canada. The Canada
Company offered emigrants good ships, low fares, tools, and cheap land
to start a new life. Now, the densely forested rolling hills were giving up
their lumber to build the rapidly-expanding village.

"The buildings look clean and nice," said Beatrice. "Not like
Newark."

"Not like Louisville, either," said Anathea.

"What do the signs say? Read them," said Freddie.

Beatrice read the sign they were passing. "Harness Shop. What's that next one?"

"Apothecary," read Anathea. "Tin Type Picture Gallery; Ladies Hats and Notions; Dry Goods."

They were at the end of the business district.

"The town appears prosperous," said Raiford.

"What's pros…" Freddie scowled.

"Prosperous means the people here work hard and have done well," Raiford explained.

"I like the gently rolling hills," said Anathea.

Raiford said, "The land at my hometown is flat as can be."

"So is Louisville where I lived," said Anathea, observing the houses as the sleigh glided past. She admired the curtains showing at the windows and wondered: *Who lives there? Will this town be my home? Is there a future for me here?*

When the two horses pranced into the semi-circular drive in front of the Cutter mansion, their jingling bells softened and fell silent. Snow dusting the wide front porch steps sparkled in the bright sunshine.

Mr. Huggins announced in a cheery voice, "Looks like they've had recent visitors."

Brown sleigh tracks were visible ahead, and footprints led up the marble steps. Raiford helped Anathea out of the vehicle while the driver helped the children.

"Hold the railing. Those steps are slippery," said the black man while looping the rein through the hitching post. "Might be the doctor visiting. Mr. Cutter has been poorly as of late, and Mrs. Cutter just got over the grippe. Are you family?"

"Yes. We're grandchildren," said Freddie before either of the adults could answer.

"Not all of us," said Raiford laughing.

Ochran heard the heavy front door knocker when he came in from the carriage house where he had taken the two-seater sleigh of the visiting men. "I'll go," he called to Zurelle in the kitchen.

In the front parlor, Joan Cutter said, "Sounds like we have more people arriving. I wonder who."

When Ochran opened the door, a gust of cold wind entered the large hallway.

Raiford introduced himself, Anathea, and the children, concluding with the statement: "These are Mr. and Mrs. Cutter's grandchildren."

"Come in out of the cold," Ochran said. "I'll tell Mrs. Cutter."

But there was no need because Joan stood at the parlor door. She had heard Raiford's introductions, approached him, and asked, "Where's Mayfield? Where's my son?"

"He's not with us," said Raiford as he came toward the frail woman in an olive green dress with rows of lace on the bodice.

Anathea, holding the children's hands, moved aside for Ochran and John to bring in the carpetbags.

"Why not?" Joan was puzzled. "These are his children, aren't they?" The old woman smiled at Beatrice and Freddie, who held tightly to Anathea.

Zurelle and Dalby came from the kitchen. Dalby ran to hold the door.

"Yes," said Anathea, and introduced the girl and boy to their grandmother.

Beatrice saw the wrinkled face of her grandmother. She looked up at the huge hallway. Her eyes widened at the sight of the animal heads with bulging, lifelike eyes. She saw a spread eagle over the stair well. She saw a bear's head with bared teeth. Bending over, she vomited on the polished tiles.

Zurelle rushed forward while untying her white apron. She wiped Beatrice's mouth as she said, "Bring her into the kitchen! There's a bucket. She might bring up more."

The others stood aside as Raiford swept the little girl into his arms and followed the black woman down the hall. Dalby carried Freddie's bag on his father's heels up the wide stairs. John closed the door and, carrying bags, followed. Willene and Fernancy, in the kitchen doorway, moved aside for the stranger with a child. Three men came out of the parlor and followed.

"Put your head over this," said Zurelle, holding out a wooden pail. Raiford held Beatrice on one knee while she leaned down and spit up a few mouthfuls of stomach bile.

Softly, Raiford asked, "Feel better now, Princess?"

The girl nodded, rested her head against him, and said, "The animals l-l-look scary."

"They are scary," said Willene. "I screamed when I saw 'em."

"I don't go in the scary place," said Fernancy, her eyes wide.

Zurelle looked at Anathea and asked, "Are you all right, ma'am?"

Raiford saw Anathea sway. Immediately, he handed Beatrice to Zurelle, stood, and put his arms around Anathea. "Are you going to faint?"

"Can't breathe," Anathea murmured. "Getting black." She was limp in his arms.

"Come here. Sit down," he said, moving her toward a chair. When she sat, her head lowered toward her knees. Raiford knelt in front of her, put his hands on both sides of her face, and tilted her face up. "Look at me, Anathea. You are not going to faint. There is nothing to fear. Beatrice was sick. That's all."

"Everything's so strange." Although Anathea's words were barely audible, Raiford heard her.

"Do you want smelling salts?" asked Joan. "Zurelle, where are the smelling salts?"

"Anathea, do you need smelling salts?" Raiford spoke softly. He rubbed her cheeks. "You know there is nothing to be afraid of. We're here – the children and me." His fingers slid across her hair at the sides of her head and back to her face. "You are safe. You are not going to faint. There is no reason for you to faint." His hands remained still on her cheeks.

Taking a deep breath, Anathea said, "The blackness is ... is dissipating."

"Good." Raiford smiled, caressed her cheeks briefly before removing his hands, and stood up. "I don't think smelling salts will be needed, Mrs. Cutter. Thank you for the offer."

Anathea sat up straight as Joan, facing the stranger, asked, "Where's my son? Is he in an army hospital? He wrote us that he was ill."

Raiford held out a chair for Joan and, when she was seated, he sat close to her and said, "I am very sorry to tell you that Mayfield is dead."

Varney came toward his wife's chair and said, "What?"

Harmon Utley said, "Oh, no."

Kirk McCarrell pressed his lips together, shook his head, and said nothing.

Raiford narrated the story of the fire, the death and burial of Mayfield Cutter. Quietly, Ochran, Dalby, and John entered from the back stairs and heard most of Raiford's explanation. When Raiford was silent, Varney asked, "Is our son dead?"

As Raiford calmly confirmed that to the old man, Harmon directed Ochran to fetch Dr. Shilliday.

"Mr. and Mrs. Cutter have recently been under the doctor's care," Kirk said to the visitors.

Joan reached up for her husband's hand, clutched it, and said, "He's left us, Varney. Our dear boy has left us." Tears trickled from her pale blue eyes.

No one spoke or moved for a long moment. Then, Zurelle came to the elderly couple and said, "Come sit in the small parlor. Ochran has a nice fire going in there."

Harmon introduced himself and Kirk. Raiford paid Mr. Huggins who left. The next hours seemed like a blur to Anathea. Dr. and Mrs. Shilliday arrived, followed by two neighbor ladies who asked if there was illness again. When the neighbors left, the news of Mayfield Cutter's death spread and several other callers came. Zurelle and Ochran put food on the buffet and watched over the old couple.

When Raiford entered the small parlor, Varney looked sternly at him and asked, "Why did you kill Mayfield?"

* * *

Having made his way to Toronto, Mechum Esling reported to Jacob Thompson at the Queen's Hotel suite. Mechum was aware of his bedraggled appearance in comparison with the three men who greeted him. After telling his adventure of escaping from federal agents on the train, Mechum ate chicken and fried potatoes from a wheeled cart and listened to the latest plans.

"We could use you on this one, Mechum," said Jake Thompson, as he paced and talked. "We've recently learned, from our contacts in Sandusky, that seven Confederate generals are being transferred from Johnson's Island prison to Fort Lafayette in New York harbor in preparation for their being exchanged."

"But they might not make it all the way there," said John Headley, sitting in the plush chair beside Mechum and crossing his legs.

"There could be an intercepting event on the train route," said Robert Martin, who stood by the tall window.

Mr. Thompson said, "I will not ask you to go on this mission unless you have confidence it will succeed. What do you think?"

John said, "We need a few more men."

Robert agreed. "I know some to enlist. Can we count on you, Mechum?"

Because his mouth was full, Mechum simply nodded.

"Who else?" Jake asked.

"Captain Beall, if he is willing," said John.

"He will be willing," said Robert.

Mechum swallowed and said, "What's the plan for getting the generals south after we rescue them?"

"They will need to be armed," said Mr. Thompson, not answering the question but thinking about the escape south.

"We can each carry extra guns," said Mr. Headley.

"They'll need money," said Mr. Martin.

"Take money from the express safe," their leader said. "Give it to the generals and take some for yourselves. You will be obliged to scatter into New York or Ohio, depending on where you stop the train."

"All we need to know is the exact date," said John.

* * *

In a calm and compassionate voice, Raiford assured Varney Cutter that he did not kill his son. Listening to Raiford's soft, melodious voice, Varney lost his belligerence and, when the tale of the hotel fire ended for the second time, the old man took Raiford's hand, shook it, and said, "Thank you for burying my son."

Joan, who had been weeping quietly, burst into sobs. Three neighbor women gathered around her chair and comforted her.

"Would you like to lie down?" Zurelle exchanged Joan's damp, lace-ledged handkerchief for a dry one.

"No. No," Joan protested, pulling her arm away. "We must see to our guests."

"Don't be concerned about us. If you need to rest..." Raiford extended his hand to help the old woman out of her chair, but she shook her head.

Raiford met the neighbors who visited with ease, but Anathea, shy amid strangers, concentrated on looking after the children. However, Raiford would not let Anathea avoid introductions. As soon as he met someone, he took that person or couple to Anathea. More than once, he explained, "The children call us aunt and uncle, but we are not related. We're friends who were in the same hotel where their father died."

So he is dispelling the myth about our being related, Anathea thought. However, she was stunned when she heard a visitor, Deering Lister, ask, "You're not married then?"

Anathea blushed as Raiford answered the older man, "No, we are not."

The conversations among the visiting neighbors were about the misfortunes of the Cutter family, with Varney's recent decline and Joan's flu. They shared memories of Mayfield, the only son and heir to Cutter Industries.

"What will happen to the place now?" Mr. Lister asked Mr. Utley, who simply shook his head and made no reply.

When the long day finally came to an end and darkness settled outside, the visitors all departed except Harmon and Kirk. Raiford excused himself to say prayers with the children before they went to bed. Returning to the downstairs hall, he saw Mr. McCarrell standing in the library doorway and motioning him to join them. Harmon was seated near the fireplace, so the young men moved chairs closer to the flames.

"The servants are helping Mr. and Mrs. Cutter to bed," Raiford said, as he sat down. *Finally, I can speak to these men alone.*

"You're an American," said Kirk.

"That's right," said Raiford "I'm from Goshen, Indiana."

"Why aren't you in the army?" asked Harmon.

"I am in the army, assigned to special duty."

"Special duty in Guelph?" asked Kirk.

"That's right."

Harmon asked, "Why?"

"We had a report from here," answered Raiford.

"Who made a report?" asked Kirk, leaning forward.

"You did," said Raiford, looking directly at the young man.

* * *

Upstairs, Anathea wondered when Raiford would return. She wanted to stay awake until he came. Talking to him before going to sleep, as they had done since they first met, became a routine which she enjoyed. Discussing the day's events relaxed her, enabling her to sleep peacefully. The children were sleeping soundly in their big bed with the yellow draped canopy held up by fat, carved, mahogany posts.

I must stay awake until he comes. I have so much to talk about with him.

* * *

Downstairs in the library, the three men continued their conversation.

"How did you know where to write?" Raiford asked.

"Guelph's constable, Milo Clark, told me about a man named Fides in Toronto," answered Kirk. "I knew only one name, so addressed the envelope Mr. Fides, United States Government Agent, General Delivery, Toronto. I guess he received it without any trouble."

"Indeed so. He shared it with me." Raiford paused before asking, "Does Mr. Cutter know about any of this?"

Kirk said, "No, I didn't want to worry him."

"I think he should be kept informed," said Raiford.

Harmon said softly, "You realize that he does not always understand what's going on around him."

"Yes, I could see that," said Raiford. "But my elderly relatives always wanted to be included. We need to tell Mrs. Cutter about these things as well."

"A woman?" Harmon scowled.

Raiford nodded as Kirk said, "Mrs. Cutter helped her husband get started in this business. She is surprisingly wise about Cutter Foundry, for a woman." He added the last three words in a lower tone.

"Well, I see no harm in advising them both," said Harmon. "Although I cannot see much good coming from it. E. L. Pearson, their manager, is so two-faced that most people are fooled by him."

"A real Uriah Heep," said Kirk, referring to the Charles Dickens' character. "As the bookkeeper, I can honestly say that Mr. Pearson does not turn in all the money he collects on sales. I am certain of that."

Harmon added, "His crafty son Elmore is following in those footsteps. We caught him stealing from my store last month. His father paid for the item and insisted I keep it quiet, but I told Constable Clark. How old is that boy, Kirk?"

"I don't know, maybe sixteen." After a pause, Kirk continued, "I had a dust-up with Pearson and told him that I won't be bullied by him or his son. Elmore comes into the office all the time just to cause trouble. He's got a pal named Tom, equally worthless."

Changing the subject, Harmon said, "Constable Clark is concerned about more weapons being manufactured. He wants to be certain that all were confiscated when Burley was arrested."

"Do you think there are more?" asked Raiford.

"I do," said Kirk. "The reason is that workmen have made tracks in the snow to the old foundry building, the one Mr. Cutter first used when he started up his business as a young man."

"That isn't enough evidence, Milo said, so Kirk is keeping his eyes peeled for something more," said Harmon.

Kirk said, "Just the other day, I overheard some of the men discussing how to keep niter from blowing up in transit."

Harmon said, "Niter is potassium nitrate used in explosives. Cutter does not manufacture anything with explosives."

Raiford nodded to Harmon as Kirk continued. "Also, those same men talked about getting paid by Pearson. Mr. Pearson does not pay the men. That's my job."

After a short silence, Raiford asked, "When Burley was arrested, did he implicate Cutter's?"

"No," answered Kirk. "But his cousin Frank Burleigh works for us. Milo Clark interrogated Frank after he arrested Bennett, but couldn't get anything out of him."

Raiford mused, "Have you searched that old foundry building?"

Kirk answered. "No. I cannot find the key. I'm sure Pearson has it."

After a moment's silence, Raiford said, "Pearson needs another buyer since Burley was arrested."

"We got a wire from a man named Jacob Thompson who is sending a replacement," said Kirk. "Do you know him?"

"Jacob Thompson heads the Confederates' secret service," Raiford informed the other two men.

"There is another scheme afoot," said Harmon. "It's unrelated to the torpedoes."

"What?" Raiford turned from eyeing the flames to face the older man.

"I just heard about an attempt to rescue seven Confederate generals, who are prisoners of war."

"Rescued from where?" asked Kirk, who was as surprised as Raiford by the news.

"Somewhere in route between Johnson's Island and New York."

"When?" asked Raiford.

"I heard the transfer is set for Thursday, December 15."

* * *

Anathea, leaning her head back on the purple velvet chair, closed her eyes but was not asleep when she felt Raiford's hand on her shoulder. She jerked and opened her eyes.

"I'm sorry to startle you," Raiford whispered.

Moving to the edge of her seat, Anathea intended to stand, but he held her down as he asked, "Can we talk? Are you too tired?"

"I'm not too tired," she said, sliding back as he went to the nearby matching chair and moved it closer.

Before sitting, Raiford looked at the children and pulled the yellow-flowered quilt snug under their chins. Taking his seat, Raiford's knees were inches from hers. He said, "Are you feeling all right now? No light-headedness?"

"I'm well," she replied. "I didn't like those animal heads any more than Beatrice did."

"Now, I have two delicate ladies to watch over," he said, smiling at her.

"It never happened like this before."

"What?"

"That I felt unable to breathe and saw the blackness starting around my vision," she said. "Such occurrences in the past were always a prelude to fainting. No one ever did anything which made those things **not** result in a fainting spell."

"You mean that my hands on your face halted your fainting?"

"I guess that was it. I don't know. How could it be?" She wrinkled her forehead.

After a moment of thought, Raiford said, "Is it possible that the feel of my hands gave you a connection to another person, so you knew you were not alone?"

"Would just that stop my fainting?"

"Apparently so."

After a long moment, Anathea asked, "Is everyone gone?"

"Yes. I had a long conversation with Mr. McCarrell and Mr. Utley." Raiford rested his head against the chair back, closed his eyes briefly, and said, "It's been a tiring day."

When he opened his eyes and looked at her, she asked, "What did you talk about with those gentlemen?"

He said, "We discussed the safety and security of our two countries."

"What do you mean?"

Raiford, keeping his voice low, said, "Mr. McCarrell, who is the bookkeeper at Cutter Industries, thinks E. L. Pearson, the manager and a Southern sympathizer, is having workmen manufacture weapons, torpedoes to be exact. A man named Bennett Burley was recently arrested for trying to ship torpedoes to Detroit. Both Burley and the weapons were taken by the constable, Mr. Clark. Kirk is certain those torpedoes were made at Cutter's foundry, and he thinks there might be more."

"Why did they reveal all of this information to you?"

Raiford hesitated only a moment before saying, "Because I am an agent for the federal government."

* * *

At the Queen's Hotel in Toronto, Rev. Kensey Stewart and Jacob Thompson sat at one of the few occupied tables in the elegant dining hall, where waiters were clearing up dirty dishes. The hotel restaurant closed at midnight, so diners were hurrying to finish.

"We need to get our men out of Camp Douglas, Rock Island, Camp Chase, Elmira, and attack ..."

Jacob interrupted by saying, "You forgot Camp Morton."

"Oh, yes, Indianapolis," said Kensey. "All efforts to release them would be futile unless we have outside cooperation. That's what I can provide."

"How?" asked the secret service commissioner.

"With men in the new Order of the Star," said the minister with dramatic flair. "This vast organization is the replacement for the Sons of Liberty, which has proven to be a complete failure. The Order of the Star, however, has all the best leaders, willing to die for the Southern cause."

Sitting at the next table, Fides and Garrett slowly ate pieces of cake and sipped lukewarm coffee as they listened to every word.

"I hope that won't be necessary," said Mr. Thompson, dabbing his mouth with a linen napkin.

"Nevertheless, they are fearless."

"Can you name some of them?"

"Oh, no, they wish to remain anonymous," said Kensey, as he took a forkful of pie. "That is why you need me. Now, to change the subject, I must have an advance on that $20,000 draft from Richmond which I have lost along the way here."

They had previously discussed Dr. Stewart's lost money draft and his need of funds.

"I have written to Richmond for a renewal, but I need money now to rent a house for my family," the Episcopal minister stated.

"I can advance you $500 in gold until you receive word from Richmond," Jacob Thompson told him.

"Is that the best you can do?" The clergyman banged his elbows on the table.

"At the present moment, yes," said Jake. "I know nothing about you except your own words. Richmond has sent me no directives about you or your plans."

"I'll tell you my plans." Without lowering his voice, Kensey said, "We burn Detroit hotels to the ground. We succeed unlike those incompetents in New York City. What failures! Greek fire is out – too unreliable. I know something better." Pausing briefly to finish his coffee, he continued, "And we'll get all of our officers off Johnson's Island just as soon as Lake Erie freezes solid."

"We will have to continue our conversation tomorrow. My wife will be wondering where I am," said Commissioner Thompson, as he signed the bill which the waiter offered.

"Can I get that $500 first thing tomorrow?" asked Dr. Stewart, following his companion's lead by rising from his chair.

Garrett and Fides waited until the Southerners were out of the restaurant before they left. Unlike the two Confederates, the federal agents did not talk in public where they could be overheard. Instead, they waited until they were at Fides' house and the door was locked before they confided their thoughts to each other and drafted a telegram for Raiford.

* * *

After Raiford revealed his true mission to Anathea, he said, "You must be tired. I woke you when I came in." Standing up, he looked at the children and asked, "Did Beatrice eat more than crackers?"

"Yes, a little more. She said her tummy doesn't hurt." Anathea started toward the door.

"That's good." Raiford followed her as he talked softly. "Ochran told me that he wants to take those animal heads down because they frighten his children, too. However, he has been too busy and it's a two-man job."

"That would be an improvement," she said.

Stopping at the open door, Raiford asked, "Where do I sleep?"

"I'll show you your room." Anathea stepped ahead of him. "Zurelle said only the master bedroom is used so five bedrooms are available. She apologized that they are not dusted and said she will do that tomorrow."

"Not on Sunday," he said, following her across the hall. "A bed in a dusty room is better than the hard ground."

They entered a darkened bedroom where the fire was dying. Raiford put more logs on the fire as Anathea used the flame to light a candle. She placed the candle on the stand near the large bed, turned, and bumped her head against his chest. Raiford caught her upper arms to steady her.

The fire light flickered on her upturned face. She made no effort to move away. Slowly, as though it was the most natural thing in the world, Raiford released her arms, slid his hands around her, and embraced her. Anathea, feeling his hands move across her back, had no desire to resist. She was tired. Everything was new and strange. But Raiford's warm embrace felt good and comforting. As her head pressed against his suit jacket, she sighed and relaxed. He tipped his chin down to feel her soft hair against his neck.

"I'm glad you're here," he whispered.

But for how long? Anathea asked herself. *Soon, all this will end. I will go away. He will go away. The children will remain. Why must it be so, Lord?*

Who moved first neither of them knew for certain. Her hands, which had been on both sides of her face, resting against the wool fabric of his jacket, felt the separation as their bodies came away from each other. Raiford lowered his hands from her back to her waist. Leaning down, he kissed her on the cheek and said, "I'll see you tomorrow."

She was at the door when he asked, "Where is your room?"

"Next to the children's," she said without hesitation.

Ten minutes later, while lying in bed and waiting for sleep to come, Anathea wondered: *Why did he want to know where my bedroom is? Surely, he will not come here. Lord, I pray not. What would I do if he did enter my room? Goodness! Such a thought! Raiford is an honorable man. He would never do such a thing.*

But across the hall, Raiford was thinking the same thing except with a different twist. *Her husband could go to her bed anytime he wanted. That is, until they divorced. Why is she divorced? She is such a wonderful woman. It felt so good to hold her in my arms. How could any man turn away from such a lovely creature? He must have been crazy. Maybe touched in the head like Varney Cutter. That poor man.* Raiford rolled onto his side. *And poor Mrs. Cutter. I feel sorry for them. But at least they have their grandchildren now. Will I ever have children or grandchildren?*

His wandering thoughts ceased and he slept.

* * *

Historic Note: With the war's progression, prisoner exchanges were not always made fast enough to keep pace with the number of soldiers captured. The official policy regarding prisoner exchanges varied during the Civil War. Because some high ranking Confederate generals were incarcerated on Johnson's Island, Union officials thought them vulnerable targets for rescue by the Confederates operating out of Canada. Therefore, orders were issued to bring seven Confederate generals from the Erie Lake island to New York where they could be processed for exchange. Getting these high-ranking officers away from a possible rescue attempt was uppermost in the minds of the federal command. As much as they attempted to keep this transfer secret, the news seeped out. Precautions were taken. Plans were made. Whether the exchange would succeed, no one knew.

CHAPTER NINE

THE BUFFALO RAID

Wherein Sue and Ned Lee prepare to travel;
Zurelle complains about the stove; Adam shoots his horse;
the newcomers attend church; Confederates plan a rescue;
Raiford goes to work at Cutter Foundry;
enemies plan revenge and robbery;
Anathea starts working at Cutter's; the Demosthenian Society meets;
Mechum mails a letter; Fides reads Mechum's letter.

The next day, Sunday, December 4th, in Lexington, Virginia, Susan and Edwin Lee made preparations to travel to Richmond the next day. They were staying with Susan's parents at the Episcopal parsonage on the hillside. Sue consulted with her mother, Anzolette Page Pendleton, about her shopping list on which she itemized what she and Ned would need before leaving for Canada. Edwin could not plan their route until conferring with Confederate officials and finding out what ships were available to run the blockade. Family and friends stopped by to bid them farewell. Although visitors were told that Ned and Sue were going to Canada for his health, some wondered if there was more to the Brigadier General's relocation. After all, he was a valuable military man, and the Confederacy needed such men desperately.

* * *

In Guelph, the Cutter household was as busy as the Pendleton parsonage. As soon as Beatrice and Freddie awoke, they hopped out of bed and went into the nearest room where they found Anathea. The children were in bed with her, talking excitedly, when Raiford knocked. In short order, the newcomers were dressed and downstairs.

They found Zurelle in the kitchen complaining about the stove.

"Don't mind her," Ochran said to Raiford. "She thinks she knows how to build a better stove."

The servants were surprised to have Anathea and Raiford help put the food in the dining room, where Joan and Varney came slowly, arm-in-arm, just before eight o'clock.

* * *

Adam Brannaman rode into the crossroads of Gnaw Bone, Kentucky, and wondered where would be the best place to shoot his horse. The animal made the decision for him. It staggered and fell into a ditch at the side of the road. Adam knew when he bought the old horse that it might not be able to make the trip to Pleasant Hill, where the Shaker village was located, but this was all he could find.

He had left Louisville after giving Barbara Dell money to provide for food and necessities for the girls. He also hired a lawyer to represent them in the will contest. His money could provide for those things but could not buy a healthy horse. The army had most of those.

A family who lived at the crossroads heard the shot and came to see what caused it.

"You reckon we could have that meat?" the long-bearded father, surrounded by six children and his wife, asked as the family came to see the dead animal.

"You're welcome to it," said Adam. "Do you know where I could buy another horse?"

"Might can," said the man. "Where you headed?"

"The Shaker village at Pleasant Hill.

"You don't want to be goin' there," the wife said, twisting her face into a grimace. "Strange people a doin' strange things live at that there place."

Adam said, "I have a relative I'm going to see there."

"We're gettin' ready to go to preachin' over at the grove," said the husband. "You kin ride along. Might be you can buy a horse from one of the fellers there."

Riding in the back of a rattling wagon with six children, Adam wondered if he should buy a mule instead of a horse. The mule pulling the wagon was slow and steady. At the church service in the grove, bonfires kept the worshipers warm. Adam saw that most of the people had walked. Only a few horses were ridden and now tied to trees.

* * *

Finishing breakfast in the large Cutter dining room, Raiford served the last of the coffee, excused the children, and returned to his chair beside Anathea. Both Varney and Joan were subdued, with Joan weeping often. Varney patted her shoulder but said little. The servants quietly removed the used dishes.

Raiford asked, "Where do you go to church?"

"First Baptist on Woolrich Street," said Joan. "But we haven't been going since Varney entered his dotage."

"That's no reason to stay away," Raiford said, sipping his coffee.

"I don't want the dear man to be embarrassed," his wife said. "He has a little trouble remembering people."

"I have that trouble at times," said Anathea, placing her linen napkin on the table and thinking: *What a pretty pattern.*

To avoid the topic of her husband's senility, Joan said, "We just completed a new building, after meeting in rented space since 1853. We have a new pastor, too."

"Rev. Clarke," said Varney.

"No, dear, that's our former pastor," his wife said. "Rev. George Grafftey is the pastor now."

"Has he been to see you?" Raiford asked.

"My, yes, he has. In fact, he stops by regularly," the older woman said. "I explained my reluctance to bring Varney to church. He understands."

"I like going to church," said her husband.

"I know but we should wait until you feel better." Joan smiled weakly.

"When will I feel better?" Varney asked.

Raiford, glancing from Varney to Joan, said, "My mother is Baptist, so I know what loving people they are. I think they would be happy to see you both in church. You know how your neighbors gathered around you yesterday. You would be a blessing to them if you allowed them to minister to you. Besides, I don't like to miss church if I can help it. I would appreciate it if you would take us as your guests."

"Yes, yes," Varney said excitedly. "Let's go to church. Let's go."

Smiling at her husband, Joan nodded agreement.

When Anathea and Raiford went up the curving front stairway to get ready for church, Anathea asked, "You said your mother was a Baptist. Was your father also?"

"No, he was raised a Mennonite, but when they married, he joined the Goshen Baptist Church." Raiford smiled at her. "He was always doing things to make her happy. She was very attached to her church family. His family understood. He even changed the spelling of his name for her."

"How was it spelled?" asked Anathea, stopping at her bedroom door.

"J-u-n-g, which is German," said Raiford. "So the English word Y-o-u-n-g is similar. Mother was so overwhelmed when he told her of the legal name change that she cried. She knew how much his German heritage meant to him, but he knew how important it was to her to be an American."

Anathea went into her room, closed the door, and wondered: *What would it be like to have a husband do something so extraordinary – change his name to please her. I had to change my name when I married. Monro would never have done such a thing for me. Everything was about him, never about me.*

Downstairs, Joan was insisting that Ochran and his family join them at church.

Ochran said, "We got those upper rooms to clean."

"Nonsense," said Joan. "You and your family are coming along with us."

"I have the dishes to do up," protested Zurelle.

"They'll wait," said Joan. "Gather the children. Hurry now. We don't want to be late."

On their way to church, Freddie and Beatrice exclaimed with delight about the fast-stepping horses pulling the sleigh.

"Isn't a sleigh ride fun?" Freddie snuggled close to Anathea.

"When I went to church with the other orphans, we had to walk two blocks," she said to the little boy.

"What church was it?" asked Beatrice.

"Methodist. The people were kind and gave us gifts at Christmas. We were their mission field."

"You were raised in an orphanage?" asked Joan.

Thus, Joan began to see beyond her grief and take an interest in the newcomers. Varney asked Raiford how the war in the states was progressing. Joan told them about the town where she lived since moving here as a bride.

Entering First Baptist Church on Woolwich Street, the people had to go up to the second level where the sanctuary was. Sunday school rooms were located on the ground level. Everyone was happy to welcome Mr. and Mrs. Cutter, who had been absent for several months. Because the news of their son's death preceded their appearance, the church members expressed their sympathy. With grandchildren, house guests, and new servants, Mr. and Mrs. Cutter used two pews.

Rev. Grafftey began the service with a special prayer for Mayfield, thanking the Lord for his life and asking comfort for the bereaved family. When the service was over, those who had not offered condolences before the service did so. Others introduced themselves to the newcomers.

Raiford felt right at home among the friendly, caring people. Anathea, however, made comparisons with the Methodists and Shakers. Although she was pleased to see the genuine concern they showed the grieving parents, she thought: *What do they believe about eternal life? Do they get their ideas from the Bible or from some founder like Mother Ann Lee?*

* * *

In Toronto, Garrett and Fides worked on coding the telegram which they would send to Raiford tomorrow when the telegraph office opened.

Kensey Stewart continued to pursue Jacob Thompson who was tiring of the minister's badgering.

John Headley enjoyed meeting old friends and making new ones as the young Confederates drank mint juleps, exchanged adventure stories, and plotted secret missions in their elegant quarters in Toronto.

* * *

Late that Sunday afternoon, when all the visitors paying respects to the Cutters had left, Anathea sat down beside Joan in the small parlor and asked, "What is this?"

The older woman twined silk embroidery threads through her thin fingers and said, "I want to make a mourning picture in memory of

Mayfield, but I don't know where to begin." Her fluttery hands wafted the threads over the piece of white linen in her lap.

"I've made a few mourning pictures," said Anathea, reaching for the velvet-covered sewing box. "Let's set things out and design a scene." Anathea took the linen, spread it on the little table, and picked up a pencil. "There should be a tombstone with his birth and death dates." She sketched an obelisk in the lower right hand corner.

"The good Lord is making it easier to face my own death," said Joan as she watched Anathea's pencil move. "I have so few ties to the world that I will be better prepared to leave it."

Raiford, carrying an armload of firewood, heard the older woman's words. As he lowered the wood to the hearth, he said, "You have your grandchildren to tie you to this world."

"Younger people like you should be raising them. I'm too old."

"Not true," he said, coming toward the women. "Beatrice and Freddie need their family." Sitting on the footstool, Raiford took Joan's vein-lined hands in his as he said, "You don't want your grandchildren to grow up in an orphanage as Anathea did."

"No. No." The grandmother said softly. "They have a home here always. So do the two of you. I need your help."

Raiford assured the elderly lady, "I will do all that I can to ease your burden."

"So will I," said Anathea, returning to her drawing on the linen square.

* * *

Monday morning, Raiford approached Joan about the animal heads.

"Mrs. Cutter, Ochran and I would like to remove the animal heads and store them in the carriage house. Would that be acceptable to you?"

"Did you ask Varney? He shot them all." Joan looked around the parlor. "Where is Varney?"

"In the kitchen with the children playing marbles."

Joan smiled and said, "He's a dear man."

Raiford said, "I did ask him. I told him those heads frighten the children. He agreed they should be removed."

"Then by all means, do so," said Joan.

The men spent the morning removing the mounted heads while the women worked on the mourning picture. In the afternoon, when the children were napping, Raiford entered the small parlor, observed the linen square, and said, "I have something you can add."

Leaving the room, Raiford returned in a few minutes with the wedding photograph which the morgue attendant found in Mayfield's pocket.

"I've never seen this," said Joan, holding the photograph. "I was not at the wedding. They were married in New Jersey."

"What was he doing there?" Raiford asked.

"He wanted to strike out on his own, to prove his worth on his own merits," said the grief-stricken mother. "Dear Mayfield did not want to inherit wealth. He wanted to be his own man."

"I can understand that," said Raiford, who recalled his joining the army to prove his patriotism.

Anathea moved the image from one location to another. Raiford, leaning over her, placed his palm on top of Anathea's hand and moved it so the photograph was in the upper left corner.

"That's where it should be," he said, lifting his hand off hers. "This provides a good balance with the tombstone and… that's where they are." His last words were in a low tone.

"Perfect," said Joan. "A perfect placement -- shows Mayfield and Adelle are in heaven. Thank you, Raiford."

Varney wandered in and sat beside his wife to watch what she was doing. Raiford decided this was a good opportunity to tell them about his conversation with Kirk and Harmon. The elderly couple listened as Raiford narrated what the bookkeeper and his future father-in-law had told him. When he was silent, Joan said, "What do you think we should do, Raiford?"

"Right now, we can be vigilant and keep alert," said Raiford.

Varney said, "You should be working there."

Joan said, "We always wanted Mayfield to take Varney's place at the foundry. Now that he cannot, you should, Raiford."

"Keep us informed," added the old man.

"That might be a good idea," Raiford replied. "But let's discuss it with Mr. McCarrell and Mr. Utley. Also, I need to help Ochran gets these heads off the wall. The children need to be settled. We need to be settled." He glanced at Anathea, who met his eyes and lowered her gaze.

Whatever does he mean — we need to be settled.

* * *

In the afternoon, Raiford and Ochran went into town. At the telegraph counter, as Raiford copied the messages he had worked out in code, Ochran watched with fascination.

"Do you know how to read?" Raiford asked the servant.

"Not yet, suh."

Raiford spoke each word as he wrote it on the paper provided by Mr. Colburn, the telegrapher. The messages appeared to be about the sale of farm equipment.

Ochran asked, "You sell farming things?"

"I'll explain later," Raiford whispered.

Mr. Colburn left the counter to record a message coming in.

"It's for you, Mr. Young," said the telegrapher, handing Raiford the paper.

After quickly scanning the message, Raiford added a postscript to his telegram, paid Mr. Colburn, and left the office.

As the men walked along the wooden sidewalk toward Aylesworth & McClennon's General Mercantile, Raiford said in a low tone, "I do not really sell farm implements but you must keep this secret."

"I can keep secrets, massa."

"I am not your master. There are no masters and slaves in Canada."

"I know. The doctor told us. It's still hard to believe."

Before saying more, Raiford looked around and, seeing no one close enough to overhear, said, "Selling plows and hoes is just a cover for my real work. I am in the army and sent here to ferret out Confederate trouble-makers."

"You're in the Yankee army?"

"That's right."

"They's goin' to free my people." The black man smiled broadly.

"Wherever they go!" Raiford returned the smile.

* * *

At five o'clock on Wednesday, Raiford escorted Kirk McCarrell and Constable Milo Clark into the home office where Joan, Anathea, and Varney sat waiting. Books lined three walls from floor to ceiling. The fourth wall had large windows which could be raised and used as low doorways.

"Harmon is unable to come due to another business engagement," Kirk said. "I told him that I would report to him on what we decide."

Constable Clark, a stocky man with muscular shoulders, said, "Mr. McCarrell has told me about the job offer extended to you, Mr. Young." He took a chair and continued. "I understand there is possibly some illegal activity going on at our town's biggest foundry, and the manager is most likely the culprit. He needs to be replaced. Are you taking the job as head man?"

"I am willing, in order to get to the bottom of this." Turning from Milo to face Kirk, Raiford asked, "Do you think Mr. Pearson will take the illegal weapon-making business to another foundry? I understand there are three other such industries in town."

"They are just small places," said Varney. "Not more than five or ten men. Isn't that right, Kirk?"

"That's correct, sir. But that doesn't mean they couldn't manufacture torpedoes or guns or whatever the customer wanted. It might take them some time to get the set up done right, but they offer good competition here in Guelph." The young bookkeeper wiped his sweaty palms onto his thighs. This was the first time he attended a meeting in his boss's home. He was nervous.

Joan asked, "How many men do we have working there now?"

Kirk answered. "Twenty right now. Twenty-three were laid off when Mr. Pearson started in September." To Raiford, he explained, "We always lay off a few men in the fall, when business slows down. We make sleighs and sleds in the summer, but during the winter, we make smaller items, so we don't need a full work force."

"But this was a larger layoff than normal, wasn't it, Mr. McCarrell?" Joan asked.

"Yes, ma'am, it was."

Raiford scowled but said nothing.

Varney, who seemed to be his old self, said, "I think a new foundry manager is in order. I will set my hand to drafting the notice."

Kirk said, "E. L. Pearson has not been doing a good job. Profits have been down since he came. He shows no initiative. He has no new ideas."

Joan said, "If he's making weapons behind our back, he's dishonest."

Varney said, "I won't have a dishonest man in my employ."

"Why did you hire him in the first place, dear?" Joan asked.

"Experience, wasn't that it, Kirk? He said he had experience."

"Yes, that's what he said."

"Do you have any experience, Mr. Young?" The Constable turned to Raiford.

"A little. I helped my uncle in his blacksmith shop."

The lawman said, "We don't want to make it too obvious that we're putting someone in charge to ferret out the weapon suppliers. You will have to do better than your predecessor at the real work which goes on there."

Kirk said, "Almost anyone could do a better job than Pearson."

The meeting continued for an hour. Anathea said little. She was intrigued by the fact that she was included in the meeting. She was glad to see Varney speaking with sense. Joan had told her that some days his mind was clear, and that he was more alert since the children came. Besides being impressed by Varney's astuteness, she was impressed with the constable who spoke of his determination to halt the illegal sale of goods across the border.

* * *

On Thursday, December 8th, E. L. Pearson was fired. He went immediately to the Crippled Deer tavern and got drunk while raving about the ill way in which he had been treated by Varney Cutter. After the Crippled Deer, he staggered home where he ranted before his son Elmore who was playing poker with Tom Donnelly.

Meanwhile, Kirk took Raiford to meet the twenty workmen who were making lanterns and candlesticks. He saw the showroom, a long low building fronting on Farquhar Street where people could see the sleighs, sleds, and smaller items for sale. Back in the office, Kirk explained the files. At noon, when Kirk suggested they go into town to eat at a restaurant, Raiford said, "No, I asked Ochran to bring us our dinner."

Five minutes later, Ochran arrived with a basket.

"Where do the men eat?" asked Raiford.

"There are tables they use in the corner of the foundry," said Kirk.

"We'll join them."

Not only was Kirk surprised, but so was Ochran when Raiford insisted he come, too. After sitting down at the long wooden table, Raiford asked if he could bless the food. None of the men objected. Raiford prayed. As Ochran handed paper-wrapped fried chicken to

Kirk and Raiford, the workmen slowly started to eat the food from their lunch buckets.

Raiford said, "I don't see any black men among you. Is there some reason for that?"

"We had three but they were first to be fired when Pearson came on."

"They were some of our best workers."

"Pearson didn't like runaway slaves."

"He said they should stay in the South where they belonged."

Raiford said, "We will have to get them back." He chewed and swallowed amid silence. "Now, tell me what each of you prefers to do here."

Not one worker had ever been asked that question. Hesitantly, they began talking, telling the new boss what aspects of their job they enjoyed, what they were good at, and who they knew was good at what. By the end of the meal, the atmosphere had changed.

"We need to expand the inventory," said Raiford, as he got up from the table. "You think about what things we should be making and let me know."

The twenty men returned to their lanterns and candlesticks with new enthusiasm. Where they had been mostly quiet in the morning, they couldn't stop talking all afternoon.

In the office, Raiford wrote letters to the men who were let go in September asking them to return to work the following Monday, if they were not otherwise employed.

That evening, Raiford heard Zurelle's complaints about the kitchen stove as she prepared dinner. He and Ochran dropped firewood into the wood box. Coming to her side, Raiford asked, "How would you improve the cook stove?"

"The wood burning ought to be in the middle, not at the side like it is now," Zurelle said. "There should be an oven on both sides with controls for each side so bread can bake in one and meat in the other." She used her hands to draw the image in the air. "There should be warming shelves above, here and here. The burners should be big and little sizes for different pots."

"You have some good ideas," Raiford said. "Let's make a drawing after the children are in bed."

Two hours later, Raiford called Ochran and Zurelle into the library where Anathea was setting out plain paper and two pencils. Raiford took one of the pencils and made a rectangle onto which he drew four feet. He sketched a center window showing flames and the other suggestions as he remembered her reciting them.

"Now what about the size of the burners?" Raiford held a pencil toward her. "You draw them."

Zurelle took the wooden instrument and stared at it.

Raiford encouraged her. "Should small burners be in the front? I don't know."

Suddenly, Zurelle burst into tears. Ochran, who was stirring up the fire, came to his wife, put his arms around her, and hugged her.

"What's wrong?" asked Raiford, surprised by Zurelle's tears.

Anathea, too, was startled by her friend's outburst.

"Is it this?" Ochran said softly, taking the pencil from Zurelle's fist. When she released the pencil and nodded against his chest, he said, "She's never held one of these things before."

"You've never held a pencil?" Anathea asked. Zurelle, her tears subsiding, shook her head and moved away from her husband's arms.

"We can do the drawing, if you would rather," said Raiford, in a soft tone.

Ochran said, "It's like drawing in the dirt. You've done that." He offered her the pencil which his wife took hesitantly. Zurelle began drawing a small burner in the front with a large burner behind, then beside that, a large burner in front and small one behind.

"Good plan," said Raiford. "Now, what about the warming shelves? Where should those be located?"

As the four people saw the design take shape, they discussed various options but Raiford insisted that Zurelle have the final word on the design. When the drawing was complete, Raiford held the paper in front of Ochran and said, "Do you think the men at the foundry can make this?"

"Seems like they could."

"I'll take this drawing to the men tomorrow." Raiford put the pencils into the wooden box on the desk.

Ochran went to the fire to screen it for the night. Zurelle, going to her husband's side, whispered to him. Ochran stopped Raiford and Anathea who were at the door.

"Sir, she wants you to know something."

"What is it?" Raiford held the door open and waited. Ochran took his wife's hand and led her toward the other couple.

"It wasn't the pencil that made her cry, sir." Ochran glanced down at Zurelle before continuing. "It was the way you treated her."

"How was that?"

"You spoke kindly to her. You listened to what she said. You care about making a better stove for her." Ochran took a deep breath before adding, "She never had a white man do such kindness to her before."

Raiford smiled, reached out, and touched Zurelle lightly on the shoulder. He said nothing. The black woman returned his smile before lowering her eyes.

Zurelle, Ochran, and Anathea assumed the workmen would make one stove for the Cutter kitchen. However, Raiford intended for this new stove to expand the inventory for Cutter Foundry.

* * *

Saida and Oscar Bolton, who had found Varney wandering when Joan was sick, were arguing.

"What does he mean by coming here and firing Mr. Pearson? He has no right!" shouted Saida, tugging on her broken-down shoes over her pudgy feet.

"The men didn't like Pearson," mumbled Oscar as he buttoned his vest.

They were in the cramped bedroom which was small and made smaller by all the miscellaneous knick-knacks she collected.

"We don't know anything about the new man or that woman he brought with him," said Saida, standing up. "Why he could be a no-account scalawag for all we know."

"He seemed nice enough when we were there at the Cutter house, consoling the old folks," Oscar replied.

"Well, of course, he would be polite in company, but look what he's doing at the foundry. I heard he's called back the men laid off. How can Old Man Cutter pay for that, when his business is slow as it always is during the winter?"

"I don't know, but it's really none of our business." Oscar left the bedroom.

"Something should be done about him." Saida trailed her husband. "You should find out about him. Talk to Constable Clark. Tell him about our concern for those dear old people. They were living happily alone but now have a houseful of strangers. No telling what the new folks are up to. Probably no good. Probably taking advantage of them, getting their money or something."

Saida was still talking when Oscar exited the cluttered house.

* * *

The next day, Anathea came into the kitchen to get the tea tray for her and Joan, and said, "I should be helping you, Zurelle. This is such a big house for you to clean by yourself."

"No, no," protested the busy woman as she poured boiling water into the tea pot. "You help Miss Joan with her mournin' picture. That's mo' important. I can do the chores."

After tea, Joan dozed off so Anathea continued working in silence. Her mind wandered to thoughts of Raiford - the first night in the Cutter house when, after all the visitors were gone, he came to talk and held her in his arms.

Why has he not been affectionate with me since then? Does he regret what he did? Does he know I'm a divorced woman and therefore unworthy? How could he know? Maybe it's because he has an occupation outside of the house now and is away from me. Maybe this is for the best. We need to become accustomed to being apart. Someday, we will separate permanently the same way Monro and I did.

As easily as Joan had nodded off, she now awoke. Her needle moved. She looked across at Anathea and asked, "What are your future plans, my dear?"

"I would like to find a job in town," said Anathea. "If I could pay for my room and board here, then I could continue to see Beatrice and Freddie."

"Why not take a job here instead of in town," said Joan.

"Here? You don't need my help here. Zurelle is very capable."

"She can't read or write," said Joan. "I need someone who can teach my grandchildren -- a governess."

Surprised, Anathea said, "But why don't they attend the town's schoolhouse?"

"Have you seen the teacher there?" Her eyes widened.

"No," Anathea answered as she saw the older woman take uneven stitches and resolved to correct them later that evening.

"He paddles the pupils. I won't have that! My grandchildren will not be paddled. They will have a governess. They love you. You're the perfect choice."

Not knowing what to say, Anathea said, "Raiford is teaching Ochran to read. He said Zurelle wants to learn, too."

"You could teach them all – the whole Wyatt family plus Beatrice and Freddie." Joan smiled happily.

"I suppose I could," said Anathea. "I helped the younger children with their school work when I lived at the orphanage."

"Good. It's settled then," said the older woman.

* * *

That evening, when Anathea told Raiford about her job offer, he smiled and said, "Then you will need to make a decision because I have another employment option for you."

"What?"

"Kirk needs you in the office to assist with the bookkeeping."

"At the foundry?" Her eyes widened.

"Yes, but only in the office, not among the workmen," he assured her. "I told him how well you maintained our financial records during the trip here. We are desperate for help."

"Why me? Shouldn't you hire a man?"

"You are as well qualified as any man."

Clutching her hands in her lap, she said, "But I would like to be the children's governess."

They were seated side by side on the settee in the small parlor. The fire in the brick-lined fireplace was blazing. Moving closer to her, Raiford took her hands in his and held them on her puffy skirt.

"I think we can work this out so you can do both," he said.

"How?"

"You teach the children in the morning, all five of them. Can you manage five?" When she nodded, he continued. "Then, I will come home for the noon meal and escort you to the foundry while the children take naps."

"I suppose that could work. Zurelle is good with the children. She can watch them while I'm away." Her fingers gripped his hands. "You know Zurelle wants to learn how to read as much as Ochran."

He, too, tightened his hold of her hands as he answered. "We can both teach Zurelle and Ochran in the evening after the children are asleep."

"You make it sound easy."

Smiling, he said, "It can be."

"Governess in the morning and assistant bookkeeper in the afternoon." Anathea pondered. Suddenly, her voice changed when she asked, "Will I be alone in the office?"

"You will not be alone. Either Kirk or I will always be there with you." Giving her hands a gentle shake, he added, "If you are not happy, you can quit."

"I don't like to quit things that I've started," she said.

"Then you will accept the job?"

"I'm still not certain. I think an office is a man's world."

"Horse feathers!" Raiford declared.

Anathea laughed. Joining her laughter, Raiford stood and pulled her to her feet. He felt a sudden urge to kiss her. Raiford dropped her hands and went to open the door.

In his bedroom, Raiford thought: *If she doesn't like to quit things, why did she quit her marriage? Am I asking too much from her? Can she manage two jobs – morning governess and afternoon bookkeeper? How will the workmen treat a woman in the office? Lord, is this plan within your divine will?*

In her bedroom, Anathea thought: *Mr. McCarrell needs me but do you? Do I dare venture into an office and do a man's work? What would the headmistress at the orphanage say? Well, I know what Miss Barbara Dell would say. Go ahead and do your best. You can succeed.*

* * *

On that same Friday, December 9, Sue and Ned Lee were enjoying the hospitality of Colonel William Lamb, his roommate from William and Mary College. Colonel Lamb, commandant at Fort Fisher, had built up the fort until forty-seven heavy guns now mounted the parapets. William and Daisy welcomed the Lees to their cottage outside the fortifications while they waited for calmer weather. A storm was raging. They planned to stay overnight, but shortly after midnight, Ned woke his wife.

"The storm has abated," he said softly. "We must go."

At three in the morning, on December 10th, they boarded the *S.S. Virginia* at Smithville. When Sue saw the arch of federal blockaders out on the water, she was scared.

"Oh, Ned, what will they do if they catch us?"

"There is no reason to fret," he assured his wife. "We are simply going to Canada for my health. I have the doctor's to-whom-it-may-concern letter safe in my coat pocket."

"But won't they know you are in the army?"

Stepping behind her as she clutched the railing, Ned put his arms around his wife and said, "Our lives are in the Lord's hands. We must trust him, whatever comes."

The moon had gone down when the *S.S. Virginia* sailed. Nevertheless, a Federal cruiser chased the *Virginia* all day Saturday. Because of the tense cat-and-mouse game between the two ships, the captain changed his course from Bermuda to Nassau. The *Virginia* finally eluded the larger ship at nine o'clock that night.

* * *

Also at nine o'clock, in Guelph, Raiford and Jesse Shilliday were hitching the horses to the sleigh in preparation for the return trip after Raiford, Anathea, Joan, and Varney had eaten dinner at the home of the doctor and his wife. The three couples had enjoyed a pleasant evening. Varney seemed like his old self, Joan said more than once.

Raiford asked, "How do you explain Varney's change in ..." He hesitated, unsure of the word to use.

"Mental astuteness," Jesse said.

"Yes." Raiford flipped the leather strap over the horse's head. "This evening, he spoke sensibly."

"But mostly about the past," Jesse said, draping the reins over the edge of the sleigh. "You noticed that, didn't you?"

"I did. But sometimes, he can't seem to talk at all."

"Joan said he has been better since you arrived, that the children perk up his spirits, and that all the activity in the house gets him involved."

"Did she also tell you that he frequently mistakes me for his son?"

"I've heard him call you Mayfield."

"What causes that – his ups and downs of mental ability?"

"I wish I knew." Jesse led the horses out of the barn. "Someday, hopefully, medical science can discover the cause."

"And the cure," added Raiford.

* * *

Later that evening, two teenagers, Elmore Pearson and his friend, Tom Donnelly, stumbled out of the Crippled Deer on Wilson Street. The intoxicated teenagers ambled along the winding road which had once been an Indian trail toward the Speed River.

"Can't buy more rum without some money. Gotta get some money." Elmore dug into his empty pockets. "Since Pa's been fired, he won't give me a shilling."

"Let's steal some," said Tom, whose acne-scarred face appeared redder in the cold air.

Elmore almost fell over a hitching post. He grabbed the beam to steady himself and asked, "Some what? Rum?"

"No, money." Tom lowered his voice although there was no reason to do so. Wilson Street was deserted.

"Old man Cutter's got money at his place. He owes my pa."

"How much does he owe?" Tom faced Elmore.

"Hundreds." Elmore kept walking.

"Hundreds o' bottles o' rum." Tom stumbled two steps backwards before hurrying to catch up.

"Money, I said." Elmore turned around and waited.

Nothing more was said that night about robbing the Cutter house but the idea was planted in the befuddled brains of the two teenagers.

* * *

The next day, at First Baptist Church, Rev. Grafftey greeted Joan and Varney, saying, "I would like to hold a memorial service for Mayfield to celebrate his life."

"That would be nice," said Varney, smiling.

"But can we wait until Anathea and I have the mourning picture finished?" asked Joan.

"Of course," said George Grafftey. "When might that be?"

"When do you think, Anathea?" Joan asked.

Anathea replied, "We can finish by next Sunday."

"We can put it on a pedestal in the foyer for the people to see," said Mrs. Grafftey, standing beside her husband.

The pastor added, "Right before the worship service begins, we'll move the pedestal to the front of the sanctuary."

"Mayfield will like that," said Varney as he turned toward Raiford and added, "Won't you?"

Many people in the crowded foyer overheard the old man's remark.

* * *

On Monday, December 12th, Anathea started working in the afternoons at Cutters. Raiford and Kirk gave her a tour of the grounds which covered three acres between the end of Farquhar Street and the Speed River. The railroad tracks bordered the eastern edge of the property and came between it and the west bank of the Speed River. Kirk pointed out the original foundry, a single stone building near the private depot from where merchandise was shipped.

"Those torpedoes were made there," Kirk said in a lowered tone.

"Looks like this property has plenty of hiding places," said Raiford, looking at the various buildings and sheds.

"You're right about that," said Kirk. "I don't know what's here and what isn't since all my time has been confined to the office."

"That's going to change now that Mr. Pearson is gone," said Raiford, waving to rehired workers arriving.

* * *

E. L. Pearson wanted revenge for his firing. He attributed this turn of events to the arrival of Raiford Young. The stocky, grumpy man also wanted to make money from the Confederates while there was still time. Frank Burleigh, the foreman of the crew who manufactured the illegal weapons for his cousin Bennett Burley, was his only hope for such a scheme. Therefore, E. L. went to Frank's modest home on Cork Street. It was after dark on Monday evening. Frank was just locking the back door when E. L. knocked at the front. Upon seeing his former boss, Frank ushered his wife, upstairs with the children, that it was a business caller.

"I'm not taking this without a fight," said E. L., stomping into the front room.

"I don't see there's much you can do about it, Mr. Pearson," said Frank, following him. "Varney Cutter made the decision."

"That old man is daft." He paced. "There's plenty I can do. I can sue."

"In court?" Frank sat in his rocking chair by the dying fire.

"Yes, in court. Where else do you sue?" He sat down in Mrs. Burleigh's rocker facing Frank.

"On what charges?" Frank reached for his pipe and proceeded to light the meerschaum.

"That Raiford fellow used undue influence on Old Man Cutter. That's what this lawyer said. Undue influence on a crazy man – that's a crime."

Taking his pipe out of his mouth, Frank asked, "It is?"

E. L. replied, "It's like some distant no-good relative getting a senile old person to sign a will and make the no-good relative the beneficiary of the entire estate, when the old person didn't even like that distant relative."

"That's what your lawyer told you?" asked Frank. "He thinks you've got a case?"

"Either for that or, maybe, Raiford Young can be accused of something more serious."

"Like what?"

"Violating Canada's neutrality. Dealing with Confederates."

"But that's what we've been doing," said Frank.

"Well, we can just turn the tables on them. Put the hot potato in Raiford Young's lap. Yes, that's what we can do. Set things up to make him look guilty."

Frank listened to his former boss rant, but was unsure if he wanted to participate in his evil scheme.

* * *

On Tuesday, December 13, in Toronto, Jacob Thompson met with John Headley, John Yates Beall, George Anderson, Robert Martin, and Mechum Esling, in his Queen's Hotel suite to make final preparation for his next scheme. The men sat in satin-covered Louis XIV chairs, smoked Cuban cigars, and drank expensive liquor.

"If these generals are being exchanged," said George, "why don't we just let the procedure go through?"

"Yes," said Robert. "We get them back on our side."

"With delays," said Jake. "Exchanges take time. We want these men on the field immediately. Their wisdom and experience are vital to our success in the upcoming battles."

"The men are ready," said Mr. Headley.

"Are you certain of success?" asked their leader.

Speaking with confidence, John Beall said, "We can do it, sir."

Mechum thought: *Do I have time to warn them? That man Fides said to leave messages with the desk clerk at the Royal Albert Hotel. How often does he go there to fetch his messages? I might be too late in warning them.*

* * *

On Thursday, Dolly and Kirk invited Anathea and Raiford to go with them to the

Demosthenian Society meeting. They rode in Kirk's sleigh which he borrowed from his landlord. The men sat in front where the wind was worse, while the two young women huddled under a buffalo robe in the lower back seat.

"Where does the Society get its name?" Anathea asked.

Dolly said, "Demosthenes was a Greek orator who lived in ancient Athens. He rebelled against Alexander the Great and ended up committing suicide instead of being captured."

Kirk added, "He lived in the fourth century B.C."

Raiford said, "You've chosen a good name for your club. What's the topic this evening?"

Dolly answered, "Is Russian serfdom more unjust and odious than American slavery?"

"Good choice," said Raiford. "Which side are you arguing?"

"I'm saying American slavery is worse," said Dolly.

"I'm taking the side of Russian serfdom being more unjust," said Kirk.

"You don't stand a chance," Dolly said as she laughed.

"They let women speak?" Anathea's voice indicated her surprise.

"Of course. Why not?" Dolly tossed the heavy robe to one side as they drove up to the town hall.

The women went into the building while the men led the horses to the stable.

During the stirring debate, Anathea was enthralled. She had never experienced anything like this gathering. As an orphan, she was taught to be silent and obedient when out in public. She had never heard women speak at a meeting of any kind. Although Raiford had not prepared ahead of time, he made several astute remarks, saying that American slavery exceeded Russian serfdom in its cruelty of separating families and prohibiting the slaves from achieving their potential. Several people opposed him, all in good spirit. Following the hour-long debate, the two dozen people enjoyed hot cider and pastries.

Later that evening, when Anathea and Raiford met in the upstairs hallway before retiring, she could not stop talking.

"I assume you enjoyed yourself," Raiford said when she stopped to catch her breath.

"I did, truly." Seeing his smile, she laughed and added, "You can tell. I've been talking too much."

"You should have expressed your opinion at the meeting."

"Oh, how could I? I didn't want someone opposing me."

"It was all in good fun, although the subject was a very serious one," he said, kneeling down to bank the fire.

"I don't like confrontation," Anathea said.

"Is that why you accepted a divorce without protest?" Standing up, he faced her and added, "At least, I assume you made no protest."

"How did you know I was divorced?"

"I saw your bill of divorcement on the dresser at the hotel when we were packing to leave." He watched her expression closely. She lowered her gaze. He rephrased his question. "Did you protest the divorce?"

"Why would I?" She raised her eyes to look at him. "If he did not want me, why would I want him?"

"I cannot understand that." He stepped closer. Only inches separated them. "How could any man reject you? You are so sweet and kind, pretty and pleasant, and very smart. He must have been crazy."

"That's kind of you to say."

"I'm not saying it to be kind. It's the truth." Reaching up to touch her hair, Raiford swiped a loose strand over her ear, and kept his hand cradling the side of her head.

Anathea shivered. The cool hallway was not the cause; the feel of his hand on her hair was. Without hesitation, Raiford lowered his hand, touched her shoulder, put his other hand around her waist, and pulled her into his arms. She rested her head against his chest and felt warm and wanted. They stood together for a long, silent moment before he spoke.

"I hope you will plan to participate at the meeting next month."

"Will we go again?"

"Certainly," he said. "As much as you enjoyed yourself tonight, I would not deny you. Besides, I think you would make a good debater." He brushed his cheek against her silky hair.

"Do you?"

"Truly, I do." He held her slightly away so he could look into her eyes. "You have a great deal of potential. I see you flowering every day, in so many ways."

"So you think I can speak in public?"

"Most assuredly." Raiford nodded and smiled.

"What's the topic next month?"

"Is memory a more prolific source of enjoyment than imagination?" he answered.

"I'll have to look up the word prolific."

"That's a good start."

"Will you take the same side as I do?"

"Wouldn't it be more fun if I took the opposite side?"

"Which one?" she asked.

"You choose first."

"I'll tell you after I find out what prolific means."

He chuckled.

Both of them assumed that Raiford would be in Guelph when the Demosthenian Society met in January. They had no thought that he might be incarcerated in a federal prison.

* * *

Weary of spy work, Mechum Esling entered the Royal Albert Hotel and handed an envelope to the desk clerk. The clerk glanced at the single word: *Fides.* He nodded, turned his back, and placed the letter in a wooden box with a lid. Within the hour, a messenger boy took the envelope, read the name, and carried it away.

When federal agent Fides read the message alerting him to the Confederates' covert operation to rescue the seven generals, he went into action.

* * *

Historic Note: Seven Confederate generals were transferred by train from Johnson's Island to Fort Lafayette on Thursday, December 15, 1864. Brigadier-General James Jay Archer, Brigadier-General William N. R. Beall, Brigadier-General John W. Frazier, Brigadier-General John R. Jones, Major-General Edward "Allegheny" Johnson, Brigadier-General M. Jeff Thompson, and Major-General Isaac Ridgeway Trimble knew nothing of the plan to rescue them. Most of these officers had participated in the failed escape attempt made during the previous winter. Several of them were leaders in the Order of the Brotherhood of the Southern Cross, the prisoners' secret society. Only after they arrived in New York harbor did they learn of the botched attempt to halt the train and free them. What went wrong was not reported in the newspapers. However, there were many news stories about the arrest of two Confederates, Captain John Yates Beall and George S. Anderson, near the Suspension Bridge over the Niagara River on December 16. The other members of the rescue team escaped capture.

CHAPTER TEN

ESPIONAGE AT ST. CATHERINES

*Wherein conspirators make plans for getting torpedoes; and
Raiford and his friends thwart those plans.*

With the failure of the rescue attempt of the seven Confederate generals, Jacob Thompson changed his focus to another scheme, getting the torpedoes that Bennett Burley had arranged to purchase. The Secret Service Commissioner had received a telegram from E. L. Pearson, asking for an urgent meeting to discuss the sale of merchandise. The telegram did not specify what merchandise. Jake knew.

"I told Mr. Pearson that I was sending a replacement for Mr. Burley," Jacob told his wife as they were preparing for bed.

"Who are you sending?" Catherine asked.

"I haven't decided. Several of our eager young men want to go," said Jake. "It's imperative that we get those torpedoes as soon as possible. Mr. Pearson is also in a hurry."

"No doubt. He wants the money." She climbed into bed and added, "I am certain you will select the best man."

"I think I'll give the assignment to Rev. Stewart."

"I've heard a rumor about him," said Catherine, wrinkling her brow. "What is it?"

"That Rev. Stewart wants your job. Have you heard that rumor?"

"I have," he said, dropping his dressing gown onto the chair and climbing into bed. "It's nothing to be concerned about. He has no authority from Richmond. In fact, he lost the draft for money which he claims our government sent with him."

"If he's so inept, why would you select him?" Catherine moved over to make room for him.

"Mainly, to get him out of my hair," said Jacob.

Mrs. Thompson smiled, moved closer, and asked, "Where is he to meet Mr. Pearson?"

"A place called St. Catherines."

"I thought you said the torpedoes were being made in Guelph."

"That's right, but Mr. Pearson wants to negotiate the sale out of town. He's probably afraid of being arrested like Mr. Burley was."

* * *

St. Catherines, an incorporated town since 1845, now had more than 6,000 residents. Cattle grazed around Martindale's Pond. Well-built houses and shops dotted the winding streets. Located only twelve miles from the United States border, St. Catherines was a convenient meeting spot for Confederates.

* * *

On Friday, December 16, as the Union Army was defeating the Confederates in the second day of the two-day Battle of Nashville, Rev. Kensey Stewart took the expense money Jacob Thompson advanced him.

"Meet E. L. Pearson at the Grimsby Hotel in St. Catherines," Jacob said.

"I'll need more money to leave with my family," the preacher said as he pocketed the bills.

"We will look after your family," said Mr. Thompson.

An hour later, when Kensey handed Emma a few bills, he said, "I have urgent business for the Confederacy. I must hurry. You can manage on this."

Emma Louisa Stewart had learned to manage during her marriage to her erratic husband. After placing the money in her reticule and waving good-bye, she sat down at the desk in the cramped, cold, rented house, and wrote an advertisement for the *Toronto Globe:* Skilled seamstress will do sewing for respectable clients.

* * *

Elmore and Tom sat at the bar of the Crippled Deer Tavern and drank their third glasses of beer.

"Pa's gone to St. Catherines," said Elmore, leaning toward his friend. "This would be a good time to rob that place. Kirk brings the profits to the house on Friday."

"Think we'll see that pretty lady when we're there?" Tom emptied his glass and called for the bartender to refill it.

"What pretty lady?"

"You know. The pretty one – Anathea," said Tom smiling as he banged his empty glass on the scarred wooden bar.

"Let's see your coin," snarled the bartender as he came toward the pair.

"You got my last one," mumbled the teenager. "Hey, Elmore, you got more money?"

"Nope." Elmore finished his drink and slid off the stool. "Let's go."

As Tom followed his staggering friend, he said, "We'll need a gun. Can't rob a strong box without a gun."

The half dozen men in the tavern turned to stare at the loud teenager.

"We'll get a gun. Don't worry." Elmore patted his friend on the back.

"Might need to shoot the lock off," said Tom as they went outside.

"Or kill someone," said Elmore before the heavy door blew shut behind them.

They went to the stable behind the Albion Hotel which was built in 1856 on the northeast corner of Norfolk and MacDonell streets. Out of the wind, the teenagers rolled cigarettes as they talked.

Taking a puff from his cigarette, Tom said, "Hey, we can use these grain sacks for masks."

"You gotta cut eye holes," Elmore licked the paper and pressed it together over the tobacco.

"I can do that," said Tom. "I got me a knife."

"We need a gun."

"Can't steal one at Aylsworth. Too many shoppers. Christmas, you know."

"Yah. Let's wait 'til after Christmas. Fewer shoppers."

They smoked in silence for several minutes.

"Would you shoot someone?" Tom asked his friend.

"I don't know." Elmore drew a long puff of smoke into his lungs. "Would you?"

"Not the pretty lady."

"How many people do you reckon are living in that big Cutter house?"

Tom held up his fingers as he counted. "Two grandkids, the two that brought them, the old folks, some runaway slaves -- how many's that?" He put his fingers down.

"Don't know. Doesn't matter. We'll rob the house at night when they're all asleep." Elmore had to relight his cigarette when the flame fell off.

* * *

On Saturday, at the Cutter mansion, the children were making Christmas gifts with the help of adults. Joan was showing Beatrice and Willene how to embroider flowers on the corners of linen handkerchiefs. Zurelle outlined Fernancy's handprint on a paper for the child to color for her papa. Dalby and Freddie glued buttons onto small wooden boxes under Varney's supervision.

Anathea was delighted to have her own money from her first week's earnings to buy presents. The Burleigh sisters were stopping by to pick her up so the three of them could go shopping. As the twins neared the Cutter house, Lynnet said, "I wish that handsome Mr. Young would go shopping with us."

"Don't set your cap for Raiford, dear sister," said Jennet.

"And why not?"

"Don't you see the way he looks at Anathea?" she asked her twin.

"Well, yes, but..."

"No 'yes, but.' You just keep your eyes off him. It is very clear that he has his heart set on Anathea." Taking her sister's arm as they went up the icy front steps, Jennet added, "You just find someone else to pursue."

"The way you pursued Eustus?"

"He pursued me!" Jennet appeared to be indignant but both young women laughed.

* * *

While the three young women shopped in town, Raiford and Ochran finished the job of removing the animal heads from the walls of the Cutter house.

"Thank you, Ochran," said Raiford. "I could not have done it without you."

"It was a two-man job for sure," said Ochran.

The two men exited the carriage house where the stuffed heads were stored. They each carried an armload of firewood.

"Have you thought about working at Cutter's?" Raiford asked. "We could use another man."

"John Higgins said you're calling back the workmen laid off in the fall," said Ochran. "You sure you won't have too many men? John says there's not much work in the winter."

"That was true in the past," said Raiford. "But we're busy manufacturing the stove Zurelle wants. Don't tell her. Let's keep it a surprise. We could use your help."

"Do you think the old couple can manage the children by themselves?"

"I've asked the twins and Mrs. Shilliday to come by every day to check on things," said Raiford. "They're happy to do that."

"That Mrs. Bolton stops by every day. Zurelle doesn't like her."

"Saida Bolton is an old busybody," said Raiford, as he shifted his load to one arm in order to open the back door.

Going first through the door, Ochran said, "I feel sorry for Mr. Bolton."

The two men chuckled.

* * *

When the three young women returned from their shopping trip, Raiford helped carry packages upstairs to hide in Anathea's room. Before she could leave, he shut the door and stood with his back to it.

"I have an idea about gifts for Varney and Joan," he said in a low tone. "I want to know your opinion."

"What's your idea?"

"A puppy and kitten," Raiford said. "The puppy for Varney and a kitten for Joan. The children could pick them out and give them. Of course, it would be a gift for the children as well, because I'm sure they would play with the pets. What do you think?"

"Do you know of puppies and kittens available?"

Raiford quickly told her of litters he knew about in the neighborhood. Anathea said, "I think it's a wonderful idea. I didn't know what to get them. They seem to have everything." She smiled.

He returned the smile, opened the door, and followed her out.

* * *

In the Grimsby Hotel in St. Catherines, Kensey Stewart met E. L. Pearson in the smoking room. They sat in a corner, their overstuffed chairs close, and discussed the sale of torpedoes. The former Cutter manager did not tell the eager buyer that he was no longer employed at the leading foundry in Guelph.

"How many have you got ready?" asked the clergyman.

"Five," E. L. answered, although he knew there were only three completed. However, he intended to get paid for more than he delivered.

"Is that all?" Kensey frowned.

"The other items were taken when Burley was arrested."

"How can they be transported?"

"Where do you want them to go?"

"To the Mississippi," said Kensey.

"Through Detroit?"

"Is that the quickest route?"

Mr. Pearson said, "Yes, but Lieutenant Colonel Bennett Hill is commander at Detroit. He keeps a close eye on Rebel doings at Windsor and hereabouts."

"Don't worry about that. Once we make the sale, you're out of it," said the minister. "I'll be taking all the risk then."

"Better hurry before weather gets too bad."

"Would snow hold up the trains?"

"Not usually." Mr. Pearson looked around to be sure no one was eavesdropping. Three other men were on the far side of the room, too distant to overhear. "Have you got the payment?"

"How much?" asked Rev. Stewart.

"Five thousand," said E.L. "Gold. No paper bills."

"A thousand dollars apiece!" The minister's eyes widened.

"That's the price," E. L. said.

The two men began to haggle.

* * *

Entering the small parlor where Anathea and Joan were seated side by side on the settee, Raiford put down the armload of wood and said, "The animal heads are all down." He began adding wood to the dying fire.

Both women looked up from the embroidery frame where they were working on the mourning picture to be displayed at church tomorrow.

"That's good. I just wish this was finished, too," said Joan, returning her gaze to the framed artwork. In a sad tone, she added, "Mayfield's death is midnight for us but a bright, sunny morning for him." She dabbed light blue water paint onto the fabric sky.

Anathea said, "We should put that sentiment somewhere, perhaps on the obelisk or embroidered in the white clouds."

"The clouds, I think," said Joan. "What do you think, Raiford?"

"I think this is the loveliest mourning picture I've ever seen." His gaze went from the framed fabric to see Anathea rub her finger tips together.

"Did you hurt yourself?" he asked.

Joan, replacing her paint brush in its holder, answered for Anathea. "She insisted on using that metallic thread to outline the sun and angels. Look what it's done to her fingers."

Raiford sat on the other side of Anathea, his hip against hers, and took her hands in his. Seeing the tiny red marks made by the stiff thread, he raised her fingers to his lips and kissed the tips. Their eyes met.

Joan, not at all surprised by his gesture, said, "I told her we could just use yellow silk but she said the metallic would look better. The dear girl needs some cream for those cuts. Zurelle!"

Zurelle came, received instructions, and went to find a jar of lotion. Raiford kept Anathea's hands in his, resting on her skirt between them.

"You both have done a beautiful piece of work," Raiford said as he looked over the decorated linen square.

"I could not have completed it without Anathea," Joan said. "She kept me on task when all I wanted to do was weep."

Joan talked about Mayfield. Zurelle brought lotion. Raiford applied the creamy white substance to Anathea's fingers. Anathea sat still and felt as though she was in a dream.

Such tender care. He is so gentle. No one ever did such a kindness for me. His hands are so warm, so large, but so, so gentle. If only this could go on.

The five children entering the room halted Anathea's thoughts. She started to pull her hands out of Raiford's hold, since the lotion was well applied. However, Raiford held her hands firmly in his and whispered, "Let me hold them until it's dry. You don't want to stain your skirt."

Varney followed the children, who were all talking at the same time, and announced, "We've got a bear. Where's my gun?"

"Don't let him shoot it!" cried Freddie. "It's a bear like mine!"

"We saw it in the back yard," said Dalby. "Near the tree line."

"Grandpa, we don't want another head hanging," said Beatrice, tugging on the old man's jacket.

Raiford stood, helping Anathea to rise at the same time, and said, "Let's see if it's still there. Mr. Cutter, bears are one of God's creatures. We must not kill."

Everyone went to see the brown bear as it lumbered away from civilization into the woods.

* * *

Also on Saturday, December 17, Mechum Esling lay in his boarding house room in Fort Erie, Ontario, two blocks from Lake Erie, and thought: *The killing might be stopped sooner because of what I've done. They will never know it was me that tipped off the federals about the transfer of those seven Confederate generals. Will it shorten the war? Who knows? At least, without competent generals giving orders, their battles are more likely to be lost. Without leaders, they might not attack. They might give up. That's all I want – for the war to end.*

He walked to the writing desk, sat down, took up a pen, and wrote: *My beloved Delphina, I am residing in Ft. Erie, in Canada West. Loyalists settled here after their side lost in our glorious Revolution. Now, loyalists, and that is what we must henceforth be, are living here once again. With our families fighting on both sides, I have resolved to change my loyalty. That will please some but not all. We will discuss the matter when you are with me and I can hold you in my arms once more. Try to come before Christmas. I am traveling to Guelph, Ontario, Canada West. Meet me there. Send word to the postmaster about your arrival date. I will come to the depot. Your loving husband, Mechum.*

As he folded the paper to create an envelope on which he placed a wax seal, Mechum realized the length of time a letter could take.

I must send her a telegram. I will hand her this letter when I see her, he thought, as he put the folded paper into his bag. *And I will send a second telegram to Cutter's.*

* * *

Saturday evening, as E. L. Pearson and Rev. Stewart continued to quibble about the price of torpedoes, Anathea and Raiford wrote letters. Anathea wrote to Barbara Dell at the Louisville Girls Home, telling her that she was well and where she was living. She also wrote to her brother Adam in California, a letter which he would never receive. Raiford wrote to his parents, telling them that he was now in Canada, having escorted two orphans home to their grandparents. He wrote nothing about the army or the war. Anathea and Raiford whispered together about where and when they would go to look at kittens and puppies.

* * *

On Sunday, December 18, Jacob and Catherine Thompson celebrated their 26ᵗʰ wedding anniversary. Jake spent the entire day with his wife, never once meeting with any of his fellow Confederates. Instead, the couple talked about their son, Macon Caswell Thompson, who recently wed Sarah Fox, and about where they would live when the war ended.

* * *

That same Sunday, Joan Cutter displayed the mourning picture which she and Anathea had made. Raiford had contributed to the artwork by writing in calligraphy the sentiment that Joan had voiced the day before. The words were written in black ink on a white cloud.

Rev. George Grafftey conducted a celebration of Mayfield's life, which brought tears to the eyes of almost everyone in the congregation. The members of First Baptist Church shared their memories of the Cutter's only son, admired his mother's needlework, and expressed their sympathy to the bereaved parents. Beatrice and Freddie received special attention from the church members. The day exhausted Varney and Joan, who both took long naps.

* * *

Also that Sunday, Adam Brannaman arrived at the Shaker village.

Greeters at the gate questioned all new arrivals. "Are you here to worship with us?" asked the first man.

"Did you see our notice in the newspaper?" asked the second man.

"No. I've come looking for someone," replied Adam, dismounting and taking his horse's reins to lead him.

As though he had not heard, the second man said, "The Meeting House is that way. You are just in time for worship."

Adam walked with several dozen people toward the large, two-story building, while looking around at the clean, orderly surroundings. The houses and barns were larger than a normal family would have. The board pathways were cleared of the light cover of snow. What would have been muddy spots were filled in with wood chips. The Shakers could be recognized by their simple, dark clothing and matching headwear. Adam was so interested in his surroundings that he did not pay attention to the two doors into the church building.

"This way to the men's door!" said a bearded man, pulling Adam's arm as he started to enter the female's entrance. Immediately, Adam saw his error as women passed him.

Inside, the men and women were seated in long benches facing each other. Adam found the arrangement strange, because he had never been in a church where the sexes were separated. But an even stranger thing was soon to come.

The sermon explained the beliefs of the Shakers. Adam let his mind wander. However, he became alert when the dance began. The dancers did a shuffle step in a circular route. Then, suddenly, the air was filled with shouts and shrieks as the dancing became frenzied. Adam could not believe what he was seeing.

Is Anathea out there on the floor? I don't see her. Surely, she does not participate in these wild gyrations. Is her husband dancing?

Not until the assembly ended did Adam have a chance to ask his question again.

"I am looking for my sister who joined your group."

"What is her name?" the man next to him asked.

"Anathea Brannaman." Realizing his error, Adam added, "Emmert, wife of Monro Emmert."

Immediately, the man glared at Adam and gave a sideways glance at the men near them.

"Are they here?" Adam asked.

"They divorced. She's gone."

* * *

On Monday morning, December 19th, Eustus Wright, the fiancé of Jennet Burleigh, stopped Kirk McCarrell before he reached the Cutter gate and told him a surprising fact. The bookkeeper hurried to the small office building, built the fire in the stove, and set the coffee pot to brew as he thought about what to do concerning Eustus' information. The room was just beginning to warm when the messenger boy, Tad, brought two telegrams -- one addressed to the Cutter Foundry Manager and one addressed to Raiford Young marked personal. Kirk read the manager's message: *Will be in Guelph on 20th to pick up order for B.B. Mechum Esling.*

A few minutes later, when Raiford arrived, Kirk handed him the two messages and said, "Eustus Wright heard that Pearson is arriving on the noon train today, and he's bringing a buyer for the torpedoes."

"Then there are more torpedoes hidden here," said Raiford as he read the telegrams.

Pouring two cups of coffee, Kirk says, "I knew there were. What's your telegram?"

Raiford, who was now familiar with the code, read the encrypted message aloud: "*Richmond sent Edwin Lee to replace Thompson. Expected first of year. Exploit change of command. Fides.*

"Who is Fides?"

"My contact in Toronto." He accepted the proffered coffee and added, "Thanks." After taking a sip, he said, "Two buyers – Mechum Esling and Pearson's man, whose name we do not know."

"What will we do?" Kirk eyed his companion over the brim of his cup.

Raiford asked, "Where did Eustus hear about Pearson bringing a buyer?"

"Frank Burleigh told him. Apparently, Eustus worked on the torpedo crew at the start, but dropped out because he knew it was illegal." Kirk sat down behind his desk. "Eustus is going to marry Jennet Burleigh, you know. He wants to be honest. Looks like Frank might want the same thing."

"Let's get them to tell us where the torpedoes are hidden?"

"We have to be cautious. We don't want the other torpedo workmen to suspect."

"I'll meet with the newly-arrived workers while you speak to Frank and Eustus," said Raiford.

The men discussed how they would go about executing their plan while allaying suspicion.

* * *

That same morning, Adam Brannaman caught the stage to Louisville. He had ridden his horse to the nearest stage stop, but the old animal was unable to go further. After selling the horse, he bought a stagecoach ticket. Now, looking out the window at the passing forest, Adam recalled his meeting with Monro Emmert. The man who told him of his sister's divorce had escorted him to the large house where Shaker men lived. Upon meeting Anathea's former husband, Adam did not offer his hand.

"Where is Anathea?" Adam had asked.

"Who are you?"

"Her brother."

"She's gone into the sinful world; deserted in the dark of night," Monro had said. "She never had a heart for the superior life we live here. She wasn't divinely called to it like I am. I never should have married her."

Adam had turned from his former brother-in-law in disgust, mounted his horse, got directions to the nearest stage stop, and departed.

* * *

Eustus was willing to help Kirk but Frank was not. Nevertheless, as soon as Kirk learned the hiding place of the illegal weapons, he informed Raiford. Within the hour, Raiford rushed into the Cutter house looking for Anathea. She was in the library office teaching the children.

"I must speak to you in the hallway," Raiford said, taking her arm and leading her out of the room. From his pocket, he retrieved the two telegrams and waited while she read them.

"Eustus told Kirk where the torpedoes are hidden," Raiford said, taking the two pieces of paper back from Anathea and tucking them into his jacket pocket over his heart. We need to get rid of them before Pearson arrives. They must not go to the Confederates."

"Is Mechum Esling the replacement Jacob Thompson was sending?"

"Perhaps," Raiford said, "Or Pearson's buyer could be that man."

"Their right hand doesn't seem to know what their left hand is doing," Anathea mused.

"That can work to our advantage."

"How?"

"By exploiting the change of command," Raiford said. "Pearson might not know yet of Thompson's departure and Edwin Lee's arrival."

"What advantage does that offer?"

"Eustus is going to tell Mr. Pearson that the torpedoes were already sold to Edwin Lee's agent who arrived ahead of him," said Raiford.

"But Mr. Esling does not arrive until tomorrow, and Mr. Pearson comes today."

"I'm not talking about Mechum Esling."

"Then who is Mr. Lee's agent?" Anathea asked.

"Me," said Raiford.

* * *

That same Monday, December 19th, border patrols were established on the Canadian/United States boundary. The added security was unknown to Delphina, who was delighted to receive her husband's wire and began packing immediately. Her father bought the train tickets. Her mother began filling a basket of food for the trip. The small household in Murfreesboro, Tennessee, was abuzz with voices and activity. Although her father wanted her to wait for better weather, Delphina was determined to leave as soon as she could.

* * *

Raiford and Kirk drove the flat wagon with sleigh runners out of the carriage house. Ochran sat on the narrow seat facing backwards and dangled his legs so his feet almost touched the ground. A large tarpaulin covered the pile of animal heads which had been removed from the interior walls of the house.

Seeing the sleigh pass, Deering Lister called, "What you boys got there?"

"Those animal heads Mr. Cutter wants us to get rid of," answered Raiford.

"They frighten the children," Ochran added.

* * *

Anathea could not concentrate on her instructing the children that morning after Raiford left. Her mind filled with thoughts of him.

Where can he be? How long will it take to get rid of those things? Will he be in any danger? Mr. Pearson will be in town soon? What will he do when he discovers our trickery?

* * *

When E. L. Pearson escorted Rev. Kensey Stewart to the old foundry building and found the three torpedoes gone, he was furious. He stormed into the Cutter office with Kensey on his heels.

"What did you do, Mr. McCarrell?" he shouted.

The minister closed the door to keep out a sharp northern wind.

"About what?" Kirk asked in an innocent tone.

"The merchandise in the old foundry! I know it was you! You're the only one who could have done it!"

"Done what? I don't know what you're talking about. Was something important in the old foundry building?"

"You know damn well there was! All your snooping around didn't fool me!"

Rev. Stewart calmly said, "I came to buy some merchandise that seems to have disappeared. Do you know where it is, young man?"

Speaking slowly and softly, Kirk said, "I have no idea."

Just then, Anathea arrived for her regular afternoon shift as assistant bookkeeper. E. L., his face red with rage, stomped toward her before she had closed the door and shouted, "This is your doing! You and that man you came here with!" Turning to face, Kensey, he added, "The two of them connived to get the old man to boot me out so they could take over and rob the Cutters blind." Facing Anathea again, he stormed, "You don't fool me, Missy! I know what…"

"I know her," Kensey said, stepping between the two. "You were on the train with my family and me."

Anathea had no time to respond because E. L. pushed the minister aside and raised his fist in front of Anathea's face. Instantly, Kirk grabbed the man's fist and yelled: "Get out! You don't strike a lady! Get off this property now or I'll call for Constable Clark!" Kirk shoved E. L. against the wall.

Kensey urged, "Come. Let us go. We don't want any trouble."

* * *

Ochran and Raiford drove the heavily-loaded sleigh out of town. The torpedoes were securely hidden beneath the animal heads, and all was covered by the big tarpaulin. Heading for the Crippled Deer, Elmore and Tom saw the sleigh but gave it only a passing glance. The teenagers were intent upon getting out of the cold and into the warm tavern.

***

Without knocking, E. L. Pearson stormed into the Cutter house. Rev. Stewart followed at his heels.

"Where is Mr. Cutter?" the former employee bellowed.

The two men looked into the front parlor, which was empty. Zurelle came out of the kitchen and stood in the doorway.

"Quiet!" she admonished. "Mr. and Mrs. Cutter are taking their naps. What do you want?"

"I demand to see Varney Cutter!" E. L. stomped toward the servant as five children gathered behind her.

"He's sleeping. You cannot disturb him," Zurelle said.

"I'll disturb him plenty!" E. L. started toward the front staircase.

Quickly, Zurelle grabbed the broom from behind the door and started after him. The minister followed, saying, "Let's not be hasty, Mr. Pearson. Let's think this through."

Before E. L. Pearson reached the first step, Zurelle swung the broom and struck his head, knocking him off balance. He fell backwards but Kensey caught him.

"Get out! Both of you!" Zurelle swung again. She missed because the minister yanked him out of the way.

E. L. yelled his demands. "I'm gonna see Old Man Cutter! Don't raise that broom to me again, you witch!" Rev. Stewart kept a firm grasp on E. L.'s arm.

Joan appeared at the top of the stairs. Her hair was in disarray. She clutched a robe closed over her chest. "What's going on down there?" she called.

"These men are leaving!" Zurelle lowered her broom and swung it back and forth as though she was sweeping them out the door. Under her breath, so Joan would not hear, Zurelle said, "Get out! Get out!"

Kensey pulled E.L. out the door while declaring, "We're leaving. Sorry to disturb you."

Zurelle slammed the door after the two, turned to the children, who had come into the hallway, and said, "See what happens if you grow up to be a bad man. Now, into the kitchen with you. We have cookies to bake."

* * *

Cookies cooled on the kitchen table when Kirk and Anathea arrived about an hour later. Freddie and Beatrice told them about Zurelle chasing two men out of the house. Joan and Varney were sitting in the kitchen waiting for Zurelle to serve tea with the cookies.

"Sit down and join us, Mr. McCarrell" said Joan. "Where are Raiford and Ochran?"

"They had some business to take care of," said Kirk, holding a chair for Anathea.

"Who were those men you shooed out of here?" asked Joan, who had not seen Mr. Pearson clearly, since he was ducking his head to keep away from the broom.

When Zurelle described them, Kirk answered Joan's question. "They were the former foundry manager, E. L. Pearson, and another man who came to buy torpedoes. They are dealing with the enemy."

"Is it Bill Johnston's gang of ruffians?" Varney asked, looking from Kirk to Anathea.

"Bill Johnston?" Anathea repeated.

Joan said, "Varney is recalling the revolution when he was a young man and fighting to free the provinces from British control."

Anathea asked, "What became of your rebellion?"

Varney replied, "We agreed to the Webster-Ashburton Treaty, which settled our differences. That was in 1842. You've heard of the Webster-Ashburton Treaty, haven't you?"

"No," she said. "Tell me about it."

They sat around the big kitchen table, ate cookies, drank tea, and listened to Varney reminisce.

* * *

Elmore and Tom were drinking and laughing at the Crippled Deer tavern when Elmore's father and the minister walked in. Hearing the teenagers, who were loudly bragging about their marksmanship ability,

E. L. stomped toward the table in the shadows and demanded, "What are you doing here?"

Tom said, "Just havin' a little drink."

"I'm not talking to you," the irate father snarled.

"Who are these young men?" asked Rev. Stewart.

"My son and his worthless buddy."

"What's wrong, Pa?" Elmore slid over on the bench so his father could sit down.

Rev. Stewart pulled up a chair, sat, introduced himself, and said, "We are most disturbed by the fact that I came here to purchase some merchandise at the Cutter Foundry, but have learned that it is gone, sold to someone else, apparently."

The bartender came to the table and took orders from the older men. When they were all drinking, Elmore said, "The old man fired you and now he's cheated you. That's terrible. What can we do to get even, Pa?"

"I don't know," E. L. mumbled into his ale.

"Varney Cutter robbed you, so we can rob Varney Cutter," said Tom.

* * *

In the Cutter kitchen, they were just finishing the cookies and tea when the Burleigh sisters arrived.

"We brought a spice cake made from a new recipe," said Lynnet. "We want you to try it."

"I might serve it at my wedding," said Jennet.

When the others protested they just finished eating cookies, Jennet appeared so disappointed that they agreed to small pieces. They told about the intruders and how Zurelle chased them out with her broom. Anathea was grateful for this distraction from these new friends, because her thoughts were on Raiford and where he was. She tried to concentrate on the twins' chatter.

Lynnet said, "We're almost finished with our dresses. Mine is pale blue. I will be her bridesmaid."

"She could have been a bride herself but she turned down her last beau," said her sister.

"I didn't love him. I wish I had, so we could celebrate a double wedding as we always planned."

"I want all of your family to come to the wedding. Your family, too," Jennet spoke to Zurelle who was clearing away dishes.

"When is it?" asked Anathea.

"New Year's Day," said the future bride. "We plan to start 1865 as husband and wife."

They went into the parlor where Kirk put wood on the fire.

"Where is Ochran?" asked Jennet. "Shouldn't he be tending the fire?"

"And where is Raiford?" Lynnet faced Anathea. "He should be home by now, shouldn't he?"

Kirk answered, "They are taking care of some business."

* * *

Historic Note: Torpedoes in the Civil War were weapons now called land mines or marine mines. Confederate Brigadier General Gabriel James Rains invented the land mine and wrote the "Torpedo Book" which gave detailed instructions on how to construct a submarine mortar battery of the non-electric type. Hunter Davidson in the Navy Department specialized in making torpedoes with an electric control system, while General Rains preferred mechanical detonators. The torpedoes manufactured at the Cutter Foundry used galvanized batteries, which Rains considered inferior to his method. Either way, torpedoes made in Canada and sent to the Confederate States of America were illegal.

CHAPTER ELEVEN

THE ICY SPEED

Wherein Raiford and Ochran dump the torpedoes into the Speed River;
Raiford falls through the ice; Ochran rescues him;
Mechum is recognized; and
Rev. Stewart plans to free prisoners.

Clutching Raiford around the waist, Ochran dragged him into the kitchen. Raiford's eyes were closed and his legs did not move. The Burleigh twins were packing their cake plate into the basket and preparing to leave. Kirk had already departed.

"What happened?" Zurelle rushed toward her husband.

"He fell in the river!" Ochran spoke over his shoulder as he pulled Raiford toward the back stairs and started up.

"Raiford." Anathea stared after the two men.

"Refill the tea kettle!"

"Heat some bricks!"

"I'll get blankets!"

"Turn down the bed!"

"Build up the fire!"

The kitchen became a maelstrom of activity. Joan, Varney, and the children entered. Jennet explained the emergency. Anathea, holding her skirt, rushed up the stairs.

In the bedroom, Ochran dropped Raiford into the upholstered red chair beside the cold fireplace, grabbed a blanket from the quilt rack, wrapped it around his hunched shoulders, and knelt to start a fire.

"Let me do that!" Zurelle pushed her husband aside. "You get his wet clothes off!"

Anathea, not knowing what to do, handed two small logs to Zurelle on her knees at the hearth. Lynnet entered with an armload of blankets. "Help me put these on the bed, Anathea."

As soon as the young women had spread out the blankets, Lynnet left the room and Zurelle called to Anathea.

"Get that other boot off."

Anathea knelt to tug off Raiford's boots. "It's frozen on."

Ochran reached over her head and yanked off the leather boot. He returned to his work of stripping off Raiford's wet garments.

Zurelle said, "Fetch a nightshirt. Middle drawer."

Anathea went toward the bureau as Zurelle took the wet clothes her husband handed her and placed them over the quilt rack.

Tugging open the drawer, Anathea almost pulled it free in her hurry and had to shove hard to keep the drawer from falling out. She grabbed a white nightshirt, neatly folded, and gave it to Ochran, who had Raiford's suit jacket, vest, and shirt removed.

Anathea stood stunned. She had never seen a man's bare chest. Raiford's smooth skin glistened with sweat and the moisture from his clothing. A small patch of dark hair grew down the center of his muscular chest. His shoulder muscles bulged. The blanket that had been wrapped around him was now only around his waist and bunched in his lap. His hands were hidden in the folds.

Anathea thought: *How handsome.* Raiford shivered. Anathea's reverie broke. Ochran dropped the flannel nightshirt over his friend's head and maneuvered his arms into the sleeves.

Zurelle removed one of Raiford's wet socks. Anathea knelt and took off the other one, while Zurelle went to bring a dry pair.

"Should have gotten his pants off first," said Ochran as he undid the waist button.

Anathea turned down the bed covers. She thought: *I wonder what Monro looked like with a bare chest.* Since her former husband always dressed in another room or in the dark, she had never seen him naked. Knowing that the servants were undressing Raiford behind her made Anathea's cheeks redden. Even when the covers were turned down, she kept her back to him.

Freddie called from the hallway: "Is Uncle Raiford frozen to death?"

Anathea went to the door, opened it slightly to block the view, and faced the five children plus Mr. and Mrs. Cutter.

"Is Uncle Raiford going to die?" Beatrice asked as tears welled up in her eyes.

"Should we send for Dr. Shilliday?" asked Joan in a trembling voice.

"Is Mayfield sick?" Varney looked over Anathea's head into the bedroom.

"I don't know about a doctor," said Anathea. "We must get him warm."

Coming from the back stairs, Lynnet said, "I have tea. Jennet is preparing chicken barley broth. You boys can carry a hot brick in a basket." She handed her tray to Anathea. "Come along, Freddie and Dalby."

"What can we do?" asked Willene, following Lynnet.

Joan ushered the others away as Anathea closed the door with her foot. She set the tray on the ornate dressing table.

Ochran helped Raiford to the bed and covered him with the pile of bedding. Raiford opened his eyes for the first time and said, in a low voice, "Thank you."

"How did this happen?" Anathea asked, kneeling on the side of the bed near his hip.

"We hauled the things onto the ice," said Raiford.

Ochran said, "Mighty thick ice. We had to use Mr. Cutter's rifles to break it so they'd sink."

"I didn't expect it to break under me."

"Were you on shore?" Zurelle asked her husband.

"Yes. He made me go ashore."

Anathea asked, "How did you get him out?"

Just then, Jennet knocked and called, "The boys have a hot brick. May we come in?"

When Raiford nodded, Ochran opened the door. Dalby and Freddie, each holding a handle, carried in a basket with the flannel-wrapped brick, which Ochran put under the covers at Raiford's feet. Jennet led in the little girls, followed by Varney and Joan. They gathered around the bed.

"Tell us what happened," Joan said in a slightly trembling voice.

Raiford said, "I fell through the ice in the river. Ochran rescued me."

"How?" asked Dalby, glancing up at his father in admiration.

"The same way that Anabaptist Dirk Willems recued his pursuer," answered Raiford, who had been reading to the children about Christian heroes. "Remember that story?"

Beatrice said, "I remember, but no one is going to get killed for this, will they?"

Raiford said, "No one will get killed."

"What were you doing on the river?" asked Freddie, climbing onto the bed to snuggle close to the man. Anathea moved to the foot of the bed.

Ochran said, "We were dumping those animal heads we took down from the walls."

"That's good," said Beatrice.

"Can you wiggle your toes?" asked Freddie, pulling back the blankets at the foot of the bed. "If you can't, we'll call the doctor."

Anathea had climbed off the bed so Freddie could un-tuck the blankets. Everyone watched as Raiford wiggled his toes through the warm socks. Lynnet came into the room with a tray which she offered to Anathea and said, "Barley broth."

Anathea took the bowl and went to the far side of the bed. There was just enough space on this side, between the bed and the window, for a small table, where she set the silver tray.

"How did the ice break?" asked Freddie.

"Isn't it frozen thick?" asked Beatrice.

"It is," Raiford said. "But we put those heads on the ice and got out our guns."

"Whose guns?" Freddie asked in an excited voice.

Anathea held a spoon to Raiford's lips. He sipped the broth before saying, "Your grandpa's, from his gun case."

"Why?" Beatrice scowled. "The animals were already dead."

Raiford chuckled. Anathea smiled at the sound. Her eyes began to tear. She concentrated on filling another spoonful of broth.

"Yes, they were all dead," said Raiford. "But we had to break the ice."

"Weren't the heads heavy enough?" asked Varney.

Ochran said, "That ice is thick."

"We wanted to sink them far enough out from the river bank so they cannot be retrieved," said Raiford.

"We didn't want to go down with them," added Ochran, putting the last log on the fire.

"As we were shooting, a funny thing happened," Raiford continued.
"What?" Freddie's knee bumped Raiford's side.
"A man rode up and asked us if we were shooting fish."
"Shooting fish?" Fernancy scowled.
Raiford smiled at the little girl and answered, "We told him that we were not."
Ochran added, "We said we were target practicing."
"Did he go away and not bother you?" asked Freddie.
"He did," said Raiford. "The man was gone before the ice broke. If he had been there, he could have helped Ochran get me out."
"Papa is strong. He could rescue you by himself," said Dalby.
Raiford said, "And he did. You have a very brave Papa."
Joan said, "You've all heard the story now, children. Let Raiford rest. Come. Out of the room."
Everyone left the room except Anathea, who continued feeding Raiford the chicken broth until the bowl was empty. Setting the bowl on the tray, she told him about her confrontation in the office.
"Mr. Pearson was very angry when he found the items gone. The man with him was Rev. Stewart from the train. He recognized me." Anathea hesitated before adding, "Mr. Pearson was going to hit me but Kirk stopped him."
Raiford pushed himself up on the pillow and repeated, "Hit you. Why?"
"He said I am to blame. You and I. He seems to think we have turned Mr. and Mrs. Cutter against him."
"I don't want you out of my sight," said Raiford.
"When we leave the house, you mean?"
"That's right. We will walk to and from the foundry together. I don't even want you to go shopping with the Burleigh ladies unless I am with you. Can you agree to that?"
"Yes." She put the empty bowl on the tray. "So you think he means to do me harm."
"He's just lashing out at whomever," said Raiford, sliding down on his pillow. Anathea pulled the blankets up to his chin. "Kirk doesn't trust him; nor do I."

* * *

In the children's bedroom, Joan and Varney said prayers with Beatrice and Freddie before going to bed.

Beatrice prayed, "Thank you, Lord, for those scary heads sinking into the river."

Freddie said, "And thank you that Uncle Raiford did not sink, too."

"Thank you that Grandpa won't shoot any more animals," his sister said.

Then the siblings took turns blessing everyone they knew.

* * *

Adam arrived at the Home for Friendless Girls in Louisville on Tuesday morning, December 20. He found the girls busy decorating the house for Christmas. They had a tree which a farmer donated. Already, they had paper chains and colorful ribbons on its branches.

"Come and see our tree, Mr. Brannaman," Barbara said as she led the way into the large parlor. The tree sat in front of the bay window.

The girls, who had been talking and laughing, fell silent when they saw Adam. They all smiled and some of them curtseyed. After admiring the decorations, he said, "You've done a lovely job but there's something missing?"

"What?" asked the oldest girl.

"Presents under the tree," he said.

The smiles vanished from the faces of the seventeen orphans.

"We need to go shopping," said Adam. He pulled his wallet out from his inside jacket pocket, opened it, and handed bills to the teenaged girls as he said, "You help the little ones shop and get whatever you think others want."

Barbara started to stop him as he passed out the money to the hesitant older girls. He said, "Do not object to this, Miss Dell. You know that if Anathea were here, this is exactly what she would want me to do. I made a lot of money in California, more than I need or want. This is the best way to use it."

"You are too kind," said the orphanage headmistress, who was close to tears.

"While the girls are shopping, we can go to the grocery and buy what we will need for Christmas dinner."

While they were at the grocery store, Adam told Barbara of his fruitless visit to the Shaker village. Upon their return to the house, they found a telegram on the hall floor. The messenger had slipped it through the door's mail slot. Picking it up, Adam read: "In Philadelphia going to New York. Will write when settled. Anathea."

* * *

Jacob Thompson did not read Kirk's telegram until the next day, Tuesday, the 20th, because he was out of town. The message asked who was the agent replacing Bennett Burley. Mr. Thompson sent an immediate reply: *Expect Rev. Kensey Stewart.*

* * *

Also that day, December 20, Bennett Young and four other men were re-arrested near Quebec and taken to jail. They were charged with raiding the town of St. Albans, Vermont, on October 19, 1864, during which three banks were robbed of $220,000 in bank notes, government bonds, greenbacks, and hard cash. Horses were stolen for the robbers' getaway. Greek fire was thrown on buildings but the flames were soon extinguished.

Their re-arrest came about because fourteen of the raiders had already been arrested while seven others escaped capture, soon after the daring raid took place. From his jail cell, their leader, Bennett Young, had placed an item in the *Montreal Evening Telegraph* stating the purpose of the raid was to retaliate for the recent outrages committed in the Shenandoah Valley and other places in the Confederate States. Nevertheless, the raiders' extradition trial began on October 24, 1864, at St. Johns near the American border. Proceedings had scarcely begun when Judge Coursol ordered the prisoners removed from St. Johns to Montreal, where the people strongly favored the Confederates. Their first trial ended December 13 when Judge Coursol declared: "I possess no jurisdiction. Let the prisoners be released."

Their second trial would begin on December 27 before Judge James Smith of the Superior Court.

* * *

Kirk met Mechum Esling at the depot and escorted him to the Cutter house. In the sleigh, Kirk explained, "Our new foundry manager,

Raiford Young, is recovering from an ordeal yesterday. He fell into the icy river while dumping some stuffed animal heads. I hope to find him well today."

Raiford was well. Wrapped in Varney's wool robe, he was sitting beside the fireplace in the library and talking to Anathea.

"I hope you were not embarrassed by my being undressed in your presence yesterday," he said.

Anathea immediately blushed. In a low voice, she replied, "I was so busy I didn't notice." She lowered her gaze to her hands in her lap.

Raiford whispered, "Is that true?" He reached across the space between their chairs, lifted her chin until she looked at him, and awaited an answer.

She shook her head no. He lowered his hand. She said, "I never saw a man's bare chest before."

Puzzled, Raiford said, "You were married."

"Always in the dark." As soon as the words were out of her mouth, Anathea could feel the heat in her face increase.

Raiford, aware of her reddened cheeks, said softly, "Don't be shy about talking to me."

She rubbed her face, wishing the blood would subside. Her skin was hot against her hands. Just then, Ochran knocked and announced Mr. McCarrell and Mr. Esling.

As soon as Mechum stepped into the room, Anathea and Raiford recognized him.

"You're the man who jumped from the train," Raiford said as he stood up and offered his hand.

As Mechum shook hands with Raiford, he said, "That is true." Looking at Anathea, he added, "I remember you."

"You kept me from falling when the train made a sharp turn," said Anathea, who remained in her seat.

Setting their chairs near the fire, the visitors assumed Anathea's rosy cheeks were caused by the nearby flames.

"So you're the buyer sent by Mr. Thompson," said Raiford.

"That's right," answered Mechum.

"We've had a little mix up with this sale," said Raiford. "Did Kirk tell you?"

"No, he said you would explain."

"It seems that another buyer, Rev. Kensey Stewart, came for them yesterday, but they were already gone."

"There was a third buyer?" asked Mechum, crossing his arms.

Raiford hated to lie. He liked the appearance of this man. However, he knew that Mechum Esling had jumped off a train to evade federal agents. He undoubtedly was a Confederate. Raiford said, "The torpedoes are under water."

"What water?" Mechum's eyes traveled from one person to the other.

"The Speed River," said Raiford.

"They were not sold?"

Raiford simply shook his head. When Mechum looked at Kirk, he too gave a negative signal. Mechum's response was unexpected even by him. He laughed.

"Under water – that's a good place for the evil things," said Mr. Esling. "I never wanted them in the first place. I just wanted to keep them out of the war, so they wouldn't kill any more men."

Raiford, Anathea, and Kirk exchanged glances. Raiford spoke. "Didn't you run from federal agents on that train ride we shared?"

"I've since changed my allegiance," Mechum said.

Then, the other three people in the room laughed. While they were exchanging information about the recent turn of events, Tad, the telegraph messenger boy, arrived.

"It's from Jacob Thompson in Toronto," said Kirk, opening the folded paper. He read: "Our agent is Rev. Kensey Stewart. Do not sell to anyone else."

The four of them laughed with delight.

* * *

On Wednesday, December 21, Susan and Ned Lee, aboard the *S.S. Darien,* under the command of Captain Cummings, arrived at St. George, Bermuda. They had spent two delightful days in Nassau, sightseeing with fellow travelers. From Nassau, Ned sent a message to Secretary of State Judah Benjamin concerning his whereabouts and plans. He used the code name W. Gray. Now, they planned to spend the week in Bermuda, far away from the war. This would be an unusual Christmas for the couple.

* * *

Adam Brannaman was climbing down the ladder after putting a big silvery star on top of the Christmas tree to replace the paper one. The orphan girls were busily wrapping gifts in various rooms of the mansion. Miss Dell was supervising pie baking in the kitchen with two of the teenagers.

"Smells good," said Adam. "What kind is that?"

"Mincemeat," said Barbara.

After putting the kettle on to heat water for tea, Adam sat down and said, "I spoke to the attorney I hired to represent the orphanage in the will contest."

"What did he say? Is he hopeful?" Barbara dusted flour off her hands onto her apron.

"I'm afraid not," Adam answered. "He said that your benefactress was not of sound mind when she made her will. There are a number of relatives and servants who will attest to that fact."

"What will we do?" Barbara frowned.

"We can find jobs," said the oldest teenager. "But what will happen to the little girls."

"Don't you worry," said Mr. Brannaman. "If you cannot live here, I can find another place for you. You will not be homeless."

* * *

Anathea and Raiford went to look at a litter of puppies at the Lister house.

"They need a good home," said Myrtle Lister. "I know that if you take one, he'll have that."

"Which one do you want?" asked Deering.

Anathea could not decide so Raiford picked the liveliest black and white puppy.

Next, they went to a small house on Heffernan Street where they saw four kittens. Anathea had no trouble selecting the motley one who nuzzled her neck when she held it.

Both Anathea and Raiford thoroughly enjoyed the afternoon selecting the pets for Varney and Joan.

* * *

On Friday, December 23, Delphina rushed into Mechum's arms when she saw him on the platform at the Guelph station. Baby Mechum, between his parents as they embraced, let out a wail. Immediately, the couple moved apart. Mechum took the baby from his mother's arms, cradled him against his chest, and smiled broadly. Delphina turned to take Maggie's hand and said, "Here is your papa."

Getting off the train from another car was the Stewart family, but Kensey was late in arriving to collect them. Emma Stewart searched the platform as her children descended the metal steps. Her minister husband was nowhere in sight.

The newly-reunited Esling family passed Mrs. Stewart as she gathered her children and luggage. Mechum had a sleigh waiting at the hitching rail.

"Where are we going? Do you have a hotel room?" Delphina bubbled and clutched her husband's arm while holding Maggie's hand. "Oh, I don't care, as long as I am with you."

Mechum shifted Baby Mechum higher on his shoulder and said, "We are not spending Christmas in a hotel. We've been invited to stay with Mr. and Mrs. Cutter and their family until we buy a house."

"Can we afford to buy a house?" Delphina whispered.

In a low tone, Mechum dipped his head toward his wife and answered, "Yes, we can. I've earned a great deal of money since we parted."

As they climbed into the sleigh, Rev. Kensey Stewart arrived.

During the ride from the depot to the Cutters, Delphina exclaimed about what a lovely little town Guelph was. Seeing the big house for the first time, Delphina said, "For goodness sakes, are we living here?"

"For the time being -- a week or two at most," said Mechum as he helped her down. "There are plenty of bedrooms and a nursery for the children."

"Oh, no, I want the children in our room." She smiled as she went up the steps. Bells jingled on horses trudging along the road behind them.

"We're here!" called Mechum, opening the front door. The hallway became instantly busy with introductions, as the residents came to greet the newcomers. Freddie shook hands with little Maggie and declared, "Now Fernancy has someone her size to play with."

The smallest Wyatt child took Maggie's hand and led her to the corner of the kitchen where she had a mat on the floor with her playthings.

Anathea quickly learned that Delphina was a chatterbox. She related news about her home in Tennessee, about her children, about how much she loved and missed her husband. Mechum, however, was much more reticent, which was a good trait for a spy. He and Raiford got along well.

* * *

Christmas Day was on Sunday, so the children had to wait until after church to open their presents and look in their stockings. Zurelle served a big breakfast, knowing that after church, they would not be ready to eat until all the gifts were unwrapped.

The church service was a joyful experience with Christmas carols and Scripture readings from the book of Luke. Various laymen and women read the familiar verses.

Upon returning home, the large parlor became bedlam as children and adults opened gifts. Raiford and Anathea had agreed to bring the new pets into the room after everything else was opened.

"What's this?" Willene asked Joan as she held up an orange she found in her stocking.

"An orange, child," the old woman said. "Haven't you seen one before?"

"No, ma'am. What does it do?"

Mrs. Cutter showed the children, who had each received an orange, how to peel it.

Sitting beside Anathea on the deep purple velvet settee, Raiford handed her a box and whispered, "Merry Christmas."

Carefully, Anathea opened the box wrapped in green paper to reveal a brightly-painted music box with a man holding a woman in a white dress. When he turned the key, Raiford watched the mechanical couple whirl in each other's arms and then looked over at Anathea. Tears trickled down her face. With his handkerchief, he wiped her eyes and said softly, "I guess this means you like it."

Unable to talk because of emotion filling her throat, Anathea simply nodded.

After the twirling dancers stopped, Anathea gave Raiford a gift wrapped in gold-colored paper. He opened it to find an elegant pen and ink bottle set with matching blotter. The blotter had a silver knob on the curving base which matched the knob of the ink bottle cap.

"It's beautiful," he said softly. Leaning over, Raiford kissed her on the cheek. "Thank you."

Anathea said, "This is the nicest Christmas I have had in a long time."

"Tell me about the last happy Christmas you had," Raiford said.

"It was when my mother was still alive and my brother was with us."

When she finished narrating that event, she asked about his last happy Christmas and Raiford told her about large gatherings of the Young family in Goshen, Indiana, concluding with the statement: "That was before the war."

Beatrice came to stand in front of the pair and asked, "Isn't it time to show Grandma and Grandpa their presents?"

"Indeed it is!" declared Raiford, standing up and taking the little girl's hand. "Come and carry one of the baskets."

In a minute, they were back. Raiford gave the basket with the puppy to Varney while Beatrice placed the smaller basket on Joan's lap. Everyone gathered around as Raiford said, "These are from all the children."

The old couple exclaimed with delight when the puppy leaped out of the opened basket and the kitten mewed and cowered in its basket. Joan picked up the trembling, black, orange, and white kitten and held it to her cheek, while the children chased the rambunctious puppy. The next twenty minutes were devoted to settling on names. Finally, the decision was made.

Joan said, "I am naming my little kitten Sheba."

Varney said, "Therefore, I will name my little dog Solomon."

Everyone agreed those were fine names.

* * *

In Louisville, at the Home for Friendless Girls, Adam sat back in the rocking chair and watched the orphans open their gifts. Barbara Dell handed him a cup of warm apple cider and said, "They have not had such a joyful Christmas for some time. You have been very generous with your gifts to them, Mr. Brannaman."

Adam said, "I keep thinking about my sister, and the Christmases she spent here. I wonder where she is now. I hope she's having a nice Christmas."

* * *

Historic Note: Savannah, Georgia, was occupied by Major-General William T. Sherman on the morning of Wednesday, December 21, after his army's long and arduous march to the sea. The next day, Thursday, December 22, the commander sent a telegram to President Abraham Lincoln in Washington City. The message read: "I beg to present you as a Christmas gift, the city of Savannah, with one hundred and fifty heavy guns and plenty of ammunition, and also about twenty-five thousand bales of cotton." Besides cotton and materials of war captured, 800 Confederate soldiers were taken prisoner. The news brought joy to the Northerners who finally caught sight of the end of the war. They were certain the soldiers would be home before next Christmas.

CHAPTER TWELVE

THE NEW YEAR OF 1865

Wherein Anathea and Raiford take a memorable sleigh ride;
Jennet and Eustus wed on New Year's Day;
Elmore and Tom commit robbery;
Edwin and Susan Lee visit Guelph.

The day after Christmas was Boxing Day, which English countries had been celebrating since the 1830s. Although a heavy nighttime snowfall blanketed the hills and houses of Guelph, holiday merrymakers were not deterred. The men had organized a sleigh ride into the country. Raiford, Mechum, and Ochran drove three sleighs, each pulled by two horses, around the side driveway from the carriage house to the front door. The drivers climbed down to help their passengers to board.

Anathea smiled at Raiford when he put his hands on her waist to lift her into the front seat. Freddie and Dalby clambered up to sit behind. In the second sleigh, Ochran lifted Willene and Beatrice to the back seat, and Fernancy and Maggie to sit beside him in front. Mechum, driving the last sleigh, had Delphina and their baby in front, while Dolly and Kirk, who had arrived for a late breakfast, rode in back. Zurelle stayed home with Mr. and Mrs. Cutter.

As the wind blew icy bits of snow at the sleigh riders, Anathea hid her face against Raiford's coat. He took one of his hands off the reins and put it over her shoulders to pull her closer. The sleighs traversed the low hills through the town and into the northern woods. Snow pellets would have clung to Raiford's beard but for the wool scarf which Joan had given him for Christmas.

Anathea thought about the coming week, when she would not have to go to the Cutter office or teach the children. Raiford had told her that she deserved a week-long holiday, and she had gladly accepted.

"Will you take the week off as well?" she had asked.

"Of course," had been his simple reply.

Elmore Pearson and Tom Donnelly saw the three sleighs head out of town with their jiggle bells rattling in the cold air. Turning to his friend, Elmore said, "Now would be a good time to carry out my plan."

"What plan?" asked Tom, following Elmore as he turned around and headed down the hill.

"Don't you remember? I plan to steal that money."

"But I heard they're keeping all their money in the bank now," Tom said.

"I think they just spread that rumor to keep the house from being robbed," said Elmore. "I bet the money Cutter got for selling those torpedoes is in the strong box. Pa said the old man keeps all his money in a metal box in his desk. I know what room his desk is in. Now's the time to find it, while the place is empty."

"Were all the people from the big house in the sleighs?" asked Tom.

"I think so. Three wagons full – that's about how many people live at the Cutters, ain't it?"

Tom shrugged his shoulders and mumbled, "I dunno."

"We can peek in the windows to see first to be sure," said Elmore.

But his plan of robbery was not to be accomplished that day, due to an accident caused by the snow. Unable to see the edge of the road because the snow made a smooth covering, Elmore stepped in the ditch and twisted his ankle.

"Ow! Damn! I turned my ankle! It hurts! Get over here! Give me some help," Elmore yelled at his friend.

"Lean on me." Tom gripped Elmore around the waist as the taller teenager pressed against Tom's muscular shoulder. "Should I pick you up? Can you walk?"

"You can't carry me in this snow," moaned Elmore. "Damn it! Hurts like the blazes!" He limped as his friend moved slowly along the road.

As the boys made their way back to the Pearson house, Tom said, "I guess this puts a stop to our robbery today, doesn't' it?"

"Only for today," said Elmore.

"We should do it some dark night anyway," said Tom.

"You're right. The neighbors might see us in the daytime."

* * *

While Emma Stewart scanned the *Guelph Gazette* advertisements for a house to rent, her husband held a long discussion with E. L. Pearson about what could be done to aid the Confederacy. Mr. Pearson had little interest in the clergyman's bizarre ideas about freeing prisoners or raiding border towns, because nothing seemed to offer him financial benefit. They were in the bar of the Albion Hotel on the northeast corner of Norfolk and MacDonell streets.

E. L. sipped his whiskey, set it on the shiny bar, and asked, "Who is this Raiford fellow anyway? You said you talked with him for hours on the train."

"He's a pleasant enough fellow," said Kensey. "He was a conscientious objector due to his father being a German Baptist, he said. He'd been doing hospital work, but had a furlough. That's why he was in one of those hotels the Confederate agents set fire to in New York. You heard about that, didn't you?"

"Everyone heard about that," grumbled Mr. Pearson. After a long moment's pause, he asked, "What about his last name?"

"Young? What about it?"

"Isn't that the same last name of the leader of those raiders that robbed St. Albans?"

Slamming his glass on the counter, Rev. Stewart said, "By Jove, you're right! Bennett Young is that fellow's name. Do you suppose they're related?"

Looking the other man in the eyes, E. L. said, "What if they were?"

"If they were, I'd say they're fighting on the same side – Bennett and Raiford."

"Whose side would that be?"

The minister answered, "Why, ours, of course."

"What should we do about it?"

* * *

Beatrice's scarf was caught on a branch as the sleigh passed close to a tree and she yelled, "Stop! Stop! My scarf!"

Ochran as well as the other two sleighs stopped.

"Let's give the horses a breather!" Raiford called, as he watched Ochran retrieve Beatrice's scarf.

The riders descended. Dolly had brought a basket of apples which she passed around. Everyone took one. Ochran cut slices of apple for Fernancy and Maggie.

Raiford said to Ochran, "Can you watch our children?" When his friend nodded consent, Raiford took Anathea's hand and led her in the opposite direction, up a slope dotted with snow-covered pine trees. Snow drifted down from the wind-blown branches. Raiford's steps slowed and stopped behind a clump of trees out of sight of the others.

"I must tell you something," he said. She waited. They were standing inches apart. "I was with my wife when she died and resolved never again to be in that situation, to see my wife die, and to endure that intense grief. I thought that meant never again to get married. But I..."

Anathea slid her hand out of her muff and touched her fingers to his lips to halt his sentence. "I understand perfectly. I, too, never want to marry again and have my husband divorce me."

Taking her hand in his gloved one, he said, "I cannot understand that – how any husband could divorce such a wonderful woman as you are."

Anathea did not know what to say. Raiford did not know what to do. Slowly, without forethought on the part of either one, they moved closer, His arms went around her. Her hands went up to his broad shoulders. He bent his head. She raised hers. They closed their eyes. Their lips touched. Their lips were cold. Raiford pressed more firmly. Her furry muff, dangling from a cord around her neck, was squashed between them.

He thought: *I want her – more than ever.*

She thought: *I never felt like this.*

Despite the cold, both of them were unusually warm. Raiford had almost forgotten what it was like to kiss a woman. It had been so long since he kissed Lenore. Since she died, he never kissed another woman until now. Having Anathea in his arms flooded him with memories of love.

Anathea had received no kisses from Monro when he was courting her, and only a few kisses during their marriage. No kiss had ever been like this. Her blood seemed to be rushing through her veins, heating her insides so the snow made no impression on her senses. Only Raiford's embrace and warm lips penetrated her mind. She raised her arms to encircle his neck.

"I don't want to love you," he murmured in her ear.

"Nor I you," she said against his cheek.

"It's too painful." His voice was muffled by her hair.

"That's true."

Pulling back slightly, she met his gaze. As his mouth came closer to hers, they both closed their eyes again. The second kiss was long and loving. All thoughts vanished from their brains. Only this moment, this embrace, this kiss had any meaning.

Suddenly, they were startled apart.

"We found you!" shouted Freddie as he raced toward them with Dalby at his heels.

"Indeed you did," said Raiford, smiling at the boy. He reached for Anathea's hand and headed down the slope to the sleighs.

* * *

On December 26, in Louisville, Kentucky, Adam Brannaman did not commemorate Boxing Day. However, it was a day of relaxation at the Home for Friendless Girls. All studies and housework were suspended. The girls were enjoying their new gifts – games, books, sewing kits, and other treasures. Adam and Barbara were in the kitchen.

Eating the last of the mincemeat pie, Adam said, "I've decided to hire a detective to find my sister."

"Aren't detectives awfully expensive?"

"You worry too much about money."

"It's a habit." Barbara smiled.

"I don't know any other way to find her."

"She said she would write to me when she was settled," Barbara reminded him.

"I know, but mail can be slow and sometimes misdirected. I don't want to delay if a detective can help me locate her sooner."

"Will you hire a New York detective?"

"Yes. That seems to be the sensible thing."

They reminisced about Anathea as they both recalled the absent sister and friend.

* * *

Before parting for the night, Raiford stopped Anathea at her bedroom door, took her hand, and led her to the dying flames of the front hallway fireplace. The fireplace at the back of the hallway was already cold. The hallway fires were not kept burning during the night.

"I need to say something to you before we retire." Raiford kept her hand in his. "We were interrupted behind the pine trees and left some things unsaid."

"What things?" she asked in a low voice.

"Despite my declaration that I do not want to love again and hold my dying wife in my arms, I do want us to remain friends," Raiford said.

Anathea nodded once and said softly, "I would like to remain friends as well."

"Good. I'm glad." Escorting her to her door, Raiford gave her hand a gentle squeeze and bade her good-night.

* * *

Having spent Christmas at St. George, Bermuda, Susan and Ned Lee packed for departure the next day for Halifax, Nova Scotia. Ned had purchased passage on the ship *Alpha*. Their rough and stormy trip took three days. Late in the day on December 30, they docked in Halifax, the capital of the province of Nova Scotia since 1749. They rented a room at Mrs. Scott's boardinghouse on Hollis Street, where they would stay until January 10, 1865.

* * *

Eustus Wright's marriage to Jennet Burleigh on New Year's Day was a joyous time for all the wedding party and guests. Therefore, when Anathea and Raiford found Lynnet crying in a storage room of the Methodist Church, they wanted to know why.

"Are the tears because you're so happy?" asked Anathea, offering her handkerchief for the damp one clutched in Lynnet's hand.

"Yes and no," said the bride's twin. "We always talked about having a double wedding – both of us married at the same time."

"Our plans are not always God's plans," said Raiford in a low voice.

"I know," said Lynnet, smiling up at him. "We even talked about marrying brothers, only... only Eustus has no brother." She wiped away a fresh flow of tears.

"Come back to the hall," said Anathea. "You are missed already. Jennet asked where you were."

"You don't want to spoil your sister's special day," added Raiford.

Lynnet dried her tears and returned to the reception.

* * *

New Years Day was special for the Stewart family because that was moving day. They departed from their crowded rooms at the Albion Hotel, to the relief of the management and guests, and occupied a rental house on Chapel Lane. Kensey left Emma to settle in while he went to visit E. L. Pearson, with whom he had spoken every day since he arrived in Guelph. However, when the former Cutter manager saw the minister through his front window, he said to Elmore, "Tell him I'm not home."

The teenager was delighted to lie to the visitor who went away discouraged.

Turning from the door, Elmore called to his father in the back bedroom: "He's got a new address! Wants to see you right away. It's urgent, he said."

"That man's whole life is urgent," grumbled E. L., coming out of the bedroom.

"I'm going to see Tom," Elmore said, as he dropped the note by the kitchen table and went out the back door.

At the Donnelly house, Tom escorted his friend into the cold basement where they could talk without being overheard by others.

"My ankle is healed now. I can run, so it's time we talked about robbing the Cutters," Elmore said.

"What's the plan?" asked Tom, pulling out his cigarette makings from behind a loose board.

"We need to take a crowbar or something to open the strong box."

"Why not just bring it with us and open it later?" Tom offered a cigarette paper to his friend who took it.

"It might be too heavy. I don't know its size."

"It fits in a desk drawer, you said."

"I wish I knew where the key was."

"We can look for it in the other drawers while we're there."

Tom and Elmore rolled cigarettes as they talked.

"We have to be quick," said Elmore.

"I know," said Tom. "Let's watch Kirk McCarrell through the window next time he takes the profits to the old man."

"Then we can see how big the box is." Elmore smiled.

"When?"

"Next Friday, the 6th."

"Then we'll rob the place on the following Friday."

"That's right," said Elmore.

"What time?"

"Midnight."

"Good time. Everyone will be asleep," said Tom.

* * *

But Tom Donnelly was wrong. Everyone was not asleep at midnight on Friday the 13th in the Cutter mansion.

In the small parlor, Anathea and Raiford had read until ten o'clock, an hour later than their usual time to blow out the candles and go to bed. The reason for reading an hour later was the exciting story of *The Coral Island* by R. M. Ballantyne, published in 1857. The novel told about three English boys, Ralph Rover, Jack Martin, and Peterkin Gay, who were shipwrecked on a deserted island. For the past few nights, the story had been peaceful, giving information about the island and the boys' adjustment to life there, until chapter 22. In that chapter, pirates arrived.

Anathea was reading chapter 23 about cannon fire. Just as she read: "the big brass gun sent a withering shower of grape point blank into the midst of the living mass, through which a wide lane was cut, while a yell, the like of which I could not have imagined," Raiford grabbed the book out of her hands and slammed it shut. He rose from his chair and paced.

Startled by his action, Anathea asked, "What's wrong?"

"It brings back memories," he growled.

"Of battles you've been in?"

"Yes."

She got up and stopped directly in front of him to halt his pacing. "Tell me about it."

"No. I want to forget." He tried to walk about her but she moved as he did, so they were two inches from touching.

"Can you forget?" she whispered.

Grabbing her by the shoulders, he held her at arms' length and declared, "I can try."

"But you're remembering it now with just a description of pirates in …"

"I know," he interrupted her. Putting his arm around her shoulders, he led her to the settee where they had been sitting at opposite ends. Now, he pulled her down to sit close to him. "I never want to think about or talk about battle. The scenes still plague me. The memories flood back at the most inopportune times."

"Like right now," she said softly.

He nodded agreement.

She said, "We've been enjoying the story."

He stopped her before she could say more. His eyes boring into hers, he said, "If I had known there would be battles on the island, I never would have suggested we read that book."

"I know what you mean," she said, meeting his gaze. "Memories come to me at the worst times, too. There is so much I want to forget but cannot."

"Forgive me," he said in a lowered tone. "I've ignored your feelings."

"No, you have not. I've never experienced war. My problems are nothing compared to yours.

"That isn't true," he said, searching for her hands, finding, and holding them.

"Maybe we should talk," she said hesitantly. "I mean, talk about memories that plague us"

Without agreeing to her suggestion, Raiford said, "I didn't think I would have to do that. The memories were fading until you came into my life."

"Me? What did I do to bring them back?"

"Don't you know?" He leaned toward her. "You're a desirable woman. I have not seen any woman who touches me as you do since Lenore."

"Oh," she whispered, not knowing what else to say.

Raiford continued, "I entered the army as a pacifist. I was told that I would not have to kill another human being, and the army kept its agreement with me. I was the one who broke the covenant."

"How?"

"I cannot tell you which battle it was. They all began to run together. It was some day in May of '63." His eyes focused on hers. "I was carrying stretchers from the front lines to the hospital tents in the rear. I saw my friends, men with whom I had enlisted, boys I went to school with, being shot, maimed, dying. I heard shouts for reinforcements. Suddenly, I don't know what came over me, but I picked up the rifle of a dead man and began firing at the enemy."

"You knew how to shoot a gun?"

"Oh, yes. I went hunting for food. I knew how to shoot and hit what I was aiming at." His gaze went from her face to the floor. They were silent for a long moment. Only the crackling fire made noise.

"You killed men?"

"Killed, wounded, mutilated. Yes. I did that. I went against all that I believed. A frenzy seemed to overcome me. I was like a madman. And when the battle ended, hours later, I was so exhausted that I could not move. I was frozen to the spot. I slept there. Someone woke me, I don't know how much longer after the shooting stopped. I was in a daze."

"Was that the last time you shot at the enemy?"

He shook his head. "No. The captain persuaded me to continue fighting. I was a good shot. They needed me. It didn't seem to matter anymore – whether I abhorred killing or not. I had already crossed the line."

"But the Lord provided a way … a way for you to leave the battlefield by coming here," she said hesitantly.

His gaze left the floor and returned to her face as he said, "Yes. The Lord did that for which I am grateful."

"I am grateful as well," she said, smiling briefly.

Raiford reached up and smoothed a stray wisp of hair behind her ear. "Now it's your turn. Tell me about the memories you wish would fade."

Hesitantly, Anathea said, "As an orphan, I dreamed of a happy home with a loving husband and five or six children. They would never be orphans. They would always have both parents living in the same house with them."

"That's why you love Beatrice and Freddie because they are orphans," he said, and she nodded assent.

"I thought my dream had come true when I married Monro, but he seemed to turn into a nightmare. He wasn't the same man as when we courted. Then, he was all kindness and gaiety. After the wedding, he was often depressed and unpleasant toward me."

"Did he ever strike you?" Raiford hated wife beaters.

"No. He would just walk away and ignore me. Sometimes, I wish he had hit me."

"No!" Raiford took hold of her upper arm and pulled her toward him. "Never wish for such a thing. Any man who hit a woman should be exiled from the human race. Forgive my interrupting you. Please go on."

"Well, my dream vanished suddenly when Monro handed me that bill of divorcement which you saw at the hotel."

"Was it totally unexpected?" He released her arm.

"Yes. I had no inkling that he intended such a thing." She glanced away at the dying fire and added, "We had visited the Shaker village on Sundays and seen their services, which he liked but I did not. I thought it was just a passing fancy of his, something new and different. I had no idea he intended to join them."

"So you did not confide in each other?"

"No. We never did. I confide in you more than I ever did him," Anathea said. "He never wanted to hear what I had to say, not the way you do. My feelings didn't matter to him."

"You know that your feelings matter a great deal to me."

"I do know that," she said in a barely audible voice.

Another silence followed as they both watched the fire go down.

"When did you decide to travel to New York?" he asked.

"I thought about it for weeks before I finally got up the courage to flee," she said. "I was so lonely. I felt so isolated. No one cared about me. It was just work, work, work, from dawn to dusk. I didn't believe anything of what Mother Ann Lee, the founder of the Shakers, taught. I was appalled by the weird dancing. My husband was lost to me."

Tears sprang to her eyes. She quickly brushed them away. As soon as she had done so, Raiford recaptured her hands and said, "I understand what that feels like. After Lenore died, I thought my life was over. My family hid the razors because they feared I would use one to kill myself." He smiled briefly and added, "So I grew a beard."

She reached up to touch his soft beard and asked, "Like this?"

"Much longer than this one."

Anathea could not refrain from asking: "You wouldn't have killed yourself, would you?

"No," he said in a low tone. "The Lord determines when we die. It is not for us to say."

They gazed into each other's eyes. The fire flickered out. Raiford stood up and pulled her to her feet. They went upstairs and parted at her bedroom door.

Two hours later, Elmore Pearson and Tom Donnelly entered the Cutter mansion by the office window. Anathea had slept restlessly. Now, she was wide awake and thirsty.

It must be from all our talking before going to bed, she thought. *My mouth is so dry. I need some water.*

As she moved through the downstairs hallway on her slippered feet, she heard noises in the library office.

Is Varney walking in his sleep? Joan will worry if she finds him gone.

Opening the office door, Anathea saw two shadowy figures illuminated by a low-burning flame in an oil lamp which Elmore carried. They had feed sacks with cutout eye holes over their heads.

"What are you doing?" she demanded.

Immediately, Elmore Pearson rushed toward her. Anathea screamed. She shoved against the teenager as he grabbed for her. She kept screaming. Tom Donnelly retreated toward the open window which they had entered. He dropped the strong box in the snow as he tumbled out the window.

Raiford heard Anathea screaming. He leaped from bed and raced toward the sound. Solomon the puppy bounded ahead of him down the stairs.

Anathea pounded Elmore's chest and back. The teenager clapped his hand over her mouth. She bit him and screamed.

"Come on!" Tom shouted, fumbling in the snow for the metal box.

Raiford entered. Elmore shoved Anathea toward him and bolted across the room. Yipping loudly, Solomon raced after the intruder. Raiford set Anathea to one side and chased the teenager across the room. Raiford tackled him, but Elmore pulled away. Raiford held onto his foot. Elmore's boot slipped off. Solomon barked around the boy's face. Anathea clutched her chest and tried to catch her breath. Sounds of people coming downstairs reached the library just as Elmore fell half-way out the window. Solomon leaped through the window after him. Tom had disappeared in the dark. Elmore fled but not before the puppy bit him on the bare ankle.

"Solomon! Come here! Come back here, boy!" Raiford called the dog as Elmore's dark silhouette disappeared at the tree line.

Raiford started to climb out the window. Anathea's quavering voice stopped him.

"Don't go!" she said.

He turned back. She ran to him. Raiford held her. Anathea wrapped her arms around him and hid her face against his nightshirt as the room filled with people.

"Call the dog," Raiford said to Mechum, who was the first to arrive.

"What happened?" asked Delphina, tying the sash of her robe.

"We had intruders," said Raiford.

"The pup isn't coming," said Mechum. "I'll go get him." He climbed out the window.

Ochran said, "Is she hurt?" He went to the wall sconce and lit a candle.

Bending his head, Raiford held Anathea slightly away and asked, "Are you harmed?"

She simply shook her head and touched her forehead against the soft flannel of his nightshirt.

"You're not going to faint, are you?"

"No," she murmured.

He pulled her into his arms again. She could feel his heart beating. She clung to him.

Mechum called: "Come on, boy! Here, Solomon!"

"Where's Solomon?" Freddie ran to the window.

"What's happened?" asked Joan.

"Thieves," answered Raiford.

"Who was it?" asked Varney

"Is that the thief's boot?" Zurelle picked up Elmore's boot.

"How many were there?"

"Did you recognize them?"

"Look what I found," said Mechum, tossing the strong box through the window. "The puppy is coming. Here he is. I got him." He climbed back in with the dog in his arms.

Raiford asked, "Is the lock intact?" He could not tell in the dim light.

"It's locked," said Ochran, as he picked up the metal container and set it on the desk.

Varney took the shivering puppy from Mechum, sat down, and talked softly to the animal. Freddie came to Varney's knee and nestled his face against the puppy's fur.

Joan went to the mantel, lifted a small Chinese urn, and said, "The key is here."

"That's a good hiding place, my dear," said her husband.

"It would be better if you didn't keep a strong box in the house," Raiford said to the older man. He smoothed Anathea's hair.

Beatrice asked, "Are you all right, Aunt Anathea?"

Anathea bend down to reassure the girl. "Yes. I am all right. I wasn't hurt, just frightened." She moved out of Raiford's arms and sat down in the nearest chair.

Raiford, with his eyes on Anathea, said, "You used a woman's best weapon." Moving close to the chair, he put his hand on Anathea's shoulder.

"What's that?" asked Freddie.

"Screaming," said Beatrice. "Didn't you hear her?"

"I heard her," the little boy said. "That's why I got up."

Varney said, "You are right, Mayfield. If the box was not in the house, this would not have happened. I am sorry you were harmed, young lady." He made eye contact with Anathea who thanked him.

"Why were you down here?" asked Delphina.

"To get a drink." Anathea replied.

"If a body is not safe to get a drink in this house," said Joan, "I'd say it's time to put all our money in the bank."

"I agree, my dear," said Varney.

Zurelle said, "Come, children, back to bed. It's too cold for you. Upstairs."

"I'm taking Solomon to bed with us," said Varney, filing out of the room.

Picking up the boot Raiford had pulled off, Mechum asked, "Do you think we can find the culprit who left this behind?"

"Just as the prince found Cinderella after she lost her glass slipper," said Raiford.

* * *

202

Arriving home, Elmore Pearson found that his icy stocking was frozen to his foot. When he was finally able to pull off the sock, he saw teeth marks and blood.

"Damn dog," he mumbled. Sitting as close to the front room dying fire as he dared, he wondered where Tom was. His friend had disappeared so Elmore had hobbled home alone.

"Same foot I twisted. Why couldn't it be the other one?" He stood up and hopped into his bedroom. After putting on a dry pair of socks, he crawled into his narrow bed and quickly fell into an exhausted sleep.

In the morning, E. L. found one boot on the cold hearth and a bloody stocking.

He woke Elmore, held the reddish sock and boot in front of his face, and demanded: "Elmore! What's this?"

The teenager opened his eyes, focused on the items in his vision, and mumbled: "Pa, I'm in trouble."

* * *

Saturday morning, Emma stirred water into porridge as Kensey added wood to the cook stove. She asked, "Will you get into trouble for these schemes you are planning?"

"Not in Canada," the minister said. "We're out of reach of the Union authorities here."

"But I've heard they have detectives and spies in Canada, just waiting to catch anyone aiding the Confederates."

"Don't worry, sweet one. I'm just doing the Lord's work, helping his poor innocent creatures escape from that horrible prison on Johnson's Island. I hope to talk with Mr. Pearson today. I need his help because he knows the area."

Dale, carrying baby Mary, came into the kitchen and said, "She's awake and hungry."

* * *

Raiford and Mechum went to see Constable Clark and report the home invasion. Putting the intruder's boot on the lawman's desk, Raiford said, "I suggest we alert stores that sell boots and ask them to watch for our thief."

"Good plan," agreed Milo. "However, I'm lacking in manpower at the present. Would you two be willing to speak to the storekeepers?"

When both men agreed, Milo Clark opened his desk drawer and pulled out two badges, which he handed to them, saying, "Pin these on as bon-a-fide lawmen. Raise your hands and I'll administer the oath."

Wearing the badges on the outside of the heavy coats, Mechum and Raiford each took one side of MacDonell Street, where all the stores were, and asked the owners and clerks to watch for someone buying a new pair of boots. The salespeople were all agreeable to help find the intruders. Needless to say, news of the attempted robbery at the Cutter house spread quickly.

When Raiford came to Harmon Utley's General Mercantile, the friendly man invited him into his office in the back and said, "I am glad you stopped by. There's a matter I need to discuss with you."

Harmon closed the door as Raiford sat down. "What is it?"

"I've heard a rumor about a possible prison break from Johnson's Island," the older man said.

Raiford knew that he would need to wire Fides. Therefore, before making the last rounds of the stores, Raiford went to the telegraph office and sent a message to Toronto.

* * *

Historic Note: On October 3, 1861, orders were issued to locate a federal prison on the islands in Lake Erie, and construction began the next month on Johnson's Island, which was selected because of its location one mile from the mainland and 2 ½ miles from Sandusky, Ohio. Johnson's Island was the southernmost of Lake Erie's islands and therefore the greatest distance from Canada West. Its 300 acres were heavily wooded, thus providing building materials and firewood. Federal officials expected to house 1,000 men there. In June 1862, Johnson's Island was designated as the prison for all Confederate officers. However, there were still enlisted men and even political prisoners confined there. By 1864, more than 100 structures dotted the island, from officers' quarters, soldiers' barracks, pest houses for contagious diseases, bakery, school, stables, to prisoners' barracks, dining hall, wash house, and condemned prisoners' cells. And, by January 1865, like all other military prisons, Johnson's Island had become overcrowded and filthy.

CHAPTER THIRTEEN

JOHNSON'S ISLAND

*Wherein Raiford and Fides become prisoners at
Johnson's Island; E.L. and Elmore Pearson leave town;
Adam and Anathea are reunited; and
General Lee and Rev. Stewart collude.*

When Fides received Raiford's telegram, he immediately made arrangements for departure on the following Monday, January 16. Using the alias William Bailey, he bought his ticket and slept most of the way. The night before had been sleepless. When he exited the Guelph Depot, he hired John Huggins to take him to the Cutter Foundry. Mr. Huggins entertained the newcomer with the exciting tale of a break-in by the Bootless Thief at the Cutter mansion.

"Are you doing business with Mr. Cutter?" asked the cab driver.

"That's right," Fides lied.

Raiford was consulting with Kirk and Ochran about the stove Zurelle had designed. Ochran had been helping part-time at the foundry since the stove went into production. He worked well with the other men who liked him. When Fides entered the small office building, Raiford nearly spilled his coffee. He was shocked to see his fellow spy.

Setting his cup on the table, Raiford said, "How may I help you?"

"I have urgent business." Fides offered his hand to first Ochran and then Kirk as he introduced himself: "William Bailey from Montreal. I should have wired but there wasn't time."

"We can confide in these men," Raiford said, shaking hands with the newcomer. "They both know the business in which we are engaged."

Fides nodded as he removed his hat and dusted off the snow. When offered a chair, he refused. Quickly, Fides revealed his mission. Raiford agreed with the strategy. Time was of the essence. Raiford gave instructions. The train whistle blew to announce its imminent departure.

"Ochran, you are to oversee the stove. Finish as many as you can. Don't overtax the men. Kirk, ask Mechum to take my place here."

"What should we tell Miss Anathea?" Ochran asked.

Raiford, donning his heavy coat, said, "Don't tell her anything."

"Won't you need a bag?" asked Kirk.

"Not where we're going," said Fides as he and Raiford stepped outdoors.

* * *

Fides and Raiford departed on the train for Detroit. As the cars left the station, Raiford wondered: *Did I tell Ochran the right thing? She can be trusted. Why did I tell him to keep my mission secret? Will she worry less if she doesn't know where I'm going? Is this the kind of relationship I want with her, keeping important information from her? What will she think when she knows I am gone?*

Fides was talking about Colonel Bennett Hill, Union commander in Detroit, so Raiford shook his thoughts of Anathea out of his mind and focused on his companion's softly-spoken words.

* * *

Anathea waited for Raiford to come home for the noon meal and to escort her back to the foundry, but Kirk and Ochran both came instead.

"Raiford was called away," said Kirk.

A cold chill ran down Anathea's back. "Called away to where?" she asked.

"We cannot say," Ochran replied.

Stepping closer to the two men in the front hallway, she asked, "Is it dangerous?"

"You must not worry," said Ochran.

Kirk said, "Raiford can take care of himself. He's with a friend."

* * *

By Wednesday, the strain of not knowing where Raiford was or what he was doing began to show on Anathea. Delphina recognized the symptoms and attempted to ease her new friend's anguish.

"I know what you are feeling," Delphina said, as the two women gave baby Mechum a bath in a tub on the kitchen table.

"About what?" said Anathea, who held the baby's back and head while his mother rubbed soap on his little body.

"Missing the man you love," said the young mother. "I was without Mechum for months that seemed like years. I especially missed him when this little man was born. I did so want his father to be there."

"Why do you call him the man I love?"

"It's apparent to everyone who sees you and Raiford together."

"It is?" Anathea was truly surprised.

"When you enter a room, you search for each other until your eyes meet," said Delphina. "It's the same with Mechum and me. My life is incomplete without him, the way yours is without Raiford."

"But neither of us wants to get married again." Instantly, Anathea realized she had said more than she intended.

"Again?" Delphina repeated.

"His wife died," Anathea said.

"You said neither of us."

"I misspoke." Anathea hesitated. *Should I tell her? No, I can't.* Slowly, she said, "That's all, just his wife died. He held her in his arms, he told me. He never wants to experience that again."

"How sad." Delphina reached for the towel and wrapped it around the baby as Anathea held him steady.

"I cannot imagine what that would have been like," said Anathea. *Since I stopped loving Monro, his death would not have saddened me anymore than a stranger's death.*

Lifting her chubby baby against her chest, Delphina carried him to the table where a blanket and his clothes awaited.

* * *

Despite how busy Raiford and Fides were as they made preparations to enter the Confederate prison, Raiford missed Anathea every minute. He wrote to her before they left Detroit for Port Clinton. He told her about the book he was reading entitled <u>The Private Memoirs and Confessions of a Justified Sinner</u> by James Hogg. Raiford had bought it at a crowded bookshop in Detroit. He thought the title sounded interesting and that it would be about a new Christian's walk with the Lord. However, he was surprised by the story. In his letter, he wrote:

Mr. Hogg's story is different than anything I've ever read and not at all what I expected. I thought it would be theological but instead it's a mystery.

Raiford dipped his pen into the ink bottle on the desk in his hotel room and recalled the beautiful ink pen set Anathea had given him for Christmas.

The story is about the son of a radical Calvinist minister in Scotland who went off on a crime spree and killed his brother and mother, while under the evil influence of a companion. The mystery is whether the evil companion really existed or was he just a part of the man's dark side.

Raiford lifted his pen, sat back, and pondered briefly before dipping the metal tip in ink and continuing.

I wonder if all people have a dark side capable of killing. Was it my dark side that came out when I was in those battles, day after day, in May of '63? Is that why I took up the gun of a dead friend and began shooting?

Dipping his pen for more ink, Raiford wrote: *Perhaps that dark side is what possessed your husband to divorce you. Certainly, it could not have been for spiritual betterment as he professed. He appears to me to be a religious fanatic like the man in Hogg's book.*

He turned his mind to the scene she had described to him, of her husband at the gate of the Shaker village handing her a bill of divorcement and Anathea fainting for the first time. He wrote: *You are such a beautiful person both inside and out. There is no earthly reason for a man to divorce you. I never would.*

Surprised by those last three words he had just written, Raiford stared at the paper and thought: *Dare I post this letter? What should I write next? I must explain that statement.*

He wrote: *I know what we said, on Boxing Day behind the pine trees, that neither of us wanted to marry again. I am beginning to change my mind on that subject. I miss you very much. I am eager for this mission to be over so I can return to you. I hope you will be open to the words I will speak. I remain respectfully yours, Raiford.*

He set the pen aside, replaced the cap on the ink bottle, and stood up from the desk.

I'll read it over in the morning and decide if I should send it, Raiford thought as he left the desk and went to the big bed, where Fides was already sound asleep.

* * *

But the next morning, Raiford slept later than Fides who went to breakfast alone, taking his own and Raiford's letters with him. He posted them before Raiford awoke. When Raiford learned that the decision to mail or not to mail the letter to Anathea was out of his hands, he dismissed the mistake from his mind, thinking: *The Lord must want Anathea to have that letter, else it would not have been mailed. Perhaps I lacked the courage to send it, so the Lord had to intervene, using Fides to accomplish his will.*

After thorough instructions at the army headquarters in Detroit, Raiford, using the name Seth Simons, and Fides, using another alias, Reddick Wadley, traveled to Sandusky on Thursday, January 19. They met with federal officials who handcuffed them and locked chains around their ankles before taking them to the dock. There, they were turned over to two guards who helped them into a row boat. The guards had no idea these were federal spies. Anyone watching the boat depart would see newly-captured Confederate officers in well-worn uniforms with their guards going to the island prison – not an unusual sight in Sandusky.

"I hope you men hear some good news for us," said the guard who limped slightly as he moved down the dock to tie up the boat. "You know us Invalid Corps cannot do much tough fighting anymore. We'd sure hate to have a prison break."

"We'll do our best for you, sir," said Fides.

The second guard, who would have been handsome if not for the ugly red scar on his cheek, said: "Have you heard what happened to Bowles and Wheeler last month, on the 13th of December?" He offered a hand to Fides climbing out of the tipping boat.

"What?" asked Raiford, eyeing the fourteen foot high stockade just twenty yards from the shore line.

"They escaped on scaling ladders," he answered.

"Only Wheeler escaped," the older guard corrected. "Bowles was shot dead on the ladder."

"What happened to Lieutenant Wheeler?" asked Fides.

"He made it to the peninsula, but some farmers heard the shots from the island, captured Wheeler, and returned him to the prison." He looked up at the sentinels and motioned for them to open the gate.

"Got a reward for it," added the younger man as the wooden gate swung wide.

As soon as Raiford entered the prison, he smelled an offensive odor. "What is that?" He covered his nose.

The older guard said, "Mr. Johnson used to haul away the garbage to slop his hogs, but he sold them all, so now he doesn't come anymore."

The younger guard added, "And the latrines overflow sometimes."

The friendly guards removed their chains and released Raiford and Fides to a federal officer who knew nothing of their real mission.

Taking the papers which the older guard handed him, the officer said, "Come with me, men. I think we can find you a bunk. It's getting rather crowded, but we put a couple of men in the hospital so you can take their places."

* * *

The New York City detective Adam Brannaman had hired reported reaching a dead end. The man wired that no Anathea Brannaman or Anathea Emmert was in the morgue. That information eased her brother's mind. The detective's telegram stated that she was not registered at any hotel. In truth, the man had not inquired at a single hotel. He was earning easy money.

Adam went for a long walk. He needed to think. *Should I go to New York myself? What could I do that this man could not? Should I notify the police there? Would they investigate a missing person or would there have to be a crime?*

Passing the post office, he wondered to whom he should write for help. He had no idea that a letter from his sister in this building waited to be sorted and delivered to the Home for Friendless Girls.

* * *

Raiford was housed in the West House, while Fides went to another building. The two federal spies knew they would not likely be housed together, which benefited them. Separate quarters would expand their knowledge base. If a prison break was being planned, it might not be camp-wide but only confined to one building. Nevertheless, Raiford and Fides were able to confide their findings when they were outdoors.

The men in the West House were reluctant to befriend Raiford, knowing that spies were often placed among them. Therefore, Raiford was cautious, reading his book by Hogg, and keeping to himself. They had asked him the usual questions about his unit and where he was captured. However, it was not until the fourth day when a tall, slender man asked, "What school did you attend?" that Raiford finally got some information he was seeking.

"My partner, Reddick Wadley, and I both went to the Virginia Military Institute."

Immediately, two fellow VMI men came close and were eager to talk. Thankfully, Raiford had studied the information in Colonel Hill's office well and could respond without mishap. One prisoner slapped Raiford on the back. Another man pulled up a keg and sat close.

After reminiscing about the military college on the hills overlooking Lexington, Raiford said, "Aren't you men sick of this place?"

The VMI men nodded agreement.

"This is no place for men of our training," Raiford continued. "Can't we break out of here?"

"You heard about the last ones who tried?"

"Yes," said Raiford. "The guards who rowed us over told us about Wheeler and another man."

"They shot J. B. on the ladder."

"But Lieutenant Wheeler made it to the mainland."

"They captured him, though. He's in a solitary cell now."

Raiford asked, "Isn't there a better way out of here?"

"Just like a new man – already thinking about escape," said a man nearby. He was not a VMI graduate.

"First thing, we have to get out of the enclosure. Ladders don't work. You're too visible."

"We should tear down the boards instead of going over them."

"Takes time and requires tools."

"Fire might accomplish that," suggested Raiford. "You heard about the New York City hotel fires."

"We heard they didn't do much damage."

"But they scared the New Yorkers," said Raiford. "Citizens along the border with Canada became fearful of an invasion."

"I wish some of those folks would invade down here," said a man from a nearby bunk.

Raiford asked, "What about bribing guards?"

The officials in Detroit had stressed the importance of finding out about untrustworthy guards.

"No, sir. That's been tried."

"There's no hope there," said a man roasting a small chunk of meat on a stick over the fire.

As Raiford listened to the discussion about possible escape plans, he learned that nothing was in the works. They knew what had been tried and what had failed.

"Our only hope is outside help," said one of the VMI men.

"Jacob Thompson could help us if he would."

"The old Mississippian is rolling in money."

The man with the roasted meat passed his stick around to the others. The men tore off a piece of meat and ate it. Raiford did the same.

"That farmer who turned in Wheeler got a hundred dollars. These Sanduskians are money hungry."

"Thompson could feed them with some of his stash."

Raiford swallowed and said, "That was good. What was it?"

"Wharf rats. We're overrun with them."

"They're fat, gentle, and easy to kill."

"Tasty, too," said the man with the roasting stick.

Raiford felt his stomach churn.

* * *

E. L. Pearson heard from his neighbor, Oscar Bolton, about the manhunt for two thieves who attempted to steal the strong box from the Cutter home office.

"Now, the Constable and his men, newly-hired men, are suspecting anyone who buys a new pair of boots," said Oscar, who had come to E. L. to borrow his axe.

"Why's that?"

"Seems like one of the robbers lost a boot when he escaped out the window."

Immediately, E. L. thought of his son. Elmore had told him he was in trouble, but not the nature of the trouble. He had said his foot had been caught in a bear trap, which E. L. had doubted because the injury was too minor. Nevertheless, the teenager refused to reveal additional information. Now, the former Cutter manager knew the truth.

"Have they got any suspects?" E. L. asked.

"Not that I know of," said Oscar. "Thanks for the axe. As soon as I get my handle fixed, I won't be needing yours anymore."

As the little man walked away, E. L. thought: *It's a good thing I didn't go right out and buy him another pair of boots. With him laid up, he didn't need them. Now, we better get out of Guelph.*

* * *

Wednesday, January 25, Adam Brannaman was nearing the end of his long journey from California to see his sister. On the train as it crossed the flat land heading north from Hamilton, he recalled Barbara Dell's excitement when she rushed into the front room with Anathea's letter. The orphanage teacher was too out of breath to talk, so handed the letter to Adam. He had quickly recognized his sister's handwriting. When he had seen the address on the envelope, he had hugged Barbara. They both laughed. Now, he was only a short distance away from the town on the envelope. Soon, he would see Anathea again.

* * *

Anathea was talking to Jennet and Lynnet in the small parlor, where they were sharing a pot of tea. It was six days since Raiford left unexpectedly with his mysterious friend. Six days of wondering, praying, and missing him..

"It was so funny," said Jennet. "You wouldn't believe those verses could be so close."

"Tell me again," said her sister. "I want to look them up." She set down her tea cup and went to the open Bible on the cherry wood bookstand.

"Eustus intended to write First John four eighteen," said Jennet.

"Wait, wait, until I find it," said Lynnet, who, when she came to that verse in the New Testament, read "There is no fear in love; but perfect love casteth out fear."

"Yes, that's it," said Jennet.

"But how did you make the mistake of reading the wrong verse?" asked Anathea.

"He smudged the Roman number one before the word John, so I thought it was the Gospel of John," said the newlywed.

"Wait now. Let me find that verse." Lynnet flipped pages back until she came to John 4:18 and read: "For thou hast had five husbands; and he whom thou now hast is not thy husband."

The three young women laughed in glee.

Amid her laughter, Lynnet said, "Did you think he was trying to tell you something – that he had found out you'd been married five times before and were now a bigamist."

"Can a woman be a bigamist?" asked Anathea. "I thought that was just Mormon men."

Jennet said, "I don't know but it was so funny. We laughed and laughed about it. I told him to be more careful when he leaves me little love notes."

Zurelle came into the parlor and announced, "There's a young man just arrived. He's waiting in the hall. He asked for you, Anathea."

* * *

Brigadier General Edwin Lee, having met with Jacob Thompson in Toronto in December, took his wife 38 miles west to Hamilton to visit his father's younger brother, Cassius F. Lee. Uncle Cassius and his family had been in Canada since July 1863. They escaped to the north after Cassius had been arrested three times for being a spy. Now, the former resident of Alexandria, Virginia, served the Confederacy by helping soldiers who escaped from northern prisons to get home. He also relayed messages, which was an important function where communication was difficult.

Upon arrival at his uncle's house, Ned was surprised and delighted to find a house guest already there – his first cousin, Daniel Bedinger Lucas. The two young men had been boyhood companions and studied law together at Lexington, Virginia, under the tutelage of Judge John W. Brockenbrough. After Susan and Edwin were settled, Dan called his friend into the small office at the back of the house.

"I need your assistance with something," Dan said, holding out a chair next to the desk. When Ned sat down, Dan continued. "I've been trying to compose a letter to General Dix."

"U.S. Major General John A. Dix in New York?" Ned sat down at the same time as Dan.

"That's right."

"Why are you writing to a Union general?"

Dan handed him several papers. There were deletions and insertions. Some sections were crossed off entirely.

"I'm offering to serve as attorney for our friend John Yates Beall. You've heard, haven't you, that he will soon be on trial for irregular warfare."

Ned nodded as he scanned the sheets of paper.

Dan continued. "I am requesting safe passage to New York to appear as defense counsel."

Ned placed the scribbled papers on the desk, reached for a pen, dipped it in the ink bottle, and began writing.

When General Dix received Dan's letter, co-authored by Edwin Gray Lee, he ignored the request.

* * *

Entering the cold hallway to greet the man Zurelle had announced, Anathea was still smiling about the mistaken Bible verse the new husband gave to his wife. Her smile widened when she heard the word, "Sister."

Anathea ran into her brother's outstretched arms. They hugged happily. Jennet and Lynnet came out of the parlor to see who it was.

Coming from the dining room, Joan asked, "Who is this, Anathea?"

"My brother! Adam Brannaman!" Her joy was obvious.

Mechum was the first to shake Adam's hand, followed by the others. After introductions, Zurelle insisted he eat. Sitting at the head of the long dining room table, Adam listened to Anathea's story with additional information interjected by others. When he finished his meal, he related his adventure of coming from California to be reunited with his sister. He told about the problems at the orphanage, about the happy Christmas the girls had, and about how he hoped to do more for Miss Dell and her girls. He did not mention Anathea's marriage. His focus was on relating his activities.

"After discovering that you were no longer at the orphanage," he said, "I went to the Shaker village."

"Stop!" Anathea held up her hands.

"What?" His expression changed as he recognized the sound of alarm in his sister's voice.

"They don't know." She spoke in an undertone and lowered her hands to clutch them in her lap.

Adam understood immediately what she meant. The people surrounding the long dining room table, the people among whom his sister had been living, did not know she was married and then divorced.

"What don't we know?" asked Lynnet.

"Do you have a dark secret?" asked Jennet.

Sitting beside Anathea, Joan put her hand on Anathea's arm, and said, "There's no reason for secrets among people who love you."

"Raiford knows, doesn't he?" asked Delphina.

"Why would you say that?" Anathea looked across the big table.

"Who is Raiford?" asked Adam.

"The man she loves and who loves her," said Jennet.

"They're very close," said Joan, nodding.

Adam smiled at his sister and said, "Does Raiford know?"

Anathea nodded and whispered, "Yes."

"Where is he?"

"Away on business."

"Should I wait for this part of the story until he returns?"

Varney said, "I think you should. I'm sure he would want to hear it, too."

So the topic of conversation changed. They talked about Guelph, the recent events and people.

Later, when the twins were walking home, Jennet said, "What is it, do you suppose, that her brother has to say about the Shaker village and why he went there?"

"What?" Lynnet asked.

"You're daydreaming," said Jennet. "Tell me your thoughts."

"Isn't Adam Brannaman the handsomest man you've ever seen?"

"No." Jennet laughed. "Eustus Wright is the handsomest man I have ever seen."

The sisters laughed together.

* * *

That evening, after the others were asleep, Anathea and Adam sat in the small parlor and talked.

"Tell me about Raiford," said Adam. "Mr. Cutter says he works at the foundry. What business takes him out of town in the middle of winter?"

"He can tell you when he returns," said Anathea. "I don't think it concerns the foundry business."

"He's not a Confederate, is he?"

"No. Certainly not."

What's his last name?"

"Young."

"Is he related to Bennett Young who robbed those banks in St. Albans, Vermont?"

"No, he isn't," said Anathea, pulling her knit shawl closer around her shoulders. "The family name was Jung, but his father, a German Mennonite, changed it to the more English name of Young when he married Raiford's mother."

"Mennonites are pacifists," said Adam. "So I guess Raiford never enlisted."

"He did," said Anathea. "He enlisted as a conscientious objector, but in May, 1863, during a series of battles, he took up a gun."

"He went against his religion?"

"I guess you would say that." She watched her brother add a log to the fire and poke up the ashes. "The decision to shoot the enemy was spur-of-the-moment, he told me. He has talked with me about his dilemma of facing his church community when he returns to Goshen, Indiana."

Returning to his seat, Adam said, "I served in a militia unit in California for a short time but disliked the captain, so I paid for a substitute."

"I am glad you did. Raiford has told me a little about the horrible experience of war." Brushing the thought from her mind, she added: "I can't wait for Raiford to get home so you can meet him. I know you will like him."

"I know you like him." Adam smiled broadly. His eyes sparkled in the firelight. "Now, if you don't mind, may we change the subject for a few minutes?"

"To what?"

"Tell me about that prettier twin, the one named Lynnet. Is she married?"

* * *

Raiford arrived home exactly three weeks after he left, on Monday, February 6. He and Fides rode the train together until they reached Hamilton, where they parted, Fides to go west to Toronto and Raiford north to Guelph. The *Hamilton Dispatch* newsboy called out the headlines to the people in the crowded station: "General Robert Edward Lee now general-in-chief of all Confederate armies! Get your papers here!"

After buying a newspaper, Fides shook Raiford's hand and said, "You did well, Olive Branch."

Raiford, too, bought a *Dispatch* and replied, "I think it was a worthwhile mission." When the newsboy had moved on, he added, "With the information we provided, lives can be saved. No one else will be shot while trying to escape."

"We can hope for that," said his friend.

"And this latest news tells us they're making a final effort." He nodded at the front-page story.

The men parted. Raiford read the paper during the remainder of his train trip. When he arrived in Guelph, he felt as though he had come home. Guelph was not Goshen with its flat land and familiar houses, but this hilly Canadian town was becoming familiar. He knew many of the residents. He knew who owned the businesses and who worked in them. As he rode Mr. Huggins' sleigh to the Cutter house, Raiford thought about making this his home.

I would not have to stand in front of my church and explain how I took up a gun and why. The Baptists have no such prohibition about fighting. Two men from First Baptist Church crossed the border to fight for the United States. They are honored in their church.

When Raiford entered the Cutter mansion, Anathea, having heard his voice, ran down the stairs. A smile illuminated her face. As soon as Raiford saw her, a memory flashed in his mind. He recalled Lenore running into his arms when he entered the house. In the same way his former wife had done, Anathea flung her arms around his neck and, standing on tip toes, pressed her cheek against his. He embraced her.

"Oh, Raiford! I have the most wonderful news! I'm so glad you're home! I want you to meet someone!"

Adam, hearing his sister's voice, came out of the dining room where he was playing checkers with Varney. When Raiford saw the handsome stranger, one thought popped into his mind.

Her husband.

Anathea motioned in Adam's direction and said, "This is my brother, Adam Brannaman."

With instant relief, Raiford laughed. He kept one arm around Anathea's waist and stuck out his hand, which Adam shook heartily.

"Glad to meet you at last," said Adam.

"I am very happy to meet you," Raiford said.

Both men smiled broadly.

"Sis has told me many things about you, but I still have a lot of questions."

"Sis," Raiford repeated as he looked down at the woman by his side. "You have your family now. You're not an orphan." She rested her head against his chest, closed her eyes briefly, and felt a wave of peace surround her.

Raiford tried to dispel the memory of Lenore from his mind. *This is Anathea not Lenore. Her brother is here. That's why she's happy. But she is also happy to see me, just like Lenore always was.*

Zurelle entered the hall, greeted Raiford, and asked, "Are you hungry?"

"I could eat," he said. "Where are the children?"

"Ochran and Mechum took them sledding on Lister Hill," said Joan, coming to Raiford's other side and receiving a hug.

In the dining room, Adam narrated his ordeal of trying to locate his sister as the other household members gathered at the big table and listened. Raiford ate the stew Zurelle served him. Anathea sat beside him. Delphina attempted to soothe baby Mechum who was fussing. When Adam came to the point in the story about the visit to the Shaker village, he asked, "May I tell this part now, Sis?"

"Yes. You might as well." Anathea lowered her head and stared at her lap. Raiford set his fork down, lifted her chin, and said, "There is nothing to hide."

Her brother said, "I think she's lucky to be rid of him."

"Who?" asked Delphina, swaying little Mechum.

"Her former husband," said Adam. "He divorced her when he joined that strange sect, the Shakers."

Just then, the front door opened and six children rushed in, followed by Ochran and Mechum. Raiford hugged Freddie, Beatrice, the Wyatt children, and shy Maggie. The men shook hands with Raiford before removing their coats. Little Mechum began crying. Delphina excused herself to go upstairs and nurse the baby.

Dalby announced, "We saw gray wolves."

Willene said, "They didn't get us."

"Where did you see wolves?" Raiford asked.

"Saw one up close, drinking water at the creek," Ochran said. "Others were up the hill."

"They looked skinny," said Mechum.

"They eat children," said Maggie.

Chuckling, Varney picked up the girl, set her on his lap, and said, "They only eat bad children so they won't eat you."

Joan swatted her husband's arm and said, "Don't tell her that. It isn't true, sweetie. He's teasing you. Wolves don't ever eat children, good or bad."

Mechum asked, "Was your business trip successful?"

"We think so," Raiford replied.

"That's good," Mechum said as he made eye contact with Raiford.

As Zurelle cleared away dishes, the children and men went to hang up their coats. Joan and Varney went arm-in-arm into the front parlor. Raiford, taking Anathea's hand to follow the older couple, leaned down and whispered, "Did you get my letter?"

Immediately, Anathea blushed.

* * *

The same day Raiford arrived home from his stay at Johnson's Island, Sue and Ned Lee began making plans to visit Rev. Kensey Stewart whose first wife was Hannah Lee, sister of Ned's father Edmund.

* * *

At the same time, E. L. Pearson and his son Elmore were traveling in the opposite direction, going east. E. L., to protect his son from possible arrest and to protect himself as well, had pulled up stakes in Guelph with no regrets except one. Having heard the constable was investigating anyone who bought a pair of boots, E. L. gave his son his old pair. They left unwanted items in their rented house, including a single boot. Departing on the night train going east, they each carried one bag. Mr. Pearson regretted that he did not get as much money from the Cutter business as he had hoped.

* * *

Adam joined Raiford and Anathea near the fireplace in the front of the upstairs hallway. The smaller fireplace in the back of the hall was already out. The three of them talked for an hour before Adam excused himself at ten o'clock. Anathea stood up intending to go to her room but Raiford stopped her with his hand on her arm.

"May we talk alone?" he asked.

She nodded. Adam smiled, kissed his sister on the cheek, and went to his room.

Raiford directed her to the settee which she had been sharing with her brother. As they sat side by side, he released her arm and asked, "What did you think when you read my letter?"

"I thought … "She took a deep breath. "I was happy … I cried... I wished you were here."

"I'm here now. Tell me why you cried."

"Because I missed you so much. I wanted to hear the words from your mouth, not just in a letter."

"I missed you as well. That's why I wrote as I did."

"Will you tell me now where you were and what you did?"

Raiford told her briefly about his mission with Fides to learn of any plans for a possible prison break from Johnson's Island.

"Were the Confederates making plans to escape?" she asked.

"Fortunately, nothing workable." He gazed at his hands. "They have developed a command structure as you would expect from soldiers. Most of them are officers. They have various ideas, but none of them could succeed without outside help."

"I've heard that many Northerners are in sympathy with them."

"Perhaps so, but not enough to jeopardize their own security." He returned his eyes to her face.

"What do you mean?"

"Anyone who aids prisoners to escape can be arrested."

"Wouldn't the winter weather be a deterrent?"

"Precisely," said Raiford. "Although the lake is frozen, enabling them to walk across to Canada, they would freeze to death before reaching shore. Their clothing is inadequate for being outside very long in this weather. They know that help from residents is essential. The authorities don't believe there are enough Southern sympathizers to provide for two thousand men on the run."

"What a shame," she said softly, but quickly added: "I mean it's a shame those men have to be locked away from their families and friends."

"I agree, since I was locked away with them albeit for a short time. I knew when I would be released. Those men don't."

Raiford took her hand in his, held their joined hands on his knee, and said, "Can we change the subject to my letter." She nodded. "I wrote during a lonely time. I'm not certain that I should have or that I expressed myself well."

Anathea said, "I understood that you changed your mind about marriage."

"That's what I thought at the time," he said as he held their hands perfectly still. "I never again want to embrace my wife as her life slips away." The memory of Lenore's death flashed across his mind. Anathea saw his unshed tears reflect the firelight.

With her free hand, she reached over to touch his soft beard on his cheek. "Then, do you mean, as you said before, that you just want us to be friends."

"Yes, I think that's what I mean." He took her hand away from his face and held it, turned to face her, and said, "The pain is still fresh although I thought it was buried. When I saw you run to me, when I arrived home, I recalled how Lenore always ran to greet me. Your delight in your brother's arrival has changed you. You're happier than I've seen you." *You remind me too much of Lenore.*

"I understand," she said softly. *You don't want to be married to a divorced woman.*

They were silent for a long moment.

"Do you have reminders of Monro when you're with me?" Raiford asked.

Immediately, Anathea declared, "Not at all! You are nothing like him. In fact, you are so unlike him that you're almost a different species."

Raiford chuckled. "Different species, huh?"

"I mean that your characteristics are nothing like his."

For the first time since he had known her, Anathea began telling Raiford about her life as Monro's wife.

"I wonder you did not run away sooner," he said when she finished.

Anathea said, "I could not bear the loneliness any longer."

"Surrounded by a village of people?"

"But they were not my friends. We were not close. I considered returning to the orphanage and asking for work there, but that would tell everyone that I was a failure. They had been so happy for me when I married. That was why I went to the big city instead. I didn't want anyone to know that I had failed. I wanted to start a new life. I wanted to succeed in what I did."

"Which you have done," he said.

"Yes, I think I have. At least, I feel better about what I'm doing now. Guelph has given me a new start, and, I think, a better one than New York would have done."

"You have people here who love you." He smiled at her.

"Yes, now that Adam is here, I do."

"Not just your brother." Lifting her hands to his lips, he kissed first one and then the other.

She stood up. He did the same. Without another word, they parted for the night.

* * *

Historic Note: As prison populations increased during the war, so did escape attempts. Sometimes, the prisoners became part of a work detail outside their enclosure and simply walked away. Other times, they attacked armed guards, stormed the barricades, tunneled under the walls and fences, crashed into the gates, or bluffed their way past sentries. Some men pretended to be dead so they would be hauled out to the burial site where they could escape. When Confederates who were confined in prisons in the far north were successful in their escapes, they fled farther north to Canada. In June 1862, a rumor surfaced about Southern sympathizers planning to free all the men incarcerated on Johnson's Island. However, after additional Union troops were sent to the island in Lake Erie, nothing materialized.

CHAPTER FOURTEEN

THE ORPHANS COME

Wherein Edwin and Sue Lee visit Guelph;
Cutter Foundry unveils its new product;
Anathea chairs the Orphans' Selection Committee; and
seventeen orphans come from Louisville

When General Edwin Lee and his wife Sue arrived in Guelph on Thursday, February 9, they went to the rented house of Rev. and Mrs. Kensey Stewart, where they were welcomed. Although the death of Kensey's first wife ended his familial connection to the Lee's, the Episcopal minister still maintained ties with Hannah's family. Emma and Sue were chatting when Kensey ushered Ned into the small sewing room which Kensey had converted to his office.

Without preamble, Kensey said, "We can capture the president. It won't be difficult. I've worked it all out."

"President Lincoln?" Ned was astounded.

"I don't mean President Davis," the minister replied.

Ned sat in the nearest chair. The strain of the trip had sapped his energy. The lung disease, which served as his excuse for coming to Canada, was worse when he exerted himself. This was one of those times.

Taking the only other chair, Kensey said, "There's a man, an actor, who was in Canada last October, I think they said." Kensey paced as he talked. "He has a team in Washington ready to kidnap Lincoln on his way to his summer retreat by the Soldiers' Home."

"For what purpose?" asked Ned, placing his hand on his chest in an effort to ease the pain in his lungs.

"President Lincoln can be exchanged for hundreds of prisoners," said the minister. "They'd want him back. They'd give anything to get him back. We could bargain for an entire prison to be emptied in exchange for that old rail splitter."

"An entire prison," mumbled Ned.

"Yes! Someplace like Johnson's Island," stated Kensey.

"Or Elmira in New York," said the younger man.

"Johnson's is filled with officers. They're needed more."

"Elmira is a hell hole."

"Either one, both, what does it matter? We need to give aid to this young actor," said Kensey.

"What aid? Money?"

"No. Thompson authorized money for him," the minister said. "They need us to provide a hiding place."

"The kidnappers plan to bring him to Canada?"

"What better place?"

Ned shook his head in disbelief. "Don't they understand what neutrality means? Do they think England would not protect her provinces? We don't want another war with England." The young lawyer tried to recall what he knew about international treaties.

"Lincoln would not remain here for long," said Rev. Stewart. "He would be exchanged quickly before the news could get across the Atlantic."

"That doesn't matter. It's a bad idea," said Ned. "We should concentrate on getting men out of prison by escape not by exchanging the Commander in Chief of their armies."

"But I tell you, this will work. You should have heard the actor. I've been told that he is very determined."

"Did you hear him?"

"No, but I was given several reports about his scheme. I'm certain it will succeed."

"What's his name?" asked Ned.

"John Wilkes Booth."

"I saw him perform in Richmond. He's very good on stage."

"So you know he will be good in this kidnapping plan."

"Not necessarily." Edwin rested his head against the back of the chair but it was hard and uncomfortable.

Kensey began to argue for his scheme. Ned did not listen. Slowly, the Brigadier General rose and said, "You must excuse me. I need to lie down. The trip has been very taxing on my strength."

* * *

Adam Brannaman could not sleep. He had dined with Lynnet Burleigh at the Royal Restaurant, a small, candle-lit eating establishment in the center of town. Joan recommended the food. Lynnet was thrilled by the invitation. Adam was spell-bound the entire evening. Now, although the grandfather clock in the downstairs hall showed ten thirty five and the household was quiet, he got up and went to the kitchen. A candle burned on the table. Raiford was warming his hands over the steam from a black kettle.

"Can't sleep?" Raiford asked when he saw Adam.

"No. You either?"

"I was heating water for tea. Want a cup?"

Adam got two cups from the shelf and carried them to the stove. After the young men were seated and sipping their tea, Raiford asked, "How was your evening with Miss Burleigh?"

"I think I'm in love with her."

"So quickly."

"I've been looking for her for a long time," said Adam. "I was beginning to doubt that my future wife even existed. Now, I know that she does and her name is Lynnet."

Raiford spoke in a low voice. "I know how that feels."

"My sister." Adam was not asking a question. He was making a statement.

Raiford smiled, looked Anathea's brother in the eyes, and nodded.

Adam said, "I suppose you know how badly Monro hurt her."

"She has told me something of her life with him."

"She should. You need to know."

"I thought you might be him when I first saw you." Raiford sipped his tea. "Anathea was so happy. I was afraid she was glad to be reunited with him."

"That will never happen," said Adam. "You ought to see that place, the Shakers' village in Kentucky. It's probably what they imagine heaven is like, all neat and clean, with everything in its place. They even hang their ladder-back chairs on wall pegs in order to sweep the floors. I couldn't stand it. There's no individual expression."

"I thought they expressed themselves in their dancing," said Raiford.

"Weird, that's what their dancing is. I can understand why Anathea ran. I'm surprised she remained as long as she did."

"I'm glad she did leave there. Otherwise, we might never have met."

"How did you meet?"

Raiford told him.

"Your meeting seems as fortuitous as Lynnet's and my meeting," said Adam. "At dinner tonight, she told me how her twin married Eustus Wright, a man who came to work at Cutter's Foundry a short while ago. Jennet believed the Lord had a hand in bringing them together."

"Did she also tell you how the twins always intended to wed on the same day?"

"No. They did?"

Raiford told Adam about Lynnet's crying on her sister's wedding day.

"I don't ever want her to cry," said Adam. "I want to make her happy, always happy."

"Do you think your intentions are reciprocated?"

"I don't know. I should ask her. Shouldn't I? What do you think?"

"I would," said Raiford.

"Have you asked my sister how she feels about you?" Adam set down his empty cup.

Raiford met his gaze. Slowly, he shook his head. "I know she missed me, as I missed her. I thought about her constantly."

"She talked about you all the time," said Adam.

"I cannot imagine my life without her. Yet, I wonder…"

"You wonder if her painful experience with Monro will spoil what you could have together."

"Yes, something like that." Raiford stood, went to the stove, set the kettle off the burner, and faced Adam. "If you knew that Lynnet had an alcoholic abusive husband who deserted her, would you be so willing to propose marriage?"

"If I knew that she loved me, I would," said Adam without hesitation.

"Hm-m," was Raiford's only reply.

"What do you think of Mrs. Cutter's opinion?" Anathea's brother asked.

"I think highly of it," said Raiford. "Why?"

"Because she said that she never saw two people more in love than you and my sister."

* * *

On Friday, February 10, attorney William Mittleberger received a telegram from a fellow lawyer in Toronto informing him that his former client, Bennett G. Burley, had been turned over to officers of the United States government. The Canadian court had decided to extradite him. William was thinking about this latest news as he walked home from his office on Cork Street. Coming toward him was a drunken youth, whom the attorney recognized as Tom Donnelly. Having difficulty standing, the teenager wandered back and forth. When he dropped something in the snow and stooped to pick it up, he fell over. William hurried to help the youth stand.

"Gotta get it," mumbled Tom, reaching for his dropped item.

The lawyer saw it was a well-worn boot.

"What's that you've got there, Tom?" asked Mr. Mittleberger, pulling the boy to his feet.

"Thas on'y thing my pal Elmore left me." He clutched the leather shoe to his chest.

"Is that his boot?" The lawyer instantly forgot his thoughts about Bennett Burley and recalled the break-in at the Cutter mansion.

"Goin' to the graveyard to bury it." Although his words were slurred, the older man understood.

"Where's Elmore? Where's the boot's owner?"

"Gone. Him and his pop. T'is all I have left of 'im. He's gone forever."

"That boot should not be buried alone," said Mr. Mittleberger in a soothing voice. "I know where its mate is." He held firmly to the teenager's arm and moved him toward the town jail. "Wouldn't you like to bury both boots together?"

"It's got a mate?" Tom's bloodshot eyes gazed at the man beside him.

"Most assuredly, and I know just where to find the mate. Come with me."

* * *

In the Stewart house, Ned Lee disagreed with Kensey's latest idea. Again, they discussed their schemes in the former sewing room with the door closed.

"We can bomb Detroit," said the minister. "You claim that Johnson's Island is out because of its location amid ice now, but Detroit can be attacked from land and water."

"For what purpose?" Ned frowned.

"The same purpose those raiders attacked St. Albans, of course," said the older man. "Wreak havoc in the north. Make the federals divert troops north to protect the citizens. Make them think we have a huge army up here just waiting to swoop down on border towns."

"Do you know the size of the army stationed at Detroit?"

"No, but we can find out. It cannot be that many. Most of the Yankee soldiers are down around Petersburg, aren't they?"

Ned simply shook his head without making any reply. The Episcopal minister continued. "However many there are, we can overpower them with excessive cannon fire. You don't need many men to fire off cannons. We've got experienced gunners up here in Montreal and Toronto. We just need to round them up."

"And where do we get the cannons?"

"Cutter's Foundry. They made torpedoes. Surely, they can manufacture cannons and cannon balls."

"In what amount of time?"

"Oh, I don't know – a few weeks, a month, maybe."

Ned, thinking what a harebrained idea this was, changed the subject. "I have some basic information about Elmira Prison in New York State."

"Why are you fixated on that place?" the minister asked, "Is someone you know imprisoned there?"

"Not that I'm aware," said Ned. "I have heard reports about what a hell it is. Our men are not provided adequate food or clothing. They're accustomed to a sunny southern climate. They cannot survive in the conditions at Elmira. We must get them out of there."

"But that's in New York," protested Kensey. "Detroit is closer."

"Detroit is not a target!" Ned's voice rose. "We will not attack a defenseless city. We are not barbarians."

"But..."

Ned cut him off and declared: "I am not considering Detroit for any military attack. We are going to concentrate on Elmira."

* * *

Adam and the children were playing a board game on the floor in the large front parlor when Anathea entered with a telegram in her hand.

"Come and join us," her brother said. "I played this game with your former friends at the orphanage." Seeing the serious expression on Anathea's face, he got up, came toward her, and asked, "What is it?"

Anathea handed him the telegram, which was addressed to them both, and said, "From Miss Dell. Bad news."

Adam had telegraphed Barbara Dell about his safe arrival in Guelph. This was the first he heard from the headmistress. He read the telegram. *Received sheriff's notice to vacate building by March 1. Please advise.*

"I left her with enough money to move elsewhere," said Adam.

"Who is moving elsewhere?" asked Raiford, coming into the room with an armload of firewood.

The serious siblings told him about the eviction notice Miss Dell received.

"It's your turn, Uncle Adam," said Freddie.

"You play my piece for me," Adam replied.

As the three adults began discussing possible options for the orphans in Louisville, Beatrice came to stand beside them and said, "Why can't they all move here?"

Raiford smiled and said, "Princess, I think you've struck upon the best idea."

"They have enough to buy tickets and come," said Adam.

"But they need places to live when they arrive," said Anathea.

"They can all get nice homes like we have," said Beatrice. "There are lots of houses here with no little girls in them."

"Why not?" said Raiford.

Thus began a conversation which continued into the evening with the adults as well as children discussing what would be required to move seventeen girls with one adult from Kentucky to Canada West.

"I am sure they could find homes," said Joan. "I know of three families right now who would love to have a daughter."

"The older girls could get work," said Anathea. "I've seen help wanted signs at the hat shop and Miss Minnie's dressmaker's shop."

"There's a sign at the laundry," said Ochran. "I read it." He smiled, happy that he was able to read.

Adam said, "We will need to advertise."

"And set up a committee to process applications," said Raiford.

"Who will be on the committee?" asked Varney.

"You should be the chairwoman," Raiford said to Anathea who sat beside him on the velvet sofa.

"Oh, no, I couldn't," she responded immediately.

"Why not?" asked her brother.

"I could not do anything like that – chair a committee."

"Of course you can," said Raiford in a low tone. "There is no one better suited to the job. You know the girls. You know which families would best suit them."

"Let Adam do it," protested Anathea. "He's met them all. He spent Christmas with them. Besides, there are four new girls that I don't even know."

"You're being stubborn," said Adam. "You know that you are the best person for the job."

"I'm not being stubborn. I just don't think it's a woman's place..."

Raiford did not let her finish. "It is your place! If you want these girls, who were your friends at one time, to live in nice homes with loving families, you should head the committee to make those decisions. I believe the Lord is calling you to this service."

Varney said, "You're like the Jewish girl Esther. She was placed in the palace for such a time as this."

Hesitantly, Anathea said, "I could serve on the committee, but shouldn't some leading citizen like Dr. Shilliday or Mr. Mittleberger be the chairman?"

Leaning toward her, Raiford whispered in her ear, "You should be the chairwoman."

Since everyone agreed with Raiford, Anathea finally consented, although she was very unsure of herself.

That evening, after the others were in bed, Adam joined Anathea and Raiford in the upstairs hallway to continue the discussion about the Orphans' Selection Committee. Both Raiford and Anathea missed their time alone together. Adam was not aware that he was intruding on what had become a special time for the couple.

* * *

The next day, as Barbara Dell read the telegram from Adam Brannaman about bringing the orphan girls to Canada, the residents of Guelph were reading in the *Gazette* about the Boot Thief being apprehended. Constable Clark sent Tad to take a message to Raiford Young, asking him to bring Anathea to his office for possible identification of Tom Donnelly. Since the teenager had sobered up, he denied all knowledge of the attempted theft of the Cutter strongbox.

They rode in the two-passenger sleigh with bells jingling and snow crunching under the runners. Anathea snuggled close to Raiford's arm as he held the reins and directed the horse.

Raiford said, "Did you see the *Gazette* story about the schoolmaster being fired and the schoolhouse being in a deplorable condition?"

"Yes," she said. "I'm glad that he was dismissed from his job. I've heard about how cruel he was to the children. I wonder why the parents put up with him."

"The paper quoted him as saying that children needed strict discipline in order to learn."

"That's not true," she said. "Children are eager to learn if the lessons are presented properly."

"Would you consider taking that job?"

"Being the schoolmaster?"

"You would be good at it," he said. "You teach the children at home."

"But I already have a job as Mr. McCarrell's assistant, and now as chairwoman of the new committee. Don't you think that's enough?"

But before he could answer, Anathea clutched his arm and said, "I know! Miss Dell! She could be the new schoolmistress!"

Raiford smiled at her and nodded agreement.

* * *

When they arrived at the Constable's stone jail, Tom Donnelly refused to look at them. After a brief discussion, Raiford said, "Rather than send him to prison for an attempted robbery, why don't we ask the judge to give him community service."

"What's that?" Tom looked up from his slumped position in the chair by Milo's desk.

"The schoolhouse needs cleaning before the new schoolmarm arrives," said Raiford.

Since the judge came to Guelph from Hamilton only one day a week, Tom had to remain in jail from Friday, the 10th until Wednesday, the 15th. Freddie had the idea of making Valentines for the lonely boy who was the only person jailed during the holiday.

Beatrice asked her brother, "Why do you want us to make Valentines for a criminal? He tried to rob Grandpa."

The little boy replied, "It could be me in that jail."

"What do you mean?" asked his grandmother.

The family was in the large parlor after supper on Sunday afternoon.

"Well, if Uncle Raiford and Aunt Anathea didn't bring us here to Canada, we could have ended up street urchins, and I could have been a criminal like Tom."

The people chuckled at the boy's reply. His sister agreed to make a Valentine and to help the others make them, too.

On Tuesday, the 14th, the children from the Cutter house personally delivered the heart-shaped cards decorated with pieces of lace and ribbons to Constable Clark's office. They handed their cards through the bars to the teen-aged boy who was as surprised as the jail-keeper. Zurelle sent cookies which Ochran gave to Tom. Raiford also accompanied them, but Anathea was too busy. She was drafting the application form for families who wished to adopt an orphan from Kentucky.

Mechum and Delphina were also busy on Valentine's Day because they were inspecting a certain house for sale. Mechum had visited several houses with a realtor and decided on this one, which was only a block away from the Cutter's house. Delphina liked his choice. They signed the sales contract as co-owners. Mechum had no problem paying cash for the two-story cream-colored stone house. He had received the money from Jacob Thompson for deeds done as well as some deeds which were not done.

Valentine's Day was also when Adam proposed to Lynnet. She joyfully said yes.

Raiford and Anathea exchanged innocuous cards. She had made hers while the children were making cards for Tom Donnelly. He had purchased one at the General Mercantile. Although they both said

"Be My Valentine" and were both signed with the word *Love*, neither recipient put any special meaning in the bright red card with fancy trim. Nevertheless, Anathea put hers in the treasure box where she kept her diary, next to the music box with dancing man and woman. Raiford saved his Valentine in the leather portfolio where he stored important papers.

After the jail was quiet, Tom opened and read the cards which he had only glanced at when the visitors were present. Inside one card, the teen read: *Do not drink beer. It is bad. Love, Dalby Wyatt.* The next card stated: *Come to dinner. I can cook. Love, Beatrice.* The other cards, from Freddie, Willene, Fernancy and Maggie, were neatly written by an adult but had a child's signature. Each one expressed a different sentiment of encouragement. All of them used the word *love,* which Tom had known little of during his sixteen years. The boy hid his face in his limp pillow on the iron cot and wept softly.

* * *

The Orphans Selection Committee met for the first time in the large parlor of the Cutter mansion on Saturday, February 18. Anathea had insisted that Raiford join the committee. He agreed only if she would serve as chairman. Adam, too, consented to participate, since he was financing the entire enterprise.

First to arrive for the seven o'clock meeting were Dr. and Mrs. Jesse Shilliday. The others – William Mittleberger, Esq.; Rev. George Grafftey, and Dolly Utley – all came within the next five minutes.

Raiford opened the meeting with prayer, asking the Lord to bless their efforts and give them wisdom to decide on the best homes for the orphan girls.

Sitting at a small table with a pile of papers in front of her, Anathea said, "We have received four more applications than there are girls."

"That's very good!" exclaimed Dolly, smiling happily.

Sheba the kitten jumped into Dolly's lap, curled up, and spent the evening there.

"I would expect such from our people," said the Baptist minister with a more serious expression.

"As I name each applicant, I will read their reason why they want to adopt a girl," said Anathea, picking up the paper on top. "Some of them have asked for two girls, or sisters, if there are any."

The group spoke agreeably about each applicant and had no difficulty, with Adam and Anathea's input about the characteristics of the orphans, in assigning Guelph families to the orphans. The first problem arose when the Bolton application was read.

"Their house is little better than a rat's nest," said Dolly.

"I wouldn't go so far as to call it that," said Harriet Shilliday. "Saida just collects too many things."

"I disapprove of the Boltons adopting," said the doctor.

Without further discussion, the vote went against the Bolton's receiving one of the orphans in their home. Following several more approvals, another problem application was read. Anathea said, "Miss Peacock, as you know, has the hat shop. She is unmarried and would like an older girl who could help her and, one day, inherit the shop. Can we let an unmarried woman adopt an orphan?"

"I don't see why not," said Raiford.

"Hilda Peacock is an upstanding woman," said William Mittleberger. "She has made a success of her business. I think she would make a good mother to an older girl."

The others agreed and voted to grant her application. The four applicants who did not receive orphans were easily decided with little debate.

The next order of business was their date of arrival, which Adam explained, and their first day.

"Mrs. Grafftey wants to hold a welcome dinner for them in the church before they go to their new homes," said George. "That way, they can meet their new families in a community environment."

"What a good idea," said Harriet. "I'll help her with the meal."

The committee concluded their work by nine o'clock. As the others left, Adam attached a leash to Solomon and said, "I'll take him for a quick walk in the yard. You two go up."

Raiford walked beside Anathea, mounting the front stairs, and said, "You did a good job. No man could have done better."

"Maybe because I knew everyone, except the lawyer, but he was nice." She held the railing with one hand and her long skirt with the other as she climbed slowly. Anathea was tired. "It won't be that easy when I have to stand in front of the townspeople and make the announcement."

At the top of the stairs, she turned to face Raiford and said, "Couldn't we just published the names of the families in the *Gazette?* Why does it have to be an announcement at your new product unveiling?"

"Because that's a sure way of bringing people in," answered Raiford. "They might not want to come out on a cold night to see a new Cutter product unless there was some other draw."

"Couldn't you read the names of the families and the girls?"

"No, Anathea," he said smiling. He took her arm and led her to the front hall fireplace where Ochran had made a blazing fire. "You are the chairwoman and should read our report."

Anathea sat on the settee while Raiford used the poker to push at the burning logs.

"There's nothing to it," he said. "You will just be reading from a paper, first telling the girl's name, her age, and something about her, followed by the name of the family who will adopt her. Mr. Mittleberger will explain about the legal adoption process. Adam or the preacher will tell about the arrival day and the dinner at church. It will be easy."

"Easy for you," she said. "You told a story about an Indian maid to a train station full of strangers without the least hesitancy. You're accustomed to talking in front of people."

"What can go wrong?" He sat beside her and took her hand.

"I'll be shaking. My hands holding the paper will shake. People will see how nervous I am."

"Do you plan to faint?"

In surprise at his question, she faced him. He was smiling. She squeezed his hand and said, "Oh, you! I don't plan to faint ever."

"I'm glad of that."

Adam appeared at the top of the stairs and saw the expression of the faces of the couple by the fire. *They belong together,* Anathea's brother thought.

* * *

The front page story of the *Gazette* for Friday, February 24, was: *Orphans Arrive Tomorrow. Families Announced Tonight at Grand Cutter Foundry Unveiling of New Mystery Product. All Are Welcome.* Although there were a few complaints by some, including Saida Bolton, that announcing the new families just the day before their arrival did not provide enough time to prepare, the citizens were pleased with the whole process. The talk in the stores and on the streets was about orphans and the mystery product.

Anathea came downstairs dressed in her newest outfit, which she had made by the dressmakers in town. Raiford met her at the bottom steps, held out his hand to her, and said, "You look lovely."

Taking his hand, she followed him into the dining room where Zurelle had prepared an early supper. They arrived at the Foundry showroom before the doors opened at six o'clock for the expected crowd. Raiford wanted it early enough so children could come, which they did. The crowd was noisy and happy as they enjoyed cake, tarts, sweet bread, and warm cider.

At six thirty, Raiford escorted Anathea up the steps of the platform at one end of the large hall. Also on the stage was a huge object covered by a tarpaulin. The people had been trying to guess what the new product was. Mechum and Ochran stood guard to keep anyone from looking under the canvas.

Stepping to the edge of the platform, Raiford said, "I would like to introduce the chairwoman of the Orphans Selection Committee, Miss Anathea Brannaman." There was polite applause. Raiford continued. "She has asked me to introduce the members of her committee. Will they please step forward when I call their names."

When Raiford came to William Mittleberger's name, the lawyer walked up the two steps to the stage and said, "I have an announcement from the School Board. As you know, our schoolmaster quit." Murmurs of approvals were voices in low tones. William continued. "The School Board met, offered the position to a newcomer, arriving tomorrow, and she has accepted." He held up a telegram. "The new teacher will be Miss Barbara Dell, formerly headmistress of the Home for Friendless Girls in Louisville, Kentucky."

The people applauded. They were familiar with the name because of the *Gazette* publicity. William waved his hand in acknowledgement of their approval and left the platform. He was followed by Constable Milo Clark, who had vouched for the good reputation of all recipients of these girls coming from Louisville.

"Thank you, Mr. Mittleberger and Constable Clark. That is good news," Raiford said. Turning toward Anathea, who stood partially behind him, he took her arm and brought her to the edge of the stage.

"Now, Miss Brannaman will read the names of the girls and their new families."

Hesitantly, Anathea lifted her single sheet of paper. She saw that her hand was steady. Raiford stayed at her side, as he had promised he would. She read the first girl's name and the couple who would adopt her. The people applauded. This continued after every matching was read, which surprised and pleased Anathea. By the time she finished reading her list, she was not nervous at all.

"You did well," Raiford whispered to her, going to the edge of the steps where Adam helped her down.

"And now for the unveiling of our new product!" Raiford placed his hand on the tarpaulin. Before pulling off the covering, he glanced at the audience to be certain that Ochran had Zurelle at his side and close to the platform steps. "This came about as the direct result of wise counsel by a woman I greatly respect." Yanking off the tarpaulin, he declared: "The Zurelle Stove!"

The guests began chattering as Ochran led Zurelle up the two steps.

Raiford said, "This is the excellent cook, Zurelle Wyatt, who inspired and aided me in designing the stove which is named for her. This is her husband Ochran Wyatt who oversaw the production of this stove and many others which are available for sale.'

"Oh, my gracious," said Zurelle as she gazed at the stove named for her. A shiny brass plate on the front read: *Zurelle Stove.*

Zurelle swatted Ochran on the shoulder and said, "I thought you were making just one for the kitchen. Why didn't you tell me?"

Ochran hugged his wife. The people laughed and clapped. Some climbed the steps to inspect the stove. Kirk opened his order book and followed them.

Raiford said to Zurelle, "This one is for your kitchen, but we have more."

"You men!" Zurelle moved toward the stairs since the stage was becoming crowded. She was beaming with delight.

As Raiford was escorting Anathea through the crowd toward the refreshments, Rev. Stewart stopped them, saying, "I would like you to meet someone."

A pleasant-looking young man with neatly-parted hair and an attractive young woman came to the minister's side.

"Allow me to introduce Edwin Lee and his wife Susan from Lexington," said the Episcopal minister.

Raiford knew immediately who the young man was – Jacob Thompson's replacement. Keeping his surprise in check, Raiford shook hands with the Confederate officer.

Susan said to Anathea, "However did you manage this adoption for an entire orphanage?"

Relieved that her first public speaking event was over, Anathea eagerly conversed with the newcomer. When Mechum and Delphina joined them, Raiford introduced the former Confederate to Ned Lee and watched his face closely, but Mechum did not betray his knowledge of the true identity of Rev. Stewart's friend. In fact, the Lees were received with hospitality by everyone they met. Both Sue and Ned had definite Southern accents. No one mentioned the fact. When General and Mrs. Lee left the town for Montreal, they took pleasant memories with them.

* * *

Saturday, February 25, was a day never to be forgotten in the town of Guelph. The orphans arrived on schedule. A line of sleighs and sleds waited at the depot to transport them to the First Baptist Church on Woolwich Street. The meal prepared was warm and welcoming. Anathea and Barbara hugged when they saw each other. Adam also took his turn to hug Miss Dell. The two women worked together in pairing up each orphan girl with the family who would adopt her. By evening, the new families were in their warm homes. As they got acquainted, they had no hint that a blizzard was heading their way.

* * *

Historic Note: The course of history has often been altered by weather. When Julius Caesar's navy attempted to cross the English Channel, they were thwarted by strong northwesterly winds and the invasion failed. In 1588, after Sir Francis Drake's naval forces defeated the Spanish Armada, those foreign ships were struck by strong winds and high seas north of Scotland and Ireland, with the result that many ships were wrecked and hundreds of Spaniards downed. In the mid-17th century, Denmark attacked Sweden during a severe winter. The Swedish soldiers crossed the ice from

Jutland to Zealand, thus forcing the Danes to surrender. In 1812, Napoleon Bonaparte's Grand Army retreated from Russia partly because of the terrible winter weather. Starting out in spring-like weather on January 1, 1862, General Stonewall Jackson led his men from Winchester to Romney in western Virginia. By the next day, snow and ice covered the path of the gray-clad soldiers. Temperature dropped to 27 degrees. The miserable march demoralized many of the Confederates.

CHAPTER FIFTEEN

BLIZZARD

Wherein Raiford and Anathea declare their love for each other;
they visit Rev. and Mrs. Grafftey;
Tom and Milo discuss his upcoming trial;
Anathea and Raiford are lost in the blizzard.

Raiford knelt in front of his bedroom window. The polished floor was hard on his knees. A coverlet was draped over his muscular shoulders, but he did not hold it closed over his chest because his hands were clasped in prayer. It was two hours since they had come home from the New Product Unveiling at the foundry showroom. The event had been a success. Raiford had praised Anathea for her calm reading of the names of those approved for adopting the orphan girls. Kirk enlisted Adam to help fill out orders for the Zurelle Stove because he could not keep up. Everything had gone well. Nevertheless, Raiford was troubled.

Aloud, but in a low tone, he said, "Lord, what am I to do? You know how much I love Anathea. Certainly you know. Love comes from you. You brought us together. Why is this so hard? Why did a vision of Lenore come to me when she greeted me upon my return home? I thought those memories were dead and buried."

A chill made him shiver. Cold air wafted between the glass and the window frame in the lower corner. He stood up, clutched his blanket tightly, and went to the fireplace where he poked the logs.

"Heavenly Father, you know how I grieved when she died. You don't want me to endure that again, do you?" He shook his head in the negative. "But why should I be immune from witnessing another wife die. Back in Goshen, there were several men who buried two or three wives, But, Lord…" He knelt on the warm hearth. "I don't want to witness Anathea's death. She is too precious to me. Don't let her die before I do. I know I don't have the right to ask you that. You have a timetable different than ours. I don't understand why you took Lenore from me when we had such happiness together. Was it so I would fall in love with Anathea? Could such a thing be? No. I don't think you did. I know the Bible says your ways are not our ways. Help me to understand. Reveal to me what you want me to do. I am your humble servant. Guide me in all your ways."

He went to the rocking chair, sat down, and, by the firelight, he read the Book of Psalms for an hour. When his eyelids became heavy, he went to bed and slept soundly. In fact, he slept so soundly that he did not awaken for breakfast.

Ochran came to see if he was sick, and returned to the dining room to report. "Raiford is fast asleep. He's too peaceful to waken."

In the library, Anathea and Barbara Dell, who was a houseguest until the cluttered rooms behind the school were cleaned, had the children in their seats at the desks Ochran had built. They were working quietly, so Anathea heard Raiford's footsteps on the stairs. In the next moment, he came to the door, greeted Miss Dell and the children, and said, "Anathea, may I speak alone with you?"

Anathea rose and joined him in the hall, where he was already reaching for her coat from the hall tree.

"Let's go for a walk."

"You haven't had your breakfast," she said, putting her hands through the sleeves of her heavy wool coat.

"I have no appetite," he said. "Too much on my mind."

Five minutes later, they were walking up the hill toward the Lister house at the end of the street.

Anathea looked at the dark gray sky and said, "Do you think a storm is brewing behind those clouds?"

Raiford steered Anathea away from a snow drift by putting his hand on her waist and pulling her toward him. Glancing upward, he simply nodded but gave her no verbal response.

How should I begin? Raiford asked himself. *What will she say?*

Reaching the top of the low hill just beyond the Lister house, Raiford turned to Anathea, placed both hands on her waist, and held her firmly at arms' length as he spoke. "I must tell you, Anathea! I have no intention of ever getting married again! It does not matter how much I love you! I never again want to hold my wife in my arms and watch her die!"

Bracing herself with her mittened hands on his chest, Anathea, in an equally adamant tone, said, "I am glad to hear you say that because I have no desire to ever marry again myself."

"Why not?" He wrinkled his forehead. "You never experienced your spouse die in your arms."

"No! My heartache took place at the gateway to a Shaker village not on a deathbed!" Her eyes sparkled with emotion as she glared at him. "My love departed not in death but in a piece of paper – a bill of divorcement handed to me at that gate."

He simply nodded once but said nothing.

"So, then, we are in agreement. I have no interest in marriage either," Anathea continued. "I never again want my husband to divorce me, to have all my worldly dreams turn to dust and to be torn asunder from the partner I expected to have for life."

"I see," he said softly.

When she attempted to move away from his hold, Raiford yanked her against his chest, and whispered into her ear: "Then what do we do about this?"

With all the love for her that he possessed, Raiford kissed her long and lovingly. For only a moment, she resisted. But his fervor opened her desire.

I love you, Raiford. I love you with all my heart. As the thoughts penetrated her mind, her lips responded to his. She kissed him passionately. Her hands moved up from his chest to his shoulders and around his neck.

His hands moved across her back. His right hand slid under her bonnet so his fingers could delve into her silky hair.

My darling, my dearest one, how can I let you go when I want you this much? How can I?

Their kiss ended. She pressed her cheek against his and felt his beard. She smelled the clean, wholesome scent of his skin. She felt his hands moving in her hair and across her back.

"I love you," he said. "I don't want to but I do. I love you, Anathea."

"And I love you, Raiford. But, since neither of us wants to marry again, there is only one solution."

"What?"

"We must part company." Anathea's words were muffled against his thick collar but he heard them clearly.

"No," was his instant reply.

"What else can we do?" She tried to pull back so she could look at his face, to see his expression, but when he felt her effort to move, he gripped her more securely against his body.

"I could not endure being apart from you again," he said. "The time at Johnson's Island was torture, not because of the conditions but because I was away from you. I thought of nothing else but you -- you and the children."

"Then what is the solution?"

Releasing his firm hold of her, he stepped back, took her upper arms to hold her slightly away, looked into her eyes, and said, "I don't know. I was up last night praying."

"Can we pray now?"

Holding hands, they continued standing as they closed their eyes. Raiford prayed, "Dear Lord, Heavenly Father, Living God, you know our dilemma here. You care for us. You died for us. We turn to you for resolution. Give us your wisdom to make the right decision, right not only for us but also for Beatrice and Freddie, for Varney and Joan, for those our lives have touched." He paused briefly. "Why, Lord? Why did you bring us together? Why did you cause us to love each other?"

Anathea prayed, "Lord, you created Raiford so different from Monro. Why do I compare them? But I do compare them less and less, don't I? Since I've come to know Raiford better, I don't believe he would ever divorce me. I believe he is honest and trustworthy. My fears become less each day. But what can I do about his fears? I have no control over when I die – before or after him. What can I do to satisfy his …"

Raiford did not let her finish. Opening his eyes, he squeezed her hands, and said, "Of course you have no control over the time of your death. What's wrong with me to expect you to …"

"But you still have that terrible memory." She opened her eyes to see his gaze intently on her.

"You have terrible memories as well," he said.

"It hurts," she said.

"To love me hurts?" he asked.

"To reconcile the painful past with what we are experiencing now is what hurts," she said, wrinkling her forehead.

Lifting her mittened hand to his cheeks, he said, "I don't want to cause you any pain. I want to resolve this dilemma today."

"I wish the same," she said.

After a moment's hesitation, Raiford said, "We need to talk to someone."

"Who? Joan? Barbara?" Anathea said. "Someone older, with wisdom, would be good."

Raiford said, "Does it have to be a woman? What about the preacher? He has experience with imparting wisdom."

"Rev. Grafftey?"

Raiford nodded.

Twenty minutes later, Anathea and Raiford sat in the parsonage parlor with Rev. and Mrs. Grafftey. Each one held a tea cup but only the preacher's wife drank the hot liquid.

"How may I be of service to you?" asked the Baptist minister.

"We're in love and don't want to be," stated Raiford. "Both of us have been hurt by past experiences. Thus, we want to avoid further hurt. Certainly, I don't want to cause Anathea any emotional pain."

Anathea blushed and lowered her eyes.

"Do you love him, my dear?" asked Mrs. Grafftey, who was sitting next to Anathea.

"Very much," Anathea said softly.

The reverend said, "This brings to my mind the story of Peter's denial of Jesus."

"Oh, George," said his wife, "What does that have to do with two young people who are in love?"

"Just listen," said the preacher. "You know how Peter claimed he did not know Jesus after the Romans arrested him." He looked from Raiford to Anathea who both nodded. "Well, when Jesus met Peter on the lakeshore, he did not look back at the dark time, when Peter was a coward, when Peter feared being arrested, too. Instead, what did Jesus say?"

"Feed my sheep," answered Raiford.

"That's right," said George. "Our Savior focused on the future, not the past. That's what you two must do. You love each other. You have a future together. Don't look to the past hurts you have endured."

Mrs. Grafftey said, "As a wedding gift, my mother gave me a sampler that says: Marriage gives double cheer and half of care."

"So true, so true," said her husband. "Clinging to past sorrow does nothing to advance the kingdom of God. You both have much to offer as a married couple. Your cheer is doubled. Your care is cut in half."

As though the tension, which had been building since they stopped on the hill beyond the Lister house, suddenly drained from both Anathea and Raiford at the same moment, he set his tea cup aside and knelt in front of her chair. Taking her hand in his, Raiford said, "Anathea, my dearest love, will you put the past behind you and enter the future with me? Will you consent to be my wife?"

Mrs. Grafftey made a slight gasp and quickly set her jiggling tea cup down lest she spill. The minister smiled.

Anathea, tears coming to her eyes, nodded and said softly, "I will, Raiford."

When she composed herself, for she was very emotional, the pastor's wife invited the happy couple to eat some pumpkin bread with a second cup of tea. Since Raiford had not eaten breakfast, he consented.

"You'll want to set a wedding date," said George. "I can't tell you what days are available until I check my calendar at the church office. Several couples have asked for spring wedding dates."

"Your brother and Lynnet Burleigh have a date set, don't they?" Mrs. Grafftey finished her slice of pumpkin bread.

"Yes, they have," said Anathea. Turning toward Raiford, she said, "Oh, I have an idea. Remember how Lynnet wanted a double wedding with her sister? Do you think she might like a double wedding with her sister-in-law?"

Smiling, Raiford said, "We must ask her."

As soon as they finished refreshments at the parsonage, the newly-engaged couple went to the door to leave. When Rev. Grafftey opened the door, he said, "Well, look there, another snowfall."

"It's coming down hard," said his wife.

"Perhaps you should wait until it lets up," said George.

"No," said Anathea. "I want to see Lynnet and ask her about a double wedding."

"We could wait to ask her," said Raiford, holding Anathea's coat for her. "This weather does not look good."

Nevertheless, Raiford agreed to go to the Burleigh's house. He had never been there. Anathea had been only once, but was talking to the twins at the time and thus paid little attention to the route. Rev. Grafftey gave them the house number, but it was impossible to see numbers from the road because of the heavy snowfall.

"I remember that the house was gray stone with dark red shutters," she said to him as they walked hand in hand down Nottingham Street.

The snow, which began as fluffy flakes, became a white sheet. The couple could not see two feet in front of them. The only way they knew they were on the street was the sight of hitching posts every so often. The flakes were icy sharp. The wind blew at thirty miles per hour. Both Anathea and Raiford had difficulty standing up and keeping their eyes open.

Suddenly, Anathea fell. Her hand slipped out of Raiford's. He bent down to help her up. She was not there. The wind had blown her backwards. She tumbled several times before she hit an object. Using the object, which was a watering tough, to help her stand, Anathea got to her feet.

"Raiford! Raiford!" she called, but her words went nowhere. The howling wind blew them back into her throat.

Several yards away, Raiford, with outstretched arms, was feeling into the blizzard for the woman he loved. But instead of a body, all he felt was cold, icy, white snow, so thick that visibility was impossible.

Have we come this far for me to lose her now? Lord, surely, this is not your will! Not after all we have shared. Why are you doing this? What is your purpose? Help me find Anathea!

Raiford shouted her name again and again as he moved in the opposite direction from the way Anathea was going.

* * *

Tom Donnelly could not believe the kindness of the Cutter family and the jailer, Milo Clark, who befriended him as well.

"I've closed the shutters," Milo said, coming back into the single room jail with two cells at one side. "You'll need to put up a blanket over the bars to help keep out the cold. Can you manage it yourself?"

"I can do it," said Tom as he took the blanket off his iron cot and moved his chair to the window.

"I'll get you another blanket for your bed," said Milo, going to the second cell which was unoccupied.

"I guess this storm means the judge won't be here for my trial any time soon," said Tom.

"I venture to say you're correct," said Milo, as he added more wood to the stove.

* * *

Anathea was dizzy when she stood up after tumbling in the snow. Waiting for the dizzy spell to abate, she wondered which direction to go. Bitter cold snow and icy wind whirled around her. She pulled up her neck scarf to cover her nose and mouth. Opening her eyes with difficulty, she tried to make out any object in her vision, but all that she saw was white, white, and white.

"Raiford!" she called. "Raiford! Where are you?"

Raiford only heard the howling wind. He saw nothing but snow. With his arms outstretched to keep from hitting something, he trudged forward. He had no idea if he had left the road. This part of town was unfamiliar to him.

Where did I see the nearest house when last I could see? The houses were far apart. I could wander off into the countryside. But I did see some barns. If I come to any structure, I'll find shelter. But where is Anathea? Has she gone inside somewhere? Is she warm and safe? Lord, help.

* * *

In the Cutter mansion, Zurelle and Ochran were worried. They were standing side by side at the front parlor window. The room was cold. Ochran did not light the fire in here. The family was all in the small parlor, which was cozy and warm.

"Where could they be?" Zurelle spoke without turning her head. Her eyes stared at the blowing blizzard beyond the glass.

"I'm sure he took her indoors somewhere," said Ochran. "He wouldn't be outside in this."

"Have you ever seen anything like it?"

"Never did, that's for certain," her husband replied.

Beatrice came to the door and asked, "Where are Uncle Raiford and Aunt Anathea?"

Zurelle went to the girl, put her hand on her shoulder, and said, "They went for a walk, but I'm sure they got inside somewhere."

"They'll come home when the storm's over," said Ochran, following his wife and Beatrice out of the cold room and into the warm one.

* * *

Raiford had stumbled into a wooden fence and was following it. He fell over the stile and landed face down in the snow. Quickly, he got up, wiped the cold, wet snow off his face, and felt a sudden urge to turn around. Without giving it a second thought, he turned. As though racing against time, he trudged as fast as he could in the direction from which he had come.

I will find her. I must. She is my life, my love. Without her, what is there? I cannot lose her, too.

Anathea banged against a wooden building and fell backward. She crawled forward with hands outstretched and felt of the wood. Still on her knees, she moved along the base of the structure. In only a few feet, she came to the corner. In another few feet she came to the next corner.

It's a small building. Where's the entrance?

As though the building answered her question, she next felt the threshold. Standing, she fumbled for a doorknob. There was no knob. She felt a bar and raised it. The wind did the rest, blowing the door wide open. Anathea entered. With all her effort, she pushed the door shut. The bar fell. She was locked in, but did not care. She was out of the wind and snow. There was only a tiny window high in the wall. Instead of glass, the window had a piece of animal skin which let in very little light. However, it was enough to see where she was.

A smokehouse, she said to herself. Anathea dropped to the dirt floor and leaned against a keg. *Where is Raiford? Will he find me here?*

By a miracle, Raiford did find her. However, almost an hour passed before he came to the same smokehouse. Lifting the bar, he entered. Shivering in the corner, Anathea had her face against her knees. She sat bolt upright when she felt the blast of air rush into the little building.

"Raiford?"

"Anathea!"

They were in each other's arms in an instant. She pressed her cheek against his ice-covered beard. He rubbed his red nose against her hair.

They clung. They murmured unintelligible words. They shook with cold, with relief, and with joy.

"I must shut the door," he said, turning from her.

"The bar will drop," she said.

"I'll fix it." He slid the bar back so it would not lock them in, and closed the door.

Returning to Anathea, Raiford said, "You're shaking. How long have you been here?"

"I don't know. I can't get warm."

Looking around, Raiford said, "At least it's a smoke house and not an ice house."

"And it's shelter."

"We can make it warmer for ourselves," he said, pulling her down to the dirt floor. "Help me find the meat to make an enclosure for us."

"An enclosure?"

"Yes, like a cocoon in which we can keep warm." He spoke while feeling around in the well-stocked smokehouse.

Within a few minutes, the two of them had lined a corner with frozen hams and turkeys and whatever meat was nearby.

"Now, we will take off our outer garments and pile them on top of both of us," he said.

"And snuggle together?"

"That's right."

Without another word, she took off her wool coat and he removed his overcoat. Raiford covered her with both coats before crawling under them, taking her in his arms, and hugging her against his chest.

"Now we must thank the Lord for rescuing us," he said.

"And for bringing us together," she replied.

* * *

Ochran asked Joan, "Do you think I should get some men to go looking for them?"

Joan had expressed her concern for Anathea and Raiford's absence as Ochran stirred up the fire in the small parlor.

"I'd be afraid you would get lost and freeze to death," said the old woman. "Where would you look?"

"I saw them walking toward the Lister house," the servant replied.

"Well, maybe you could ask Deering Lister if they've found shelter at his house, but come right back and report," said Joan. "We don't want you to get lost in this weather."

Ochran's walk to the Lister house and back took almost an hour. When he got there, Mrs. Lister insisted that he warm up before returning home. Ochran reported that the neighbors had not seen Anathea and Raiford.

The blizzard came as it went – gradually. The wind died down. The snow tapered off. Raiford and Anathea slept. When they awoke in late afternoon, Raiford listened for the howling wind and heard nothing. Gently pushing Anathea off his chest, he crawled from under their coats and went to the door. He opened the wooden door causing snow to fall from the roof. The sky was gray. Nothing moved.

"Anathea, we had better go home," he said coming to her. He took her coat and helped put her arms in the sleeves before donning his own coat.

"Has the storm stopped?" She looked beyond him to the open door.

"It has." Taking her arm, Raiford pulled her to her feet.

Upon leaving the smokehouse, they looked around to see where they were. Only one house was in sight, so they went to it. When a man opened the door, he immediately held it wide for them to enter. Raiford introduced himself and Anathea.

"I know who you are," said Abijah Jennings. "I work at Cutters."

"Yes, you look familiar," said Raiford, shaking hands with Abijah.

Mrs. Jennings gave them hot cider while Mr. Jennings hitched up the sleigh to take them home.

"I'm glad our smokehouse kept you alive," said Abijah, flipping the reins over the horse's back. The sleigh moved easily on the newly-fallen snow.

"You'll find your meats a little rearranged," said Raiford. "We moved them to provide warmth for us."

"Think nothing of it," said the friendly man. "After all you have done for Cutters and this town, it's little enough I can do for you."

"Do you mean about the new stove Cutters will be manufacturing?" asked Anathea, nestling close to Raiford in the back seat.

"That new stove!" Abijah laughed. "Now the misiz wants me to buy her one."

"We have a discount for employees," Raiford said.

"You're too good to us," said the older man, turning his head to smile at the couple behind him.

"You are hard workers and deserve some benefits besides just your pay," said Raiford.

"But we never expected what you did for us at Christmas," said Abijah.

"What did he do?" asked Anathea.

"Gave us all the week off between Christmas and New Years," said Abijah. "With full pay," he added, smiling.

"The workmen had off?" Anathea lifted her head from his shoulder to look him in the face. "I thought it was just us that had the week off from work between Christmas and New Years."

"Oh, did I forget to tell you about that?" Raiford smiled at her.

"Yes, you did." She put her head down on his shoulder again. "Don't forget to tell me important things like that in the future."

"You're sounding like a wife already," Raiford said and kissed her on the forehead.

* * *

Historic Note: The American Civil War effectively ended when General Robert E. Lee surrendered his Army of Northern Virginia to General Ulysses S. Grant at Appomattox Court House, Virginia, on April 9, 1865.

The End

EPILOGUE

Anathea and Raiford had a double wedding with her brother, Adam Brannaman, and Lynnet Burleigh on Saturday, April 1, just eight days before General Robert E. Lee surrendered the Army of Northern Virginia, to General Ulysses S. Grant at Appomattox Court House, Virginia, thus ending the Civil War for all intents and purposes.

They had four children. Their first son, born in 1866, was named Ulysses Grant Young, whom they called Grant. He became a lawyer in Guelph. Their second child, Barbara Dell Young, born in 1869, married a prosperous businessman in Hamilton, Ontario. Conrad Grebel Young, named for a famous Mennonite, was born in 1872, and became a Baptist minister. The youngest child, Analisa Joan Young, was a school teacher before she married a university professor and moved to Toronto. All four children provided grandchildren for Raiford and Anathea.

Varney Cutter altered his will to divide his estate between Freddie and Raiford with provision that they care for Joan, Beatrice, Anathea, and all descendants. The will also made provision for Ochran Wyatt and family, who continued to serve at the Cutter house, and then at the Young house.

When Tom Donnelly faced a judge, Raiford, Anathea, and several citizens spoke on his behalf. The judge sentenced him to community service of cleaning up the schoolhouse and keeping it clean. Barbara Dell tutored Tom, who built up a harness making business, joined the church, wed, and had a happy family. He never heard from his boyhood friend, Elmore Pearson, or Elmore's father.

All the orphan girls who came from Louisville settled easily into their new homes in Guelph. Miss Dell taught school there for many years before she retired to marry a widower and adopted three children from one family when the parents died.

Edwin Gray Lee remained in Canada while his amnesty request was going through channels. In his application to President Andrew Johnson, Ned stated that he had gone to Canada for his health and not to pursue any activities against the United States. He received a pardon signed by the president and Secretary of State William Seward on July 22, 1865. Ned died of tuberculosis on August 24, 1870. Two months later, on October 22, 1870, his second cousin once removed, Robert Edward Lee, died in Lexington, Virginia.

Anathea's wish came true. Raiford never divorced her. At each wedding anniversary, he told her that he loved her more than the year before, although he did not know how such a thing was possible.

Raiford, too, had his wish. He did not see his second wife die. Raiford went to be with the Lord when he was 95 years old. He died of pneumonia. Anathea followed him two months later. People said she died of a broken heart.

RESOURCES

Andrews, Edward Deming, *The People Called Shakers,* Dover Publications, 1963.

Bassett, John M., and A. R. Petrie, *The Canadians, William Hamilton Merritt,* Fitzhenry & Whiteside Limited, 1974.

Bell, John, *Rebels on the Great Lakes, Confederate Naval Commando Operations Launched from Canada, 1863-1864,* Dundurn, Toronto, 2011.

Boatner, Mark Mayo, III, *The Civil War Dictionary,* David McKay Company, Inc., 1959.

Brandt, Nat, *The Man Who Tried to Burn New York,* Syracuse University Press, 1986.

Clark, Thomas D., and F. Gerald Ham, *Pleasant Hill and Its Shakers,* Pleasant Hill Press, 1996.

Frohman, Charles E., *Rebels on Lake Erie,* The Ohio Historical Society, 1965.

Headley, John W., *Confederate Operations in Canada and New York,* Collector's Library of the Civil War, The Neale Publishing Company, 1906.

Horan, James D., *Confederate Agent, A Discovery in History,* Crown Publishers, 1954.

Johnson, Clint, *"A Vast and Fiendish Plot," The Confederate Attack on New York City,* Citadel Press, 2010.

Kinchen, Oscar A., *The Rise and Fall of The Patriot Hunters, Liberation of Canadian Provinces from British Thraldom,* Bookman Associates, 1956; *Confederate Operations in Canada and the North,* The Christopher Publishing House, 1970; *General Bennett Young, Confederate Raider and A Man of Many Adventures,* The Christopher Publishing House, 1981.

Levin, Alexandra Lee, *"This Awful Drama," General Edwin Gray Lee, C.S.A., and His Family,* Vantage Press, 1987.

Lloyd, Julie, *A Pocket Guide to Weather,* Paragon Books Ltd., 2007.

Mayers, Adam, *Dixie & The Dominion, Canada, the Confederacy, and the War for the Union,* The Dundurn Group, 2003.

Military Commission, *Trial of John Y. Beall as a Spy and Guerrillero,* D. Appleton and Company, 1865.

Rush, Daniel S., and E. Gale Pewitt, *The St. Albans Raiders,* McNaughton and Gunn, 2008.

Singer, Jane, *The Confederate Dirty War, Arson, Bombings, Assassinations and Plots for Chemical and Germ Attacks on the Union,* McFarland & Company, Inc. 2005.

Speer, Lonnie R., *Portals to Hell, Military Prisons of the Civil War,* Stackpole Books, 1997.

Tidwell, William A., with James O. Hall and David Winfred Gaddy, *Come Retribution, The Confederate Secret Service and the Assassination of Lincoln,* University Press of Mississippi, 1988.

Towne, Stephen E., *Surveillance and Spies in the Civil War, Exposing Confederate Conspiracies in America's Heartland,* Ohio University Press, 2014.

Winks, Robin W., *Canada and the United States, The Civil War Years,* The Johns Hopkins Press, 1960.

BOOK CLUB AND CLASSROOM DISCUSSION QUESTIONS

1. The Confederates purpose in burning the New York City hotels was to shorten the Civil War. Do you think terrorism accomplishes any worthwhile goals?

2. Do you believe people spread gossip about others in order to keep gossip away from themselves, as Saida Bolton did? Is there ever a good reason for gossip?

3. Did you sympathize with Joan Cutter who felt ashamed of her husband's mental decline and tried to hide him? Do we still feel this way about older people?

4. What do you think of Raiford's plan to get rid of the torpedoes? Would you have done something different?

5. Did you understand Anathea's shame of being divorced? How have times changed in that regard?

6. Did you agree with the decisions of the Orphans Selection Committee? Should Saida Bolton have been denied? Should Hilda Peacock, a single woman, been allowed to adopt?

7. Could learning to read and write solve problems of inequality between people?

8. How did the simple kindness of giving Valentines to Tom Donnelly change his life? Do you see any application in your life?

9. Discuss the differences between Civil War prisoners, both north and south, and prisoners of other wars.

10. What have you learned about the Civil War that you did not know previously?

11. Have you changed any of your opinions since reading this book?

INDEX TO HISTORIC NOTES

End of Chapter

Printed in the United States
By Bookmasters